No More

Spirit Creek Series, Book One

BRENDA SINCLAIR

Brenda Sinclair

No More is a work of fiction. All names, characters, places and incidents are the product of the author's imagination or are used fictitiously. Any resemblance to actual events, locales or persons, living or dead, is entirely coincidental.

ISBN 978-0-9919492-7-4

DEDICATION

To my husband Bruce, my son Gary and daughter-in-law Jean, and my youngest son Terry who've all cheered me through the writing of this series, beginning years ago when the first book was just an idea for a story that popped into my head one evening. Thanks, guys, you're the best!

ACKNOWLEDGMENTS

Thank you to Victoria Chatham, Doreen Logeot, Sherile Reilly, and Sharon Vierboom for beta reading and providing constructive critiques and catching those pesky inconsistencies. You gals know how much I value your friendship and appreciate your willingness to spend a little time with my characters.

Thank you to Ted Williams for his excellent line editing. Because of his patient explanations, I'm catching more and more mistakes every time. He needn't worry about putting himself out of a job, however. He still finds things that I miss, even when I believe my manuscript is darn near perfect. Won't happen.

And thank you to the talented Su Kopil from Earthly Charms at http://www.earthlycharms.com for the beautiful cover. Look up patience in the dictionary and you'll find Su's picture. Thank you, Su, for helping me design the perfect cover every time.

Thanks also to the friendly folks in Miles City, Montana including the hotel proprietors, the waitresses at the various eating places, grocery store clerks, and everyone who provided directions and answered my inquiries during my two visits to your fine town. I enjoyed myself immensely while completing my research, once in early May and again a few years later during a chilly October.

During both visits to Miles City, I checked out the Range Rider Museum over on West Main Street. What a lovely facility! The knowledgeable folks working there patiently answered my questions and often volunteered additional information and insights into the topic at hand. Thank you so much! Readers, if you find yourselves in Miles City and you're of a mind to shake hands with history, wander on over and spend a few hours walking through the various interesting displays. You won't be disappointed.

I also dropped by the Miles City Library and talked with the very helpful and well-informed librarians. The Montana room upstairs is a goldmine for someone like myself doing research on the area history. And the rolls of microfilm, especially the old newspapers from my era of interest, were invaluable. I'm certain your town is understandably proud of that library.

Lastly, thanks to my family for their patience and understanding during the writing of this series.

NO MORE

Chapter 1

Spirit Creek, Montana
Wednesday, May 29, 1889

A high-noon sun beat down on Maggie Burns stumbling along the muddy street in the part of town where no one considered wooden sidewalks necessary. Despite the hint of rain that still lingered in the air after last night's downpour, she breathed through her mouth in an attempt to avoid the objectionable odor of horse manure and kitchen slop. Although distracted by her mission, she minded where she stepped, avoiding the rain-filled puddles as best she could. But her buttoned-up fancy boots might be ruined, regardless.

Maggie's temples throbbed. She couldn't believe her situation had come to this. Three short weeks ago she'd been a happy wife and mother, content with her lot in life. The bullet that pierced her husband's heart had shattered her existence as well. And never in her wildest dreams would she have imagined herself in this area of town.

Finally, she arrived at her destination and, as she had hoped, the street appeared deserted. Grasping the whitewashed handrail, she sprinted up the four wide wooden steps, raced across the narrow veranda, and slipped through the intricately-carved swinging doors of The Joker's Wild Saloon.

Maggie paused for several seconds while her eyes adjusted to the dark interior. She felt as nervous as a fattened goose the day before Christmas, and the unfamiliar atmosphere induced an involuntary shiver. The odor of stale beer and unwashed bodies assaulted her nostrils. She coughed, patted her chest, and resisted the urge to dig her perfume-scented handkerchief out of the pocket in her long, black skirt.

Maggie gazed at the mahogany arch supported by sturdy pillars that towered above the curved wooden stage where red velvet panels with gold-tasseled tie-backs framed each side. On the wall behind the mahogany-inlaid pine bar hung a rectangular mirror flanked on either side by polished wooden shelves containing liquor bottles and assorted glasses.

"Fellers only, missy. Saloon's no place for uppity ladies like yerself," muttered an old codger, slumped in one of the low-back mismatched chairs surrounding the wooden tables. He glowered at her and sent a stream of tobacco juice sailing toward a brass pot situated on the sawdust-strewn plank floor. Muttering to himself, he finished plugging his pipe with tobacco and lit it. Although his clothes looked like they hadn't been washed in months, the hand clasping the glass of beer appeared surprisingly clean. He drank deeply and set the glass aside, returning the pipe to his mouth.

At another table, a pair of scruffy-looking cowboys openly ogled Maggie and, judging by their raucous laughter, exchanged inappropriate comments about her. She cringed and turned away.

A red-headed young Irishman wearing a grimy white shirt with frayed Kelly-green suspenders popped up from behind the bar like a mischievous leprechaun. "What are *you* doing in the saloon?" he demanded. A small curved pipe hung precariously from the corner of his mouth. "We don't allow respectable women in here."

His angry brogue startled Maggie. "I…I wish to speak to the owner." If it wasn't for the pipe, she would have believed the youthful-looking fellow had been hiding in the saloon, hoping to avoid his lessons at the schoolhouse where she'd once taught.

"Darby O'Dell at your service." A nod accompanied his introduction while piercing blue eyes peeked over his round, wire-rimmed eyeglasses.

"*You*…are the proprietor?" Maggie almost asked his age but caught herself.

"Aye, I am. State yer business and then be on yer way." The fellow frowned and crossed his arms.

Maggie's resolve faltered. But she'd come this far. No turning back now. Having failed to acquire a job or sell her furniture, Maggie feared Mr. O'Dell was her last hope of rescuing her four-year-old son, Sam, and herself from total ruin. She squared her shoulders, determined to see this embarrassment through for her son's sake. "Do you own a piano, Mr. O'Dell?"

"Aye, over yonder." Darby pointed toward the far corner of the room.

Maggie's gaze followed his hand and she gasped when she spied the object. One pedal was missing and the keys were yellowed and chipped. The warped lid sat askew on the badly stained and dented wooden case, and one leg on the bench appeared shorter than the others. If the poor thing was a horse, she'd insist one of those ill-mannered cowboys dispatch its life with a bullet and put it out of its misery.

"For heaven's sake, look at that thing!" she exclaimed, meeting Darby's eyes. "I own a like-new, perfectly-tuned piano of the finest quality. I'll part with it for two hundred dollars."

"Two hundred dollars! Are ye daft, woman? Fifty," countered Darby.

"Fifty! Father bought that piano for me as a wedding gift. Knowing my father, it's the best instrument money can buy and easily worth what I'm asking. I'll not settle for a penny less." Maggie's knees shook beneath her skirts, but her voice never wavered and she hadn't blinked an eye.

"Well, the customers have been complaining about the piano. Suppose it could be considered a lifetime investment. Sold!" Darby slapped the bar and stuck out his hand to seal the deal.

"Thank you, sir." Maggie vigorously shook his hand. Feeling her face redden from her unseemly display of enthusiasm, she dropped her hands to her sides. "Kindly fetch my payment, please."

Inwardly, she cheered her success. She couldn't wait to toss the money in that miserable bank manager's face. She'd rip up Banker Peterman's foreclosure notice on her house in front of him, toss the pieces into the air, and dance a jig on them when they fluttered to the floor.

"Aye…the matter of the money." Darby shoved both hands into the deep pockets of his baggy trousers, extracting several bills. "Would the fifty dollars I offered be satisfactory as a down payment?"

"You don't understand." Maggie wagged her gloved finger in

Darby's face. "I require *all* the money today before the bank forecloses on my house."

"Peterman's an ornery bast… feller. Would force his own ma out in the street if she missed a payment." Darby shook his head. "Imagine that devil foreclosing at a time like this. You're the sheriff's widow, aren't you?"

"Yes, I am," she replied in a whisper. Realizing the barkeep couldn't pay, Maggie turned her back to him and dabbed at her tears.

"Mrs. Burns, I'm real sorry about your husband's death. He was a fine sheriff."

Maggie recalled the reason why she'd found herself in such dire straits, but she'd been taught the virtue of forgiveness. Mr. O'Dell hadn't put the cards in her husband's hands and forced him to gamble away all their money. She met the barkeep's eyes. "Thank you for your kind words, sir."

Darby grabbed a bottle off the shelf and poured a shot into a clean glass which he placed on the bar in front of her. Without thinking, Maggie raised the glass to her lips and downed the contents in one gulp.

The fiery liquid stung her tongue and burned a path down to her stomach. Her eyes watered and her vision blurred. The room began slowly spinning, and she slumped against the wooden bar for support. As she furiously fanned her flaming cheeks with one hand, her reticule slipped off her other arm and landed in the beer-soaked sawdust on the floor. Her lungs ached as if she'd narrowly escaped from a burning building.

She gasped for breath.

She was dying.

"Are you all right, missus?" inquired Darby, sounding genuinely concerned.

Maggie could only shake her head. And then an unseen hand pounded her back, and she sucked in precious air.

"There now! She'll be as right as rain in no time," spoke a chipper female voice.

"Goodness, Belle, I hope you're right, lass," replied Darby.

"Thank you," whispered Maggie, blinking to clear her blurry vision.

Maggie gasped when the saloon girl stepped out from behind her. The barmaid wore a red lacy creation, the flouncy skirt ending well above her knees, and a sky-blue plume protruded from a thicket of pumpkin-orange hair. A sickening floral scent enveloped her skinny, long-legged body, and the garish red color applied to her plump cheeks and full lips aged her several years, no doubt intentionally.

Forgetting her proper upbringing, Maggie turned on Darby. "What the hell was that?" she demanded.

"Whiskey, missus." Darby's face reddened.

"That concoction could pickle your insides!" Maggie had never tasted whiskey before, and now she understood why. "Are you attempting to kill me and just steal my piano?"

Darby paled. "I was feeling sorry for you, being in such a troubling situation."

"Kindly refrain from extending additional liquid offerings of sympathy. I won't survive it." Maggie bent to retrieve her reticule. Overcome with dizziness when she straightened, her knees buckled and she collapsed in a puddle at Belle's feet.

And then everything went black.

"Mrs. Burns! Wake up, Mrs. Burns!"

Maggie heard a muted voice calling her name from the bottom of a well. Or was she in the well? The buzzing of the thousand bees that had taken up residence in her head prevented any clear thoughts from forming.

"Is she kilt?" inquired a male in a codger-like rasp.

"Charlie, she fainted."

Maggie recognized Belle's voice.

"Looks kilt to me."

Codger again.

"Mrs. Burns!"

Belle, patting her hand.

Maggie forced open her eyes. "What…what happened? Why am I on the floor?" She felt her cheeks heat from embarrassment.

"Up you go, missus," warned Darby.

Before Maggie realized what was happening, the barkeep grabbed her by one arm, hoisted her to her feet, and busied his hands brushing sawdust from her skirts. Maggie teetered on her fancy boots, too befuddled to object.

With Darby's assistance, Maggie stumbled out the door a few minutes later and slumped onto a warped wooden bench situated on the veranda. "Thank you, Mr. O'Dell. I'll be myself in a minute," she mumbled, arranging her skirts.

Darby observed her for a few seconds and then scurried back inside.

"What will I do now?" Maggie whispered aloud and fought back tears. The day had proven a total waste of time and her efforts almost killed her, death by whiskey that tasted like lamp oil.

Why was this happening to her? She'd always been independent to a fault, due mostly to unaffectionate parents concerned more with their social lives and professions than with her. All of her life, she'd voiced her own opinions and stood up for her beliefs. Even though her parents had forbidden it, eight years ago she'd struck out on her own for Montana to fulfill her dream of becoming a schoolteacher. Now, she couldn't secure a job or raise sufficient funds to save her home. She hated feeling so ineffectual and helpless. Had marriage and motherhood changed her that much?

Her final option had failed, and she knew for certain her time was up. The whole situation seemed hopeless. She and Sam would be out on the street, homeless and penniless, by Friday.

Maggie burst into tears.

* * *

A rose-patterned teacup slipped through Luke Carlyle's hands and shattered at his feet on the kitchen's dingy plank floor.

"Dammit, I hate washing dishes," he muttered, and then grimaced at his verbal slip in front of his eleven-year-old daughter. His thoughts had distracted him. He'd been mentally formulating his plan for days, but that didn't excuse his outburst.

"Sorry about the cussing, Lucy," offered Luke, wearing sturdy denim trousers, a blue plaid work shirt and a yellow-striped apron. Until two years ago, a gun to his head wouldn't have gotten him into an apron, but his wife's sudden death had changed a lot of things.

Lucy finished drying the dishes with a tattered tea towel, and then stuffed everything into the wooden breakfront. "Papa, I'm heading upstairs to fetch Patti for school."

"Your little sister surely can dawdle," observed Luke, unrolling his shirt sleeves. He'd been silently prioritizing the dozen barnyard chores that raced through his mind. But there was one item on his list of things awaiting his attention that had niggled at his conscience for days now, not giving him a moment's peace. He fully intended to tackle it today.

"The more I tell her to hurry, the slower she goes." Lucy stood, arms crossed.

"Honey, I'm so proud of you for helping with Patti and the housework since your ma passed." Luke kissed the center of her forehead, and then trailed his fingers through his daughter's shoulder-length, golden curls identical in color to her mother's. He noticed the hem of Lucy's dress ended well above her ankles, and he recalled Patti was outgrowing her dresses too. He'd neglected his girls' needs, giving him one more reason to carry out his plan. And he would order new clothes for them while he was in town.

"Thank you, Papa." Lucy hugged his waist, beaming from his praise. She scooped a small pile of folded clothes off the table and slipped out of the kitchen.

"You work too hard, sweetheart," called Luke, remembering that horrible day, two Aprils ago, when his beloved wife died of a frightful case of influenza before the doctor arrived. In his opinion, her mother's passing forced Lucy to grow up much too soon, but she never complained about any of it.

"Mornin', Sonny Boy," greeted Ned Armstrong, fumbling with the screen door handle. The ranch foreman stumbled into the kitchen lugging a large basket filled with eggs. The old fellow wore sturdy overalls, one strap hooked and the other flapping loose, over a red and white plaid shirt.

"Good morning," replied Luke, slapping his father figure on the back.

Luke's heart still ached whenever he thought of losing his father days after he'd turned twenty-one. Ned had considered him still wet behind the ears and willingly offered an invaluable helping hand. With Ned's help and his own expertise, a passel of hard-working ranch hands and a generous portion of good luck, Luke had turned his pa's ranch into an even greater success over the past fourteen years. Everyone considered him one of the wealthiest ranchers in the vicinity, and Luke felt justifiably proud.

"I hate washing dishes, cleaning house, cooking meals," growled Luke, sending the apron sailing through the air, landing on one of the eight mahogany chairs circling the enormous kitchen table.

Ned dragged his old felt hat off his head, and a healthy patch of brown hair liberally streaked with gray stuck out in all directions. He tugged on his bushy gray moustache. "Reckon I agree with ya."

Even with Ned's help, Luke felt overwhelmed with all his responsibilities and raising his daughters alone. "I wish we weren't lassoed with this damned housework. We're too busy with ranch work, branding time, and the cattle rustling problem. We can't keep up with it all."

"So, hire yerself a woman to help out." Ned set the egg basket on the table, sank onto the closest chair.

"Do we want a woman interfering in things?" Luke never hinted to anyone what he'd been planning, and the fact Ned had arrived at a similar conclusion surprised him.

"Well, Sonny Boy, do ya want help or not?" Ned's gnarled hands massaged his knees. "Tripping over female frippery and toleratin' a few tears once in a while would be a small price to pay, if'n yer askin' my opinion."

Luke contemplated his plan. The idea of any woman other than Catherine occupying the house felt like a burr beneath his saddle. Could he accept another woman cooking in Catherine's kitchen? Touching Catherine's things? Another woman's finery hanging on the clothesline? Another woman's scent teasing his nostrils whenever she passed by him?

For his daughter's sake as much as his own, he would do it.

"We need help. And I know the ideal woman for the job." Luke charged out of the kitchen, heading upstairs to his bedroom.

* * *

Maggie dried her tears, hearing her Aunt Penny's voice in her head. *Tears never solve anything, only actions.* Feeling fresh out of actions, she'd lost track of time, sitting outside the saloon, contemplating the sad state of affairs her life had become. She was pulled from her thoughts when an elegant carriage with ornate harness shining brightly and jangling rhythmically halted in front of The Joker's Wild.

Luke Carlyle jumped down from the bench seat and marched up the wooden steps. Dressed in a finely-tailored suit, white shirt, tie, and polished boots, he crossed the veranda, paused, and rested his hand on one of the swinging doors.

Maggie lowered her head, fervently praying he wouldn't recognize her. But in this small town, of course he would.

"Mrs. Burns?"

"Yes, it's me," she whispered, feeling her face redden to her hairline as her worst fear was realized. Luke Carlyle of all people discovered her sitting outside the saloon in broad daylight. She wished the veranda floor would open and swallow her whole.

Mr. Carlyle removed his silk-banded black bowler and dragged a tanned hand through the thick brown curls that tickled his shirt collar. "Mrs. Burns, I understand your pain, your recent loss, having been there myself. But turning to drink is not the answer."

"I assure you, sir, I am *not* turning to drink!" Maggie leapt to her feet. Overcome with dizziness, she would have fallen had Mr. Carlyle not reached out and steadied her.

He frowned, not appearing to believe her denial. "Please accept my condolences once again. William's death was a tragedy."

"Thank you, Mr. Carlyle." She shook the handsome widower's outstretched hand and forced herself to make eye contact. His intense wren-brown eyes seemed to gaze right into her soul, and she quickly glanced away.

Luke cleared his throat. "After I…exchanged a word with Darby, I intended to head over to your house to discuss an important matter."

Maggie's hands shook, hidden in the folds of her skirts. Why would Luke Carlyle don his Sunday best to meet with her on a Wednesday afternoon? Her intuition warned her that if Luke required Darby's liquid fortification prior to speaking with her, this matter wasn't of the good-news variety.

"Perhaps we should converse at my home." Maggie squared her shoulders and pointed in the direction of her house. At least, it was still her house today. Renewing her resolve, she vowed that the minute she settled things with Mr. Carlyle, she would formulate another plan to raise money. She refused to allow that heartless, miserly banker to put her out of her home.

"Please allow me to escort you in my carriage." Mr. Carlyle smiled, offered her his arm, and guided her down the steps.

Maggie declined his suggestion that she ride inside the carriage, hoping the fresh air might eliminate the whiskey-induced spots that danced before her eyes. But seated in close proximity to him on the bench, her knees shook beneath her skirts and her heart beat like an Indian war drum. She inhaled deeply to calm her nerves. She'd worked with his late wife on church projects, but she and William had never socialized with Luke or Catherine beyond a polite hello after church.

Mr. Carlyle commented on the weather, but Maggie barely heard a word. She dared to sneak a peek at him. Their eyes met for a moment, and then his attention returned to the rutted road ahead. Did William have unfinished business with Mr. Carlyle? Owe him money as he did the bank? She would drive herself mad with speculation. Between her husband's untimely death and the disagreeable business with Mr. Peterman, she wouldn't survive any more bad news.

Finally, they arrived at her small house.

Mr. Carlyle set the brake and leapt to the ground. Before Maggie could extend her hand for his assistance, he planted his hands on her waist and lifted her down from the seat. Hearing her gasp he stammered, "I apologize, Mrs. Burns. I'm so accustomed to lifting my daughters down, I forgot my place."

"Apology accepted," she mumbled and flew into the house, hoping to calm her pounding heart by distancing herself from the man, if only for a moment or two.

She removed her small hat and set it atop her reticule and gloves on the hallway table. She felt as wilted as the forgotten wildflowers stuffed into the Mason jar that she'd almost tipped over in her haste. She watched as Mr. Carlyle hung his bowler on the peg William always used.

Maggie smoothed the fitted black jacket that covered her simple black shirtwaist—gone were the days of the satins and silks of her privileged upbringing. "Please, make yourself at home," she offered as she led the way into her parlor.

The room felt cool with the sun traveling west. Maggie perched on the edge of the sofa and placed her hands in her lap while Mr. Carlyle occupied William's rocking chair.

"May I offer you something to drink?" she inquired, remembering her manners despite the stressful situation.

"No, thank you. Your home is lovely, Mrs. Burns. May I call you Maggie?" Mr. Carlyle rushed ahead without waiting for her reply. "Maggie, Spirit Creek is a small town and people talk. I'm aware of the foreclosure on your home, and I doubt you've found work."

Maggie twisted her embroidered handkerchief in her hands. "Mr. Carlyle, you have no idea how hard I've tried."

"Please, call me Luke."

Before she could stop herself, Maggie blurted out her tale of failed attempts to procure a job and her fruitless efforts to raise money by selling her furniture. She even recounted today's dealings with Darby O'Dell before she could stop herself.

"So when you stumbled outside the saloon…" Luke's expression softened.

"Still a bit dizzy from the whiskey. Thank you for steadying me." Maggie blushed, unable to fathom why she had shared the embarrassing incident with him. Was she losing her mind?

"No job. No money. And you must vacate this house by Friday." Luke summarized her situation with a hint of sadness in his voice.

She nodded in answer, not trusting herself to speak, as unshed tears blurred her vision.

Luke slid forward in the rocker and balanced on the edge of the seat. "As you know, since my wife passed I've been raising my daughters alone. But I require help with the housework: cooking, cleaning, laundry, mending, and gardening. The things a wife would do."

"I'm quite familiar with housework." Maggie's spirits brightened immediately, realizing this could be the solution she'd prayed for. Was Luke offering her a job as his housekeeper? Surely, the banker would allow her to keep her house if she became gainfully employed.

Luke stared into her eyes and continued. "More importantly, I require a lovely lady in my daughters' lives to encourage them, guide them into womanhood. You'd be perfect."

"My training as a teacher would serve me well in that capacity." Maggie attempted to slow the pounding of her heart. Did she dare hope her problems were behind her?

"You're well-liked in the community, and I believe we'll get along." Luke's broad shoulders reclined against the back of William's rocking chair, and he appeared confident and relaxed with his hands dangling over the arms. Maggie's breath caught at the picture Luke made. If her late husband had spent more evenings relaxing in that rocker instead of playing cards in the saloon, she wouldn't be in this predicament.

Maggie's thoughts shifted back to the matter at hand. No doubt her visitor required household help. Last Sunday, she'd noticed his daughters had outgrown their clothes, but she didn't dare chastise the man for neglecting his children's needs. But could she trust him? If they argued, would Luke dismiss her as his housekeeper and clear the way for the banker to turn her and Sam out on the street?

"The more I think about this, the more it makes sense." Luke intently examined her face.

Maggie shifted in her seat, frazzled by his close scrutiny. What did he expect to discover hidden in the depths of her eyes? She'd lived in Spirit Creek for years. If he didn't know her character by now, he never would. She considered herself a reputable person, a church-going former teacher, and until recently, wife and mother. Now she and Sam were the extent of her family.

"Let me consider the position for a little while," she blurted. Just sitting in William's rocker, Luke had unnerved her. How could she work for him every day? Maggie leapt off the sofa and strode toward the parlor's doorway, hoping he would follow.

"There's no more time to think." Luke stood, frowning. "Unless you were planning to return back East."

"Absolutely not! Spirit Creek is my home." Maggie would beg in the streets before she'd move back to Philadelphia to endure Aunt Penny's continued disappointment in her. Returning to her privileged upbringing wasn't an option.

"Then you should accept my offer." Luke stepped toward her.

Maggie raised her hand, stopping him in his tracks. "If I was tempted to accept, which I'm not saying I am, there's something you should know. I consulted Doc Fitzgerald earlier today. I've been too preoccupied to realize the reason for my malady."

"Maggie, are you ill?" Luke whispered the question, paling visibly.

She regretted bringing the subject up, but she had. And his reaction to her news would reveal the sincerity of his job offer. "I'm with child again," she whispered. Despite her tenuous future she couldn't help rejoice with the news.

Luke stumbled back a step, as if a thousand-pound steer had

kicked him square in the chest. "You're having a baby?"

"This child is a final gift from William. But I suffered absolutely debilitating bouts of morning sickness with Sam. In time, carrying this baby may hamper my ability to keep house properly." Maggie wrung her hands. The job offer would be her salvation. But should she accept the position doubting her capacity to fulfill her obligation?

"Carrying a baby won't be a problem. I employ ranch hands for hauling water, splitting wood, heavy lifting." Luke's eyes crinkled at the corners, dimples straining.

Was it her imagination? Luke appeared delighted with her revelation about the baby. "I wouldn't be earning my pay. I must decline your kind offer." Maggie swung away, but a sob escaped her lips.

Luke turned her, gently enveloped her in his arms, surprising her. Without thinking, she leaned into his embrace and rested her head against his muscular chest. For a few brief moments, she inhaled the forest fragrance of his soap, the freshly-washed scent of his shirt, relished the comforting warmth of his strong arms. And then she gasped and broke away from him.

His cheeks flushed. "I apologize for holding you like that, but you were crying. I've no excuse, no right. You haven't accepted yet."

Purely mortified, Maggie wondered what he must think of her. A widow for three weeks, and she'd clung to him in the most shameful way. Would returning back East to face the elderly aunt she'd disappointed eight years ago be as embarrassing as facing Luke every day after her scandalous behavior in his arms?

"I cannot accept your offer. I'm sorry," she insisted.

"You are the most exasperating woman." Luke shook his head, spreading his arms wide before her. "I'm the most eligible bachelor within miles. Mothers are throwing their daughters at my feet. You require a husband in the worst way, and yet, you won't even consider marrying me?"

"Marrying you?" Maggie collapsed onto the sofa, barely able to catch her breath. "I assumed you were offering me a job as your housekeeper."

"The gossips' tongues would be wagging in no time if we shared my home without the benefit of the 'I do's'. It's better if you become my wife."

Maggie stared at Luke. Why was he so adamant that they marry? Was his only intention to help with her desperate situation, acquire help with his housework? Or was there more to his offer? Something he wasn't sharing with her?

"I'm in mourning," stated Maggie. No matter how angry she was with William, Untamed West or not, she lived by the standards she was taught. Widows did not remarry for at least a year.

"Maggie, if you become my wife we'll share companionship and support. Our children will benefit from proper care provided by both a mother and a father. Marriage will solve all our problems." Luke crossed his arms, suggesting that he considered the matter settled.

"The two hundred dollars I require to save my home will solve my problems. Not a scandalous marriage." Suddenly, Maggie's eyes lit up and she leapt to her feet. "Mr. Carlyle, *you* could buy my piano. You can certainly afford to pay me in full, and I'd save my home. Sam and I would still have a place to live. And I'll gladly give your daughters lessons…"

"Whoa! Just one minute, Maggie." Luke raised his hands to halt her verbal onslaught. "There's an old piano at the ranch. Catherine was teaching the girls how to play. Besides, earning a few dollars from the sale of your piano won't solve your problems."

Maggie raised her voice. "Don't you realize how much this home means to me?"

"Saving your home is the least of your worries. How will you live?" Luke scratched his head. "Unless you move back East, marriage is your only option."

"This whole idea is preposterous!" exclaimed Maggie. One second William was alive, and the next second he was gone. And she'd lost the battle with Mr. Peterman to keep her home. Now, Luke Carlyle was introduced to the mix. At every turn something new thwarted her happiness and threatened her sanity. Whatever had she done to deserve this?

Should she have forgiven William for his foolishness? For putting her and Sam's futures in jeopardy? For squandering away all their money gambling and then borrowing against their home to boot? She could never admit this to anyone, but anger had replaced her love for him. Was this her punishment for her steadfast refusal to forgive William for what he'd done?

"I suppose there's the matter of the marriage bed." Luke appeared deep in thought, and she wondered if he intended to speak the words aloud.

Then Maggie's eyes blazed, understanding dawning. "Your priority isn't your children or the housework. You just want a woman in your bed!"

"I'm determined to marry you, no more housework for me. But you're still in mourning and I respect that you're not ready to move on."

Maggie took a step back, taking a minute to think. Of course she wasn't ready to move on. At the moment, she doubted she'd ever trust another man as long as she lived. But was she being foolish? Everyone in town admired Luke Carlyle. Even William had spoken highly of him. Handsome, well-educated, wealthy, kind-hearted and generous. Would being his wife be so unbearable? Sam's face popped into her mind, and she immediately regretted even considering such a thing.

"I could never betray William's memory by marrying you, no matter how desperate my situation." She stood, head held high, challenging Luke. Despite his shortcomings, William was still her children's father. Regardless of her low opinion of him, she wouldn't shame his memory for Sam's sake. "But I desperately need a job. I'll gladly work as your housekeeper."

Luke's expression softened. "The townspeople will understand the necessity of our marriage. In the eyes of the church and our children, we'll be married. In truth, our marriage will be a simple agreement, a marriage of convenience, to benefit our children, nothing more. The marriage will not be consummated, until and unless you're ready. Could you live with that?"

Maggie felt somewhat relieved. She cringed at the thought of ever trusting another man enough to welcome him into her bed.

Luke reached for her hand and continued pleading his case. "You'll be providing your children with food on the table and a roof over their heads. William would expect that."

Maggie studied Luke's face; his eyes spoke volumes. By all appearances, he genuinely cared about her and her children. "I'll be your wife in name, but your housekeeper in reality."

"Exactly, if that's how you want to look at it. I promise you. Everything will work out." Luke smiled and she wanted desperately to believe him.

Maggie closed her eyes and prayed she was doing the right thing. She hadn't realized she was crying, until she opened her eyes. She brushed the tears away, brushing her doubts away with them. "Because of Sam and my unborn child, I'll marry you."

"Then it's decided. We'll be married on Friday morning." Luke patted her arm.

Maggie nodded in agreement.

"You won't regret this." Luke smiled, broadly.

God help her. Luke had won. His words sounded so final, but somehow so right. *Everything will work out.* She almost believed him.

Chapter 2

Maggie closed the door behind Luke and slumped against the solid pine wood. If not anchored by the door's substantial weight, she would spin out of control like a popped balloon soaring about the room before plummeting to the floor.

"What have you done?" she whispered aloud. What appeared to be a sensible decision moments ago, now seemed the height of folly. Or was it? Marriage would solve her problems, and his. That was a good thing. Wasn't it?

She inhaled deeply, stood tall, and pulled her shoulders back. She could either accept her fate or sink into a pool of self-pity, as broken and deflated as that imagined balloon.

"Elizabeth will know whether I'm being foolish or not." She grabbed her shawl, hat and reticule, and dashed out the door.

Ronald Waverly, the proprietor of The Spirit Creek General Store, glanced toward the entrance when the small silver bell over the front door tinkled loudly. Maggie blanched as she charged into the store like a stampeding steer. She slowed her pace, thankful there were no customers to witness her arrival.

"Good day," called Ronald, stacking canned goods on a middle shelf.

"Good afternoon, Ronald. Where's Elizabeth? I must speak with her immediately." She hoped Ronald wouldn't notice her flushed face and rapid breathing from her haste.

Ronald turned, clasping a can of baked beans in an arthritic hand. "The missus is in back. Go on ahead and you'll find her." He nodded, but a worried frown wrinkled his brow.

So much for appearing unruffled. Before her friend's intuitive husband could start asking questions, she wended her way through an obstacle course of pickle barrels, wooden crates, and articles of clothing that hung precariously from overfilled shelves. A pair of dungarees caught her hat, knocking it askew.

"Oh fiddle," she muttered, shoving the trousers back onto the shelf and straightening her hat.

"Elizabeth," she called a warning before entering the living quarters in back of the store. This time, she didn't bother to hide her flustered state. Her best friend would understand.

At fifty one, Elizabeth was twenty years older than Maggie and infinitely wiser in the ways of the western life. Hearing her name, the matron poked her head out of the pantry, and a broad smile appeared on her face.

"It's so good to see you. You haven't dropped by for a few days, and I was becoming a little concerned." Elizabeth wiped her hands on the pale blue apron that covered a simple calico housedress before crushing her visitor against her ample bosom in an enthusiastic embrace.

Maggie relished the warm hug, her heartbeat still racing. "I've missed you."

Elizabeth leaned back and met her friend's eyes. "What are you doing all dressed up in your Sunday duds?"

"You won't believe my news," whispered Maggie, her hands visibly shaking.

"Sit down and I'll make a pot of tea. You're wound up tighter than an old ball of yarn." Elizabeth poured water into the tea kettle, set it on the woodstove, and added a log to the fire.

Maggie hung her shawl over the back of a wooden chair and seated herself at the square pine table. Golden afternoon sunshine reflected off the cheerful yellow walls, and the aroma of fresh-baked bread lingered in the air. Her stomach grumbled and she glanced at the wall clock. Two p.m. She'd forgotten about dinner, unforgivable when carrying a baby.

Elizabeth set out crocus-patterned china teacups. "I baked two loaves of bread this morning. We'll have a slice with our tea."

She placed a white glass cream jug and matching sugar bowl on the table and then gently clasped Maggie's freckled face in both hands, examining her like a concerned mother. "You look tired, dear."

"Well, that's because I'm with child." Maggie smiled and stood, accepting her friend's embrace. Despite her turmoil, she welcomed the new life growing inside her.

"That's wonderful news." Elizabeth's eyes misted.

"I've been worried about Sam, accepting William's death, dealing with his deceptions, and heartsick about the foreclosure on my house. I missed all the signs." Maggie recalled how foolish she felt at Doc Fitzgerald's clinic when the kindly old fellow asked a dozen questions during the course of her examination. Suddenly, it occurred to Maggie why she felt so poorly, and she startled the old doctor with her loud gasp.

Doc confirmed her suspicions, and she couldn't be happier.

"Wouldn't a little sister for Sam be special?" Elizabeth beamed, clapping her hands.

"A little girl, a little boy, I really don't care. As long as the baby is healthy, that's all that matters." Maggie eyes filled and she whispered, "I've wanted another baby since Sam turned two, but nothing happened. This baby is a final gift from William, a miracle."

"Every new life is a miracle," agreed Elizabeth, pouring boiling water into the teapot.

Maggie heard the wistfulness in her friend's voice. Elizabeth and Ronald had never been blessed with children. But Maggie had delayed explaining her purpose for the visit long enough. Stomach flutters caused further pause; she hoped Elizabeth wouldn't think her foolish. "I have more news."

"Well, spill it." Elizabeth set the teapot on the table. "Although I don't know what would top your news about the baby."

"Luke Carlyle asked me to marry him." Maggie listened to the wall clock ticking in the room that seemed as quiet as The Spirit Creek Church during Sunday sermon.

And then Elizabeth burst into laughter.

Maggie's mouth dropped open at her friend's unexpected reaction.

"That's a good one." Elizabeth swatted Maggie's arm. "I almost believed you there for a second."

Maggie wasn't certain whether she should feel annoyed or relieved. At least, Elizabeth hadn't fainted. "I've agreed to marry Luke Carlyle on Friday," she insisted.

"Oh, go on with you." Elizabeth sat on the chair across from Maggie. "Be serious now."

"It's no joke, Elizabeth." Maggie buttered her slice of bread too enthusiastically and ripped a small hole in the middle.

"You're getting married?" Elizabeth straightened in her seat. "To Luke Carlyle?"

"Yes." Maggie took a large bite, nearly starving.

"How on earth did this come about?" Elizabeth sobered as the realization that Maggie was indeed totally serious dawned on her.

Maggie related the details of her morning between bites, including her unsuccessful attempts at selling her prized piano, and her encounter with Luke Carlyle. She continued her story, "Everything he'd said led me to believe he was offering me a job as his housekeeper. Then he suddenly inquired why I wouldn't consider marrying him. The question knocked me over."

"Why marriage?" Elizabeth poured their tea.

"He's gallantly saving my reputation from the town gossips." Maggie chuckled at the irony. "I've no doubt damaged my reputation beyond repair sitting on a bench outside that saloon in broad daylight."

Elizabeth frowned. "A healthy young man without a wife…I suspect he's scheming something other than having hot meals and clean socks."

Maggie recalled the moment she'd arrived at the same conclusion and called Luke on it. "Luke certainly didn't back down when I told him about the baby. Perhaps I'm being naïve, but I believe he's sincere. And this marriage will solve all my problems."

Elizabeth sipped her tea, deep in thought for a moment. "You hardly know him. Sitting across the aisle from someone in church every Sunday is quite different from being married to them."

"Luke promised a home for me and my children. His daughters will acquire a mother, and Sam a new father. Once you become accustomed to the idea, it's really a sensible plan. Besides, I don't have a choice. I must vacate my home on Friday, but I'm taking everything of worth with me: my son, my furniture, and my memories." Maggie grimaced with the realization that William had controlled every aspect of her life. Was she willingly setting herself up for more of the same? At least, Luke was wealthy and it seemed unlikely he'd leave her penniless and without a roof over her head.

Elizabeth patted Maggie's hand. "Stay with Ronald and me. Let Luke court you. Take time to discover your feelings for him before considering marriage."

Maggie was tempted by the idea, but their union would be only a marriage of convenience. "In no man's land Montana Territory, a soul has to do what a soul has to do. I'll be fine, Elizabeth. You needn't worry about me."

"You shouldn't be so trusting. You and Luke are practically strangers."

"I shouldn't trust Luke?" Maggie failed to stem her annoyance, and blurted, "I trusted William through two years of courting and six years of marriage. And you know how well that ended."

"Well, yes, dear. But that was different," suggested Elizabeth.

"How so? Considering all the deceptions and lies, William now feels as much a stranger to me as Luke does." Maggie took a deep breath to calm herself.

"That's just the grief talking."

"No, it's not. Luke has offered me safety, security, and companionship. That's more than I got from William. Luke Carlyle won't leave me home alone every night while he's off gambling away every penny he's ever earned." Maggie fought back tears. She'd tried to put the hurt behind her, but evidently it still lived near the surface of her feelings.

Elizabeth's voice softened. "What will happen when Luke has you…behind closed doors?"

Maggie couldn't meet her friend's eyes. Her arrangement with Luke should stay just between the two of them. How she hated lying to Elizabeth, even lying by omission.

Elizabeth continued her warning. "Many a woman has been fooled by sweet words and big promises. I don't want you to discover Luke has a dark side, after the 'I do's' are said."

"Really, Elizabeth," scoffed Maggie. "Luke Carlyle is about as violent as a new born puppy. I've seen him with his wife before she died: courteous, soft-spoken, and respectful. He's a gentle soul, with a kind heart and an agreeable disposition."

"But…"

"I'm positive Sam and I will be well cared for, Elizabeth. I trust him." *Trust.* She almost choked on the word, and her heart raced just saying it aloud. Considering how well William had fooled her, she prayed her instincts about Luke served her better. Yes, she would extend Luke Carlyle the benefit of the doubt since she had no choice. But she'd never let her guard down and allow him to fool her the way William had. Initially, she would trust her new husband, but Luke must earn her continued loyalty.

"If there's even a hint of mistreatment, promise me you will tell me immediately." Elizabeth wagged her finger at Maggie.

"I promise, Elizabeth." Maggie raised her hand, solemnly swearing like a witness before a judge. Appearing before a stone-faced judge would be downright preferable to facing a disgruntled Elizabeth. "I'm certain your fears are unfounded."

"Well, let's hope so." Elizabeth hugged her. "All things considered…"

Maggie never could keep a secret from her friend, and today was no different. "You do realize this marriage is just an arrangement to suit both our purposes, especially for our children. There'll be no mention of love. Luke's only interested in providing his daughters with the security of both a mother and a father. And I want the same for Sam and this baby." During her confession, Maggie refilled her teacup while contemplating whether she should risk another slice of the fresh-baked bread. She hoped her iffy stomach was due to nerves and not the onset of morning sickness.

"Of course, I suspected as much. But what if Luke expects more one day? You won't be mourning William forever. What will you do then?" Mistrust was written all over Elizabeth's face.

Maggie refused to consider such a thing. "I'll take care of the house and the children, and he'll operate his ranch. A partnership based on common sense for a mutual purpose. We've both had our chance at love. Neither of us desires another."

"I pray you won't regret this one day." Elizabeth lectured, in a motherly way.

Maggie's eyes filled with tears, realizing what her life had become since her husband's death: no more home, no more hope, and no more options.

Except one.

"Elizabeth, I've exhausted all attempts at raising money, and I refuse to move back East. I'm getting married on Friday." Maggie's mind seemed at peace, at last.

"Are you certain there's absolutely nothing else you can do?" Elizabeth grabbed Maggie's hand, like she would a drowning person going down for the last time.

"I could sing at The Joker's Wild," teased Maggie. She laughed at Elizabeth's horrified expression. "I met one of Darby's ladies. Merciful heavens, Elizabeth, you wouldn't believe the outfit she was wearing. If I donned that clothing, or should I say lack of it, God would strike me dead!"

"This is no laughing matter," huffed Elizabeth. "Your mind is definitely made up?"

"It's what I'm prepared to do." Maggie needed to treat her situation with humor, knowing if she started crying she would never stop.

In truth, the whole idea of this marriage of convenience terrified her. But what choice did she have? "William loved Sam and he would insist I protect his child, no matter the means. My children's needs must come ahead of my own happiness. I'm marrying Luke Carlyle." Maggie surprised herself with the conviction she heard in her voice. And, frankly, after what William had put her and Sam through, she secretly didn't care what he would think. But she'd never dare speak the thought aloud.

"I understand you're doing this for your children." Elizabeth sounded resigned to the idea. "So I'll help you with the wedding plans."

"No, no, no." Maggie shook her head, emphatically. "I remember the hours of planning that went into my wedding to William as if it were yesterday."

"You were the most beautiful bride." Elizabeth sighed, and then she frowned. "And you were madly in love with the groom, as I recall."

"That's not fair, Elizabeth." Maggie's anger flared. She wasn't entering this arrangement with the starry-eyed innocence of youth. No doubt, her future held a bushel of loneliness and a peck of unhappiness, but Sam and her unborn child were worth it.

"You're right. I'm sorry." Elizabeth patted Maggie's hand.

"Apology accepted," conceded Maggie.

"I assume the wedding will be held at The Spirit Creek Church."

"Luke agreed to speak to Reverend Gerald about a simple

ceremony: just Luke, me, our children, and our witnesses." Maggie's tone sounded firm, and she prayed Elizabeth was listening.

"Under the circumstances, I suppose something simple would be best," Elizabeth muttered to herself.

"You'll serve as my witness, won't you?" Maggie reached for her friend's hand. "Please, once again?"

"Of course, dear," Elizabeth smiled in agreement.

"Thank you." Maggie intended to occupy herself with packing her belongings and block the upcoming nuptials from her mind.

At that moment, Ronald strolled into the room, grabbed a dipper full of cold water out of the pail by the kitchen sink, and drank deeply. He wiped his mouth with the back of his hand and asked, "What are my two favorite ladies plotting now?"

"Maggie is marrying Luke Carlyle on Friday." Elizabeth blurted out the news. "And you're giving the bride away."

"Well, I'll be jiggered." Ronald scratched his head. "That explains the list of goods Luke dropped off. I collected up most of the grub and household supplies, but he requested Elizabeth organize the clothing for him. Something about knowing the proper sizes. He'll have the whole lot of it picked up tomorrow afternoon."

* * *

Parallel rows of mature cottonwood trees lined the winding lane leading to the Diamond C Ranch's majestic main house, shading the way as Luke's carriage rumbled along. The trees' leaves moved in the afternoon breeze, whispering a welcome home. Luke caught himself humming a tune.

After bidding Maggie adieu, he'd conferred with Reverend Gerald concerning a simple wedding on Friday. The reverend voiced his concern that a recent widow would remarry so soon, but Luke explained the necessity for the rushed nuptials. The minister agreed to perform the ceremony as Luke requested. Luke didn't doubt for a second the good reverend would drop by Maggie's home to assure himself that the bride wasn't marrying under duress. Hopefully, the reverend wouldn't talk the bride out of the whole affair. Then where would they be?

"Nope. Positive thoughts," he muttered to himself. Maggie

understood the necessity for the marriage, and she wouldn't be dissuaded from their plans.

Before heading home, he'd stopped at the general store, and then dropped into the bank to negotiate a little business. And on his way out of town, he'd placed his order at the feed store, completing his very productive day in town.

Luke caught sight of Ned, busy removing laundry from the sagging old clothesline, folding each item, and tossing it into a nearby basket. Ned had signed on with Luke's father over twenty years ago. At the time, had the old fellow considered the possibility that someday his duties would include laundry and housework? Luke smiled at the thought and shook his head. How would he have survived the past two years without Ned?

Luke tied the tired horses' reins to the whitewashed hitch. As he strode across the yard, his old dog, Skipper, lumbered along beside him. Nothing went on around the Diamond C Ranch that the dog wasn't aware of. Luke had discovered both two-legged and four-legged varmints shaking in their hide when he investigated an episode of frenzied barking and spine-tingling growling.

"How-do," called Luke as he approached.

"Sonny Boy, what in tarnation kep ya in town so long? Didn't reckon it'd take all day hirin' a housekeeper." Ned's twinkling blue eyes belied his annoyance.

"Actually, I didn't hire a housekeeper." Luke bent to scratch Skipper's ears.

"Hell and damnation!" Ned cursed at his boss. "I was aprayin' this was the last time I'd be washin' yer danged dirty socks."

"It's the last time." Luke extracted a half-eaten cookie from his pocket and fed it to the dog. Skipper gulped down the treat with one bite.

"How ya figurin' that?" Ned tossed a folded towel into the basket.

Luke took a deep breath. "I've asked Maggie Burns to be my wife."

"What?" Ned whipped around and scowled at Luke, disappointment evident on his face. "Have ya been too long in the saloon?"

"Stone sober, Ned. You heard me right. I'm marrying Maggie Burns on Friday," repeated Luke as his faithful canine sat at his feet, tongue lolling, waiting for another treat.

"I reckon the poor widder lady don't have much choice." Ned squinted, studying Luke's face. "Does Maggie Burns know she's gettin' a man who's still nursin' a broken heart?"

Luke stared at the old fellow while pondering the question. Was he still mourning his wife? Or was he ready to move on? Perhaps it didn't really matter one way or the other. There were more important issues to be considered here. "My daughters are my priority; they deserve a mother. And Maggie's little boy needs a new father."

"That ain't no reason fer gettin' hitched." Ned shook his head. "I figure ya best be lovin' the filly ya tend to corral for the rest of yer life."

Love? Maybe again, some day.

Luke recalled his panicky moment when he thought Maggie's visit to Doc Fitzgerald meant she was seriously ill. He'd returned to those horrible hours when his dear Catherine fought for her life, and lost. He'd loved that woman more than life itself. Now, whenever one of his daughters coughed, it required all his willpower to stop himself from summoning Doc.

Luke smiled at their secret… Maggie's with child. His soon-to-be wife's news tickled his sensibilities; he loved babies. And if Maggie birthed another baby boy, by law he'd have two sons. But he wouldn't share their secret yet, even with Ned.

"It's the best solution for both of us." Luke hoped he sounded sold on the idea. He'd convinced himself of it. At least, he was pretty sure he had.

"I'll say no more. Yer a growed man. Should know what yer doin'." Ned folded the last towel and tossed it on top of the pile of clothes in the basket. "Cain't say I'll miss this woman's work."

"I've got one request, Ned." Luke smiled at his friend. "Would you be my witness at the wedding on Friday?"

"Ya know dang well I will." Ned grinned.

"I better share the news with the girls." Luke headed toward the house, and Skipper leapt to his feet and loped along beside him.

"Good luck with that wedding news, Sonny Boy," called Ned, bending down to grab the clothes basket. "Them girls think yer hirin' a woman to clean house and cook meals couple days a week."

"This might prove interesting." Luke retreated to the carriage, untied the horses' reins, and started toward the barn.

"Where ya goin' to?" asked Ned, supporting the basket's weight on one hip.

"I require some time to prepare my words."

Ned cackled, and Luke thought he heard the old guy mumble something about a coward, but he continued walking.

* * *

At six o'clock, Luke joined his daughters for supper at the huge kitchen table in the main house. Ned had left a stew simmering on the woodstove when he headed off to join his wife for their evening meal together, after she fed the ranch hands in the cookhouse.

"Before we say grace, I have news to share." Luke couldn't delay any longer. He'd thought long and hard about the plan he'd formulated and brought to fruition this afternoon. Now, he just prayed his daughters would see the wisdom of his decision and the logic behind his reasoning when he divulged what he'd done.

"What's your news, Papa?" inquired Patti, sitting a little straighter in her chair.

Luke reached over and playfully tweaked her nose. The seven-year-old giggled and leaned back in her chair out of her father's reach.

"I've made arrangements today that will greatly improve our situation," began Luke, grimacing at his understatement.

"That's wonderful, Papa." Lucy settled in her chair and rearranged her skirts like a young lady should.

So far, so good.

He took a deep breath and continued. "You girls deserve more free time instead of helping Ned with housework. I appreciate all you've done, but children should enjoy being children."

"Papa, I don't mind helping." Patti smiled.

"I like cooking, Pa," added Lucy. "Besides, Mama would have wanted me to take care of her house."

"Not true, Lucy. The responsibility was mine, but the cooking and cleaning are behind us." Luke squared his shoulders. "I've asked Mrs. Burns to marry me."

Luke studied his daughters' shocked expressions. He braced

himself for their reactions; he didn't know what to expect. Had he been courting someone for several months, his announcement would have been a natural evolution in the relationship. But thrusting such sudden news on his daughters seemed almost unfair. Even though he was remarrying for their benefit more than his own. At least, that's the argument he'd used to convince himself he was doing the right thing.

"You're marrying…another woman?" whispered Lucy, aghast.

Luke leaned back in his chair and crossed his arms. "Yes, I'm marrying Mrs. Burns on Friday. Then, she and Sam will move out here to the ranch. She'll take over the cooking and the cleaning and such."

Lucy's eyes filled with tears. "Don't you love Mama anymore?" she whispered.

"Mama's gone, sweetheart. But there will always be a special place in my heart for her." Luke reached across the kitchen table and gently clasped his oldest daughter's hand. "You girls require a mother. Ned and I need to concentrate on running this ranch, instead of cooking meals and washing dishes and scrubbing floors."

"I don't want another mother." Lucy yanked her hand free. "Please, Papa, we don't need her here. I'll help Uncle Ned with chores all day long..."

"You won't miss any school days! Your education is not negotiable." Luke had always assumed his girls would consider the possibility that he would remarry someday. He hadn't anticipated Lucy's strong objection to another woman stepping into the role of her mother.

"Papa?" Patti whispered and skipped over to his side.

"What is it, sweetheart?" Luke scooped her skinny body onto his knee, tucking her flowered skirt underneath her.

"I want a little brother. I like Sam. Sometimes we play together after church." Patti rode his leg like a pony.

"I'm sure you'll have a lot of fun with Sam." Luke gently tugged on his daughter's pigtails.

"Can I be the boss?" inquired Patti.

"Yes, sweetie. You're three years older than Sam, so you can be the boss." Luke noticed a new crop of freckles appeared on her pretty face every day. "But there's a difference between being the boss and being bossy. Just teach Sam the rules to keep him safe on the ranch."

"I'll be a very good big sister." Patti hopped down and returned to her chair.

Lucy crossed her arms. "I don't want a new mother or a stupid little brother. Everything is just fine the way it is."

Luke stifled a groan. What had he gotten himself and Maggie into? Somehow, he had to convince Lucy his plan would work, that he'd made these arrangements for her sake. "Well, regardless of your individual opinions on the matter, both of you will be in attendance when I marry Mrs. Burns on Friday morning. Then Sam and his mother will move to the ranch."

"But, Papa!" exclaimed Lucy.

"There will be no further argument. Let's have our supper." In Luke's mind the matter was settled as the family joined hands for grace.

Lucy bowed her head and whispered her fervent prayers. Luke had a feeling they had nothing to do with the food she was about to receive.

* * *

"I'm home, Mama." The screen door slammed, and a trail of small muddy shoeprints followed her son across the kitchen floor. With rosy red cheeks and a dirty face, he beamed from ear to ear.

Maggie arranged for Sam to spend the day with his best friend at the neighbor's house while she attended to her mission at the saloon. Seeing him so happy, she just couldn't scold him for making a mess on her floor. "Did you have fun today?" she inquired, stirring the pot of leftover stew warming on the woodstove. Sam hadn't smiled much in the past three weeks.

"The mostest fun ever, Mama. We played with the puppies and walked with Robbie's ma to the creek for a picnic. His ma said it was too cold, and we couldn't even stick a toe in the creek, but we caught bugs and frogs." Sam giggled, grinning. He struggled out of his jacket, tossed it onto a chair, and kicked off his muddy shoes.

"Hang up that jacket on your hook, young man. And wash up for supper, hands and face." Maggie wiped the floor and set the muddy shoes beside the back door.

"Mama has something to tell you," she called, setting plates and forks on the table.

Sam crept back into the kitchen and slumped into his chair. "Is it something bad…like when Papa died?" he whispered.

"No, sweetheart, it's nothing like that." Maggie sat on the opposite chair, heart breaking a little more at seeing her son's pain-filled eyes. She took a deep breath. "We must change things now that Papa isn't here."

Maggie had convinced herself while talking to Elizabeth that she'd made the right decision. But searching Sam's eyes, she wavered. Doubts crept around her resolve, attempting to plant their roots in her mind. Would speaking her plans aloud one more time assure her that this arrangement could work?

"We must leave this house in two days, muffin. So, we're moving to a ranch. Mama's marrying the gentleman who owns the ranch, and we'll live with him and his daughters."

"Why?" Sam scratched his freckled nose.

"We can't stay in this house; we have to move. The ranch will be our new home." Maggie hated uprooting her son this way, shattering his sense of security.

Everything was William's fault. The gambling. The lies. The secret loans. While he couldn't help being killed protecting the citizens of this town during an attempted bank robbery, leaving her penniless was unforgivable. Had he even once considered the untenable situation he'd leave his family in if something should happen to him?

"What ranch?" asked Sam.

"Do you remember Mr. Carlyle? He sits across the aisle from us in church, with his daughters, Patti and Lucy."

"Uh-huh." Sam shifted in his chair.

"His ranch will be our new home. Mama will care for you and Patti and Lucy. I'll cook the meals, clean the house, and wash the clothes. Same things I do here, except I'll be doing it at the ranch."

"Why do we gotta go there?" Sam crossed his little arms, a defiant expression on his face.

"Remember Mama said I needed a job?" Maggie smiled as Sam bobbed his head in answer. "Well, this is Mama's new job, and you get a new father…"

"I don't want a new father," blurted Sam, his eyes filling with tears. "I want *my* Papa back."

Maggie grasped his small hands and fought back tears of her own. Her heart bled for him; he was simply too young to understand the ramifications of what was happening. "I'm so sorry, muffin, but Papa can't ever come back."

"What if Papa comes home and I'm not here?" Sam sounded panicked by the possibility.

"Papa won't come home, ever, but he'll be happy that you're in a safe new house with a new father and two new sisters." She hated throwing his life into turmoil. Someday he'd realize she'd agreed to this arrangement for him. For now, how would she convince him this plan served their best interests? How indeed? Was she even convinced herself? Believing she was doing the right thing was so difficult when all she saw was confusion in her son's eyes.

"I don't want a new father and sisters." Sam pouted.

"Living on a ranch will provide opportunities for wonderful new adventures."

"What's a 'venture?" asked Sam.

"An adventure is something fun. We'll see long-horned cows and magnificent horses. There'll be wide open spaces to explore. And we'll meet new people."

"Can I have a puppy?" Sam's wren-brown eyes peeked up at his mother.

Maggie considered his question for a moment. Would asking for a puppy be overstepping the bounds of her agreement with Luke? William had promised Sam one of the neighbor's new puppies, but she'd had to renege when her husband died and their housing situation became so uncertain.

"Maybe the Carlyle family already has a dog on their ranch?" she suggested.

"They have a dog?" Sam brightened and leapt onto his mother's lap.

"I'm not certain, muffin. But surely a ranch isn't complete without a dog." Maggie tenderly hugged her young son and brushed his curls out of his eyes. He needed a haircut. Would there be a dog on the ranch? She had no idea. Maggie kissed his forehead. "I guess we'll find out on Friday."

* * *

On Thursday evening, after packing the last of their possessions into two small suitcases—Luke's ranch hands had picked up everything else that afternoon, including her piano, and taken it to the ranch—Maggie and Sam stopped by the town's churchyard on their way to Ronald and Elizabeth's house for supper and to spend the night.

A crude wooden cross honoring Sheriff William Burns protruded from the fresh mound of rock-covered dirt occupying the far corner of the church's small graveyard. Three weeks had passed since the bullet from a bank robber's pistol ended her husband's life, but it seemed like yesterday.

She'd been so proud of William when she heard he died during a heroic act. At the time, she'd never loved him more. But she recalled that horrible day when, hours after burying her husband, Banker Peterman presented her with the foreclosure notice on her home, knowing she couldn't pay back her husband's secret gambling loans. Now, apprised of his unforgivable lies and deceptions, she wondered again, what had William been thinking?

Sam stood silently beside her, a corner of his navy blue shirt hanging out of his trousers. He slipped his small warm hand into hers, seeking comfort.

"Where's Papa?" he asked, a few tears sliding down his chubby cheeks.

He'd asked her the same question dozens of times these past few weeks. Maggie knew his young mind didn't comprehend the fact his father wasn't returning home again. She forced her answer past gritted teeth. "Papa's in heaven with the angels, muffin."

She pulled a dandelion out of the ground and blew the white fluffy seeds into the wind. If only she could blow her troubles away as easily. She tossed the dandelion remains aside and brushed the dirt from her hands, brushing away any lingering feelings for William as well. He'd hurt her so badly; losing the home she'd loved so much had been the last straw. But she would play the role of the grieving widow and publicly mourn her husband for Sam's sake.

She strode across the uneven ground, mindful of turning an ankle, as they exited the graveyard. She grabbed their suitcases and prayed Sam wouldn't see the anger on her face as he trotted along beside her. That miserable banker had sorely tried her Christian conviction to never hate anyone. *I want you and your son out of the house by the end of the month.* The banker's heartless pronouncement had struck fear in her heart. She'd decided then and there to never trust another man as long as she lived.

But here she was, already putting her and Sam's entire future into the hands of a virtual stranger. She'd failed to save her home, but she'd do anything to ensure Sam and his unborn sibling were safe.

Anything.

Even marrying Luke Carlyle.

Chapter 3

Friday, May 31, 1889

Maggie awoke, neck-deep in rumpled covers with sunshine streaming in through the open window, fearing she'd overslept. Was Elizabeth hoping she'd miss her own wedding? She glanced at the clock on the vanity table, ten minutes past eight. After listening to the clock's ticking for hours, she'd finally fallen asleep with Sam snuggled against her last night, but his side of the bed was empty now.

The intoxicating aroma of coffee and fried bacon teased her nose, while bits of excited conversation drifted into the bedroom from the kitchen. Although she couldn't hear their words clearly, Maggie identified the familiar female voices—Elizabeth and Sarah Grayson, a widow held in high esteem by all citizens of Spirit Creek. Her late husband, Graham, had owned the bank now run by Mr. Peterman for the new owners in Boston

Maggie disentangled herself from the covers and leapt out of bed, tugging her nightdress over her head as she crossed the sun-warmed plank floor. She donned a housedress, and quickly put up her hair in a bun.

"Good morning," she called, entering Elizabeth's sunny kitchen. "Where's Sam?"

"Good morning, dear," responded Elizabeth. "Don't worry. He's in the store with Ronald."

"Morning, Maggie. You know me, always busy. Sorry, I can't stay and chat," called Sarah, waving as she hurried out the door.

"What were you and Sarah discussing?" inquired Maggie,

pouring herself a cup of coffee from the pot on the woodstove. "I hope you didn't mention the wedding plans."

"Now, why would I do that? What with you considering the nuptials a secret and all." Elizabeth didn't meet Maggie's eyes. "Sarah invited me for afternoon tea to admire her lovely flower garden."

Maggie detected something amiss. Did Elizabeth still doubt the wisdom of this wedding? "I've overslept, so this cup of coffee will do." She seated herself at the kitchen table, hoping Elizabeth would discuss what was bothering her.

"Your baby needs a good breakfast. Can't expect a healthy baby if you're just drinking coffee." Elizabeth chattered nervously, as she dished up a plate of food at the woodstove.

"What's the matter, Elizabeth? Why are you so rattled?"

"Don't worry about me. I'll be fine once you've walked down the aisle. Now, eat up." Elizabeth placed a plateful of eggs, bacon, fried potatoes and buttermilk flapjacks in front of her.

"My word, Elizabeth, I'll never finish all this."

"Just eat what you can," suggested Elizabeth, pouring herself a cup of coffee.

Maggie consumed every bite and then handed her plate and cup to Elizabeth. "I was starving, wasn't I?"

"Feed that baby three good meals a day. I want a healthy baby girl." Elizabeth hummed a familiar hymn while washing the dishes.

Maggie grabbed a tea towel off the rack, noticing her friend had conquered the nervousness. "When we finish these dishes will you help me dress?"

"Certainly, dear, I'd be honored." Elizabeth's eyes misted. "I can't believe I'm helping you prepare for another wedding."

"How do you think I feel?" whispered Maggie, squeezing the blue and white china cup she was drying. Fortunately, it didn't crack.

A few minutes later, Elizabeth joined Maggie in the bedroom. Maggie had made the bed and performed her ablutions in record time before donning her petticoats and seating herself on the padded vanity chair facing away from the mirror. Elizabeth grabbed a brush and tackled Maggie's unruly curls.

"I popped into the bank yesterday, and informed Mr. Peterman that I would be vacating the house as agreed." Maggie wrung her hands as she spoke; she'd never done anything so difficult in her life.

"That must have been unpleasant for you," said Elizabeth, intuitive as ever.

"I'd come to grips with my decision." Maggie stared out the window, hearing a songbird chirping from a nearby tree branch. "What truly floored me was his revelation that he'd already sold my house."

"Go on with you." Elizabeth tipped Maggie's head up and then continued brushing the bride's locks. "Before you even moved out?"

"That greedy man couldn't wait to make a profit." Maggie sniffled, regained her composure, and moved the conversation to a more pleasant topic. "I dropped around to the clinic and told Doc Fitzgerald about Luke and the wedding, too."

"What did Doc think about your plans?" Elizabeth fussed with one unruly tendril.

"He wished me good luck. Even admitted that at one point he'd considered asking Sam and me to move into his 'lonely old mansion', as he called it. I suppose to help with his doctoring."

"Oh, that's rich!" Elizabeth hooted. "How could you help with any doctoring?"

"I have no idea." Maggie sighed, recalling her confused frenzy whenever faced with an emergency. If one of her students fell in the schoolyard or became ill in the classroom, she'd felt as helpless as a newborn kitten and sent one of the students for help. "I doubt he requires assistance. Just being his kind-hearted self."

"You're probably right." Elizabeth handed Maggie a small hand mirror and whispered, "Take a peek."

Delicate white daisies entwined throughout Maggie's long, flowing auburn hair, secured in place with the pearl-encrusted combs that were a gift from her Aunt Penny. Twin curly tendrils framed her smiling face. "It's beautiful, Elizabeth. Thank you so much."

"Sarah's daisies deserved a better purpose than sitting atop my kitchen table." Elizabeth patted Maggie's shoulder.

"They're perfect." Maggie peered into the mirror and inspected herself from all angles. "Sarah doesn't realize how special these blooms are."

Elizabeth turned away from Maggie's gaze. "Pinch your cheeks for some color."

Maggie quickly obeyed. "Please fetch my fancy boots from my valise."

Elizabeth extracted them and passed them over. "Here you go."

"Thank you." Maggie reached for the shiny boots that she'd spent hours cleaning after trekking through the mud to the saloon. She certainly couldn't afford a new pair, and her Sunday footwear looked decent again. "Except for our nightclothes and wedding duds, I shipped everything we own, even my piano, to Luke's ranch yesterday."

"When Mike picked up Luke's parcels at the store, he mentioned heading over to your house next."

"For an abandoned orphan, Mike matured into a wonderful young man." Maggie finished buttoning the boots with her hook and tossed it back into her bag.

"Luke's foreman and his wife adopted the boy."

"Wife? I didn't know Ned was married!" blurted Maggie, taken aback.

"Mind you, I've never met her." Elizabeth appeared deep in thought. "But I'm certain he's married."

"Well, I'll probably meet his wife when I move to the ranch." Maggie stood and shook out her petticoats.

"Now, let's hope this old wedding dress of mine isn't too big on you." Elizabeth bustled across the room. "This dress has remained hidden away in my trunk, waiting for my daughter's wedding. But children weren't in God's plan for Ronald and me, so I insist you wear it."

"Thank you so much." Maggie dabbed fragrance on her neck and wrists, then silently questioned why she bothered. This wasn't a real wedding, and Luke wouldn't notice such things. Why should he? But her favorite lilac scent might help calm her nerves today.

"Raise your arms, so I won't muss up your hair." Elizabeth guided the medium-blue silk gown over Maggie's head as her slim arms worked their way through the long, lacy sleeves. Her hands caressed dozens of seed pearls sewn onto the bodice, but the high stiff lace collar scratched her neck until Elizabeth finished buttoning it in place.

"Shake out the skirts," ordered Elizabeth.

When Maggie obeyed, the generous skirts billowed around

her slim body. "It's so beautiful."

"I'm happy we're putting it to use," insisted Elizabeth, still fussing with the skirt's voluminous folds.

Looking at herself in the cheval mirror, Maggie imagined a much-younger Elizabeth as a bride. Ronald and Elizabeth adored each other, and Maggie hoped the dress would bring her good luck, if not love.

Elizabeth draped a white lace shawl around Maggie's shoulders, and then exclaimed, "You look absolutely lovely!"

"Thank you, Elizabeth. I'm doing the right thing, especially for Sam and the baby." Maggie smiled at their reflections in the mirror and wondered which of them she was trying to reassure.

"I'll leave you alone while I change and check that Ronald and Sam are getting dressed. I'll meet you down in the parlor in a few minutes, dear." Elizabeth patted her hand, and then hurried from the room.

Maggie stared at her reflection in the mirror, and her thoughts shifted to William. "How did our lives take such an unexpected turn?" Realizing she'd spoken aloud, she half expected William to answer her.

What if she was making the worst mistake of her life? No, her children were her only concern. Standing tall and prepared to face her future head on, Maggie pulled her shoulders back, held her head high, and stepped into the hallway.

* * *

"I hope things'll work out fer ya, Sonny Boy. I sincerely do." Ned's arthritic fingers skillfully adjusted Luke's western bow tie.

"Thank you for saying that. Catherine's been gone for two years now, and I'm moving on," stated Luke and the two men shook hands.

"Never thought I'd hear 'em words outta yer mouth, knowin' how much ya loved Catherine." Ned shook his head. "But out here in the West, a feller's gotta make his own happiness. Always somethin' awaitin' round the corner to ruin things fer ya."

"So very true, Ned." Raising his foot onto the entryway chair, Luke swiped the dust off one boot, and then switched and did the other. He tossed the rag into the entryway table's drawer and closed it.

Would marrying Maggie assure his happiness? And hers? It certainly couldn't hurt. At least he'd have the satisfaction of knowing he'd done the right thing, rescued her and Sam from an impossible situation. What had William Burns been thinking? Luke shook his head. He could never leave his family faced with such a precarious future.

He pulled himself from his musings. "Right now my main concern is Lucy. What's that girl thinking? Does she perceive Maggie as a threat? Believe marriage to Maggie means I've forgotten her ma?"

"I'm plumb outta ideas as to what that girl's thinkin', but she's some unhappy." Ned shrugged his shoulders. "Let me look ya over."

Luke slowly turned in a circle for final inspection. His hands had shaken while he'd fumbled his way into his new black trousers, white dress shirt, and waistcoat upstairs in his room. And then he'd scolded himself. Just going through the motions. Not a real wedding.

"Ya look right proper, fer a feller about to git hitched," announced Ned, grinning.

"I'm a tad on edge," he admitted, as he slipped into his Sunday-best frock coat. "Should have dropped by Barney's Barber Shop, got my ears lowered." Luke's nervousness annoyed him.

"Stick yer hat on, and nobody'll notice yer dang hair," advised Ned.

"I can't very well wear my bowler into The Spirit Creek Church, can I?" Luke sounded more annoyed than he intended. Maybe he should just slap his old Stetson on his head. He smiled, knowing his proper English mother would roll in her grave if he set foot in church in that thing.

"Dang it. I forgot about the churchin' part." Ned adjusted his own string tie and checked his appearance in the large gilded mirror in the entryway. "Don't worry, Sonny Boy. Ya look fine."

Patti swept down the long staircase like a princess departing for the royal ball. Smiling from ear to ear, she curtseyed and proclaimed, "I'm all ready to go."

Luke laughed at her playful antics. "And looking exceptionally pretty in your new pink dress."

"Thank you, Papa." Patti held a matching pink ribbon in one

hand and tiny white gloves in the other. White cotton socks and shiny new black leather shoes completed her attire. "Will you please tie up my hair, Uncle Ned?"

"Where's yer sister?" inquired Ned, reaching for the hair ribbon.

"That's an excellent question. We should have left five minutes ago," added Luke, checking his pocket watch. Standing at the foot of the long winding staircase, he called, "Lucy, hurry up or we'll be late."

"Stand still if'n ya want this bow tied proper-like," scolded Ned. Patti stood as still as a palace guard, allowing his arthritic fingers to tie a neat bow with practiced efficiency.

While Luke waited at the foot of the stairs for Lucy to appear, thoughts of Catherine popped into his mind. He recalled their wedding day; he was scared skinny and twice as nervous as today. But having made this decision, he'd promised himself he'd endure a loveless marriage to ensure a promising future for his girls. He knew Catherine would approve.

"Lucy, hurry up!" repeated Luke, one foot resting on the bottom step.

"I'm not going!" Lucy replied.

"The devil you're not."

Lucy stood in her nightdress at the top of the staircase, glaring at her father. "I am not going!"

"Oh, you're coming with us. I'm your pa, and you will obey me." Luke started up the long curved staircase, fists clenched at his side, eyes blazing. They were running late already, and he didn't have time for her histrionics. "Get into one of your new dresses and brush your hair. We're leaving in five minutes."

"Why would you shame Mama this way?" Lucy burst into tears.

As Luke reached the top step, he unclenched his fists and softened his words. "I loved your ma more than life itself. But she's gone, sweetheart. You and Patti need a mother to answer your questions about becoming a woman, to impart wisdom, to encourage your dreams."

"I don't want another woman in Mama's house." Lucy swiped at her tears and then crossed her arms, eyes blazing. "This wedding is the stupidest idea I've ever heard!"

"Well, you're entitled to your opinion, but you're attending the wedding, either in a pretty gown or dressed as you are. If you don't change now, I'll toss you into the carriage, nightdress and all!" Luke felt his face heat with embarrassment.

He'd never before spoken to his daughter this way, but her behavior was so infuriating. For the first time in his life, Lucy had questioned his authority, his decision. He felt ill-prepared to deal with such an independent, headstrong daughter. Thankfully, she'd acquire a new mother by day's end.

"Fine, I'll go. But I hope you see reason and change your mind before it's too late." Lucy stomped into her bedroom and slammed the door closed.

His daughter returned almost twenty minutes later, but she was dressed in her newest finery: a pale blue satin dress trimmed with white lace, shiny black leather shoes, and white gloves. Long blonde hair hung down her back, held in place with a blue ribbon. She looked so beautiful.

But she hadn't removed the scowl from her face.

* * *

Elizabeth borrowed Doc Fitzgerald's elegant carriage for the bride's trip to the church in order to better accommodate the wedding gown's billowing skirts. Ronald and Sam led the way in Ronald's buggy.

Elizabeth and Sam disappeared inside the church, leaving Maggie in the carriage with Ronald for company, until Elizabeth fetched her for the ceremony.

"This is ridiculous," complained Maggie, shifting in her seat. "Why must I bide my time waiting in this stifling carriage, Ronald?"

"I have no idea, but that's my orders," stated Ronald, emphatically.

"Why should it matter whether I wait in this carriage or in the church? What's the delay?" Maggie attempted to peek out through the small window, but Ronald blocked her view.

"I don't know, my dear. But Elizabeth accomplishes more by noon than most people finish by sunset. So when she gives orders, I obey with no questions asked." Ronald picked a piece of lint off his trousers and then straightened his bowler.

"Well, it's absolutely ridiculous. This isn't even a real wedding. We're only going through the motions." Maggie slumped in her seat.

The next time she checked her watch pin, almost an hour had passed. She might have actually dozed off for a few minutes. "What on earth is the hold up?" she complained.

"Perhaps Reverend Gerald has been delayed." Ronald relaxed in his seat.

Maggie crossed her legs, and then uncrossed them again. Suddenly, her eyes grew wide. "Oh fiddle, this can't be happening."

"Maggie, are you ill?" Ronald reached out his hand, but she brushed it aside.

"It's not Reverend Gerald at all. It's Luke!" Maggie's eyes blazed. "He's changed his mind. He intends to leave me at the altar!"

"I'm certain he's just running late." Ronald met her eyes, and added, "But when he arrives he'll have me to deal with. Leaving you cooling your heels like this is unforgivable."

At that moment, Elizabeth stuck her head through the carriage window, knocking her new navy-blue chapeau askew. "How are we doing?" she chirped, straightening her hat. Noticing Maggie's murderous expression, she asked, "Oh dear, what's wrong?"

"Maggie believes Luke changed his mind, and he's not coming." Ronald shifted nervously in his seat.

"Elizabeth, Luke's realized this ridiculous marriage is a terrible mistake. Or perhaps, he's testing my gullibility." Maggie whispered, "At least only you, Ronald, and Reverend Gerald know about Luke's devious plan to leave me at the altar, looking like a fool."

"Why would any man plot such a hurtful trick on a poor widow? I'm betting he's just running late." Ronald glared at his wife.

Elizabeth yanked the carriage door open, hoisted her skirts, and climbed inside.

"I can't believe I fell for his silly idea. Desperation goes hand in hand with stupid decisions," rationalized Maggie, shaking with fury. "I'm such an imbecile. If I wasn't so gullible I'd have guessed Luke's intentions. Remember what William did to me? And now Luke's done the same. Ronald, take me back to the house."

"You can't just leave, Maggie!" A horror-stricken expression creased Elizabeth's face. "What will people think?"

"Only the Reverend knows. We'll say there's been a misunderstanding," suggested Maggie, accepting the fact she'd been duped by a man again.

Elizabeth's fingers played with her lacy white handkerchief. "Maggie, I have a confession. When I begged Sarah for some flowers from her garden to decorate the church, she browbeat me until I divulged the reason I required them. Together, we invited some folks to your nuptials."

"You did what?" blurted Maggie, aghast.

"We wanted some semblance of normalcy for you, considering the circumstances of your union with Luke. I admit I'm feeling rather guilty now." Elizabeth's pained expression didn't elicit Maggie's forgiveness.

"Well, everyone in town will certainly remember the day Luke Carlyle made a complete fool of Maggie Burns." She turned in her seat, giving her friend the cold shoulder. "Perhaps I should return back East after all. It couldn't be any worse than what's happening right now."

At that moment, Luke Carlyle popped his head through the open doorway. "There's the bride. Sorry we're late, folks. We experienced some difficulty with Lucy, but I'll explain about that later."

"It doesn't matter. I've changed my mind." Maggie spoke through clenched teeth. "I'm moving back East after all," she lied, desperate to escape the embarrassing situation.

Luke's gaze flew to Elizabeth, then to Ronald, and back to Maggie. "You can't change your mind."

Maggie placed her hands in her lap. "You concocted this ridiculous idea to humiliate me by leaving me at the altar. I don't trust you enough to even pretend to be your wife."

"I would never humiliate my wife, even a pretend one. We are getting married today. Let me help you out of this carriage." Luke proffered his hand.

Elizabeth leapt up and clasped his hand. After Luke safely assisted Elizabeth out of the carriage, Ronald followed. Maggie glanced from Elizabeth to Ronald. Finally, her eyes settled on Luke, but she remained seated.

"Are you coming, or not?" asked Elizabeth, impatiently.

Everyone waited a half minute for her response.

"Help me out of this carriage, Luke. We need to talk." Maggie stuck out her hand and ducked her head. When her feet touched the ground, she politely added, "Thank you."

"Excuse us for a moment, please." Luke guided the bride-to-be toward a massive cottonwood tree several feet away. His expression told Maggie he had no idea what she intended to discuss with him. Luke stood, hands clasped behind his back. "Perhaps it's for the best if you return back East, Maggie. I'll purchase tickets for you and Sam and forward your belongings from the ranch."

Maggie blanched. William wasn't the only one with limited gambling skills; Luke had called her bluff. Forced to fess up, she hissed, "I have no intention to move back East." She swiped at a stray lock of hair and then glanced away.

"I suspected as much." Luke turned her toward him, lifted her chin with his hand, and forced her to meet his eyes. "If you won't marry me, how do you intend to support yourself?"

"I don't know. But I refuse to marry a man I don't trust." Maggie realized that marrying Luke was her only means of staying in Spirit Creek, but what common sense told her, her ego refused to admit.

"Maggie, I'm the most respected man in Spirit Creek." Luke threw up his hands. "Why don't you trust me?"

"How could you leave me waiting for an hour before putting in an appearance at your own wedding?" Maggie glared at him, feeling betrayed and embarrassed. She'd convinced herself Luke wasn't coming, but he stood before her now. Was her wounded pride overruling levelheadedness? She pulled the wrap a little tighter around her shoulders, suddenly chilled despite being close to suffocating a few minutes ago in the stuffy carriage.

"Lucy doesn't believe I should marry you," blurted Luke, frustration evident in his voice.

"Perhaps Lucy's right." Maggie fought back tears, silently reminding herself to keep a clear head and not to succumb to her emotions. But she'd never felt more confused. Should she trust her instincts, or should she trust the stranger standing before her?

"Lucy's defending her ma's memory. She doesn't realize you're homeless, penniless." Luke leaned closer and whispered close to her ear, "She doesn't know you're with child."

"And you're certain I'm doing the right thing?" Her shoulders slumped. She yearned for a guarantee that this arrangement would work, for Sam's peace of mind more than her own. But life didn't provide guarantees.

"I am, and deep down you know it, too. If you refuse to move back East you have no more choices." Luke searched her eyes.

Maggie pursed her lips. *No more choices.* It galled her to admit Luke was right. Besides, she'd said yes to this proposed arrangement, and she'd been taught that a person's word was as binding as a legally-notarized document. She turned and walked back to the carriage.

* * *

Luke followed, walking a step behind his betrothed, hoping he'd successfully convinced her to go ahead with the wedding. She didn't trust him, and he couldn't blame her after all she'd endured. Until this very moment, he hadn't realized how badly William Burns' deceptions had hurt her.

"Elizabeth, I'm ready now," mumbled Maggie, bunching the wrap in her hands and tossing it through the carriage door before straightening her skirts.

Luke grimaced. She'd uttered the statement like a prisoner's coerced confession; words everyone wanted to hear but weren't necessarily true. *I'm ready now.* Was her mind made up? Was her heart prepared? Or was she simply resigned to whatever fate awaited her?

"Ronald, walk me into the church, please." Maggie's sorrow-filled request sounded wrenched from her, spoken against her better judgment, but she extended her trembling hand. Without hesitation, Ronald smiled and tucked her hand into the crook of his arm.

Luke exhaled in a rush, unaware he'd been holding his breath. He barely stopped himself from wrapping her in his arms and squeezing the distrust and uncertainty he saw in her eyes from every fiber of her being.

"Thank you, Maggie." Luke whispered the words like a prayer. "I believe you're doing the right thing, and I'm hoping someday you'll believe it, too."

Maggie only offered him a weak smile.

Luke grimaced. She doesn't believe a word of it, fears she's making the worst mistake of her life. Would they remain married long enough for her to realize his intentions were honorable and sincere? Or would she insist on a divorce, scandalous though it would be, the first time they argued? He just needed time to prove to her that their arrangement could work.

Luke walked toward the church with Elizabeth on his arm. For a moment, he glanced back at Maggie standing beside Ronald. She looked as dejected as a child abandoned outside an orphanage. The sight almost tore his heart out of his chest.

Ned, Lucy and Patti waited for Luke at the bottom of the wide whitewashed church steps, and he smiled as he approached. "Everyone is ready. Let's go inside."

Ned placed his gnarled hands on Lucy's thin shoulders and urged her forward. But she reached for her father's hand and pleaded, "Papa, she doesn't want to marry you. Forget this, and let's go home."

"Lucy, go inside," ordered Luke.

After a moment's hesitation, his willful daughter stomped up the church steps with Ned shuffling along behind her. She never looked back, just disappeared inside.

Elizabeth grasped Patti's hand. "Come sit with Sam and me up front, dear."

Luke inhaled deeply, blew out his breath, and then followed. Just inside the door, he removed his bowler and then froze in his tracks. Almost every pew was occupied. He glared at Elizabeth and growled, "This is an exceptionally well-attended private wedding."

Several heads turned their way, hearing Luke's raised voice.

"Sarah Grayson provides the flowers for weddings and funerals. No one died. She dragged the wedding news out of me," whispered Elizabeth.

Luke lowered his voice to reply. "And then, the two of you planned all this?" He suspected a limited amount of 'dragging out' occurred, knowing women and their fondness for weddings. Elizabeth no doubt willingly served as Sarah's accomplice.

"Yes, and I won't apologize for it. We wanted to make the day special for Maggie. And you'd better do the same for the rest of her life." Elizabeth poked him in the chest for added emphasis and then scurried toward the front pew where she seated Patti beside Sam.

Luke rubbed the spot where she'd jabbed him and then

strode up the aisle behind them.

"Where's Mama?" whispered Sam, smiling when Luke winked at him.

"She'll be along in a minute, dear." Elizabeth patted his leg.

Luke faced Reverend Gerald standing under a huge arch in front of his congregation. "Morning," he said, shaking the fellow's hand.

"Not exactly the wedding we planned on Wednesday afternoon," observed Reverend Gerald, smiling at the groom. "But you know what women are like when it comes to a wedding."

"I'm beginning to remember," muttered Luke, passing his hat to Ned while silently praying Maggie wouldn't bolt from the church when she realized what her friends had done.

The groom smiled at his daughters and then nodded a greeting to his closest neighbors, Robert and Hattie Morgan and their two sons, R. J. and Donnie. He pulled his watch from his waistcoat pocket. It was twenty minutes past eleven, and he'd told the preacher ten o'clock.

"Sorry for the delay, Reverend."

"Quite all right, Luke. I haven't seen every pew filled in ages." Reverend Gerald rocked on the balls of his feet and smiled at his fold. Luke suspected news of the unexpected nuptials explained the unprecedented turnout.

Kenneth Wallace, the liveryman, and his wife, Wilma, caught Luke's eye and he smiled. His gaze tripped across the aisle toward Sheriff Franklin Smith, seated beside Ellie Thomas, the schoolteacher. Luke recognized several ranchers and their families, and he nodded a greeting to old Doc Fitzgerald. But he didn't recognize the portly gentleman standing in the back corner.

Luke caught a movement out of the corner of his eye and turned. Maggie's voluminous skirts billowed around her and she appeared to float towards him on Ronald's arm. Absent of expression, his future wife might as well be heading to the gallows. His stomach knotted. For better or for worse, he was getting married.

* * *

Maggie gasped as Ronald guided her into the church. Hushed voices reached her ears when she paused just inside the doorway, allowing her eyes to adjust to the interior light. Many citizens of Spirit Creek and area were crammed into the pews. She nearly swooned and leaned on Ronald for support.

"Oh, fiddle. Why are all these people here?" Maggie whispered through clenched teeth.

Ronald replied, a deadpan expression on his face. "There's a wedding in town today."

Maggie couldn't stop herself from smiling. Ronald's bit of humor would help her through this. She startled when Sarah Grayson pressed a small bouquet of spring flowers into her hands. Although stunned, she whispered, "Thank you."

Grasping Ronald's arm tightly, Maggie journeyed down the narrow aisle on shaky legs, forcing herself to smile at the assembly of Spirit Creek citizens and their children, many of them former students. She stumbled once, distracted by the lavish decorations, but Ronald kept her from falling.

A sprig of ponderosa pine tied with a handful of larkspur, bluebells, and daisies greeted her from the end of every rustic hewn pew, and a cluster of lilacs adorned each window ledge. A garland of blue-green sagebrush sprigs and blooming lilac branches lay across the top of the piano. Large milk crocks, filled with a rainbow assortment of blooms, surrounded the altar. Luke and Reverend Gerald stood under an arch, fashioned from ponderosa pine boughs, with small pink peony blooms attached.

Candles burned in holders arranged throughout the church, an unseemly waste in Maggie's opinion on such a sunny May morning. But the hypnotic atmosphere and intoxicating scents stole her breath away. Recalling the whispered conversation in Elizabeth's kitchen this morning, Maggie fought back tears, overcome by the ladies' thoughtfulness.

Arriving at the arch, she turned and searched for her son. Elizabeth, without a hint of guilt, met Maggie's eyes and waved her ever-present handkerchief. Whether attending the wedding of her best friend or a total stranger, Elizabeth would shed an equal number of tears.

Sam sat beside Elizabeth in the front pew, swinging his short legs. Doubts overwhelmed Maggie's thoughts. Am I doing the right thing? Will Sam be happy living with strangers? Her normal school training taught her that young children quickly adjusted to change.

Luke's youngest daughter was holding Sam's hand, and both she and Sam waved. Luke's oldest daughter slumped in the seat beside Ned, arms crossed, a scowl on her face. Oh my, she recalled Luke's warning that Lucy didn't approve of their marriage.

Luke's eyes met Maggie's, and her heart skipped a beat. Perhaps she should stop this silliness right now. And then what would she do? She silently cursed William for leaving her in this situation. There was no turning back now; she must go through with this charade. For better or for worse, she was getting married.

"Dearly beloved, we are gathered…" Reverend Gerald began the solemn ceremony and his smiling face turned toward Luke and then back to her. She watched the minister's mouth form words, but her vision blurred and her hearing evaporated. She was vaguely aware that Ronald released her arm and seated himself beside his wife.

Was this loveless marriage punishment for her anger toward William? When she'd spoken the vows during her wedding to William, she'd meant every word. Today, she would vow to love a man she considered almost a total stranger. Was Luke equally uncomfortable with his lie? He didn't love her. Without a doubt, he'd loved Catherine when he'd married her. Was Luke experiencing similar distress?

As if stepping into sunshine while walking in fog, her senses cleared. Luke was staring at her, but she couldn't read the odd expression on his face. She must have spoken the 'I do's' when prompted, but she recalled nothing. And then she heard Reverend Gerald's words. "Luke, I said you may kiss your bride."

Maggie's heart almost stopped.

Chapter 4

You may kiss your bride.

The Reverend had spoken the words twice. Was Luke waiting for her permission?

Her body stiffened when Luke gently brushed her cheek with the softest of kisses, but his lips burned her skin like the brands ranchers use to denote ownership of their cattle and horses. She couldn't stop her hand from touching her cheek. Had Luke's kiss just marked her as his own?

"You smell very pretty. The same as the other day. Lilac scent must be your favorite," whispered Luke, smiling.

Maggie met his eyes. The fact Luke noticed the fragrance boggled her mind. William had never once complimented her on her scent. "Thank you, and thank goodness that's over," she muttered, relieved that she'd survived the ceremony. She just wanted to collect Sam and head to her new home as soon as possible while still making a gracious exit.

"Ladies and gentlemen." Reverend Gerald smiled at Sarah Grayson standing at his side. "Your presence is requested at Mrs. Grayson's lovely home for the wedding luncheon and the opportunity to extend your congratulations and best wishes to the newly-married couple."

"Thank you for making the announcement," said Sarah, smiling.

Maggie almost swooned, but Luke slipped his arm around her waist. The reverend's words shattered her momentary relief. She'd survived the ceremony, but a luncheon loomed ahead. How would she keep up this pretense?

As if he'd read her mind, Luke whispered, "You can do this. I'll remain at your side for support. Everything will be fine." His eyes met hers, and he smiled.

She needed his support but was his concern genuine? She wanted desperately to believe he'd remain at her side. That he'd help her through the remainder of the day while she faced the inevitable questions from half the population of Spirit Creek.

"Mama, I'm hungry." Sam tugged at her skirts, bringing her back from her thoughts.

Luke scooped Sam up into his arms and ruffled his hair. "Well, son, it's official."

"You're my new papa?" whispered Sam, wrapping one small arm around Luke's neck.

"I surely am," answered Luke, grinning. "Now, let's get you something to eat."

Maggie rode alone with Luke inside Doc's carriage to Sarah's house, while Ned took Lucy, Patti and Sam in Luke's carriage. Luke made no attempt to engage Maggie in conversation, perhaps suspecting she required time to regain her composure. Why wasn't Luke overwhelmed by the surprise preparations? The groom appeared totally unfazed by the whole affair. Was Mr. Take-Charge, Always-In-Control Carlyle never riled by anything? Luke acted exceptionally easy-going, a very agreeable trait in a husband.

"Lord only knows what's awaiting us in this marriage," she whispered, and then blushed when she realized she'd spoken the thought aloud.

"Did you say something?" Luke glanced her way.

"Did you know about the townsfolk attending the wedding? The flowers? The luncheon?" accused Maggie, as the carriage pulled up to Sarah's house.

"Never heard a peep. Your friends are a crafty pair." Luke assisted his new wife out of the carriage and then thanked Doc for driving the rig to the luncheon.

Cradling her elbow, Luke guided her along the pathway leading to the backyard. As they rounded the corner of the mansion, Luke and Maggie stopped in their tracks and stood gaping. Meticulously-maintained flowerbeds overflowed with a spectacular array of flowers and shrubs. Towering cottonwoods and ponderosa pine trees shaded a dozen rectangular tables set up in the large garden. A short glass vase of colorful blooms served as the centerpiece on each table draped with a lace-trimmed white tablecloth.

"I'm speechless," whispered Maggie, taking it all in.

Elizabeth and her accomplice approached the bride and groom. "I'm responsible for divulging your wedding plans. And Sarah insisted we go all out with the decorations," confessed Elizabeth.

"And we invited everybody we crossed paths with and then some," added Sarah, smiling unashamedly. "I hope you're not too angry with us, but we won't apologize. You deserve a memorable wedding celebration."

"It's such an unexpected surprise. I'm in shock." Maggie threw up her hands. "But you're both forgiven. I'll never forget this day."

"Allow me to add my thanks, ladies," said Luke, smiling. Maggie startled, having forgotten he was standing beside her. "Everyone's enjoying themselves, including me."

Luke's intense gaze undid Maggie, and her heart flipped over in her chest. While he searched her eyes so intently she wondered what he saw. Her sorrow, her anger, her regrets? Her uncertainty? Or had he caught a glimpse of their future together?

If she possessed a crystal ball like the gypsies she'd read about in childhood storybooks, perhaps she could preview her life. What if the future held even more pain and heartache? She banished such a terrifying thought from her mind. *For better or for worse*, she reminded herself.

Luke and Maggie cordially accepted congratulations and best wishes from the guests. Everyone assured the bride that they understood her situation and believed she'd made a wise decision. Maggie pasted a smile on her face, relieved she hadn't become a social outcast.

China platters overflowed with cold meats, cheeses and sandwiches. Colorful glass bowls contained an assortment of pickles and preserves. Generous slices of fruit pies and cakes sat atop small dessert plates on one long table. Gallons of tea and coffee awaited the adults, and a huge platter of cookies and pitchers of cold milk tempted the children.

"Luke and Maggie, I believe you two are well suited as a couple, and I wish you both a long and happy life together," offered Sarah, escorting Luke and Maggie to their table of honor where fragrant wildflowers adorned the posts on two ladder-back chairs.

"Thank you, Sarah." Maggie avoided Luke's eyes. Only time would tell.

An enormous, rectangular cake with white icing occupied a place of honor on the table in front of the bride and groom. Their names were scripted across the top in the exact shade of blue icing as her borrowed wedding dress. Maggie experienced a moment of disbelief, having her name associated with Luke's. Wasn't it only yesterday she'd married William? Now, in the blink of an eye, she'd become Mrs. Luke Carlyle.

Two teenaged girls set a plateful of food each in front of Maggie and Luke, and the newlyweds ate in silence for several minutes.

"We experienced some difficulty with Lucy this morning," mumbled Luke, almost to himself. "She's too independent, stubborn, and strong-willed. She's only eleven, and I'm losing control of her." Luke related the nature of his conversation with Lucy.

"Hopefully, we'll convince her that we have her best interests at heart." Maggie patted his hand. "Patti and Sam are accepting this sibling business. Did you notice the two of them holding hands in the church? She's just adorable, Luke." Maggie followed Luke's gaze.

A young man raced across Sarah's lush green lawn, headed for Doc Fitzgerald. Words were exchanged, accompanied by arm flailing and finger pointing. The old doctor dropped his napkin on his plate and lumbered toward his carriage.

"I hope no one is injured or seriously ill." Luke craned his neck, observing the frantic exchange. "Perhaps a woman is birthing a baby?"

"I hope Doc moves that quickly when it's my time." Maggie blushed, realizing she'd blurted her thoughts aloud.

"Amen to that," whispered Luke.

Maggie sat, speechless. Luke's instant agreement confirmed his caring nature; this kind-hearted man she'd just married couldn't abuse anyone. Her new home would be a safe haven. She'd done the right thing in that regard.

The young girls returned to the head table several times, their arms overflowing with gifts which Luke and Maggie opened. Afterward, the couple mingled with the guests, extending a thank you for the generous gifts and for attending on such short notice.

After the wedding cake was served, Ronald handed Luke a cigar, which he lit. The sudden whiff of smoke sent Maggie's stomach roiling. Refusing to ruin the day with a display of morning sickness, she wandered away in search of Elizabeth.

"Hello, Maggie." A portly gentleman appeared at Maggie's side. "It's been years since I saw you last. I was engaged at the time."

Maggie leaned closer, looking the vaguely-familiar fellow in the eye. "Arthur MacDonald? I don't believe it. How are you?" She shook his hand enthusiastically, her queasy stomach forgotten.

"Don't blame you for not recognizing me right off. We were acquainted about sixty pounds ago." Arthur patted his ample middle. "I'm working for a fellow in Miles City, owns the Yellowstone Journal. I've been traveling around Montana visiting local towns. In November, I'll be covering the big news when Montana receives statehood. Won't that be an exciting day?"

"Everyone I've talked to is delighted. Becoming citizens of the great United States of America will be life-changing for so many people." Maggie recalled William's dream of being named a U. S. Marshall, but he'd died before realizing his goal. "Are your travels a holiday of sorts? Or are you working on an assignment?"

"Actually, I've been visiting local towns in hopes of starting up my own newspaper. With my employer's blessing, of course. Now that I've met up with you again, perhaps I should give Spirit Creek special consideration."

"Arthur, a newspaper would be so welcome. Even with the telegraph and the stagecoach coming through twice weekly, news takes forever to reach our little town." Maggie admired Arthur, a very likeable chap. And she'd never understood what he saw in the extremely opinionated and very spoiled debutante he'd been engaged to. She'd heard he called off the wedding, and she hadn't been surprised.

"Maggie, I've spent considerable time learning photography from a slightly-eccentric local woman, in my opinion anyway, who travels around the area taking photographs. I've brought my camera with me. I've mastered the contraption, so please come by the hotel after the luncheon. I'll take your picture with Mr. Carlyle, a wedding present for you both." Arthur waddled toward the hotel before Maggie could reply.

Elizabeth strolled across the lawn and stood beside Maggie. With tears threatening to undo her stiff British composure, Elizabeth placed her wrinkled hands on Maggie's cheeks. "You keep getting married. One night under my roof, and here I am saying goodbye again."

"I'll only be a few miles from town. You'll see me often." Maggie hugged her friend. And then her eyes wandered toward Luke, standing on the opposite side of the yard, deep in conversation with Ronald. "What do you suppose our men are discussing?"

Our men? Maggie felt her face warm. She'd used the expression often when married to William. That the words rolled off her tongue so easily, having just wed Luke, momentarily shocked her.

"Could be anything," said Elizabeth, with a dismissive wave of her hand.

Had she even noticed Maggie's choice of words? "Quite an intense topic, judging by their expressions," she observed.

"Ronald enjoys a good chin wag." Elizabeth shook her head. "It's a wonder he ever accomplishes anything at the store."

"If the topic concerns us, we'll learn soon enough." Maggie reached for her friend's hand. "Let's share another piece of Sarah's delicious cake."

"Heavens! Do we dare?"

"Yes," answered Maggie, laughing. "Sarah won't divulge her grandmother's recipe, so we might as well enjoy her masterpiece."

* * *

Luke wasn't fond of cigars, but he wouldn't refuse Ronald's offer. "Doc rushed away like the devil was licking at his heels. Do you suppose someone's been injured?" questioned Luke, searching for an opening topic of conversation.

"I overheard something about a baby coming." Ronald puffed on his cigar. "That young lad was one of Florence Jones' boys. This one must be what, twelve for her now?"

"Sounds about right." Luke noticed the older man wouldn't meet his eyes. "What's on your mind?" He blew a smoke ring while waiting for Ronald's answer.

"You've just married a woman I consider my daughter." Ronald looked Luke in the eye. "This conversation is as close to a father-of-the-bride speech as you're going to get."

"All right, let's have it." Luke stood with his arms crossed, carefully avoiding burning a hole in his best frock coat with his cigar.

"Maggie's pretty tender of heart; she's lost William and she's lost her home. Found herself in a sticky financial situation. I'm proud of you, son, for stepping up and helping her out like you did." Ronald's eyes drilled into Luke's like the concerned father he claimed to be. "She's a very loving person, son, and I wouldn't be surprised if she came to love you one day, but I'm hoping you'll take her feelings into consideration and give her a little time for now."

"Maggie became my wife today, and I'll treat her as such. She'll be given all the time she needs to grieve. But you know that, Ronald, or you wouldn't have allowed me to marry her." Luke puffed on his cigar. Ronald had known Luke since he was a teenager, and his character and upbringing spoke for him.

"You're right, Luke, but the words needed saying anyway." Ronald slapped Luke on the back. "You best stay behind when Ned and the children leave for the ranch in your carriage. The girls loaded up all your presents, won't be room for you and Maggie anyway."

"What do you have in mind for us?" Luke raised one eyebrow. Had Ronald and Elizabeth arranged a room for them tonight at The Spirit Creek Hotel as a wedding-night gift? Was June, the hotel owner, in on the wedding surprise as well?

"I'll lend you my buggy, give you newlyweds some time alone on the ride out to your ranch. Just arrange for one of your ranch hands to return the rig to town tomorrow." Ronald puffed on his cigar.

"Thank you for your thoughtfulness. I'd enjoy a private talk with Maggie." Luke shook hands with the man he now considered his father-in-law.

Luke wasn't certain he was relieved or disappointed to hear he wouldn't be spending the night alone with Maggie at the hotel. Of course, nothing would have happened between them. Tonight wouldn't be a proper wedding night. Still, he looked forward to spending time alone with her to just talk and get to know each other better. And who would say no to a starlit ride with a beautiful woman, especially a fellow's wife, on a lovely May evening.

Ronald smiled and slapped him on the back again. "It will give Maggie a chance to catch her breath after all this ballyhoo today."

Luke threw his head back and laughed. "Between you and me, Ronald, I think you're spot on. But you best hope our wives don't hear you referring to this wedding as ballyhoo." He strolled across the yard and explained the change of plans to Ned who quickly rounded up the children. All three of them circled Luke, waiting to hear his news.

Luke glanced at his new wife and smiled. "I'll explain in a minute." He whispered his plans to Ned and the children. He kissed Patti and Lucy on their cheeks while Sam hugged his mother and assured her he wanted to go with Ned and the girls. Luke and Maggie watched the two younger children race each other to the carriage with Ned and Lucy lumbering along behind.

As the carriage headed down the street, harness jangling, Luke slipped his arm around Maggie. "The children will be fine. Ronald offered us his buggy to provide some quiet time together after this busy day."

"But…Sam…" stammered Maggie.

Luke caught the hesitation in her eyes. His new wife appeared as skittish as an abused mare, and equally untrusting. What would it take to dispel her fears? "Wouldn't you enjoy some private conversation while riding out to the ranch?"

"Sam appeared happy enough," conceded Maggie. She pulled back her shoulders and smiled at him. "All right, we'll ride together in Ronald's buggy."

"Good." Luke tucked Maggie's arm around his, ignoring her reaction when she jumped at his touch. "Mrs. Carlyle, let's extend a final goodbye to our guests. Then, we'll head home."

* * *

Fifteen minutes later, Ronald and Luke strolled across Sarah Grayson's lush green lawn, deep in conversation and laughing at a shared joke. Elizabeth and Maggie, arms entwined, followed behind them. Maggie noticed how much it felt like old times when she and William had spent a day together with her two favorite people.

The foursome approached Ronald's handsome buggy where

one of Sarah's hired grooms held the horse's bridle. The newly-painted black frame and fire-red wheels shone in the late afternoon sunshine. Maggie recalled many a comfortable ride on the upholstered benches, and Elizabeth had insisted on the covered top which protected everyone from the elements. The open sides provided an unobstructed view of passing scenery for the riders out on an excursion.

Twelve-year-old Molly playfully nudged Ronald's hand, and he dug something out of his pocket and fed the mare a treat. In spite of her age, Molly danced a lively two-step, eager to begin her journey.

"Take good care of my girl, Luke," ordered Ronald.

"Do you mean Maggie or your mare?" teased Luke, grinning.

"Both of them." Ronald chuckled and rubbed the horse's neck.

"They're both safe with me." Luke shook the older fellow's hand.

"I snuck home and fetched your bags." Ronald pointed to Maggie's valise sitting on the back bench. "Sent Sam's bag with Ned."

"Thank you." Maggie stood on her toes and kissed Ronald's cheek.

"You're welcome, my dear girl. I want nothing but happiness for you and this fellow," he whispered in her ear.

"Me, too," she replied, blinking back tears.

Elizabeth hugged Maggie as if she were embarking on an extended stay overseas. "I'll miss you so much, my dear."

"Me, too," repeated Maggie, sniffling.

Luke sighed as he watched them embrace. "My house is situated on the northern corner of the ranch, only five miles out of town."

Maggie tossed him a sharp look. "It's not the same as living a few streets away."

"We're burning daylight. If that MacDonald fellow expects a good photograph we should be going." Luke shifted his weight to his other foot.

"Photograph?" inquired Elizabeth, a puzzled expression on her face.

Maggie explained Arthur's offer while Luke climbed into the buggy and took up the reins. And then Ronald helped the bride with her voluminous skirts onto the seat beside the groom.

"Good day, folks," called Luke, flicking the reins. Molly snorted, and the buggy lurched forward.

Maggie waved until her friends disappeared from sight, and then she faced forward on the bench and arranged her skirts. Peeking sideways at her new husband, she confessed, "When Arthur offered to take our picture, I intended to refuse his generosity. But he rushed away before I could decline graciously."

Luke glanced at her. "A wedding picture will lend credibility to this marriage, especially for the children's sake."

Maggie considered the possibility she'd intentionally failed to decline Arthur's offer. After all, what bride wouldn't desire a wedding picture? Would she treasure the memory of this wedding someday? Only time would tell if this marriage proved itself a blessing or a curse.

A few minutes later, the newlyweds arrived at The Spirit Creek Hotel and discovered June Davidson stationed at the front door.

"Congratulations!" she exclaimed, vigorously shaking their hands. "Mr. MacDonald and his camera are waiting for you in the courtyard in back."

"Thank you, Mrs. Davidson," offered Luke. "We'll find our own way."

Luke guided Maggie out the side door where curved flowerbeds circled a grassy expanse. Several wooden benches provided seating areas for hotel guests. Songbirds chirped overhead in the shady cottonwood trees, and a mixture of floral scents hovered in the air.

Maggie introduced her new husband to Arthur who extended his congratulations to them. For several minutes, the photographer worked around what remained of the natural daylight, moving Maggie and Luke from one spot to another to another.

"Did Maggie mention I'm considering starting a newspaper somewhere in the vicinity?" asked Arthur.

"I'll put in a good word with the mayor to garner the town council's approval to set up your new business in Spirit Creek," offered Luke.

Maggie recognized the suggestion as a shameful bid to tip the decision in his town's favor. She suspected Luke might badger the newspaperman to make his decision as soon as possible. Even this marriage proved Luke Carlyle pursued what he wanted until he got it. Arthur didn't stand a chance.

"Thank you for offering, Luke, but that won't be necessary," mumbled Arthur, concentrating on his preparations. "I met with Randy Barker earlier today, and he sounded quite taken with the idea."

Luke smiled. "I'm delighted to hear it."

Finally, Luke sat tall in a low-backed chair with his hands resting on his thighs while Maggie stood slightly behind her husband, her left hand resting on his right shoulder. She flushed at the contact and attempted to still her shaking knees.

The sparkling opulence of her wedding ring caught her eye; its dazzling brilliance almost blinded her. Most of the marriage ceremony remained a blur, and she couldn't even recall the moment Luke had slipped the ring on her finger. And where had Luke obtained such a magnificent ring on such short notice? The question was forgotten when Arthur declared his preparations complete.

"Now, folks, hold your breath, don't blink, and don't move a muscle." His slightly-balding head disappeared under a black cloth.

Luke and Maggie inhaled a breath and stared into the eye of the small box that possessed the magic of photography. After what seemed an eternity, Arthur's head reappeared and he declared, "All done!"

Maggie gasped, filling her aching lungs with precious air. "Arthur, my word, any longer and you'd have a picture of a blue-faced bride sprawled on the ground."

"Feared I'd shame myself by slumping over in the chair," added Luke, taking a deep breath and grinning broadly.

"Sorry, folks, unavoidable." A sympathetic expression blossomed on Arthur's face.

"Thank you so much for this thoughtful wedding gift," gushed Maggie, as Arthur walked them to their buggy.

"We promise to keep in touch," said Luke. "I'm hoping we'll hear that you've decided to start up your newspaper here."

"Won't be making a decision for a few months yet. But I'll definitely keep Spirit Creek in mind." Arthur shook Luke's hand, hugged Maggie warmly and then waved goodbye. As they climbed into the buggy, he returned to his camera.

"Do you require another stop? Have you forgotten anything?" Luke held the reins aloft, awaiting her answer, while she adjusted her unruly skirts.

"I don't believe so, but thank you for asking."

"Then we're off." Luke flicked the reins, and Molly darted forward tossing Maggie against the back of the seat.

"Thank you for encouraging Arthur to open his newspaper in Spirit Creek." Maggie straightened, sitting rigid and tall. "I met Arthur years ago in Philadelphia; he's a true gentleman. And wouldn't a town newspaper be wonderful?"

"It would indeed." Luke smiled at her, and then returned his attention to the dusty street.

"If Arthur resided in town there'd be no waiting months for a traveling photographer." Maggie forced herself to relax. "After the questionable welcome that trouser-wearing woman received last summer, I doubt she'll be back."

Luke chuckled. "Oh, yes, she surely created a stir."

"Arthur mentioned she'd instructed him in his photography." Maggie recalled the outrage generated by the woman's riding skirt, fashioned as trousers to eliminate the need of a side saddle. Surely, Luke didn't condone such a scandalous costume. William had hired the woman to take his picture with Sam, without telling her. Another deception. Mind you, she'd never have permitted the picture had she known. Now, the final picture with his Papa provided a wonderful keepsake for her son. Perhaps it was meant to happen.

"I approve of Arthur's wedding photograph, and Elizabeth and Sarah certainly provided you with a wedding to remember." Luke met her eyes. "I'm indebted to you for seeing the wedding through. Regardless of the purpose of this marriage, I hope you'll fondly remember today."

Maggie heard the hopefulness in his voice. "Most of the ceremony remains a blur, but I'll cherish my friends' thoughtfulness."

As they rode past The Joker's Wild Saloon, piano music drifted out through the swinging doors and at least a dozen horses lined the hitching posts.

"Judging by that equine head count, it'll prove another lively Friday night at Darby's," observed Luke.

Maggie felt her face redden.

"Were you recalling your recent visit to his establishment?"

Luke winked at her.

"Instead of reminding a lady about it, a gentleman would forget that that unfortunate incident ever happened. I chose that saloon on purpose, being it's located in the farthest corner of town. And still, you discovered me there." She glared at her new husband, but a smile creased her face before she could stop it. He'd understood the necessity for her venture into the most-seedy area of town. "Considering the shabby condition of Darby's piano, it doesn't sound too bad."

"That's not Darby's relic. I recalled your story, and when your magnificent piano arrived at the ranch, I donated our old one to the saloon."

Maggie sat, speechless. The gift was just another example of Luke's generous nature.

Rounding the corner, they caught sight of Stanley Wakeman locking up the feed store for the night. Luke halted the buggy and greeted Maggie's former neighbor. "Good evening, Stan."

"Delivered your order after the wedding, Luke. You require anything else?" Stanley Wakeman rested his hand on a substantial metal padlock. Maggie suspected Luke was the feed store's best customer, and he would willingly open the store again. Stan had managed the store for the late Ellwood Barker and now for his son, Randy.

"Nothing more, Stan, I've got everything I need." As he spoke, Luke smiled and then winked shamelessly at his new wife.

Maggie caught his double meaning and felt herself blush.

"Good night then, folks." Stan tugged on the locked padlock and turned toward home.

Luke gently flicked the reins, and they continued on their way.

"Stan's son is Sam's best friend." Maggie choked on her words and whipped around on the seat.

"Robbie is a fine lad," agreed Luke, glancing over to see what had spooked her.

Maggie heard his sharp inhale of breath.

Chapter 5

"I'm sorry. I should have taken an alternate route out of town." Luke's expression told her he'd totally forgotten they would pass by the jail where William's killers awaited the circuit judge's arrival to preside over the would-be bank robbers' murder trials.

"I can't avoid this street for the rest of my life." Maggie straightened her spine. "I promised myself I'd face the future with strength and conviction, but it's proving more difficult than I imagined." She wiped away a tear with her handkerchief.

Luke patted her hand. "Let me know if there's anything I can do. You're not alone in this any longer."

Maggie smiled through her tears. Of course she was alone. William was dead, and she'd lost her home. If it wasn't for Sam and the baby she carried, she'd have nothing. Had Luke forgotten their marriage was a sham?

Thankfully, her parents weren't alive to witness their daughter hitting rock bottom. She'd gone from privileged debutante to housekeeper on a cattle ranch. Her socialite mother would be scandalized, and her father would be extremely disappointed in her.

The newlyweds rode in silence for several minutes, lost in their own thoughts. Maggie avoided Luke's eyes, mortified by her emotional display while passing by the jailhouse. What must he be thinking? Had his opinion of her slipped a notch or two? Did he consider her a weak, overly-emotional female? She hated feeling so powerless every time a wave of what-might-have-been washed over her.

Maggie held her head high while she observed her

surroundings for the first time since leaving the rutted streets of Spirit Creek. A sweeping landscape of blue-green sage, massive cottonwoods, brown tufts of vegetation, and colorful wildflowers spread before her, thrilling her senses. "Isn't this land beautiful? Some would see only harsh wilderness while others appreciate its beauty and wonderment."

"You've summed it up." Luke smiled. "And the air is extremely invigorating."

Maggie swiveled in her seat, attempting to gain her bearings. "Five miles from town is farther than I thought."

Luke stared ahead at the endless landscape. "I'm taking the scenic way home."

Home. Maggie grimaced inwardly at the word. She shook off her moment of melancholy and then glanced at a hillside sliced open by years of abusive weather displaying layers of soil: gray, gold, pink and red. "Such beauty."

"You remind me of Catherine," blurted Luke, paling a moment later.

Maggie wondered if he intended to speak the thought aloud. "In what way are we similar?" She heard a falcon's angry scream and searched the sky for the source.

"You're both well-educated, well-bred young ladies hailing from the East. You're warm-hearted, charitable, caring, and wonderful mothers."

"Where did you meet Catherine?" Maggie's curiosity surprised her, and she hoped Luke wasn't offended by her bold question.

"Her father instructed at the college I attended, and we were introduced at a social one evening. Her intelligent conversation mesmerized me." Luke's eyes indicated he approved of her questioning.

"My father practiced law, and my busy socialite mother volunteered for a variety of charities," offered Maggie in the spirit of sharing. "I arrived late in their lives, an only child. They provided me with every comfort imaginable and limitless opportunities." She almost added 'while demonstrating limited affection' but caught herself. "My parents died together in a carriage accident less than a week before Sam's birth. Doc forbade me to travel to their funerals. Unfortunately, grief marred my initial happiness as a new mother."

"What a shame. I'm an only child, too."

Maggie detected a hint of wistfulness in Luke's voice. Did he regret growing up alone, as she had? She would have given her eye teeth for a sister. "I loved reading, and Father insisted I pursue higher education. But I dreamt of teaching young children, and after endless arguments Father abandoned his lofty college plans for me. I graduated top of my class from The Plymouth State Normal School in New Hampshire." Maggie hoped she didn't sound boastful. It hadn't been her intention.

Did her parents know about Sam and the new baby? Did they know about her heartache? She gazed at the endless blanket of white fluffy cotton which hung just above the horizon and spread across the evening sky. Patches of bright blue promised a sunny day tomorrow.

"My father insisted a man should learn about the world. I've read almost every book in our library." Luke smiled and continued. "Matthew Carlyle taught me that a man's true strength doesn't come from muscle and sweat, but from honesty, loyalty, conviction, and integrity. What a man accomplishes for others counts most, and I've lived my life to that end."

Maggie patted his arm. "Your father would be proud of you."

"Father died in a riding accident a few days before I graduated from college. His horse spooked and threw him; he broke his neck and died instantly. Mother was riding nearby and witnessed it." Luke's voice caught as he finished.

"How awful!" Maggie gasped.

"A shock for all of us, to say the least." Luke cleared his throat. "Catherine's father forbade us to marry. *You will not whisk my only daughter away to a land of heathens and outlaws* were his exact words. Being of age, Catherine married me anyway. We moved to the ranch and I assumed ownership. The college mailed my diploma."

"What a tragic beginning to a new life together."

"I'd only turned twenty-one the week before, scared skinny at the responsibility. But Ned proved an invaluable mentor. And Mother adored Catherine, welcomed her into the family with open arms."

"I imagine your mother loved Catherine like a daughter, having borne no other children." Maggie was reminded of her own relationship with Elizabeth.

"You're wearing her ring." Luke pointed at her hand.

Maggie blanched and whispered, "This was Catherine's ring?"

"Heavens, no! I'm sorry you misunderstood." Luke's face turned scarlet. "That was Mother's ring. Father presented it to her the day I was born."

"Why would you give me such a precious keepsake?" gasped Maggie.

"Two years after Father passed, Mother died of a broken heart. The ring's been hidden in safekeeping for too long. You're Mrs. Luke Carlyle, and Mother would be pleased you're wearing it." Luke's fingers caressed the beautiful stone.

Was he fondly remembering his mother? Or was he thinking about the devastating loss of his first wife? "Did Catherine wear this ring?" she blurted. The question seemed petty, but she had to ask.

"I offered it to Catherine, but she refused. She loved Mother dearly, and she couldn't bear to wear her ring. Catherine's wedding ring is safely locked away, for Lucy someday."

Maggie released her breath, relieved that Catherine hadn't worn her ring. *Her ring?* She silently scolded herself for such a foolish thought. What did it matter who'd worn this exquisite piece of jewelry before her? The ring represented a sham of a marriage, and no doubt Luke would insist she return it when he came to his senses.

"I hated the social scene in the East: charity balls, fancy gowns, afternoon tea with society ladies. If I'd listened to Mother and hadn't refused to attend those social functions, perhaps Catherine and I would have crossed paths and become friends." Maggie never would have imagined those words coming out of her mouth, regret for not following her mother's example and stepping out in society.

Luke laughed. "My Philadelphia debutante evolved into a true rancher's wife, equally comfortable sipping tea with Mother in the parlor or attending an ailing calf in the barn."

Maggie's marriage to Luke evolved purely as a business arrangement; she'd hired on as housekeeper and stepmother to his children. Most likely, she'd disappoint Luke when her swollen belly grew cumbersome and hampered her housekeeping. Even her stepmother abilities might fall short of the mark if Lucy never accepted Maggie in her father's life. No, she'd never match Catherine's high standards.

She grimaced, recalling the path her life had taken recently.

With her luck, in a month or two Luke would scandalize Spirit Creek by demanding a divorce. In the meantime, she would take her role as Mrs. Carlyle seriously, for her son's sake.

"My parents regretted instilling independence in me, after I announced I'd accepted a teaching position in Spirit Creek," she offered, choosing to continue contributing to the sharing. "Father ranted and Mother took to her bed. Aunt Penny swore I'd regret my decision. But I'd recently turned twenty-three and yearned for adventure. I selfishly scorned their concerns and departed without a backward glance."

"How did you enjoy your journey to our little town?"

"During the endless stagecoach ride, we stopped every half hour or so to change or rest the horses. The cantankerous driver was the most disagreeable man I'd ever met. I was thrown from my seat on one occasion as a result of the jerky ride. I arrived in Spirit Creek, positively ill from the whole ordeal. Thankfully, Elizabeth whisked me off to her home for a hot bath and a long rest, or I would have returned to Philadelphia."

"But you excelled as a teacher."

"I soon recovered from the trip and never looked back. Now, I can't imagine living anywhere else." Maggie smiled at the truth of her statement. After all, she'd chosen to marry a stranger in order to remain here.

"No regrets?"

"I regret disappointing Aunt Penny, Father's sister. She'd influenced my life in many positive ways, and she still writes occasionally." Maggie looked away, tears threatening. She preferred to believe arthritic fingers explained the increasingly infrequent letters and not her aunt's continued disappointment in her. Only wishful thinking on her part, she suspected.

Luke reined in the mare, giving her a much-needed rest. He turned on the bench seat and met his wife's eyes. "For the most part was William a good man?"

Maggie sat, totally stunned by the unexpected question. After a moment, she recovered and realized Luke was waiting for her answer. "Being the son of an army officer, William thrived on discipline and honor. He abhorred the lack of law enforcement he encountered while working in the mines. In 1882, he moved to Spirit Creek and accepted the position of Town Sheriff which he loved despite the risks. After we married and Sam was born, he swore he'd be careful, but fate took him." Maggie sighed.

"Fate can be cruel," whispered Luke. "No one knows that better than us."

"William borrowed against our home to pay his poker losses. I'm still angry with him." Maggie's hand flew to her mouth as she uttered her secret aloud. What would Luke think of a widow speaking so poorly of her departed husband?

Luke reached for her other hand. "William wasn't perfect, Maggie, and sometimes a man's poor judgment catches up with him. You're entitled to your anger, but don't let someone else's poor choices ruin your life."

His sympathetic words surprised her, filling her eyes with tears. She quickly turned away. *Don't let someone else's poor choices ruin your life*. She'd lost her home and married someone she barely knew because of William's betrayal. If that didn't qualify as a ruined life, what did? No, she admonished herself, she couldn't think that way.

"I'll survive this," she whispered. "William crippled me financially, but I won't allow his deceptions to harm me mentally, emotionally, or physically."

"Good for you." Luke flicked the reins, and Molly leapt forward, rested and eager to continue the journey. The buggy passed by a gnarled tree resembling a stooped cowhand who'd spent too many years in the saddle.

"My father always said everything happens for a reason." She smiled at the memory. For all his indifference in her formative years, he'd become her mentor in her adult life. The wedding vow *for better or for worse* popped into her head. Would she someday believe her arrangement with Luke happened for a reason? Happened for the better?

Suddenly, a lone brown hawk screamed from overhead, soaring, perhaps searching for a prairie mouse or similar tasty morsel for his dinner. Had Maggie believed in the Indian's way of life, she might consider her father's spirit inhabited that hawk and he was watching over her from above. Maggie smiled. Anything was a possibility.

"In a way, Fate brought us together," observed Luke.

"I suppose you're right. Fate cruelly stole my parents from me, and then William, and finally my home." Maggie heard the bitterness in her voice. Her life had spun out of control. If Fate had additional challenging situations in store for her, count her out.

"Fate took my parents and Catherine, too," countered Luke, sadly. "We're quite the pair."

Maggie realized their lives paralleled in so many ways: only children who'd lost both of their parents, privileged upbringings, similar educations, a love of books, and a first marriage destroyed by sudden death. A soft breeze whispered in her ear, and one buggy wheel's persistent squeak intruded on her thoughts. The buggy passed by a small cluster of cottonwood trees, standing in a creek, covered to their knees with murky water.

Luke gently squeezed her hand and then released it. "My parents, Matthew and Ruth, were raised in England, privileged children with nannies, governesses, and servants. As a married adult, Father enjoyed the comforts of a well-to-do English gentleman: fox hunts, tennis, cricket, and high tea. But he received reports from his contacts in the colonies: stories of the Wild West involving detailed descriptions of encounters with cowboys and Indians, tales of millions of buffalo roaming the range, and updates on the civil war between north and south."

"And it all sounded quite intriguing?" Maggie tilted her head.

Luke nodded. "In 1864, Father boarded ship for America destined for Montana Territory in particular. He assured Mother and me that we would join him once he became established."

"Did he intend to prove he could be successful on his own?" Maggie turned her full attention to Luke's story.

"And to escape his mischief-making twin brother. Uncle Michael dallied with other fellow's wives." Luke whispered the scandalous admission, even though they were miles from anyone. "Father feared being mistakenly shot by a jealous husband."

Maggie's hand flew to her mouth. "Oh, my."

"Yes, well," mumbled Luke, appearing lost for words to elaborate on a situation that required no further explanation. "For two years, a few male relatives visited Father in the colonies and returned to England bringing with them stories of savage Indians and splendid hunting and vast untamed wilderness."

"Goodness. It's a wonder your mother ever left England." Maggie laughed for the first time in three weeks.

"The fellows also reported on Father's success; his fortunes swelled from his mining endeavors. But he dreamed of something more permanent for our future: a magnificent cattle ranch. In 1866, Father heard the account of Nelson Story driving longhorns to Montana from Texas. Two years later, Father hired a pack of drovers and personally supervised the journey of his own one thousand longhorns from Texas to his Montana ranch."

"What an adventure!" exclaimed Maggie.

Luke slowed the buggy and pointed west. Several cows patiently stood at attention while their hungry calves suckled mother's milk and swished their small tails in contentment.

"Aren't they adorable?"

"Adorable?" Luke laughed.

"All four-legged babies are adorable," insisted Maggie. An image of cuddling a fat, squirmy puppy in her arms flashed before Maggie's eyes. Recalling her son's tears and heart-breaking disappointment the day she'd retracted William's promise, she wondered if she could someday muster up the courage to request a puppy on Sam's behalf. And then she reconsidered the whole idea. She'd have enough on her plate working as Luke's housekeeper and caring for three children and expecting another. The last thing she needed in her life was a new puppy!

Luke flicked the reins and they continued on their way.

"Father and our foreman, Ned Armstrong, became lifelong friends while working in the mines together. Having been raised on a cattle ranch in Texas, Ned was hired by Father to accompany him to Texas and back, staying on as foreman. Once the cattle operation was running smoothly, Father hired a crew of fellows to construct a proper house before sending for Mother and me in 1869."

"How old were you when you arrived in America?"

"Fifteen, and itching for a great adventure, not realizing the long hours of hard work awaiting me." Luke produced a large quilt from behind the seat and handed it to her. "That's a brisk wind tonight. Wrap this around your shoulders."

"Thank you." Maggie stood, cocooned herself in the quilt, and sat down again, warmed immediately. Luke had reached out a hand to steady her. She shouldn't be surprised by his thoughtfulness, but she was. "At least we won't be bothered with mosquitoes."

Luke continued his story. "The cattle operation thrived until the disastrous blizzards of '86-87 struck. The snow fell two feet deep, and its surface crusted in the extreme cold. The cattle couldn't find feed, and often cut their noses attempting to break through the snow's hard surface. Some cut their legs when they broke through the sharp crusts. With raw, bloody and swollen lower extremities, even the strongest cattle froze and perished. Weaker cattle just lay down and died. We lost almost half our herd."

"How devastating!" Maggie never once considered the hardships ranch folks faced, and the bravery required to start over again after such a loss.

"And then Catherine died of influenza that April," whispered Luke, shaking his head as if reliving the pain again. "All of it nearly killed me, but Ned pulled me through."

"I've lived in a similar purgatory these past few weeks: losing William, learning of his lies, losing my home." A single tear slowly trailed down her cheek, unchecked. Admitting her pain to someone felt good, but would Luke interpret her admission as complaining about the hand life dealt her?

She didn't want him to think she'd been fishing for sympathy. She knew he understood the devastation of losing a spouse. The finality of a death with no warning and no time to prepare for the inevitable, unlike what a lengthy illness afforded those left behind to mourn. For a brief second Luke's hand touched her arm, and she startled at the unexpected contact. She met his eyes and he smiled in a way that meant he understood what she'd endured. Was still feeling.

"There's Robert Morgan's ranch. He raises cattle and breeds Morgan horses…imagine." Luke chuckled at his own joke, perhaps believing a bit of humor would help them overcome the awkward moment. "Robert is a distant relative of Justin Morgan Sr., founder of the Morgan horse back in the last century sometime. Robert and I became the best of friends, shortly after I arrived here. Like our fathers before us. Actually, he's more like a brother than a friend. Robert married a mail-order bride about ten years ago. Hattie and Catherine were best friends, like Robert and me, and our children adore each other."

"I've spoken with Hattie at church, but I don't really know her." Maggie recalled the ranchers' wives seldom socialized with the town ladies, and she wondered why that was. She must ask Luke about it in the future.

Night fell upon them like an unseen hand had tossed a

blanket over the land and smothered the last fiery flames of daylight hovering on the horizon. But they needn't light a lamp; the moon shone brightly overhead.

"Today, The Diamond C is perhaps second or third largest in Montana. There's a fellow over Beaver Creek way rightly boasts the largest operation, but my ranch continues to prosper. We've been plagued by cattle rustlers lately though, and we're missing several head of cattle. But we'll find the guilty parties in time. The losses won't break us; our family will never want for anything. It's the principle of the thing. Stealing another man's property is just plain wrong."

"I agree. And I'll earn my keep." Maggie had turned her back on the material life in Philadelphia, and she harbored no regrets. She ignored Luke's *our family* remark, knowing this arrangement was a farce invented to ensure their children's sense of security and nothing more.

But the thought of her new husband dealing with cattle rustlers frightened her. Having been married to a sheriff, she knew these outlaws carried pistols and they wouldn't hesitate for a moment to use them. Could his life be in danger? Surely, he'd leave such things to lawmen and not take unnecessary risks, being a family man. She banished the troublesome thoughts from her mind, not wanting to mar the end to the day.

"My girls and I will benefit from our union equally as much as you and Sam." Luke pointed and her eyes followed.

Two impossibly tall, thick, pine poles bore the weight of an equally sturdy crossbar. An enormous wrought-iron sign with *DIAMOND C RANCH* lettering burnt into the wood was suspended in the center. They soon passed underneath and continued along a dusty path leading down into the valley below.

"Thousands of acres encompass the ranch. When we're closer I'll explain the purpose of all the buildings you'll soon see in the distance." Luke's voice shattered the still of the night. "In the meantime, tell me your thoughts on child-rearing?"

"I'm all in favor of it," Maggie teased. "I have a child of my own."

"Seriously, we must present a united front." Luke looked into her eyes. "Do you believe the principle 'if you spare the rod, you spoil the child'?"

"I never spank Sam. Mind you, he's a very well-behaved little boy." Maggie reconsidered her answer for a minute. "There was the time he let a baby skunk into the house, calling it 'kitty'. Fortunately, it never occurred to the baby skunk that he shouldn't be in our house. But I shooed the creature out the backdoor and spanked Sam before I realized he might not know any better, having just turned three."

"A skunk in the house?" Luke grinned and shook his head. "What have I gotten myself into?"

"Boys possess more energy than any creature ever invented, and I marvel at the way his mind works. He's equally fascinated with a butterfly's wings or by the way his elbow bends." Maggie laughed.

"I'll raise him as my own, and he'll thrive on the ranch." Luke patted her hand.

"Robbie Wakeman's dog birthed seven puppies a while back. I should warn you that Sam wanted one, but our lives seemed too unsettled." Maggie's voice caught.

"We have an old dog at the ranch. Sam will have fun with Skipper."

"What *are* all these buildings for?" Maggie's head swiveled, taking it all in.

"That's the horse barn and smaller cattle barn and corrals to your right. The hen house and goose house are beyond that. To your left are the two bunkhouses, home to our ranch hands. An ice house and a root cellar are hidden behind the cook shack over there. Across the path are Ned's house and two empty cabins."

The buggy rumbled along the slightly rutted and grassless path beaten down by years of use. The buildings appeared to be painted a dark shade of red, but she couldn't be certain in the moonlight. Knee-high grass surrounded the buildings, and Maggie was shocked at the degree of disrepair she observed, witnessing little pride of ownership.

As if he'd read her mind, Luke continued. "The ranch is in shambles; we've neglected things shamefully. But Ned and I won't be preoccupied with housework any longer."

Maggie blurted, "I've arrived in the nick of time."

"That you have." Luke's expression indicated no sign of hurt feelings over her outburst. "Up ahead is the main house."

"The ranch must look amazing in daylight." She couldn't wait to see things tomorrow. Returned to shipshape condition, she imagined the property would take her breath away.

"The garden is hidden over there. More weeds than vegetables to be seen right now I'm afraid, but we'll get it cleaned up. A creek runs alongside it."

The buggy rumbled down the curved, tree-lined driveway, which abruptly opened into a magnificent yard. As the rig continued along the circular path, she almost rubbed her eyes, believing she was dreaming. When she caught sight of her new home, she almost fainted.

"*This* is your house?" she gasped.

Chapter 6

The house—wouldn't the term mansion seem more appropriate?—stood three stories high. She'd eat her sunbonnet if it measured less than five thousand square feet. Luke slowed the buggy as they approached from the south-east corner.

The wooden exterior was painted white with green trim, and a small covered porch stuck out in back, perhaps leading to the kitchen. A large third floor dormer towered directly above the back porch. To her left, light from twin lamps flickered in a main floor bay window. The buggy rounded the corner, and another smaller dormer caught her eye. Maggie turned in her seat for a better view of the massive turret with three windows on each of three floors facing the north-east corner.

"My goodness, this is magnificent," she exclaimed, meeting Luke's eyes for a moment.

He jumped down from the buggy and secured the reins to the hitching post while her attention returned to the house. She felt like a child on Christmas morning.

The generous placement of windows throughout the three floors would maximize natural light in the home. Lamplight peeked through a few windows, and twin wrought-iron lamps flanked the massive front door, lit to welcome home the master of the house.

The quilt slipped from around Maggie's shoulders, and Luke assisted her from the buggy. "When you promised a safe home for Sam and me, I never imagined…" she whispered, incredulously. Luke grabbed her valise and guided her towards the front door.

Sturdy, plain white columns of substantial breadth supported both the covered front entry and the small balcony above. Six wide wooden steps led to a broad veranda where its cover was supported by smaller pillars similar in design to the columns. Thin square spindles supported the narrow sloped railing where she trailed one hand, her glove catching on peeling paint.

"I never dreamt such a stunning home existed in this barren frontier." For a moment, Maggie envied Catherine who no doubt had cherished the lady-of-the-house title. Don't even contemplate such silliness, she silently chastised herself, housekeeper is your official title.

Luke's expression, blank and devoid of emotion, sent a shiver up her spine. What was he thinking? Was he already regretting his decision to marry her and bring her to his home? She banished such negative thoughts from her mind. She'd felt quite comfortable with him, exchanging their past histories with each other during the ride. Besides, Luke had offered her and Sam a home, and she'd accepted. For better or for worse, they were here.

"You'd cringe at the overgrown vines and climbing roses along the front of the house. And the grimy windows covered with prairie dust. The grass requires cutting, and the flowerbeds need weeding. But we'll work on it." Luke swung the massive oak double doors open while still carrying her valise in his other hand. "Mother loved this house. She brought all her furnishings, china and crystal dishes, fancy linens, Axminster rugs and whatnot from England. Most of it is still in use."

"I'll see to the buggy and mare, Mr. Carlyle."

Luke and Maggie startled as the ranch hand stepped into view and nodded politely in their direction. Tall with boyish good looks that belied his age, he grasped the mare's reins with practiced confidence.

"Thank you, Scotty. That's very kind of you," said Luke.

"Think nothing of it, sir. Good night, Mr. and Mrs. Carlyle." Scotty and the rig disappeared into the night as the moon played hide-and-seek with the dark clouds.

Luke extinguished the outdoor lamps, closed the doors, and then set her valise on a spindly-legged chair in the entryway. "News travels fast. Already, my ranch hand addressed you as Mrs. Carlyle." He pulled a pistol from somewhere on his person. Without a word, he extracted a key from his pocket, unlocked a drawer in the hallway table, placed the gun inside, and locked it again.

"Do you carry a weapon everywhere? William wore pistols, but he represented the law." Maggie's voice wavered. What sort of gun-toting frontier rancher had she married?

"Out on the range, a man requires protection from all manner of critters. Mostly four-legged ones, sometimes two-legged. A man is safe if he's prepared."

Maggie stood, speechless.

"We're law-abiding folks," continued Luke. "I haven't fired that pistol in years, not since I frightened off a bear on my way into Spirit Creek. The guns in the house remain locked up and unloaded at all times. The children are safe. Don't be concerned."

Maggie removed her gloves and laid them and her reticule on another small table beside the front door. *The children are safe*. Was Luke including Sam in that statement? Would Luke treat him as his own as he'd promised? She wandered across the entryway. Heavy, intricately-carved square posts fronted a gracefully-curved mahogany staircase leading to the second floor. A wide wooden handrail was supported by substantial spindles simply designed with a single swelling.

"What a marvelous staircase." Maggie turned toward her new husband.

Luke cocked his head, listening. "The house is so quiet, the children must be asleep, exhausted from their big day."

Heavy footsteps could be heard, and Ned wandered into the front hallway. "How-do, folks. The young'uns are asleep. Yer here now, so I'll be headin' off to bed."

"Thank you for bringing the children home, Ned." Luke shook his foreman's hand.

"No trouble. That little feller is a hoot, ma'am." Ned chuckled and opened the front door on his way out to his own cabin.

"Thank you," called Maggie, smiling at Ned's comment and wondering what Sam had said, as the front door closed. She twiddled her thumbs, feeling rather foolish just standing in the entryway.

"Forgive my manners, please come in. Let's start the tour of the house in my study." Luke lifted the lit lamp off the entryway table and led the way down a narrow hallway to a small square room on the right.

Floor-to-ceiling wooden bookcases painted dark-green lined

three walls, and a small stone fireplace occupied one corner of the fourth wall. An impressive mahogany desk with a black leather-upholstered chair commanded the majority of the floor space. Two side chairs and a small round table stood to the left of the desk. Liquor decanters and crystal glasses huddled together upon a silver tray on a narrow painted table just inside the door.

"What a marvelous gentleman's room," observed Maggie, dragging her fingers along a row of leather-bound titles. Straining her eyes in the low lamplight, she recognized many favorites.

"It's a nice place to escape to, unless I'm recording the ranch's financial activity in my ledgers. Bookkeeping is a necessary evil of any enterprise. I prefer burying my nose in a good book." Luke's easy smile and casual manner relaxed her, as she followed him out of the room.

Farther down the narrow hallway, they entered a substantial parlor. Two groupings of large sofas upholstered in sky-blue silk and overstuffed chairs covered in floral-patterned materials stood atop two luxurious Axminster rugs. Small side tables and high-backed chairs stood in the corners. The wide plank floor appeared dusty. Large pictures depicting a fox hunt, a sea-faring ship, and a still-life of flowers hung on the walls. A silver tea set resided on a dust-covered table in the far corner.

"Did your mother bring these beautiful rugs from England? Mother owned a rug similar to that red and white floral one."

"Most of the rugs, pictures, crystal, china and a few pieces of furniture accompanied Mother here. But Father commissioned a fellow to build all of the tables, chairs, beds, and armoires." Luke strolled around the room, holding the lamp aloft for her benefit.

A rifle hung above the enormous stone fireplace. The wide solid-wood mantle displayed assorted framed family photographs and exquisite silver candlesticks. Her prized piano occupied the far corner, and she silently trailed her hand along the familiar keys.

"Your ranch hands took exceptional care with my piano. I don't see a mark on it."

"I'll tell Scotty and Mike that you appreciated their attention to the task. Come along, Mrs. Carlyle, there's a lot more to see."

Maggie smiled weakly, knowing she'd never become accustomed to the name. She still considered herself Maggie Wentworth Burns, and she imagined she always would.

The kitchen was situated at the far right of the hallway, exactly where she'd guessed it would be, having seen the porch from the outside. They inspected the surprisingly bare pantry and small laundry, and then strolled outside to the back veranda where moonlight lit the back yard.

"Father forged a double swing from two huge wagon wheels and other salvaged materials from around the ranch and tucked it beneath that large cottonwood tree. Mother and Father spent endless hours just swinging while dreaming of their future. I regret they never lived to watch their grandchildren grow up." Luke's voice quivered.

"I know how you feel. My parents died before Sam was born."

"Can you see the wooden bench and metal birdbath beside that small thicket?" Luke pointed and then continued. "Mother and Catherine were avid gardeners, and there are several curved flowerbeds overflowing with flowers and shrubs. Those women would cringe if they saw their garden now. I don't know the difference between a turnip and a tulip."

"Luke, I can distinguish a turnip from a tulip, and a potato plant and a petunia. I love gardening. It's hard work, but sharing time with nature is relaxing. Does that make any sense?" Maggie felt herself blush with her spontaneous admission.

"Not to me, but you're welcome to spend all the time in the gardens that your heart desires. When the flowerbeds are properly maintained, you cannot imagine the splendor. During the next few days, we'll hire sufficient help to ensure everything is brought up to your standards."

"I recall you hired *me* to serve as the hired help," protested Maggie.

Luke waved away her words. "I wouldn't expect you to tackle such an extensive revitalization by yourself. But you'll be able to maintain it all once things are set to rights."

"Thank you for your consideration." She smiled, having no intention of shirking her duties. She was hired as his housekeeper, and she intended to fulfill that commitment.

Back in the kitchen, Luke continued the tour. "The ranch hands will top up these wood bins every day, and they'll chop kindling for this box here."

Maggie's small kitchen was less than half the dimensions of

this room. "Look at the size of that woodstove. And all these cupboards. That long worktable will be a pleasure to use. This kitchen must be the heart of the home," she mumbled, thinking aloud. She approached the massive breakfront cabinet and swung open the center doors. "You own the exact same patterned dishes as mine!" she exclaimed.

"Maggie, those are your dishes," said Luke, chuckling. "We put your things away; I wanted everything ready for your arrival."

"Everything?" gasped Maggie. She hadn't expected her lady's unmentionables to be unpacked by strangers.

"Everything but your clothing; those boxes are piled upstairs. There's a large armoire for that purpose." Luke studied her, his gaze intense. "You've entrusted me with your possessions. Have I overstepped my bounds?"

Maggie smiled, remembering how few those possessions numbered. She'd lived a simple life with William, certainly frugal in comparison to her life in Philadelphia. She wasn't overwhelmed by Luke's splendid house; she'd been raised in similar luxury. But would she adjust to her new home? To working as his housekeeper?

"Not at all. Thank you for your thoughtfulness." Maggie turned away as the room began closing in around her. Luke shouldn't be discussing her personal items with her, husband or not. They barely knew each other. "Where does this door lead?" she asked, attempting a change of subject.

"To the dining room, but we haven't used it since Catherine passed," explained Luke, leading the way inside.

Maggie noticed that someone had piled their wedding presents atop the massive dust-laden mahogany table. Twelve ladder-backed chairs, the seats upholstered in a gold silk, surrounded the table. No doubt, the ranch hands had helped unload the gifts, and that explained why their marriage was now common knowledge.

Luxurious velvet panels in deep golden hues framed the bay window and appeared to shimmer in the flickering lamplight that she recalled seeing through the window as the buggy passed by. Luke extinguished the two lamps and then stared out into the night. She wondered what he was thinking, but she suspected he'd share his thoughts with her if they were important.

A breakfront cabinet covered one whole wall and displayed a dusty collection of several china patterns, crystal bowls and platters, and assorted glassware. She opened a drawer and caressed a collection of intricately-embroidered tablecloths. Another drawer held dozens of tea towels and every-day tablecloths. Others were filled with candles and assorted linens.

"Death lived alongside us in this house for the past two years, but it's time death moved on. We should be entertaining, using these linens and dishes again." Luke left his spot by the window.

Maggie had agreed to portray the happy couple, a charade for the children's sake, but she had no intention of entertaining guests for the sole purpose of dragging out a tablecloth or a set of dishes hidden away for two years. But she was too exhausted to argue about it tonight.

They made their way back to the front entrance and Luke grabbed her valise, pausing at the foot of the winding staircase. "It's past ten o'clock. Would you like a cup of tea or a bite to eat before turning in?"

"No, thank you, I'm exhausted. Please just show me to my room," she replied.

Luke led the way to the second floor with Maggie following in his footsteps, but then he continued up the stairway to the third level. It made sense that the hired help slept near the children. Dust bunnies cowered in the corners of each step, and as they topped the staircase the smell of fresh paint assaulted her nose.

"Would you like a peek at the children before we turn in?" whispered Luke.

"Yes, please. Sam is sleeping in a strange house," said Maggie. Her son was a very outgoing child, but she hoped he hadn't thought she'd deserted him.

Luke and Maggie stood in the large bedroom doorway. Sam slept soundly with his arm tightly wound around his toy dog. In an identical double bed on the opposite side of the room, Patti slept with the covers pulled up to her chin and a large doll tucked in beside her. Shelves covered with dolls and books lined two walls, and a large rocking horse stood in one corner.

"Angels when they're asleep," he whispered.

"Sam is sharing a room with Patti?" Maggie had assumed Sam would be assigned his own room in this enormous house.

"Not for long. His room was freshly painted yesterday. I warned Patti that Sam would only share her room until his room was finished. It requires another coat of paint, and we're building some new shelves for toys." Luke studied her eyes, no doubt awaiting her agreement or disapproval.

"Sharing temporarily is a sensible decision; Sam will be less frightened by the move. He was quite happy with Patti's company at the wedding." Maggie smiled at her son sleeping without a worry in the world. If only she could sleep so soundly.

"Patti is tickled silly having a little brother. I predict they'll be getting into mischief together in no time." Luke silently closed the door.

"That's Lucy's room. She is not happy with us right now." They peeked inside at the sleeping child and then Luke silently closed the door. "There are guest rooms on the other side of the hallway."

Returning to the second floor, Luke opened the double doors on a large painted cupboard. "This is the linen closet. If there's anything lacking, don't hesitate to order it from the general store."

"Have my linens been added to these?" asked Maggie.

"I believe so," said Luke closing the door. "Ned's wife handled the unpacking. You should ask her tomorrow. Another two guest bedrooms occupy this side of the house as well as the bathing room."

Maggie hesitated for a moment and then followed Luke inside. An enormous claw-foot bathtub stood in the middle of the floor. She imagined herself lying back in that beautiful bathtub filled with hot water, lathering her aching body with her lilac-scented soap. A half-circle washstand stood under a small window, which was covered with a floral-patterned curtain. She crossed the floor and drew aside a matching floor-length curtain and discovered an indoor convenience. She felt her face redden.

Luke cleared his throat. "I don't believe in using outhouses during the winter months, especially when there are women and children in the house. But we use the outdoor facilities during the summer when the ranch hands are too busy to maintain indoor conveniences. I intend to rig up a waterworks system when time permits. I've been studying the apparatus and it seems simple enough."

"That's very thoughtful of you," stammered Maggie, certain her face was scarlet. She dashed out of the room and Luke followed.

"The last room is the master bedroom. There's a small

nursery in there." Luke pointed to a door on his left. He opened a set of double doors leading into the bedroom which spanned the whole front of the house. "There's an adjoining door to the nursery inside here."

Maggie stepped through the doorway and her breath caught. A magnificent four-poster mahogany bed stood against the far wall. Plump pillows rested upon a massive patchwork quilt, obviously hand-made with love and hours of patience. A lacy throw lay across the foot of the bed, and a floral-patterned Axminster rug peeked out from underneath.

"Who made this wonderful quilt?" asked Maggie, standing on one side of the bed and looking across at Luke. The bedcovers appeared rumpled, the pillows slightly askew. Had Luke hurriedly made the bed himself this morning? She decided he genuinely required the services of a housekeeper.

"That is one of Catherine's creations. She loved making quilts." Luke spoke softly, trailing his hand along the length of the bedcovering before setting her valise on the bed.

Maggie quickly looked away. He's still in love with Catherine, she thought. Will he regret bringing her into his home? Will he consider her an unwelcome intrusion in his life?

A set of silver candlesticks kept each other company upon the mantle of the small brick fireplace. Six tall, narrow windows wore matching blue-velvet panels falling gracefully to the plank floor. William's desk and chair fit nicely inside the semi-circular area of the turret.

"The natural daylight would be perfect for writing letters," she observed, slightly annoyed that Luke had confiscated her husband's desk for his own use. But Luke had rescued her and her children from homelessness and starvation. She hadn't any right to complain.

From the master bedroom, a door opened onto the covered balcony she'd seen above the front entry. Maggie stepped outside and discovered a rocking chair hidden in the far corner. She pictured Luke sitting alone on warm summer nights, mourning his wife while recalling their happy times together. She shook the image from her mind and peeked over the waist-high railing at the ground far below. Immediately, her equilibrium wavered and she staggered back inside.

"I won't be peeking over that railing again anytime soon. I get dizzy standing on a chair."

Luke smiled at her comment but said nothing.

She turned away, feeling like a total ninny. This was Luke's bedroom for heaven's sake. Except for changing linens or making his bed each morning, what reason would she have for being in his room? And she'd certainly have no excuse for looking over his balcony.

She gazed around the spacious room. Two large armoires—one his and one for his wife, she reasoned—rested against the opposite wall. A lady's vanity and tufted stool occupied the far corner of the room. A chaise longue covered in a red-floral pattern called to her from the opposite corner. "Catherine must have enjoyed many hours relaxing in that comfortable chair. I know I would." Maggie blushed, realizing she'd spoken her thoughts aloud.

Luke made no comment.

She scrunched her shoulders toward her ears, tipping her head back, willing the knots in her neck and upper back to relax. As she turned to inquire which room was hers, she spotted three boxes—weren't those the boxes she packed her clothes in?—sitting beside one of the armoires.

"Your ranch hand mistakenly deposited my clothing boxes in here." She grabbed her valise off the bed and headed for the door. "We can move them tomorrow. Just show me to my room, please."

"There's no mistake. We'll be sharing the master bedroom," declared Luke, matter-of-factly.

"What...did...you...say?" Maggie's words slithered across the room, like a venomous snake intent on inflicting a poisonous bite.

Chapter 7

Luke repeated with conviction, "We're sharing the master bedroom."

Maggie's valise slipped from her hands as she stumbled across the floor and collapsed onto the chaise. Trembling fingers massaged her throbbing temples, easing the beginnings of a full-blown headache. The wedding day sorely tried her patience, but the wedding night promised far worse.

"You cannot be serious," spat Maggie.

"I'm quite serious." Luke stared at her as if she'd sprouted a third eye.

Had her initial suspicions been correct? Was Luke only interested in having a woman in his bed? "You expect me to share your bedroom? What are you up to?" Maggie leapt to her feet, hands fisted.

"Expecting my wife to share my bedroom is a reasonable assumption." Luke slammed his hands into his pockets.

"Reasonable assumption, my foot! There's only one bed in here, and there are several rooms available in this house." Maggie paced in front of him, controlling the urge to slap his face. "Just when I foolishly began trusting you…."

"There are several guest rooms, but you are not a guest. *You* are my wife. I agreed to an unconsummated marriage, but I never suggested separate bedrooms." Luke strode across the floor and closed the double doors.

Maggie planted herself in front of him and leaned into his face. "Elizabeth warned me that you might be pulling something, and that I'd be sorry I agreed to this marriage. I'm of a mind to collect my son and return to Spirit Creek this minute."

"I will not have my wife and son riding around the countryside in the dead of night!" Luke wagged his finger in Maggie's face.

"Your wife and son!" gasped Maggie.

"Surely, you don't consider yourself anything less than my wife," he stated.

"I consider myself your housekeeper, as per our arrangement. And I suggest you assign your housekeeper a room on the third floor close to her son." Maggie headed for the door.

In two quick strides, Luke blocked her exit. "If you were only the housekeeper then occupying rooms on the third floor would be appropriate. But you are my wife, Mrs. Carlyle. To convince the hired hands and our children that we are indeed husband and wife, you must remain in this room, every night, till death do us part." Luke stood firm, blocking her only means of escape with his hand glued to the doorjamb.

"The ink isn't dry on the marriage documents and already you're issuing orders. You are the most stubborn man I've..." Maggie burst into tears, mortified that she was crying again. She'd spent the entire day alternately spilling happy tears or sobbing from one anguish or another. Luke probably considered her an emotional ninny, without a backbone or sensible thought in her head.

"Come and sit down for a minute." Luke seated her on the end of the chaise and crouched in front of her. "Maggie, please listen to reason. You require a good night's rest. In the morning, this stipulation will seem reasonable. Trust me."

"There's that word again. Can I trust you? Or was it a mistake coming here?" Maggie searched his eyes for answers, but only saw wren-brown pools filled with confusion. Had either of them really thought this whole arrangement through?

"What possible mistake could you have made agreeing to a roof over your head and food in your belly?" Luke rested his forearms on his thighs. "Your only mistake would have been refusing to marry me."

"I never dreamt you'd expect me to share your bed. You promised no consummation, but are you a man of your word?" Maggie clenched her handkerchief in shaking hands. She felt light-headed from lack of sleep, from crying, and from the day's stresses. She wanted to roll into a ball and disappear into a comforting cocoon and not wake for months. Instead, she had to face this situation and settle things now.

"Perhaps I should summon the town's barrister, Robert Rutherford, and instruct him to prepare a binding legal document. *I hereby swear to completely ignore my wife whenever she sleeps in my bed*," he dictated jokingly, a smile creasing the corners of his mouth.

"Now you're just making fun of me." Maggie attempted to stand, but Luke gently pushed her back onto the chaise. His hands remained on her arms, annoyingly warm and comforting.

"I'm sorry if I made light of our situation. Before the wedding I promised you this marriage will remain unconsummated until you are ready, and I intend to keep my word. I'm not a young stallion unable to control my manly urges. I won't ravage you some night in a fit of unbridled lust. You're as safe with me in this bed as a babe asleep in a cradle." Luke's hands slid down her arms, and he clasped her hands.

"There's no need for sworn statements. I'll accept your word that you will honor our agreement." Maggie realized that what Luke Carlyle wanted, Luke Carlyle got. She had as much chance of winning this argument as she had of being elected mayor of Spirit Creek.

"Let's set down some ground rules," he stated, meeting her eyes. "Firstly, you are Mrs. Carlyle and you are the lady of the house."

"I'm your housekeeper..."

Maggie's protest was waved aside by Luke's hand. Ignoring her correction, Luke continued, "Secondly, I'm hiring sufficient help to return this house and the grounds to their proper splendor at the earliest possible date. There are plenty of ladies in town who've helped at the ranch before, and the ranch hands will assist with the grounds. It should only require a couple of day's work." Luke crossed his arms, obviously anticipating another argument.

She wouldn't disappoint him. "How will I fulfill my part of our arrangement, if you're hiring every woman in town to do my chores?"

"Once everything is set to rights, you'll assume responsibility for maintaining the house and gardens." Luke's shoulders slumped. "Seeing the ranch through your eyes tonight, I'm ashamed that I've allowed things to deteriorate to this condition. Rule number two: the ranch will be returned to rights as soon as humanly possible, and hang the cost."

"But what..." Maggie was quieted again by his finger on her lips.

"Rule number three: you are the mother of my children, and from this day forward I consider myself Sam's papa. We'll raise the children as husband and wife, father and mother, equally responsible for their upbringing. Are we in agreement?" Luke tilted his head, waiting for her answer. While his expression conveyed his determination, she detected something more. Was he silently pleading with her to meet him halfway?

Maggie nodded. "We're in agreement."

"Then that's settled." Luke stood.

Maggie peered up at him through her lashes. "That's all well and good. But we haven't settled the sleeping arrangements."

"This monstrous bed can easily be shared without any physical contact. I insist on marital appearances for the children's sake. What number was I at, three? Rule number four: We will share this room and this bed. End of discussion."

Maggie sighed, feeling like a child having a parent dictate terms as a result of poor behavior. She hated surrendering, agreeing to Luke's dictator-like pronouncements, especially since she didn't agree with him one iota. But she felt too exhausted for further argument.

"Enough rules, it's time we both got some sleep." Luke removed his waistcoat and hung it over a chair.

Maggie gasped, as he casually disrobed. Although numb with fatigue, every nerve ending in her body ignited. Surely he didn't intend to strip naked in front of her! The idea was both intriguing and horrifying in equal measure. The fireplace hadn't been lit, but Maggie suddenly experienced an unexplained rush of heat throughout her entire body, and her face felt flushed.

"I'll retire to my study for a half hour while you prepare for bed. And there'll be no more talk of running off back to town." Luke rolled up his shirt sleeves, lit a candle to illuminate his way downstairs, and disappeared through the double doors, quietly closing them behind him.

Maggie stood, tempted to sneak upstairs to another room. But he'd only drag her back down here again. She considered locking the door but he'd probably splinter it with a well-placed boot, just to make a point.

What was the point? She and Sam had legally joined Luke's family today. Luke became Sam's father, and she acquired two daughters. While married to William, she'd often prayed for a daughter, but never in her wildest dreams... And the new baby was growing inside her. Like it or not, Maggie Burns had become Mrs. Luke Carlyle.

While she unbuttoned her fancy boots, a dozen jumbled thoughts raced through her mind. She'd survived William's death, faced his deceptions, and accepted losing her home. But for some reason she suspected sharing a bed with her new husband would prove her greatest challenge yet.

How could she grieve for everything she'd lost? Since her husband's death she'd cried her heart out in the dark every night. She hated Luke Carlyle for stealing her privacy, her tears, and her grief. He'd given her his name, a home, a future, but her exhausted mind found his generosity falling short of a fair trade. And she wanted nothing more at this moment than to cry herself to sleep.

She tossed her boots aside and unbuttoned the borrowed wedding gown. Sighing, she remembered she'd willingly agreed to this arrangement. But in hindsight, would the price be higher than she'd anticipated? A woman of her word, she would fulfill her commitment. *For better or for worse.*

Maggie struggled out of the wedding dress and hung it in the armoire amongst Catherine's dresses and things. She rummaged through her boxes for a nightdress and donned the first one she found, a long pink cotton gown with short sleeves. Seated at the vanity table, she yanked the daisies and combs out of her hair and quickly brushed out the long curly strands.

She discovered a chamber pot under the bed, used it, and then leapt under the bedcovers. She tugged the beautiful quilt up to her chin, her entire body trembling. She wasn't certain if frazzled nerves or cool sheets caused her shivering. She yawned loudly before leaning over and extinguishing the lamp.

Soon, she relaxed and her body stilled. And then she waited. And waited. And waited. True to his word, Luke hadn't returned unexpectedly. She felt foolish, rushing through her bedtime preparations. Every muscle in her body ached. For a few minutes she listened to her own breathing.

"I cannot face another argument tonight," she whispered into the darkened room. She breathed deeply and squeezed her eyes shut intending to just pretend she'd escaped to dreamland when Luke returned.

In less than a minute, she was sound asleep.

* * *

Luke paced in his study, carrying a glass of whiskey clenched in his hand. Now that he'd acquired a new wife, the majority of his time could be spent on the operation of his ranch. But even though all of his waking hours would be occupied with work and making plans to capture the cattle rustlers, he needed to set aside time to arrange for the ranch revitalization.

"I'll assign Mike, Charlie and Willie to clean up the grounds. A couple of the older fellows will do the whitewashing and painting." Luke took a sip. "The grass needs cutting and the hedges need trimming. Ranch hands can do that. Oh, damn," cursed Luke, realizing he was talking to himself. But a multitude of restoration plans competed for attention in his head. Cleaning the house from top to bottom required a dozen women, and Maggie should organize and restock the pantry.

He'd been such a damn fool, he chided himself, taking another sip of his scotch. For the past two years, he'd believed Ned and he had handled the parental responsibilities and done a fair job of the housekeeping and ranch work. Now, he realized the extent of his neglect. Shortly after his wife's passing, he should have hired a gray-haired matronly housekeeper to eliminate any hint of scandal but who possessed all the necessary qualities like a caring nature and efficient homemaking skills. Too late now.

His father had taught him to respect his property and maintain it. And to appreciate material rewards earned through hard work. *Never take your good fortune for granted*, he'd preached. His father, mother and Catherine would be ashamed of his neglect. But with Maggie's help, he would do better in the future, and the children would grow up surrounded by beautiful trees and flowers, thriving on homegrown produce and proper meals, and sleeping peacefully each night knowing they were safe and loved.

He pulled out his pocket watch. Thirty-five minutes had passed since he'd slipped out of his bedroom. He couldn't believe how his new wife had gotten under his skin in such a short time. But the woman had refused to listen to reason.

"How long do you reckon it takes a lady to prepare for bed?" Luke asked Skipper, lying on the rug beside his desk. The faithful old dog raised one eyebrow, then closed his eyes and returned to sleep.

"Some help you are." Luke gulped the last of the drink, set the glass on his desk, grabbed the lamp, and exited his study.

Luke slowly climbed the long staircase and paused outside his bedroom for a few seconds. He cracked open the door, peered inside, and discovered Maggie at the far side of the gigantic bed, her slim body a mere bump under the covers. Soft, even breathing indicated his new wife was definitely asleep, not pretending. Moonlight poured through the narrow windows, illuminating her pale face and her dark auburn hair cascading across the stark white pillowcase. Until this moment, he hadn't consciously realized how absolutely beautiful she was.

To his horror, his body responded in the age-old way a man reacts when attracted to a woman. Luke silently cursed. Holding true to this unconsummated marital arrangement may be more difficult than he'd bargained for. How long could he hide his obvious physical attraction to her?

She frowned in her sleep. What subconscious thoughts run amok in that lovely head? Did she regret this marriage? Did she truly distrust his intentions? He hadn't forced her to marry him. Had he? Perhaps he'd taken advantage of her situation, but providing Maggie and her children with a secure future was the right thing to do, for all of them.

Luke closed the door, crossed the room, and set the lamp on his bedside table. He pulled off his boots, set them beside the chaise and tossed his socks on top. He undressed, hanging each item of his Sunday best clothing in his armoire. In consideration of his skittish new wife, he didn't remove his underwear.

He crossed the room and extinguished the lamp. The bed dipped and shimmied when he crawled in and settled himself. She never stirred. He clasped his hands behind his head and stared at the ceiling. He felt different somehow. And then he realized that for the first time in months, he felt content.

"I'm a married man again," Luke whispered aloud, smiling. He turned toward his new wife. "Good night, Mrs. Carlyle."

He sighed and rolled onto his side. In an instant, he was fast asleep.

* * *

"Sam!" Maggie screamed, panic rising and threatening to take her breath. Her heart stopped when she lost sight of her son in the darkness. "Where are you, Sam?"

"Here, Mama." Sam grabbed her hand.

Maggie's heart resumed beating and she forced back tears. "Sam, no matter what, don't let go of my hand." She'd never been so cold or so frightened. Where were they? She couldn't discern anything familiar in the dead of night. She tripped on a clump of sagebrush, almost falling, but caught her balance.

"I'm scared, Mama." Sam almost ran in order to match his mother's stride.

"I know you are, sweetheart." Maggie knew they were lost, but she'd never admit it aloud. Frightening Sam even more than he was already, just wasn't an option.

For what seemed like hours, she'd pushed onward, struggling to find their way in the dark. She almost crashed into a cottonwood branch hanging at eye level, but she ducked in time. Every rock, every bush appeared menacing. Where were they?

Suddenly, she heard heavy footsteps behind them, moving closer.

"What was that, Mama?" whispered Sam.

"Don't look back, muffin. Just keep running." Maggie quickened her pace, dragging her son along beside her and fearing she'd wrench his arm from its socket as she hurried onward.

"I'm tired, Mama. Let's stop," pleaded Sam.

"No, we can't stop. We need to hurry." She refused to glance back to see who was following them. Was it a man? An outlaw?

"I'm scared, Mama," repeated Sam, sobbing now.

"We must keep going." Maggie stopped and lifted her son into her arms. And then she sprinted forward, running, running, running.

Sam's arms encircled her neck and he buried his face in her

hair. Her cheek felt wet; Sam's tears mixed with her own. Who was chasing them? Perhaps a feral nocturnal animal?

And then something leapt at her from the darkness…

Chapter 8

Luke bolted upright in bed, jolted awake by a blood-curdling scream. For a second, he sat dazed and disoriented, and then he noticed his new wife thrashing about in the bedcovers like a victim fighting off an attacker.

"Maggie, wake up. You're having a nightmare. Sweetheart, wake up." Luke scrambled out of bed, struck a match, and lit the bedside lamp. He raced around to his wife's side of the bed, pulled back the covers, and gently shook her arm. As soon as he touched her, Maggie's eyes popped open, wild with fright.

"You're safe, Maggie. You were dreaming." Luke brushed her hair out of her eyes and wrapped her in his arms.

"Where…where am I?" Maggie squinted in the lamplight.

"You're at the ranch with me. Remember?" Luke tightened his hold. "We were married today."

"Where's Sam? Is he safe? Sam and I were lost in the darkness. Something was chasing us. I was so scared." Maggie wiggled out of his embrace.

"Sam is sleeping. You were just dreaming," insisted Luke.

Maggie nodded her head and whispered, "I'll…I'll be fine now."

"Good. You took several years off my life." Luke dragged a hand through his hair.

Maggie took a deep breath. "I apologize for frightening you. Everything seemed so real. And something jumped out at me."

"This is my fault." Luke's shoulders slumped. "I planted the idea in your mind, being alone out on the range in the dark, when you threatened to leave the ranch earlier tonight. I'm sorry."

"I've had nightmares since William died, woke up paralyzed with fear," admitted Maggie. Before it had been someone pointing a gun at her. "I've felt as lost in life as I did in that nightmare. Maybe I'm afraid of being alone or afraid of what the future holds for me." She flopped back against the pillow.

"You're safe now." Luke tucked the quilt under her chin. "And we'll work on that fear-of-being-alone business."

"Why do you care?" whispered Maggie. The question just slipped out.

Luke met her eyes. "You're my wife, and I'm responsible for you. Anything that I consider mine, I protect."

"Am I just another possession? Your latest acquisition?" Tears threatened behind her eyes.

"No, Maggie, never! You're family." Luke touched a strand of hair shining in the lamplight. "There are men in the world who demand control, submission. They ridicule and degrade women. I'm not like that, Maggie. A gentleman considers his wife someone special, someone to share his life with. Share his secrets, his fears, his successes and failures. Regardless of our arrangement, you're my wife and I'll always treat you as such."

"Banker Peterman should take lessons from you." Maggie's heartbeat had returned to normal again. Luke's words provided some assurance she'd made a wise decision and laid to rest her trepidations for the time being.

Luke chuckled. "No one would mistake Peterman for a gentleman. But I've always felt protective of women and children. There, now you know one of my secrets."

Maggie turned on her side. "Thank you for being so kind and understanding. I'm not accustomed to such tender care when waking from a nightmare. Usually, I lie in bed trembling in terror for several minutes and then burst into tears." She sighed. "Perhaps I shouldn't have confessed all that."

"Any time you're frightened by a nightmare, wake me up. No one will lie in bed trembling in terror in my house." Luke extinguished the lamp and crawled into bed, snuggled under the covers.

It took every bit of self-control to stop himself from wrapping Maggie in his arms and holding her until she slept. But he knew she'd never permit it. Likely accuse him of taking liberties if he even tried such a thing.

"Good night, Luke." Maggie closed her eyes.

"Good night, Maggie." Luke whispered, mesmerized by the beautiful face he could only faintly distinguish in the moonlight. "Sweet dreams."

Saturday, June 1, 1889

Maggie awoke with a start, and for a moment she couldn't recall where she was. Then she remembered. She now resided at the Diamond C Ranch, and she occupied Luke Carlyle's bed. Thankfully, her new husband wasn't sleeping beside her. To say that would have been awkward would be an understatement.

Immediately, her thoughts flew to Sam.

Where was her son?

She tossed the bedcovers aside and leapt out of bed.

Sam woke her up every morning, reliable as a rooster. Pulling her nightdress over her head, she noticed steaming water in the floral porcelain jug inside the matching basin. Had Luke been so thoughtful? She'd wash later she decided. The first order of business was finding her son!

Out of habit, she donned a wrinkled black housedress she dug out of one of her boxes. She twisted her hair into a bun while a dozen questions plagued her mind. Had Sam slept well during his first night on the ranch? Had he been frightened and confused when he first awoke this morning, unable to find her? Or was he happily playing with the other children?

Throwing open the bedroom door, she counted the grandfather clock's chimes as she strode down the hallway. Ten. Good heavens, she'd slept until ten o'clock in the morning! Some hired help she was proving to be.

Maggie's feet flew down the long staircase, and she rushed into the kitchen. Her heart stopped as she froze in mid-stride. An Indian woman wearing a deerskin dress and moccasins stood at the opposite side of the kitchen table, holding a small knife in her hand.

Oh, God, where was Sam?

Maggie's heart pounded with fear and several means of

escape raced through her mind. Should she slowly retrace her steps, back her way out of the kitchen? Should she turn and run, praying the woman didn't chase her? Maggie discredited all of these ideas. With her feet rooted in place, she couldn't move if she'd tried.

"Good morning, Mrs. Carlyle. I make you breakfast." The Indian set the small knife on the table, and Maggie realized the woman had been peeling potatoes.

Smiling, she motioned for Maggie to sit, while pouring coffee into a china cup and bringing it to the table. Maggie's heartbeat continued racing, and her feet remained nailed to the plank floor while the native woman casually filled one of Maggie's own dinner plates with eggs, sausage, and a biscuit.

"Who are you?" whispered Maggie, finding her voice at last.

"I am Morning Star, Ned's wife." She placed the plate on the table.

Maggie relaxed and her heartbeat slowed while she scrutinized the native woman's appearance. She couldn't even guess her age. Her flawless cocoa complexion enhanced an attractive round face. Raven black hair hung down her back in a single braid secured at the end with a thin rawhide strip tied in a bow. A beautifully beaded and fringed deerskin dress covered her slim body, and fur-trimmed moccasins adorned her small feet. "I'd heard Ned was married…" she muttered aloud.

"I sorry give you fright. Mr. Carlyle say make breakfast for children, then little ones play outside. I peel potatoes while wait for you."

Maggie flopped onto the kitchen chair. Her heart no longer threatened to leap out of her chest, and the food's tantalizing aroma teased her nose. "Is Sam playing outside?" she asked, reaching for the fork.

Morning Star nodded and smiled. "Little Sam good boy. Thank me for breakfast."

"This is absolutely delicious." Maggie caught herself talking with her mouth full and swallowed. "Please forgive my shameful behavior. I was startled. I…" Maggie's jaws clamped shut. How did one apologize for believing their life was in mortal danger?

Morning Star poured herself a cup of coffee. "Do not feel bad. If white woman suddenly appear in my mother's tent, face would look same." Morning Star's stern expression turned into a grin and she laughed. "May I sit with you, Mrs. Carlyle?"

"Please do, and call me Maggie." She smiled and popped another bite into her mouth. "How long have you lived on the Diamond C? And how did you meet Ned?"

Morning Star settled into a chair opposite Maggie. "I tell you about me. My story begins over twenty years ago when one of the ranch hands working for your husband's father found me stumbling around his ranch. I'd been raped by a white man some time before and after I mended in my aunt's tent, I left my Cheyenne tribe worried that I might be carrying a white baby. I couldn't bring shame to my family. A Cheyenne fellow named Wounded Wolf worked for Mr. Carlyle and he translated my words. I'd been two weeks on the rangeland, alone after being thrown from my brother's horse. I suffered from thirst and hunger and many bug bites, but Mr. and Mrs. Carlyle took care of me while I healed."

Maggie shook her head. "You poor thing, I can't imagine anything so horrible." She leapt out of her chair, almost toppling it, and threw her arms around Morning Star.

"You…you very kind," she stammered, appearing startled.

"How did you become Ned's wife?" asked Maggie, refilling their coffee cups.

"I am daughter of a Cheyenne chief. Ned spent hours talking to me while I got stronger each day. I not understand most words, but he sounded like very kind man. I liked him much, and I felt very safe. Ned ask Mr. Carlyle could I be his woman. If I carrying baby, I need someone to look after me. Later, we learn there wouldn't be a baby, ever." Morning Star paused for a second and wiped a tear from her eye with her finger. "Mr. Carlyle was Christian man and he say Ned must marry me. For two weeks, Ned and Mrs. Carlyle teach me say white man wedding words with hand signal for 'I do' and 'I will'.

"You didn't understand English?" blurted Maggie.

"At time, only a few words that they teach me. Wedding in flower garden behind main house. Ned give signal and I say white man's wedding words. I become Mrs. Ned Armstrong." Morning Star grinned. "The reverend believe I understand every word."

The ladies shared a hearty laugh. "I can tell we're going to be very good friends," said Maggie.

"I think that, too," replied Morning Star.

* * *

Luke strolled toward the main house to check on Morning Star and his new bride. He couldn't contain his curiosity a moment longer, concerned how well the two ladies from very different cultural backgrounds were getting along.

"All I ask is for peaceable coexistence between the deerskin and the calico," he muttered aloud. He stepped into the kitchen, tugged his Stetson off his head, and stood speechless. Morning Star and Maggie were laughing and hugging each other like old friends.

"Maggie, I go cook. Hungry men come soon for dinner. It was nice meet you." Morning Star beamed.

"It was nice meeting you, too." Maggie smiled.

Morning Star turned to Luke. "Good morning, Mr. Carlyle. I like new wife very much."

"Thank you, Morning Star." Luke scratched his head as the Indian woman grabbed her bowl of peeled potatoes and headed toward the back door. "I like her very much, too."

"Luke Carlyle, where is my son?" demanded Maggie, hands on hips, the moment Morning Star left the house.

"Sam and Patti are playing in the backyard." Luke tossed his Stetson on the table and planted himself in front of his wife. "I sent a ranch hand to town with Ronald's rig, and I instructed him to warn Ronald that we wouldn't be attending church tomorrow."

"We can't miss church…" she began.

Luke grasped Maggie's hand. "We'll let the townsfolk work the gossiping out of their system."

"I demand to see my son this minute. And I'd like to know why no one mentioned Morning Star to me. I made a complete fool of myself when I walked into the kitchen."

Luke held the screen door open for her. "What happened?"

"When I dashed into the kitchen I discovered her there, holding a knife. I thought I'd be murdered on the spot." Maggie glared at him. "Now, I feel like a total ninny. She was peeling potatoes."

Luke laughed uproariously. "Morning Star has a wicked sense of humor, and we love her dearly. She won't think you a ninny." Luke led Maggie out to the backyard.

The second Sam spotted his mother, he raced to her and she

scooped him up in her arms. Maggie forced back her tears. He'd never felt so good, wrapping his arms around her neck and smiling broadly.

"Guess what, Mama?" exclaimed Sam.

Chapter 9

Maggie buttered bread for sandwiches for dinner, recalling how excited Sam had been earlier. *Guess what, Mama?* Of course, he'd discovered the dog on the ranch and spent the entire morning playing with his new four-footed friend.

She'd learned from Luke that the old dog they called Skipper was part Collie and part Shepherd. He hadn't left Sam and Patti's side all morning. She would never worry that the children might stray too far from the house, knowing Skipper would keep an eye on them. Hopefully, she'd heard the last of Sam's puppy woes.

Just as she finished preparing dinner, the screen door creaked open. Maggie looked up from setting the table to discover Luke standing in the doorway. His presence seemed to fill the room.

"What are you doing here?" she blurted, and then wished she could call the words back. Such a stupid question. After all, it was his house, his kitchen.

"It's dinner time. I'd be much obliged if you'd set a place for me." Luke smiled at her and for some unexplained reason, her heartbeat quickened.

"Of course…you just surprised me…Morning Star mentioned you eat dinner with your men in the cookhouse. I…I didn't expect you until supper." Maggie's sweaty palms fumbled the cutlery into place on the table while she felt herself redden like a silly schoolgirl.

"I thought I'd join you and the children today." Luke washed up at the sink and dried his hands on a tea towel.

Maggie held her tongue and made a mental note to leave a

hand towel there in future. Had he wanted to spend time with her and the children, or was he checking on her efficiency?

"What have you been up to this morning?" he inquired.

"I wrote out thank-you notes and put our wedding gifts away," she reported, smiling. "I'll hand out the notes after church next Sunday."

"Thank you for doing that." Luke grabbed the dipper from the water pail beside the sink, gulped cold water, tossed the dipper back in, and wiped his mouth on his sleeve. "What do you have planned for this afternoon?"

"I'll iron the basket of clean clothes I found hidden in the dining room of all places." Maggie didn't add that she suspected Lucy hid them there on purpose to discredit her. "Then I'll tackle my unpacking."

"You only have your three boxes left. I apologize. I haven't packed up Catherine's clothing." Luke grimaced with his confession.

"I don't mind undertaking the task. I imagine you've been too busy to worry about such things." Maggie smiled warmly. Or perhaps you couldn't bring yourself to do it, she thought. Elizabeth had helped her clear out all of William's personal belongings shortly after she'd learned how badly he'd deceived her.

"I'm truly sorry. Thank you for being so understanding." Luke dragged out a chair and sat at the table, one arm hooked over the chair post. "My assistant foreman recently left my employ when he came into an inheritance. Bought his own ranch and moved his family out, kit and caboodle. We stored most of your furniture in the empty cabin. It's well-built, no risk of varmint infestation."

"Thank you, Luke." Maggie pushed open the screen door and called, "Patti, Sam, dinner is ready!"

The children washed up and Lucy wandered into the kitchen from the parlor. Finally, everyone took their seat, Luke said grace, and the family ate with gusto. Everyone that is, except Maggie. She picked at her sandwich and hoped no one noticed how little actually reached her mouth. She'd finished a large breakfast not too long ago. Now, her stomach had started to rebel, either from nerves at being on the ranch or a threatened onset of morning sickness. She prayed it wasn't the latter.

After dinner, the two youngest children raced outside to play and Lucy disappeared upstairs. Luke gulped the last of his coffee, reached across the table and touched her hand. "I'll be back late tonight so don't wait supper. I'll be riding from ranch to ranch, meeting with several of my neighbors about taking steps to capture these dang cattle rustlers."

"Shouldn't that be a job for the law?" blurted Maggie. As if she knew anything about catching cattle rustlers.

"The new sheriff will be called in to help once all the ranchers determine the extent of their losses, whether we figure it's just a couple rogue thieves, or it's an experienced gang."

"Please be careful. It sounds like it could be dangerous." Maggie had just buried one husband and she didn't want to bury another one days after the 'I do's' were spoken.

"Don't worry. We're in the early stages of deciding what steps to take." He leapt to his feet, grabbed his hat off the peg, and rushed out the door before Maggie could respond.

"See you later," she whispered into thin air, seconds too late for him to hear. The room seemed so empty when he left.

Maggie washed the breakfast and dinner dishes, then climbed the stairs to their bedroom. Firstly, she must remove Catherine's clothes from the large armoire, but she'd forgotten to inquire whether or not Luke intended to donate them to charity, since it would be years before Lucy or Patti would fit into any of them. She considered the possibility Hattie Morgan could make use of them. Although her own wardrobe was scanty, there was no way Maggie would ever wear any of his late wife's clothes. She'd ask Luke what he'd intentioned tonight.

While packing the clothes in boxes for disposal later, Maggie discovered Catherine's wedding dress in a decorative box atop the armoire. Maggie admired the magnificent creation of snow white silk covered in pearl beading. This she would keep for Luke's daughters to wear on their wedding days.

"Are you stealing Mama's wedding dress?" screeched Lucy, bursting into the room through the open double doors.

Maggie jumped a foot and her hand flew to her heart. She turned and glared at her new stepdaughter. "My goodness, you frightened me."

"Most thieves are frightened when caught." Lucy wrenched the dress from her stepmother's hands.

"I was simply admiring how beautiful the gown is. Your

mama would expect you to wear this dress on your wedding day, and we'll keep it for that purpose." Maggie grabbed the dress back.

Lucy rushed across the room to the vanity table and yanked open her mother's jewelry box. She peered inside and then glared at Maggie.

"You honestly believe I'll make off with your mother's jewels, too?"

Lucy's eyes squinted. "Papa doesn't love you. He'll send you away."

"Believe what you will. But your papa and I married to form a family for you and Patti and Sam. I'm not here to replace your mother or steal her things. I only want to be someone you can rely on." Maggie attempted to calm herself. Why did this girl rile her so?

Lucy stomped her foot. "I don't want you here."

"Unless your father asks me to leave, I'm not going anywhere." Maggie gently took the girl by the arm and guided her toward the bedroom door.

"I'll be watching you. I won't let you ruin Mama's things. Papa will come to his senses soon enough and send you away," spat Lucy, yanking her arm free.

"I have no intention of ruining your mother's things." Maggie gently shoved her out the door and closed it. Frustrated, she yelled through the door, "And there is nothing wrong with your papa's senses."

Maggie listened for the girl's response, but only heard her stomping upstairs to the next floor. Lucy was a charming child, intelligent and well-liked by everyone in the community. Having Maggie as a stepmother, however, hadn't set well with Lucy who believed the worst of her new parent.

"Well, young lady, that can't be helped. I'm here to stay, and you had better get accustomed to the idea," she muttered aloud.

But what had Maggie been thinking, shouting like a lunatic at her new stepdaughter? Maggie had trained as a schoolteacher, learned methods to reason with children, not to resort to a shouting match. Her instructors at The Plymouth State Normal School would be horrified at her behavior. Returning to her task, she vowed next time to act like a responsible, level-headed adult.

Tuesday, June 4, 1889

"Stop giggling and finish your breakfast," scolded Maggie.

Patti and Sam busily argued the finer points of catching frogs while they polished off their toast and gulped down their milk. The two of them were inseparable, and Maggie was pleased that her son was adjusting to his new family.

"I like having a little brother," said Patti, beaming.

Sam giggled again. "I like having a big sister."

Children were so resilient. But would Sam accept his new papa as easily as he accepted Patti? And then there was Lucy. Maggie refreshed her cup of coffee from the pot on the woodstove, and then slumped back into her chair.

Sam appeared at her side and encircled her neck with his chubby arms.

Maggie squeezed him until he squirmed out of her embrace. "Mama's going into Spirit Creek today to hire some ladies to help clean up this place. Do you want to come and play at Robbie's house?"

"Yippee! I can play with the puppies!" Sam danced in a circle, shattering his mother's hopes for no more talk of puppies.

"Lucy and Patti will be coming with us."

Lucy entered the kitchen at that moment. "I'm not going anywhere with you!"

Maggie silently counted to ten to control her temper. "You'll be coming to town with us. You can't stay here alone."

"I'll go the barn and…"

"You're coming to town with me," repeated Maggie. "And there'll be no argument from you, young lady."

Lucy stamped her foot and glared at Maggie.

"Go change your clothes and be ready to leave in ten minutes," she warned her stubborn stepdaughter.

Lucy swung around and stomped out of the kitchen.

Everyone changed into proper going-to-town clothes and then climbed into the buggy she arranged with Luke. Maggie shared the bench seat with their driver, Mike, while the children rode in back.

"Let's go, Mike," she said, with a mischievous grin. "We're burning daylight."

Mike tipped his head back and laughed. "You sound like Mr. Carlyle, ma'am."

They dropped Sam and Patti off at Robbie's house to play with the puppies all afternoon, while Lucy visited her friend on the other end of town. Mike completed errands for Ned and Luke, and Maggie and Elizabeth hired every lady they could find willing to help at the ranch tomorrow. After a cup of tea and a tearful farewell with her friend, Maggie dropped by Doc Fitzgerald's office.

"Good afternoon, Doc. I couldn't come to town without dropping by to say hello." Maggie hugged the kindly old gentleman, one of her dearest friends. His snow white hair and laughing blue eyes warmed her heart; he was like a grandfather to her. At least what she imagined a grandfather to be. He always fussed over her, concerned for her well-being. The competent and caring doctor brought Sam into the world, and she'd be forever beholden to him for his kindness over the years.

"And how is my Maggie today? You're carrying that little one, so don't be overdoing." Doc Fitzgerald guided her to a chair and then pressed his stethoscope to her chest.

"I experienced a bit of queasiness this morning and I'm concerned morning sickness is on the way, same as when I was carrying Sam." Maggie knew her ghostly-pale complexion and the dark circles under her eyes wouldn't go unobserved by Doc.

"You look tired, dear. No late nights sewing those quilting squares you're so fond of. You require extra rest, especially if the vomiting starts. It takes a lot out of a body." Doc Fitzgerald patted her on the hand. Laughing, he added, "No pun intended."

The door stood ajar, and a man in his early thirties strode into the room bold as could be. Maggie gasped at the unexpected intrusion.

"Benjamin, my boy, come meet one of my favorite patients." Doc Fitzgerald stepped aside and motioned the young fellow further into the room. "Maggie, I'm pleased to present Doctor Benjamin Johnson, newly-arrived yesterday from Philadelphia. Benjamin, this is my dear friend Maggie Carlyle."

"Pleased to meet you, Doctor Johnson." Maggie extended her hand, deciding her initial reaction uncharitable, the man being a doctor and all.

"So, you're the Maggie I've heard so much about. I'm

delighted to meet you." The slim young doctor stood six feet tall in good quality woolen trousers with his crisp white shirt rolled to the elbows. A watch chain hung from his waistcoat pocket, and a stethoscope circled his neck. Piercing dark blue eyes peeked out from under a mop of pale blonde hair, and Maggie suspected few things escaped his close examination.

"Benjamin is married to Pearl Jones. She worked for your husband, and then she left town to train as a nurse."

"Yes, I recall Pearl visiting her mother last Christmas…a lovely young lady."

"Maggie is with child, Benjamin. I'd be obliged if you keep abreast of her condition." Doc Fitzgerald's voice oozed affection.

"Congratulations, Mrs. Carlyle. A new baby is always a welcome addition to every family." Again, those piercing blue eyes met hers, accompanied by a wide smile.

"Thank you." Maggie turned and stared at her old friend. "Doc, you never mentioned plans to hire another doctor?"

"The citizens of Spirit Creek keep me pretty darn busy, Maggie. Now I hate to admit it, but my age is starting to show around the edges." Doc Fitzgerald laid a fatherly hand on the young man's shoulder. "It's rather pleasant, sharing the work with such a competent young fellow."

"Thank you, Doc," said Benjamin, smiling.

"Where are you and Pearl staying, Doctor Johnson? I'd love to call round and visit Pearl." Maggie stood, shook out her skirts.

"They're staying with me." Doc Fitzgerald turned away, coughing into his handkerchief.

"Pearl helps us out in the office most days. She's in the back room fetching some bandages. Stop and say hello on your way out." The young doctor held the door for her. "And call me Doc Benjamin."

"Thank you, Doc Benjamin. I'll do that. And Doc Fitzgerald, please drop out to the ranch for supper some evening real soon. Bring your new colleague and his wife, too. Luke would love to meet our new doctor." Maggie kissed the old fellow on the cheek.

"I just might take you up on that offer." Doc escorted her out of the room. "I'll give Bertha the day off."

After exchanging a few words with Pearl, Maggie exited Doc's office and waited on the sidewalk for Mike. Within seconds, the young man pulled the buggy up beside her. He set the brake, jumped down, and helped her get settled on the wooden bench.

"How was your day, Mrs. Carlyle?" inquired Mike, while she arranged her skirts. "I picked up your order at the general store."

"Thank you for doing that. My day has been quite productive." She folded her hands in her lap. Mike flicked the reins, and they were off to collect Lucy first.

Soon Robbie's house came into view, and they stopped to collect the other two children. A lump formed in Maggie's throat when she glanced over at her old home, but she straightened her spine and shook off the 'what ifs'. Maggie thanked Mrs. Wakeman while Mike lifted the children into the buggy. And a few minutes later, they were headed home.

Everyone seemed in good spirits, even Lucy, and their conversation was cheerful and lively. In time, however, the jostling buggy ride proved too much for Maggie. She shouldn't have had that cup of tea and cookie with Elizabeth.

"Stop the buggy, Mike…now," whispered Maggie, urgently.

As soon as the buggy ground to a halt, Maggie hoisted her skirts and leapt to the ground. She stumbled, righted herself. Gulping, she forced down the contents of her stomach until she staggered behind a nearby thicket, and then she vomited.

Maggie heard Mike order the children to remain in the buggy. A second later, he rounded the thicket on the run. "Are you ailing, Mrs. Carlyle?"

"Return to the buggy, Mike. I'll be fine." That said, she turned away from him and vomited again.

"I'd best drive you back to town to see Doc, ma'am." Mike's voice wavered.

"No need for doctoring."

"Mrs. Carlyle, anything happens to you Mr. Carlyle's gonna skin me alive." The young man's entire body shook.

"Oh, for Pete's sake, Mike, I'm not dying." She leaned closer and whispered, "I'm carrying."

"Carrying what, ma'am?" Mike looked bewildered, and then he blushed. "Oh! Mr. Carlyle has me hauling water and such because you're having a baby?" he asked in a whisper.

"Yes, but this must remain a secret for now." Maggie patted her forehead with a crumpled handkerchief and then wiped her mouth. She blinked back the tears burning behind her eyes, knowing this first bout of morning sickness meant weeks of misery ahead. But having a new baby in the end would be worth it.

"Wild horses heading to Hades couldn't pull a secret out of me, ma'am," stated Mike, solemnly. Then he smiled and whispered, "Congratulations, Mrs. Carlyle."

"Thank you, Mike."

"I confess I'm guilty of uncharitable thoughts, ma'am, concerning the water carrying and all. Figured you looked able-bodied enough. Please accept my apologies."

"You didn't know, Mike. No need for an apology." Maggie straightened her spine. "Let's continue on home now."

On their way back to the buggy, Mike quickly picked a handful of wildflowers. Without a word of explanation, he shoved the impromptu bouquet into Maggie's hands. The young man assisted her into the buggy, and then leapt up beside her.

"We'll be on our way again," said Mike, glancing back at the children. "Your mama saw these wildflowers, and she just had to have them." Mike met Maggie's eyes, and he winked.

"Why couldn't I pick flowers, Mike?" asked Patti, pouting.

"I would have picked flowers, too," snarled Lucy, frowning at Maggie.

"Snakes, girls," said Mike, smiling at his little white lie as he winked at Maggie again. "This area is just crawling with them."

Maggie turned aside, smiling with appreciation of the young man's quick thinking.

As the buggy rolled toward the ranch, Sam and Patti chattered non-stop about puppies while Lucy stared at the horizon, ignoring everyone. Maggie burst into a well-known children's song and even Mike joined in.

The buggy rumbled up the driveway at exactly six o'clock. Lucy leapt out and stomped into the house. Mike lifted Sam and Patti down. Morning Star waved from the back veranda, and the children raced to the house for supper. Mike helped Maggie out of the buggy and set the wooden box of food staples from the general store on the veranda.

Maggie smiled and patted his arm. "Thank you, Mike, for driving us to town. And thank you for keeping my secret a while longer."

"Don't mention it, ma'am. Just doing my job." He tipped his hat, jumped aboard the rig and with a quick wave headed toward the barn.

Maggie set her bouquet of wildflowers atop the wooden box and then silently snuck up the back stairs and peeked through the screen door. Morning Star, Sam and Patti were seated at the kitchen table stuffing themselves with hearty soup and biscuits, while the children expounded on their afternoon with the puppies. Lucy nibbled on a biscuit with her nose in a book, totally ignoring her siblings' chatter.

Stepping away from the door, Maggie smiled. She'd formulated the revitalization plans in her mind and then made several lists during the past few days. The completed work lists burned a hole in her pocket; she couldn't wait to get started.

Only one more job remained to complete her revitalization preparations, set to begin tomorrow morning. Maggie steeled herself and prayed. Please, Lord, help me through this.

Chapter 10

Maggie took a deep breath, straightened her spine, and stepped across the threshold into forbidden territory: the cookhouse during the ranch hands' evening mealtime.

Whitewashed walls stood out against the grime-covered windows located on opposite sides of the large room, and two enormous wooden tables stood parallel along the full length. Second helpings of the evening meal waited in pots and metal bowls on a narrow metal table near the door.

No one had noticed she'd slipped into the room.

"Excuse me, gentlemen. May I have a word with you?" Maggie heard the nervousness in her voice. Would Luke's ranch hands forgive her intrusion? Would they listen to her?

Every man swung around and glared at the female interloper. Four men leapt to their feet, almost tipping their chairs over. Obviously, their mamas taught them to stand when a lady entered the room. At least a dozen others simply leaned back in their chairs, draped an arm over the back, and stared at her. Three ranch hands, heads together, appraised her from head to toe as if she were a prize heifer up for auction. Heat radiated through her entire body, and she felt herself blushing.

One dark-skinned fellow, probably of Spanish descent, coughed and spluttered.

"He swallered his coffee the wrong way," offered the man sitting next to him while thumping the fellow's back with his hand. "He'll be to rights in a minute, ma'am."

"I apologize for interrupting your supper." Maggie's innards twisted, and she fought the urge to turn tail and run.

"What can we do for you, ma'am?" asked a silver-haired fellow, standing close to Maggie. He winked at her and she inhaled sharply. His boldness eased her nervousness, as he'd probably intended.

She squared her shoulders, clasped her hands behind her back, and addressed the men with confidence. "Gentlemen, as you are aware, the Diamond C is a beautiful ranch. But, it's fallen into…well…the ranch is…" She placed her hands on her hips. How should she phrase this without offending anyone?

A familiar looking freckle-faced lad with a cowlick occupied the chair beside her. He whispered, "It's looking poorly, ma'am."

"Thank you…" Maggie's eyes encouraged an introduction.

"Scotty, ma'am." The young man turned crimson, earning himself a round of jeering from the other cowboys.

"Thank you, Scotty." Maggie patted his shoulder, recognizing the fellow who handled Ronald's rig and mare the night she arrived at the ranch. "The Diamond C is looking poorly, and I'd appreciate your assistance in putting things to right."

"It'd be a pleasure, ma'am." A tall, blond-haired fellow bowed at the waist, like a butler in a proper English manor house, inciting laughter and jeering.

A slightly stooped, bow-legged fellow stood. "Be honored to hep yer out, ma'am."

"Me too, ma'am," added an Indian fellow.

Was he Morning Star's translator of years ago? Still working for the Diamond C? "Would you happen to be Wounded Wolf?" asked Maggie.

The Indian stood and met her eyes, but he didn't appear surprised when she addressed him by name. "Yes," he answered, simply.

"Pleased to make your acquaintance." Maggie smiled at him.

Wounded Wolf shook her hand, his grip firm and confident, and a full set of perfect pearly-white teeth smiled back at her. He stood tall with a lean waist and broad chest. His hair was cut short—no braids for this Indian—and his weathered complexion looked slightly pocked.

Within a minute, Maggie acquired another ten volunteers. Confidence soaring, she rested her hands on the back of the vacant chair in front of her.

"Please consider the revitalization work secondary to your commitment to Mr. Carlyle. Your regular duties take priority."

A rumble of agreement rolled throughout the room like thunder on a hot summer day.

Maggie extracted a slip of paper from her dress pocket. "These are the chores requiring your assistance." It was sheer folly to expect most men to recognize the obvious. Best spell things out in black and white. She read the list aloud. "Gentlemen, please do not hesitate to add anything you deem necessary that I may have missed."

"Ma'am, please forgive me for being forward and all, but I'd be right honored to oversee things and assign duties. The men could direct their questions to me, and not bother your pretty head about it." The silver-haired fellow who'd winked at her smiled.

Maggie's fists clenched at the 'pretty head' comment, but she let it pass. "Does anyone object to this fellow overseeing your work?"

Someone from the back of the room muttered, "The old bastard's the only feller in here who can read yer damn list."

The silver-haired man gasped. "There'll be no cussing when there's a lady present." Turning to Maggie, he added, "Sorry about that, ma'am. My humblest apologies."

"Apology accepted." Maggie considered it the least she could do. After all, she'd encroached on their personal time and territory. Several men exchanged glances, but no one spoke up. "Then I'm placing this fellow in charge, and I thank all of you for your assistance."

"Does Mr. Carlyle know about this?" The fellow spoke with a French accent and glared at Maggie, hiding behind a flea-infested beard. Stringy brown hair hung well below his shoulders, a battered, dusty hat teetered on his head, and he sucked on yellow, chipped teeth. His clothes were unwashed, and Maggie wisely stood downwind of him.

"Does Mr. Carlyle know about what?" Luke's voice ricocheted off the walls.

Maggie startled and whipped around. Her husband's murderous expression indicated he expected an explanation for her presence in the cookhouse, and it had better be a good one.

"Excuse us for a minute, gentlemen." Luke grasped his wife's arm, and her fancy boots barely touched the ground as he escorted her outside.

"What in blazes are you doing? The cookhouse is off limits to womenfolk." Luke spat the words, but he released his grip on her arm.

"What would you suppose I'm doing? Inviting them to afternoon tea? I'm garnering volunteers for the ranch revitalization," hissed Maggie, fuming. Her husband had hauled her outside like a misbehaving child who'd embarrassed its parent.

"Why didn't you clear this with me first?" Luke crossed his arms.

"When was I supposed to clear *anything* with you? You sneak out of the house before the rooster's awake, and you seldom return until everyone's retired for the night and asleep in their beds."

"I'm too busy with ranch work for sit-down-to-tea-discussions with you." Luke poked her lightly on the shoulder.

Maggie slapped his hand away and glared at him. "Well, I'm busy planning the revitalization, and I don't have time to search thousands of acres of rangeland in hopes of discussing every little detail with you."

"I intended to delegate the outside work to the men myself." Luke paced in front of her.

"You ordered the ranch *returned to rights as soon as humanly possible*. Rule number two, if I'm not mistaken." Maggie stood hands on hips. "How dare you accuse me of interfering with your men when I'm carrying out your instructions?"

"You're forbidden to issue orders to my men." Luke dug in his heels and glared at her. "What were you doing in there?"

"Making arrangements to whip this embarrassment you call a ranch into some semblance of presentable." Maggie was building up a head of steam. "If I'm forbidden to issue orders to anyone, why did you hire me to work for you?"

"I did not hire you, I married you," muttered Luke. He looked heavenward for a second and then grasped her arm and guided her back inside the cookhouse.

"Let go of my arm," whispered Maggie through clenched teeth. Luke released his grip and planted her in front of him, his hands resting affectionately on her shoulders. She was sorely tempted to plant an elbow in his ribs, but restrained herself.

"Gentlemen, the Diamond C requires extensive repairs."

Luke's voice echoed throughout the silent cookhouse while every eye rested on him. "The main house has been neglected…"

"The main house is on par with Darby's cleaning of The Joker's Wild." Maggie didn't realize she'd whispered her thoughts aloud until she heard Scotty's gasp.

The young cowhand's eyes widened, and their eyes met. "Mrs. Carlyle, when were you in Darby's saloon?" he whispered.

"Shut up, Scotty," ordered Luke and Maggie in unison.

Luke cleared his throat, glared at her. "The revitalization of the Diamond C is of utmost importance. Please give Mrs. Carlyle's list of chores your immediate attention, gentlemen."

Maggie had overstepped; she realized that now. Next time, she would remember Luke's penchant for a little palavering before issuing orders to his ranch hands. His tanned hands rested atop her shoulders, their warmth burned clear through her calico dress. She managed to stifle a shiver from the pleasure of it. While his words had infuriated her a second ago, his touch felt hot as a brand. Why did something so simple magnify itself in her senses?

"Mr. Carlyle, we'll start first thing in the morning." The silver-haired fellow she'd put in charge of the volunteers extended his hand to the boss.

* * *

"Thank you, Third." Luke addressed the entire room. "Gentlemen, there'll be extra dollars in the pay envelopes for every man who assists with the clean-up." Luke locked eyes with the stringy-haired, foul-smelling cowhand. "Enough incentive for you, Frenchy?"

The ranch hand sneered, turned his back, and hunched over his supper.

Luke recalled the drifter's reluctance to take orders, and on several occasions, Ned reported finding Frenchy sitting under a tree out on the range, perfecting his talent for afternoon napping.

"Appreciate your help, Frenchy." Luke patted the cowhand's shoulder, noticed his flinch. Had someone rubbed him the wrong way? Luke respected his men's right to privacy, but he intended to keep an eye on the disgruntled drifter.

"Mighty generous, sir." Third initiated a round of applause

for the boss, and then added, "Finish your vittles, fellas, and get your behinds into bed. Big day ahead of us tomorrow."

Garbled bits of conversation followed Luke and Maggie outside.

* * *

A warm evening breeze carried a mixture of scents. Maggie's nose twitched, and her eyes smarted. Would she ever become accustomed to barnyard stench?

"I overstepped, Luke," admitted Maggie. "It won't happen again. I'm sorry."

"You're forgiven." Luke reached for her hand and headed for the main house.

"Did you address that older fellow as Third?" Maggie tipped her head to one side.

Luke chuckled. "Years ago, three trail-weary cowhands rode onto the ranch. Father hired the first two men, but the third fellow appeared drunk. The other men vouched for him as being a good worker, but the fellow's brains were addled from one saloon brawl too many. The poor man couldn't remember his own name. The last of the trio to be hired, Father called the nameless fellow 'Third'. We still don't know where his kin hails from, or if he even has family alive."

"What a sad story. He's never regained his memory?"

"Not even a smattering." Luke shook his head.

Maggie hurried to match Luke's stride. "I can't imagine not knowing my own name or where I hailed from. Third is fortunate your father gave him a job, a home."

"The Diamond C's success evolved from the sweat, blood and sacrifices of our hired men. Any fellow who provides years of dedicated, hard work earns himself a permanent home at the Diamond C. And a bonus always boosts morale." Luke tightened his grip on her hand.

"Your generous offer will ensure the work is completed quickly." Maggie flushed with heat. Was her rapid heartbeat due to Luke's warm hand or her increased pace?

"Saw right through that ploy, did you?" Luke grinned mischievously.

"It didn't take a genius." Maggie met Luke's eyes. "Thank you for your support. I wasn't certain your men would co-operate with a female doing the asking."

Luke brushed her hand with a kiss. "You're Mrs. Carlyle, and my men best respect you as such. Or I'll be having a loud discussion about it with those fellows."

Maggie's heart pounded. Would she ever become comfortable with the title 'Mrs. Carlyle'? Being the wife of one of the wealthiest ranchers in Montana Territory bordered on royalty in these parts. But she'd never felt special in her life: not as a lonely debutante in Philadelphia, not as a frontier schoolmarm, and not as the sheriff's wife. Now, she'd become Mrs. Luke Carlyle. She found the whole idea more frightening than flattering.

"When do your hired ladies arrive?" Luke guided Maggie up the back steps. He handed her the wildflowers and carried the box of supplies into the kitchen.

"First thing tomorrow morning. A dozen busy women willingly agreed to drop everything to help me out. *It's just the neighborly thing to do*, they said." Maggie marveled at small town generosity

"Did you talk to Hattie Morgan?" asked Luke, closing the door behind them and setting the box on the table.

"She's coming but she refuses to take any payment."

"Hattie and Catherine were best friends. She's as familiar with this home as I am."

"We chatted at the wedding, and she extended a standing invitation for tea, surprisingly. Usually never says two words to me after church."

"You were a 'town lady' before." Luke smiled at her confused expression. "The ranchers' wives are common folk: no fancy clothes, no fancy educations. Town women intimidate them with their uppity, highfalutin ways."

"I do not consider myself highfalutin, thank you very much," protested Maggie.

"Town ladies parade about in their fancy silks and satins and feathered hats, while the ranchers' wives wear calico and gingham and sunbonnets."

Maggie hadn't worn silk and satin since marrying William. He insisted she could only afford calico dresses on his sheriff's salary.

And now, regardless of their arrangement, she'd be considered the wife of a wealthy rancher. Did she qualify as highfalutin or a simple rancher's wife? "This is ridiculous. Town ladies are no different than the ranchers' wives. Education or finer clothing doesn't make us better people. I admire the grit and fortitude of the ranchers' wives." Maggie paled and turned away.

"What is it?" Luke swung her around to face him.

"I know nothing about cattle, geese or chickens." Maggie sighed. "I'm no longer a town lady, and I'm going to fail miserably as a rancher's wife. I won't be welcome by any of them."

Luke met her eyes. "When Hattie arrived as Robert Morgan's mail-order bride, she didn't know the difference between a hen and a Hereford. You'll do fine as a rancher's wife."

"I do enjoy feeding my chickens," admitted Maggie. "But that bossy rooster chased me away from the hen house twice. I'll win him over yet. Your geese are another matter."

"What crime have the geese committed?" Luke snickered and Maggie poked him in his muscular chest.

"I set out my tin flowerpots filled with colorful pansies, petunias and marigolds. The beggars pecked the daylights out of the metal containers, dented them something awful, and ruined my flowers."

Luke washed up in the basin while Maggie served up the hearty soup and biscuits left warming on the woodstove.

"Well, *my* geese weren't at fault." Luke spoke with a judge's authority, proclaiming the accused innocent of all charges, and then sat at the table. "Those *other* geese are to blame."

"*Other* geese?" Maggie tilted her head.

"If my goose sees its reflection in something shiny, like your tin flower pot, she'll peck at the other goose she sees." Luke raised the spoon to his lips, sipped his soup.

Maggie stood hands on hips. "Are you testing my gullibility?"

"It's perfectly logical if you're a goose," insisted Luke, grinning. "Set your tin flower pots up on the veranda, not on the ground."

"Fine lot of good that piece of advice is now." Maggie pursed her lips, pushed her supper aside. Would Luke notice how little she'd eaten?

"Once the flowerbeds are tidied up, you'll have more flowers than you know what to do with. I'm sorry about the flower pots. Buy some new ones." Luke buttered the last biscuit and popped it into his mouth.

"Well, I'll know better next year." Maggie sucked in her breath. Living on the ranch four days, and she was talking about next year? Why would she say such a thing? Would this ranch become home sooner than she imagined?

"Leave these few dishes for morning and let's turn in. There's a busy day ahead of us tomorrow." Luke escorted Maggie to the bottom of the staircase.

"Will you involve yourself with the clean up? Or is Third totally in charge?" asked Maggie, yawning.

"Third is capable of handling things." Luke frowned. "I'll be riding out early to discuss the cattle rustling matter with the men working the range. I'll be home late tomorrow night, so don't wait supper."

"All right, but you might not recognize your own ranch when you arrive home," teased Maggie.

Luke brushed her cheek with an unexpected kiss. "I'm having a brandy before I retire. I'll be up in a half hour."

"Good night," whispered Maggie, smiling. Their nightly ritual continued—she retired first and he followed later—and she appreciated Luke's thoughtfulness.

"Good night, Maggie." Luke headed toward his study.

Maggie would need a good night's sleep in preparation for the busy day tomorrow, and she hurried upstairs to their room. She shed her clothes, hung them to air, donned her nightdress, and quickly brushed her hair. She slipped between the cool sheets, considered everything on tomorrow's agenda, and whispered a prayer that she hadn't bitten off more than she should have.

Chapter 11

When Luke entered their bedroom thirty minutes later, Maggie slept soundly, arms flung wide, her long auburn hair flowing across the stark white pillow. He stared at his angelic wife for several seconds, and then gently tucked her arms under the covers and pulled them up to her chin. Before he talked himself out it, he brazenly kissed her on the mouth. Was it simply his imagination, or had Maggie smiled in her sleep?

She never stirred.

A certain part of his anatomy leapt to attention, however.

How would he get any sleep now? He would never have imagined how attracted he'd become to his new wife. And he'd never survive their arrangement unless Maggie cut her grieving short and agreed to consummate their marriage.

Luke shed his clothes, climbed into bed wearing only his long johns, and buried his head in the feather pillow. After a minute, he punched the pillow in frustration. Maggie looked so beautiful, especially when he could watch her unobserved, sleeping soundly. How long could this arrangement continue? He should have spelled out a timeline. Six months? Four months? Two?

Damn. He couldn't think that way. He'd promised to wait until she was ready to move on. But time crept along like a snail with a gimped leg. Did snails even have legs? Finally, he'd almost drifted off to sleep when he heard Sam screaming. In a flash, he leapt out of bed and raced upstairs to the third floor.

Maggie had woke immediately and followed on his heels.

"What's wrong?" asked Luke, rushing into the room Sam and Patti still shared.

"I heard...a ghost," sobbed Sam, shaking like a cottonwood leaf in a wind storm.

Maggie scrambled past Luke and engulfed her son in her arms. "There's no such thing as ghosts, honey. You probably just heard the wind."

"No...it was...a ghost," insisted Sam, clinging to his mama like a burr on a hound dog.

Luke strode across the moonlit room and lightly touched his youngest daughter's arm. A moan erupted from Patti's lips.

Sam howled, "There it is, Mama. There's the ghost."

Luke placed his hand on Patti's forehead. "It's not a ghost, Sam. Patti's burning up with fever." Luke headed for the door, paused with one hand on the doorjamb, and met Maggie's eyes. "I'm going for Morning Star. Stay with the children."

* * *

Maggie flopped onto Sam's bed for a moment, stunned, listening to Luke's boot steps pounding down the stairs. At least he remembered to slip into some footwear before racing out of the house.

If the situation hadn't been so serious, she might have smiled at the picture he would make, streaking across the yard wearing nothing but his long underwear and his boots. Instead, she crossed to the small table beside Patti's bed, struck a match, and lit the lamp.

Maggie's hand brushed Patti's forehead. "Sweetheart, let's get you cooled off."

Sam tiptoed across the floor and hopped onto his sister's bed. "Is Patti going to die?" he whispered.

Maggie noticed the tears in her son's eyes; he cared for his new sister as much as Patti cared for him. "No, sweetheart. We'll make her well. Don't worry. I'm going to fetch a basin of cold water and a washcloth to bathe her." She kissed him on the forehead and rushed out of the room.

Maggie strode across the third floor landing and knocked on Lucy's door. "I'm coming in," she shouted and then charged into the room. She poured water into Lucy's basin from the matching jug and then grabbed several washcloths.

"What are you doing in my room?" growled Lucy, rubbing her eye while rousing from sleep.

"Patti is burning with fever." Maggie grabbed the basin and raced out of the room.

Lucy scrambled out of bed and followed her. "Patti, what's wrong?" Lucy grabbed the wet washcloth from Maggie's hand and placed it on her sister's forehead.

"We should undress her and bathe her whole body to reduce the fever," ordered Maggie.

While Lucy whipped the covers off and pulled her little sister's nightdress over her head, Maggie led Sam back to his own bed. This was no time for an anatomy lesson, differences between girls and boys. "Sam, go back to sleep. There's no ghost, and Patti's going to be just fine." She tucked him in with his toy dog.

At that moment, Morning Star slipped into the room with a tin cup filled with a steaming brew in her hand. "This will stop fever. Step aside, Lucy."

Lucy crawled across Patti's bed and continued her ministering from the other side. While Morning Star spooned her medicinal tea into her, Patti spluttered but swallowed most of it.

"What is that, Morning Star?" inquired Maggie, pointing to the cup.

"Tea brewed from snowberry twigs. Very good for fevers. But for child only small amount." Morning Star spooned a bit more into the little girl's mouth.

Maggie peeked into the tin cup and turned her nose up at the brown liquid. "I'd have to be near death to ingest that."

"If Morning Star says it'll work, then Patti's drinking it," muttered Luke.

Maggie startled; she hadn't heard him enter the room. Obviously, Luke believed in Morning Star's doctoring and held the native healer's talents in high esteem. His decree induced a smile from the native woman.

Thirty minutes later, Lucy placed her hand on her sister's forehead. "She seems a bit cooler, Papa? Don't you think?"

Luke stepped forward, leaned around Morning Star, and placed his hand on his daughter's cheek. "I believe you're right. The fever is going to break."

"Everybody go sleep. I stay with little one. Give more tea until fever breaks." Morning Star dismissed everyone with a wave of her hand.

Reluctantly, Maggie set aside the washcloth. "Are you certain you don't need any assistance?"

"Tea working. Patti be fine, Maggie. Go sleep." Morning Star dragged the only chair in the room closer to the little girl's bed. She stretched her back, sat down, and then peered over at Sam. "Your little man sleep, too. Everything fine now."

"Good night, Morning Star." Luke patted the native woman on the shoulder. "And thank you so much. What would we do without you?"

Lucy returned to her room down the hall, and Luke and Maggie descended the stairs to the second floor. Maggie slipped under the covers, and Luke crossed to his side of the bed and removed his boots.

"Patti took a few years off my life tonight. I was scared to death for her," whispered Maggie.

"How do you imagine her father felt?" Luke crawled under the covers. "I greatly appreciated having you here with me during a scare like that. Thank you."

"You're welcome. It's called being a parent." Maggie yawned. Had Luke been reminded of Catherine's ordeal? Had the notion that Patti might die crossed his mind? Thankful that everything had turned out well, Maggie drifted back to asleep.

* * *

Luke recalled kissing Maggie on the mouth earlier when he'd found her asleep. It seemed ages ago, but in truth, only a couple hours had passed. He didn't dare attempt a repeat performance for fear he'd wake her. Having endured such a harrowing ordeal, she needed her rest. After all, she carried the unborn child he now considered his.

"*His child*," he whispered aloud. A legal marriage ensured certain benefits. And he hoped some day he and Maggie might have children of their own. He adored Sam but he'd like nothing better to have his own flesh-and-blood son.

Although he wasn't foolish enough to believe his children

wouldn't try his patience and threaten his sanity on future occasions, he wouldn't trade one second of parenthood for anything.

In a minute, Luke drifted off to sleep, smiling.

Wednesday, June 5, 1889

Blinding sunshine greeted the day and a warm breeze wafted across the lush valley where the Diamond C main house, barns, and corrals were nestled. The ranch hands wolfed down their breakfast and hurried through their morning chores, knowing only a damned fool would turn down the opportunity to fatten his pay envelope. True to their word, Third and his volunteers had tackled their cleanup chores promptly at six a.m. Considerable progress had already been made.

At seven-thirty, Maggie sat on the rocking chair, hidden from view on the small balcony above the main house front doors. She peeked through the rail's thin spindles—she still couldn't bring herself to look down over the railing as she had her first night on the ranch—and watched unobserved while a dozen ladies arrived in buggies and carriages. Two of Florence Jones' teenaged daughters rode double on a slightly swayback horse, and she smiled as Scotty raced out to greet the twin girls and offer to care for their mount. They giggled and handed over the reins to the handsome young ranch hand.

Dozens of butterflies fluttered inside Maggie's stomach as she watched the women arrive. Some were dear friends, and others she'd only exchanged a quick hello with in passing, on the sidewalk outside the general store or on the church steps after a Sunday service.

Maggie smiled. Her children were playing in the backyard. There'd been no sending them to school, with all the excitement going on at the ranch today. She'd allowed them to stay home from their lessons on this special occasion.

She slipped back into the master bedroom and headed downstairs to greet the ladies assembled in the front entryway, laughing and chatting together while awaiting her instructions. She was overwhelmed with everyone's willingness to help out.

"Ladies, thank you for coming. Your generosity means so much to me." Pausing to collect herself, she took a deep breath and fought back tears. "Elizabeth will help me with assigning jobs. Choose whether you'd like to work on the main floor or upstairs. Team up in groups of two or three. We'll take a break at noon for dinner together, and hopefully we'll finish up in time for supper."

"Wonderful," said Bertha Watson, beaming with enthusiasm. For many years, she served as Doc Fitzgerald's housekeeper, and at forty-five, Spirit Creek's old maid was no stranger to hard work.

"Let's get busy, ladies," added June Davidson, a sturdy widow in her early forties and now the sole owner of the Spirit Creek Hotel. Two of her maids had accompanied June to the ranch today.

Maggie shook Rebecca Simpson's hand, noticing the septuagenarian's firm handshake belied her years. "Rebecca, why don't we assign you something where you can sit. Perhaps cleaning the silver."

"Thank you for your thoughtfulness, Maggie. These old knees aren't much good at scrubbing floors anymore. And I didn't get home until after midnight last night, delivering a baby at the Decker's ranch." Rebecca smiled and hugged Maggie warmly, before heading for the dining room. Despite her years, Rebecca still served as Spirit Creek's only midwife.

"Thank you so much for inviting me and my twin sister," said Agnes Jones. "Angela and I would never pass up the chance to earn some extra money."

Maggie imagined every cent in the household budget counted with a dozen children in the family. "You're very welcome. I know what hard workers you girls are," said Maggie, smiling. The twins had been favorite students, years ago when she'd first been hired as Spirit Creek's teacher. The sisters hurried off with Lucy on their heels to clean the dining room.

While everyone scrubbed and polished in the main house, Morning Star prepared a sumptuous and hearty chicken dinner with iced tea in the cookhouse. At noon on the dot, Hattie Morgan helped Morning Star serve the meal on tables in a shady corner of the backyard, which the ladies enjoyed amid animated conversation. The ranch hands ate inside the cookhouse. Soon everyone finished their meal and Morning Star waved off all offers to help with the dishes, encouraging the workers to finish their chores.

The ladies assembled in the parlor and Elizabeth assigned duties. Sam and Patti ran errands for the ladies, fetching clean cloths and brooms and carrying armfuls of dirty linens downstairs to the laundry. With so many helping hands, the chores progressed at a remarkable pace.

"Maggie, did anyone remember to sort out the root cellars?" asked Hattie, as they stood outside Luke's study.

"Oh fiddle! I totally forgot to add that to my list." Maggie's shoulders slumped.

"Come on, I'll give you a hand," offered Hattie. "We'll start with the indoor one."

Finally, the day's work ended shortly before five o'clock and Morning Star served up afternoon tea with cookies and small cakes with Ellie Thomas' help; the schoolteacher arrived just in time to help finish the chores. Amid complaints of aching muscles and sore backs, the ladies shared their pride in a job well done. And they'd finished in time to hurry home to collect their children from the neighbor who'd babysat and get supper on the table for their husbands and children.

Maggie fetched a wad of money from a cigar box, hidden in Luke's study. As instructed by her husband, the new Mrs. Carlyle distributed suitable compensation to all of her helpers, refusing to listen to suggestions of overpayment while thanking them profusely for their hard work. Everyone left for home, except Elizabeth.

After supper, Maggie and Elizabeth put the children to bed and then shared a cup of tea at the kitchen table. Although Elizabeth would never admit it, Maggie knew both of them felt done-in after such a busy day. Being with child, Maggie wanted nothing more than to fall into bed an hour ago when she tucked Sam and Patti in after a story.

"Goodness, I almost forgot." Maggie dug her lists of household supplies and children's needs out of her apron pocket and handed them to Elizabeth.

"This marriage of yours is proving very profitable for Ronald and me," joked Elizabeth, taking a peek at the lists. "Most of these items are on the store shelves, and anything I order should arrive in a few weeks."

"Thank you, Elizabeth. The house looks wonderful, and the ranch hands did a marvelous job of the grounds and outbuildings. Those fellows worked every bit as hard as the ladies. They even weeded the vegetable garden."

"The lot of them probably feared being shown up by the womenfolk." Elizabeth laughed as she filled the teacups. "There's just the flowerbeds left. We'll have those completed by tomorrow."

"I can't wait to show William. He won't believe how much we've accomplished today." Maggie yawned loudly and glanced at Elizabeth, unable to interpret her friend's strange expression. "What?"

"Do you realize what you just said?" whispered Elizabeth.

"What I just said about what?" Maggie shook her head and set her teacup down. She must be tired, she couldn't recall saying anything unusual a minute ago.

"You said *I can't wait to show William.*" Elizabeth searched Maggie's eyes.

"I never said William," she blurted the denial while her heartbeat raced. She felt light-headed and totally stunned, knowing Elizabeth wouldn't lie about what she'd said.

Why would she say such a thing! She'd attempted to put William Burns behind her and move forward with her life, accept that her future was with Sam on this ranch, working for a wealthy man as his housekeeper to keep her children safe and happy. But thoughts of her late husband had surfaced despite her best intentions to put the most horrendous time of her life behind her.

"I realize you meant to say Luke. But, dear, you distinctly said William. It's perfectly understandable, a simple slip of the tongue." Elizabeth patted Maggie's hand.

"Oh fiddle, Elizabeth. What if I'd said that in front of Luke? I'd be mortified!" Maggie propped her elbows on the table and cradled her head in her hands.

"Luke would understand, dear. There wasn't any hurtfulness intended. It just slipped out." Elizabeth rubbed Maggie's back. "You're probably overtired."

Maggie noticed the undeniable concern in her friend's eyes. Should she be concerned, too? Was the strain of this marriage affecting her mind? William's death had sent her life plummeting into a downward spiral of grief, distress, and uncertainty. But her life righted itself more with each passing day. Surely, only the day's stress caused the slip.

"You're right. I should just watch what I'm saying. I won't allow it to happen again, Elizabeth." With a steady hand, Maggie lifted the teacup to her lips.

"Well, I'm getting too old for all this cleaning nonsense in one day. I'm off to bed. I sent word to town with Bertha, to assure Ronald I'm only staying one night." Elizabeth kissed Maggie's cheek. "Otherwise, he'll complain bitterly about how lost he is without me."

"Good night, Elizabeth." Maggie stood to hug her friend. "And thank you for everything. I couldn't have survived the day without you."

"Don't wait up too long for Luke's return." Elizabeth wagged a finger at her friend. "You need your rest. We'll get an early start in the morning."

"I won't wait up for long. I'm dead on my feet." Maggie hoped her expression didn't reveal her little white lie. She intended to wait up for Luke until dawn if necessary. She couldn't wait to see his expression when she showed him all they'd accomplished.

Maggie kissed her friend's cheek and received another hug in return. "Good night. Sleep well," she called as Elizabeth headed up the staircase to her guest room.

While she awaited Luke's homecoming, Maggie wandered throughout every room on the main floor, inhaling the fresh scent of soap and furniture polish, running her hands along the gleaming furniture. She walked silently across the dust-free rugs settled back in place upon shiny plank floors.

"I can't believe it's possible to accomplish so much in a single day." Maggie blushed, realizing she'd spoken aloud. She turned her attention to the old dog sleeping beside his master's rocking chair in the parlor. "I was talking to you, Skipper. Are you listening?"

Hearing his name, the senior canine raised his head. Maggie bent down and scratched his silky ears. She'd swear the dog smiled at her. Soon, the hound closed his eyes and slept again.

Maggie admired the spotless parlor with a place for everything and everything in its place. She picked up a photograph of Ruth and Catherine: smiling faces, arms entwined, laughing together. Did they approve of her living in their home, sleeping in their bed?

"Ladies, I sincerely hope you would commend our efforts today, returning your home to its original magnificence. As long as I reside here, I'll never permit such neglect to occur again," she vowed aloud.

Her voice caught, and she returned the picture to the mantle, realizing with shocking clarity that she truly yearned to feel at home here. Mind you, who wouldn't want to live on this beautiful ranch in this exquisite home? She should just be thankful for the positive turn her life has taken. Had Luke Carlyle not come into her life when he did, she could be living in the street, or worse yet, with Aunt Penny and that frightful housekeeper she employed back in Philadelphia.

Maggie returned to the spotless kitchen and poked her head into the neatly-organized pantry. She touched the secret section of shelving Hattie showed her that shifted and led down a set of stairs to the hidden root cellar. The majority of the preserves and root vegetables were stored there. No wonder the pantry had appeared bare before. She closed the door, smiling with the secret. The laundry room stood silent for the first time today, but a hint of soap and starch still lingered in the air. In adjoining places on the table, sat cookie crumbs and empty milk glasses, remnants of the youngest children's bedtime treat. Those two were plumb tuckered out, as Ned would say. Her children had beamed with pride when Elizabeth announced the ladies completed the work ahead of time due to their help. She set the glasses in the washtub alongside the teacups and brushed up the crumbs.

Maggie returned to the front entryway and skimmed her hands along the gleaming wooden railing as she climbed the staircase. All the beds were made up with clean linens, the rugs were back in place, the floors waxed and polished. Everyone's clothes were washed, ironed, folded and neatly hung in the organized closets and scented armoires. The children's toys were sorted, and their books were arranged on clean bookcases.

She yearned for a hot bath to ease her sore muscles, but she hated the thought of messing up the gleaming bathroom. She buried her nose in a fluffy yellow towel and inhaled its fresh-air scent, before hanging it back on the side of the claw-foot tub. Mike had promised to haul hot water from the kitchen, after he'd completed the last of his chores in the horse barn. He hadn't shown up and maybe it was for the best. She might have dozed off and drowned while enjoying a long luxurious bath.

Tip-toeing into her son's bedroom, she found her little angel sound asleep after such an eventful day. With Elizabeth's help, Sam had lugged all his toys, books, and clothes into his own room this afternoon. Mike removed his bed from Patti's room; no more sharing with his sister. She smiled, recalling his proud insistence, *I'm a big boy, Mama. This is my room!* How had Sam developed such confidence and independence by age four? She remembered herself as an extremely withdrawn child, painfully shy, and terribly lonely. Their housekeeper had been her best friend.

Sam's birthday was December 5th. He'd soon be telling everyone he was four and a half. "Sleep tight, angel," whispered Maggie. She touched her son's downy-soft hair and kissed his forehead.

Maggie peeked into Patti's bedroom next. The little girl slept soundly, snuggled under the covers, hugging her favorite doll. Absent of Sam's bed, her room appeared quite spacious. Patti's dolls stared at Maggie with unblinking eyes from their places on the painted shelves. There wasn't a farm animal or wooden block in sight. Maggie bent and kissed the little girl she'd already come to love so dearly. "Sleep tight, sweetheart." Would Patti miss her brother's company? Probably not, she acted as independently as Sam.

Maggie slipped into Lucy's room and found her sound asleep, unusual for the family night owl who enjoyed reading until ordered to snuff out the lamp. Lucy had worked diligently today and reluctantly admitted to Elizabeth that she approved of the revitalization plans. But would today's improved attitude carry into the future?

"I doubt it," muttered Maggie as she stepped into the hidey-hole formed around the third floor turret. The upholstered bench surrounding the windows provided a secret place for a girl to lose herself in a good book, or in needlework, or in dreams for her future.

Maggie gently kissed Lucy's cheek, hoping she would soon accept her stepmother's presence at the ranch. With no more cooking and cleaning and fewer chores to do, Lucy's time was freed up, as her father intended. Lucy spent hours in the horse barn with the new mare Luke bought her. And every evening Lucy curled up on one of the sofas in the parlor with a book, glaring at Maggie when she slipped into what had been her mother's rocking chair to work on her quilting patch. Apparently, Lucy hadn't yet realized that having a new mother was a good thing.

She glanced at the clock atop Lucy's vanity table which indicated it was a few minutes past eleven o'clock. What on earth was keeping Luke so late?

In the darkened room, Maggie almost tripped over the trunk

which contained a dozen of Catherine's wonderful quilts. Like a mother bear watching over her cubs, Lucy supervised the freshening up of the quilts which were gushed over, aired out, neatly folded and promptly returned to the trunk. Obviously, her mother's quilts meant the world to Lucy.

Maggie stared at the sleeping girl, envying her such a wonderful legacy. She'd never felt a close connection to her own mother. Born the year her mother turned forty, Maggie often wondered if her mother had even wanted her. She'd always suspected she'd been an accident, a mistake, an inconvenience in her mother's busy social life.

Forbidden to travel, Maggie birthed Sam two days after her parents' funeral. It still hurt that she couldn't attend and say goodbye. Aunt Penny had handled all the arrangements for her and never mentioned any legacy from her parents. Perhaps they'd never forgiven her for moving out West against their wishes. She shook the melancholy thoughts from her mind.

When she turned to leave the room, her heart almost stopped.

Chapter 12

Maggie shooed her husband out of Lucy's room. "Luke Carlyle, you just took ten years off my life."

"Sorry about surprising you." Luke sounded sincere.

"You're forgiven. Have you seen the work your men did?" Maggie felt herself beaming.

"I arrived home just before dark, and you were right. I thought I'd wandered onto the wrong ranch." Luke scratched his head. "Third showed me everything. As well as completing your list of chores, the boys nailed some loose boards on the barns and repaired some horse troughs. And a few other things that needed doing."

"Those fellows worked from dawn till dusk. I was extremely pleased when I ventured outside. They even weeded the vegetable garden!" Without thinking, Maggie clasped her hands around his arm, but Luke didn't appear shocked by the unexpected contact. She decided against releasing her hold.

"I've been occupied in the horse barn with Mike. One of my horses needed tending." Luke kissed her cheek. "I apologize for coming in so late."

"That's all right. Now that I have your undivided attention, I'm not relinquishing it. At least, not until you've seen evidence of the ladies' hard work." She smiled, squeezed his arm. "I have proof that I'm fulfilling my commitment to our arrangement."

Together, they toured almost every room on all three floors.

"Everything looks wonderful," proclaimed Luke, as they entered the kitchen.

"We accomplished so much in one day," Maggie gushed, breathlessly running on adrenaline. "Tomorrow, there are the flowerbeds to weed and we're finished. Hattie even helped me sort out the root cellars. All that remains is restocking the pantry when I pick up my order on Wednesday. I've ordered new clothes for the children, and Elizabeth assured me that most things are in the store." Maggie pointed to the ceiling. "Elizabeth's staying the night in that one guest room we didn't enter to get an early start again."

"Order yourself some new dresses and such, too. You deserve some new things for your hard work." Luke tucked a wayward strand behind her ear. For a moment she feared he'd kiss her on the mouth. Instead, he turned her around and gently massaged her shoulders. "You must be exhausted."

"That feels wonderful." Maggie sighed. And then she blushed, realizing the intimacy of the moment. She pulled away from Luke's touch and looked into his eyes. "I'll think about your offer of a new frock or two. Although, I can't imagine where I'd wear them, except to church. And soon enough, they won't fit anyway."

Luke yawned and then turned her around and resumed his ministrations to her neck muscles.

"How was your day? Did you learn more about the cattle rustlers?" asked Maggie, nearly purring like a kitten as Luke continued the massage.

"Almost every one of my neighbors has cattle missing, too. We're going to palaver with Sheriff Smith next Friday night to decide how best to put an end to this."

"Well, just as long as you're careful. I imagine these fellows are the least reputable people around."

"I'll be wary. We won't be confronting them any time soon until we determine what we're dealing with." Luke bent and kissed the back of her neck, sending shivers throughout Maggie's body. "Don't worry. I'll be fine."

Mike knocked, charged into the kitchen, and tugged off his hat. "Sorry I took so long, Mrs. Carlyle. Hello, sir. One of the horses took to limping, so we tended to him. He's going to be fine, ma'am, but I couldn't get away until now."

"Tending Luke's horse was more important. My bath can wait until tomorrow night. Thank you for coming up to the main house even though you're clearly exhausted." Maggie smiled and herded him out through the kitchen door to the back veranda. "Off to the bunkhouse with you." Mike was such a wonderful young man; Ned and Morning Star must be so proud. If Sam grew up like him—hard-working, considerate, and kind-hearted—she couldn't ask for more.

"Good night, Mike." Luke leaned forward and shook the young man's hand. "Thank you for taking the extra time with Ranger. That horse is one of my favorites."

"Thank you, and goodnight, sir." Mike beamed at the boss's praise. "And goodnight to you, too, ma'am."

Luke and Maggie watched from the porch and exchanged a smile. Whistling, the twenty-year-old disappeared into the night.

"You look lovely in the moonlight, my dear, but you also look totally tuckered out." Luke grabbed the oil lamp off the back porch railing where he'd set it down and guided his wife through the kitchen door.

Maggie gaped. She looked lovely? She'd caught a glimpse of herself in several mirrors during their brief tour of the house: her dress stained from cleaning and her hair falling out of her combs. He probably required eyeglasses, she decided.

"Are you feeling all right?" asked Luke.

"I'm a little tired, but that's to be expected with the day's excitement." Maggie felt considerably more than a little tired, but she couldn't be happier. Even in the wretched stage of neglect the mansion had appeared grand, but now, her home looked absolutely magnificent. *Her home*, she repeated the thought. And then she smiled.

"I don't want you overdoing it." Luke took her hand. "I'm planning a surprise for you."

Maggie met his eyes expectantly. She couldn't remember William surprising her with anything. No, she corrected. He'd surprised her, once, with a small bouquet of flowers picked from her own garden.

"What kind of a surprise?" she whispered.

Monday, June 10, 1889

Luke worried about all this latest business with the cattle

rustling while working in the cow barn. Dammit, he and his neighbors had to get a handle on the situation and fast. Everyone lost too much stock already.

He heard a noise and turned, discovered Sam standing just inside the barn door. "What are you doing down here?" he blurted.

Sam appeared ready to run.

"Come over here, son," he quickly added, softening his voice. "Why aren't you up at the house? Playing with the dogs and your sister?"

"Patti is playing with her stupid dolls." Sam remained by the door.

Luke chuckled. "I guess that explains it then."

"Can I ask you a question, Mr. Carlyle?"

Luke paused before answering, thinking 'Mr. Carlyle' seemed too formal for a father and son, even a stepfather. Already, he loved this little fellow like his own. His sweet disposition, his easy smile, and his contagious giggle endeared him to everyone on the ranch. Patti thought the sun rose and set on her little brother.

"Why don't you call me Papa?" inquired Luke, crossing the barn floor and resting a hand on the little boy's shoulder. The pain-filled expression on the child's face almost brought Luke to his knees. Sam appeared ready to burst into tears.

"Papa's in heaven. Mama says he can't ever come back," whispered Sam.

Luke detected the same sadness in the boy's voice that he'd heard two years ago when his daughters lost their mother.

"I'm sorry about that, Sam. But 'Mr. Carlyle' seems a tad formal to me. Perhaps you should call me Luke?" He squatted to Sam's level, meeting the little boy's eyes. He rested his forearms on his thighs, waiting for a response.

"Mama says little boys gotta say 'Mister'. I always gotta show respect to my elters." Sad innocent eyes searched Luke's distracting him for a second. The little guy's eyes were the same shade of brown as his own, and Sam's curly brown hair matched his perfectly. A stranger could mistake the two of them for kin. Come to think of it, he and William Burns had resembled each other quite a bit. Odd, considering they certainly weren't related. Just a coincidence, no doubt.

"That's correct, Sam. Little boys should respect their elders.

But your mama married me and I'm legally your pa now. So, how about Papa Luke? How does that sound?" Luke stood and extended his hand.

Sam looked way up and met Luke's eyes, apparently thinking it over. He slipped his small hand into Luke's large, callused one and shook on it. "Papa Luke," he repeated.

That being settled, Luke stood with his hands on his hips. "Now, what was your question, Sam?" Maggie had warned him that Sam was very intelligent and outspoken for a child his age. Luke realized she wasn't boasting; it was the truth. This precocious little fellow would challenge every parenting skill he possessed.

"What are you doing with those bells?" Sam hopped from one foot to the other.

Realizing he towered over the little fellow, Luke crouched down to his level again. "This here's a cowbell," explained Luke, reaching for one.

"A cowbell," repeated Sam, nodding his head.

"We hang it around a cow's neck. It tinkles when she walks around, and we can locate her in the dark." Luke decided there was no time like the present to teach the next generation of cattlemen. Unless Maggie agreed to a proper marriage in the future and honored him with a son of his own, Sam could be his only male heir. Assuming the new baby wasn't a boy, of course. But secretly, he wanted another son to even up the numbers. He'd wanted a son with Catherine and that had never happened. How did the saying go, what you see is what you get?

"You must have a lot of cowbells, Papa Luke. 'Cause you got a whole lot of cows." Sam nodded his head as he spoke.

Luke chuckled. "Cows are sociable animals, and they tend to stick together in groups. So we only hang a bell on a few of them. If you find one in the dark, you'll find a herd of them."

"All the cows eat together?" Sam's eyes lit up. "Like a picnic? I went on a picnic with Robbie and his mama."

"That's exactly what I mean. Lady cows socialize like regular folk. They stand around together chewing their cud and watching over their calves. Like regular ladies stand around talking."

Sam thought about this for a minute; Luke could visualize the cogs turning in his small head. "Like the ladies at church on Sunday? Mama says those ladies are gosspering."

"Gossiping." Luke corrected.

Sam nodded his head and whispered, "Mama doesn't like gossiping."

"Well, Sam, I don't rightly know whether cows gossip or not. Maybe you could ask Ned that question. Tell him Papa Luke would be right interested in hearing his opinion on that." Luke grinned, imagining the expression on Ned's face when Sam inquired about gossiping cows. Yes sir, being stepfather to this young man was going to be a pleasure. Do cows gossip? Hell if he knew.

"You run along and play with Skipper." Luke's suggestion was met with a pained expression. "What's wrong, Sam?"

"Skipper chases the ball a couple of times, and then he flops down under a tree. And he won't move no matter what I do." Sam's eyes dropped to his small dusty shoes.

His dejected spirit tugged at Luke's heartstrings.

"Well, maybe we'll have to do something about that. For now, you run along and play with Patti. The ranch hands are too busy working to watch out for a little boy. I don't want you anywhere near the barns and corrals, you hear?" Luke spoke sternly on purpose. If anything happened to his new son, he'd never forgive himself.

"Patti's playing with a bunch of dumb dolls. It's boring." Sam shrugged his shoulders.

"Let's go find Mike in the horse barn. He'll saddle up a pony and give you a riding lesson." Luke strolled outside with Sam holding his hand and skipping alongside him.

Sam didn't notice his mother striding toward them arms pumping, but Luke did. Dang it. There was a woman on a mission. She likely intended to rip a strip off his hide for allowing her son near the barns. He mentally braced himself for a tongue-lashing, but Sam kept walking and dragging him along, too.

They spotted Patti outside the horse barn, peeking through the corral rails.

"Patti!" Sam broke away from Luke's grasp and raced to his sister's side. "Mike's giving me a pony lesson."

"Hi, Sam." Patti threw her arms around her little brother. "You mean a riding lesson."

"I thought you were playing with your dolls?" Sam wiggled out of his sister's embrace.

"I was, but I want to ride my pony now. Mike's getting him

ready." Patti smiled at Sam.

"Maggie, what brings you out here?" asked Luke, as his wife approached them. "Is there some trouble up at the house?"

"I intended to hang laundry on the clothes line, but I discovered both children gone. I came looking for them." Maggie appeared exhausted, but Luke made no comment, knowing full well she'd only deny it.

"You chose the perfect time to visit the horse barn." Luke caught himself grinning like a schoolboy.

"Are you up to something?" Maggie wagged a finger at him.

Luke sauntered up to the corral with Maggie in pursuit. "Hello, sweetheart, do you want to ride your pony?" Luke tugged on one of Patti's pigtails.

"Uh-huh. And Sam can ride Lucy's pony. She never rides him anymore now that she's got her new mare." Patti beamed at her father.

Mike Armstrong strolled out of the barn's side door. At age five, Mike had arrived at the Diamond C as a homeless, abandoned orphan, and Morning Star took him under her wing like a fussy mother hen. The young man thrived under Luke's tutelage and earned the title of Head Horseman, in charge of training, taming, breeding and handling the horseflesh on the Diamond C.

"Mr. Carlyle, do you reckon anyone around here wants to ride a pony today?" asked Mike, rubbing his chin.

"I do, I do," shouted Patti and Sam, jumping up and down and giggling.

"There's your answer. Saddle up their ponies please." Luke stood with his arms crossed.

"All done, sir. Two ponies are tied up to the corral out back." Mike shook hands with his boss.

"Thank you, son." Luke couldn't be prouder of the young man, capable and resourceful.

"Morning, ma'am. How are you feeling today, Mrs. Carlyle?" Mike tipped his hat to the boss's wife.

"Fine, thank you for asking, Mike," answered Maggie, with a wink.

Luke noticed and understood its meaning. His wife explained that, out of necessity, she'd confessed her condition to Mike one day on their way home from town.

Sam and Patti trotted back behind the horse barn.

"Those two are certainly excited," observed Maggie, following Luke and Mike.

As the children cautiously approached the two saddled ponies, Sam reached for his sister's hand. One of the ponies stomped his feet and danced about, sending Sam high-tailing it behind Patti.

"Where did he come from?" Patti glanced at her father and then leaned toward Sam and whispered, "That isn't Lucy's pony."

"It isn't?" Sam stood wide-eyed.

Patti shook her head.

Luke hunkered down and smiled at Sam. "He's your pony, son."

Sam stared open-mouthed at the animal. "He's *my* pony?"

"Sure is, and his name is Spots. He's saddle-broke, and he can't wait to meet his new master," said Luke.

"Isn't that R. J.'s pony?" inquired Patti.

"When I mentioned buying a pony for Sam, Robert told me he'd just bought a new horse for R. J. and I knew Spots would be perfect." Luke glanced at Maggie and saw tears glistening in her eyes. He extended his arm, and Sam scooted over to his papa's side. "R. J. outgrew Spots, and he's all yours now, son."

Luke rested his hands on Sam's shoulders. "Spots, this here is Sam Burns, and he's your new owner." The pony bobbed his head, as if he understood every word. "You treat him right, you hear? Behave yourself whenever he's riding you, and Sam will sneak you an extra ration of hay."

With his hands tightly clasped behind his back, Sam leaned around the pony and stared into the animal's eyes. "Hi, Spots," he whispered.

"Come closer, Sam, and pat him on his side." Luke watched as the brave little boy extended one small hand and slowly swiped it across the pony's side. The pony's hide rippled, as if the child's touch had tickled.

"He's soft." Sam patted the pony again.

Luke peeked over at Maggie, catching her wiping away a tear. He winked at her, and her radiant smile told him she approved of his gift.

"Come here, Sam." The little boy skipped over to Mike's side. "Up you go." The young rider grabbed the saddle horn when his trousers landed in the saddle. Mike showed him how to hold the reins, and the riding lesson began.

"Mike's a really good teacher, Sam. He taught me how to ride," announced Patti, climbing into her saddle, parading her pony around like a pro.

"Old Sam here looks like a born cowboy to me." Mike patted Sam's leg and walked beside the pony holding the reins as they strolled into the corral. "He'll be riding the range looking for strays in no time."

Sam beamed from ear to ear, swiveling slightly in the saddle searching for Luke, as if hoping for his new papa's approval.

Luke blinked, momentarily undone by his emotions. He couldn't love that little boy more if he were his own flesh and blood. "You're doing a great job, Sam. I'm proud of you, son." Luke called out the encouragement he suspected his son sought.

"Yippee!" shouted Patti, bouncing up and down in her saddle. Her well-behaved pony never batted an eye. "When can I go riding with Sam, Papa?"

"Better give Sam a couple weeks to get the hang of it, and then Mike will accompany the two of you until Sam's older." Luke patted Patti's pony as he wandered by.

"I'll show Sam where I meet Donnie and R. J. after school. And we'll hunt frogs in the creek. And we'll watch clouds and rush home before it rains, like you taught me, Papa."

"I'm sure you and Sam will share many happy excursions on your ponies. But first, Sam learns to ride as well as you do."

Patti beamed at her Papa's compliment.

Mike turned the pony, and Sam waved at his mother. "Mama, I can ride a pony!"

"You're doing a wonderful job," called Maggie, sniffling. She smiled at Luke. "Thank you. You're a very generous man."

"Every boy raised on a ranch deserves his own pony. In a couple years, he'll want to ride Thunder." Luke pointed over his shoulder at the magnificent stallion bucking up a storm in an adjoining corral.

Maggie gasped.

"Relax. I said he'll *want* to ride Thunder. I didn't say I'd let him. Nobody rides that horse but me." Luke slipped his arm around Maggie's shoulder, squeezed lightly. When she tensed up, he lowered his arm to his side.

Just then Lucy galloped up to the corral and reined her new mare to a stop. She wore boy's trousers, a plaid shirt and boots. She'd stuffed her long golden locks up inside a floppy felt hat. Luke smiled, recalling the new cowhand who'd mistaken her for a boy yesterday. His spunky daughter set the fellow straight in no uncertain terms.

Lucy remained in the saddle and glared at her father. "Why would you buy the brat a pony when you'll be sending him and his mother away soon?"

Sam slumped in the saddle and glanced over at Luke, wariness evident in his eyes.

"Neither Sam nor his mother are going anywhere. And it's time you got that through your head, young lady," ordered Luke, through clenched teeth.

Lucy reined her horse around and raced across the valley, heading west toward the Simpson place.

Luke shook his head, noticing that Robert Morgan had ridden up on his jet-black gelding. His best friend dismounted and tied the horse to a hitching post before wandering over to Luke's side.

"How-do, neighbor. Lucy sure can handle her new horse. I bred that mare with her in mind. Where's she heading off to in such a hurry?"

"Good day, Robert. She has gotten herself in a snit, but she'll be fine. She'll return in her own good time." Luke's daughter rode as well as any cattle hand on the ranch, and she'd be careful even if her mind wasn't totally on riding.

"That's enough for today, Sam," suggested Mike.

"Sam and Spots are certainly getting along," said Luke, grinning at his best friend.

Robert slapped his friend on the back. "The pony was a big hit with the little guy?"

"Oh, yes. This is the first time he rode him, and that grin won't be leaving Sam's face for any time soon." Luke imagined his own grin matched his new son's.

Mike nodded, acknowledging Robert's arrival. "Walk him into the barn, and I'll show you how to brush him. Caring for your horse is a cowboy's most important job. A dedicated cowboy loves his horse as much as he loves his wife." He winked at Luke and Robert. "You have a wife, Sam?"

"No, Mike, I'm only four." Sam giggled, holding up four fingers. Mike headed Spots toward the barn door. "Thank you for my pony, Papa Luke," called Sam before he disappeared inside.

"You're welcome, son." Luke and Robert followed Maggie toward the barn.

"You call my pa, Papa Luke?" Patti stood arms crossed, watching Sam brush Spots. "Then I'm calling your ma, Mama Maggie."

"That's okay, I guess. 'Cause my mama is your mama, too," reasoned Sam, gently brushing the pony.

Luke and Maggie exchanged a smile. Obviously, Sam loved his new sister, and he didn't mind sharing his mama with her.

"Papa said we're a new family," whispered Patti.

Luke realized his youngest daughter loved having a little brother and enjoyed being part of a family again. If only Lucy would come around. Luke hadn't heard a harsh word about their marriage for a few days now, but her recent display of temper spoke volumes.

Regardless, Luke smiled at Maggie. Whether his eldest daughter thought so or not, marrying this woman was the smartest decision he'd made in ages. And he couldn't wait to consummate the marriage. But, being a man of his word, he would.

"Could I have a word with you, Luke?" asked Robert, absently-mindedly patting Spots' neck.

"I'll wait for the children, if you gentlemen would like your discussion to be private?" offered Maggie.

"I don't imagine that's necessary," answered Luke. "What do have on your mind, Robert?"

"I rode over here to let you know I'm missing more steers. Wondered if you've noticed anything here?" Robert's one eyebrow rose.

"I'd wager we're missing at least a hundred head, stolen over these past few months. There's no way you can blame coyotes or wolves for those numbers." Luke paced. "I'm getting more annoyed by the day."

"This whole business is too well-organized for my liking." Robert took a step closer and lowered his voice. "I'm beginning to think it's an inside operation. What if ranch hands are doing this? Who better to know when our guard is down? Who better to know which animals are prime stock?"

Luke had considered the possibility also, and it amazed him how much he and Robert still thought alike after all these years of friendship. "I'd arrived at a similar conclusion. Do you think we could be on to something?"

Robert tugged his Stetson off his head, dragged his hand through his hair. "I don't know. Except for a couple of hands, I've had the same help for years."

"We have men coming and going all the time on the Diamond C, and I've got men who've worked here for over twenty years. Men who worked for my pa." Luke shook his head. "There are cattle missing from so many ranches, it could be hands from just one or fellows from several ranches doing this."

"Well, keep your eyes peeled for trouble." Robert stuck his Stetson back on his head, started walking toward the door. "I'll see you folks at church on Sunday. We can discuss this some more after services."

"Give our best to Hattie and the boys," called Maggie.

"Will do," Robert replied and disappeared outside.

* * *

After the noon meal, Luke pushed his chair away from the table and suddenly announced, "Ned and I are heading into Spirit Creek, got business in town. We're taking Sam and Patti along, too." Luke sauntered down the hallway toward the front door.

"You're what? You're taking Sam? Does this have anything to do with the cattle rustlers?" Maggie heard the panic in her voice; she simply wouldn't allow her son out of her sight. If Sam was leaving the ranch with Luke, then so was she. She whipped her apron off, tossed it onto a chair, and followed Luke out of the kitchen.

"Nothing to do with that business. Just a trip to town, picking up some supplies. You best take advantage of this opportunity to get some extra rest this afternoon. You're looking some peaked. Been overdoing things the past couple days, with all the cleanup ballyhoo." Luke grabbed his going-to-town Stetson off the hallway hook and slapped it on his head.

"Sam is not going to town or anywhere else without me."

"Afraid you're wrong about that, my dear. You're staying home to rest." Luke blocked her exit and steered her towards the staircase. "Sam will be perfectly safe with us. We'll see you around 6 o'clock. Have supper ready."

Maggie gaped as Luke spun on his heels and strode out the door, with Sam and Patti skipping along behind him.

Sam called over his shoulder, "Bye, Mama."

"Bye, Mama," echoed Patti, as the screen door slammed behind them.

Immediately, the silence in the house was deafening. "My son will be fine. Luke wouldn't let anything happen to Sam." Saying the words aloud, she almost convinced herself she believed them.

All morning, while hunched over a laundry tub of hot water, she would have given anything to rest her aching muscles and weary body. Be careful what you yearn for, she thought. Climbing the stairs, she admitted to herself she felt totally exhausted. No time like the present to begin trusting her new husband.

"If anyone asks, tell them I'm busy taking a nap," she whispered aloud and smiled.

Sleeping in the afternoon seemed the height of laziness to her, but perhaps it would settle what little dinner she'd eaten which threatened to perform flip flops in her stomach. She clambered atop the bed, kicked off her shoes, and pulled the lacy throw over her shoulders. Within a minute, she drifted off to sleep.

* * *

At six o'clock on the dot Maggie heard the wagon rumble up the curved driveway and halt in back of the house. She flew across the kitchen and raced outside, almost tripping over Skipper in her haste. Luke stood, tying the horses' reins to the newly-painted hitching post.

"Made good time home, Maggie. Is supper ready?" Luke turned, smiling broadly. That look warned Maggie something was up.

"Never mind supper. Where's my son?" Maggie strode toward the wagon, holding her skirts above her ankles to prevent tripping. Ned lifted Patti down while Sam stood waiting his turn, clutching a wooden box in his arms.

Maggie stood looking up at her son, her heart racing. "Sam, are you all right?"

"I've got Rags, Mama!" he replied.

"What on earth do you want with a box of rags?" Maggie frowned and took a step closer.

"He's my new puppy!" Sam crowed, triumphantly. "Mrs. Wakeman named him Rags because she always found him sleeping in her basket of cleaning rags."

Maggie couldn't have heard her son correctly. "You've got a new puppy?"

"Yes, he does," confirmed Luke, standing beside her. Maggie jumped at the sound of his voice. "Sam promised to feed him, play with him, and clean up any mistakes in the house."

"I warned you Sam wanted a puppy." Maggie glared at Luke.

"I never told you Sam couldn't have a puppy. Skipper's getting up in years, and he's not partial to chasing a ball all day long. A boy needs a dog he can have some fun with." Luke whispered near Maggie's ear, "All the way home, Sam held Rags in a death grip like that puppy might sprout wings and fly off to the highest branch of a cottonwood tree. William promised him a puppy. His new papa just made sure he got one."

Maggie stood, speechless.

"Thank you for Rags, Papa Luke. He's the one I wanted." Sam set the box on the ground, hugged Luke's leg, and then plucked a squirmy brown and white-spotted puppy out of the box.

"You're welcome, son. Now you better convince your ma to hunt up an old bowl for him and an old blanket for his bed. Until he's house broke that puppy sleeps in the back porch." Luke tousled the boy's hair.

"Luke Carlyle, what have you done?" Maggie finally found her voice.

"We've been blessed with a new family member, Maggie." Luke beamed proudly. "And once you get accustomed to the idea, you'll agree that puppy is rather cute."

Luke seemed quite pleased with himself for putting that smile on Sam's face. "Cute, my foot. I'll be the one cleaning up after him and feeding him." Maggie's annoyance slipped a notch, watching Luke's smile. Suddenly, she recalled her husband's love for animals. "You're as taken with that darn puppy as Sam is."

"Could be. Not admitting to anything." Luke ruffled the puppy's ears.

"I'll take real good care of Rags." Sam hugged the wiggling

puppy in his arms.

"I know you will." Luke patted his son's shoulder, matching smiles plastered on their faces.

"You're really enjoying this, aren't you?" whispered Maggie. "Well, you can tend to that pup at two o'clock in the morning when he's howling and missing his mama."

Just then Lucy strode around the corner of the house, having returned from her ride. "What's that?" she inquired, glaring at the small ball of fluff in Sam's arms.

"My new puppy," whispered Sam, stepping closer to his new pa. "Don't you hurt him."

Lucy glanced at her father and shook her head. "What a brat," she muttered and stomped across the yard. She raced up the veranda stairs, yanked the screen door open, and slammed it closed behind her.

"She won't hurt your puppy," said Luke, ruffling Sam's hair. "She might be prone to a bit of temper, but she'd never hurt an innocent animal."

Maggie followed Lucy up the back steps and disappeared into the house, slamming the screen door again for good measure. A minute later she returned with an old porcelain bowl filled with water, another filled with kitchen scraps, as well as an old gray blanket. She set the bowls beside the back door and tossed the blanket into the corner.

"If this is your idea of a surprise, Luke Carlyle, I am not the least bit impressed." Maggie stood, arms crossed and eyes blazing.

"This isn't *your* surprise. I got the puppy for Sam." Luke climbed the back steps, holding the large box of kitchen staples he'd picked up in town. "Rags won't be missing his mama in the middle of the night, will he?"

Maggie smiled wickedly and sashayed into the house.

On his way through the door, Luke whispered, "Lord, what have I done?"

* * *

The moon hid behind low-hanging clouds and a cool breeze blew across the range. Frenchy high-tailed it over Diamond C land, hell bent on meeting with his partners. He cursed the ominous black clouds overhead. They held rain; he could smell it in the air.

His long brown hair kept blowing in his face. Cursing, he pulled his mount up short. He removed his battered Stetson, secured his hair with a strip of rawhide and slapped his hat back on his head. He dug his bony knees into his horse's sides and continued on.

Maybe they shouldn't have chosen tonight to grab a few more head and stash them with the others. Showing up back at the Diamond C lookin' half-drowned would be a little difficult to explain. *Couldn't sleep so I went for a little ride.* Ain't nobody gonna believe that bull.

As he approached their usual meeting place, Frenchy reined in his sorry-ass mount. The poor old critter looked near death compared to the frisky Morgan gelding Carlyle provided for him while he rode the range lookin' for strays. He laughed aloud. If Carlyle only knew what Frenchy did with half those strays. *His* strays now, he corrected, grinning in the dark.

"Frenchy! That you?" whispered a familiar voice to his left.

"*Oui*," he replied in his native tongue. "Where are the others?"

Sammy rode up beside him. "Pete and Bobby are checkin' on the cattle we got hidden."

Frenchy nodded and smiled. Sammy worked for the Maxwell outfit a few miles from here, and Bobby worked on the Simpson ranch. Pete stayed with the animals and arranged to sell them to smaller outfits looking to build up their herds. Pete pretended he represented the men who owned the cattle and always sold animals with the same brand to each customer. The man could sell water to an island dweller. Pete's younger brother helped drive the cattle to their new homes.

"Let's steal us a few more head and then git back home before we get wet," suggested Frenchy.

"Maybe we should call it off? If there's thunder on the way, them cattle will be mighty hard to control." His co-conspirator spit tobacco juice out the side of his mouth.

"Dammit, Sammy. Didn't come this far for nothin'." Frenchy swore under his breath.

"Up to you, boss."

Frenchy considered his options for a moment.

"You got some strays ready to go?" inquired Sammy.

"About a dozen. Luke Carlyle doesn't know his ass from an anthill. I've stolen close to fifty head right out from under his nose this month and he hasn't caught on yet," scoffed Frenchy. "And those fools he has workin' for him, ain't caught on either."

"Same thing over at the Maxwell ranch. I've been there well on six months now. Borrowed me over twenty-five head every month." Sammy laughed uproariously.

"Quiet! You idiot!" spat Frenchy, reining his mount behind some bushes. "Horses coming this way."

Sammy followed his lead.

Pete and Bobby rode into view.

"How are the cattle?" inquired Frenchy, leaving his hiding place.

"All there, boss," answered Pete, dressed in his usual trail coat over denims and plaid shirt.

"A little nervous with the storm coming," added Bobby, sheepskin jacket flapping wide open. As usual he couldn't get it to fasten across his enormous belly.

"What say we head home and wait for better weather?" suggested Pete.

Frenchy glared at him. "Got me a dozen head hidden five minutes from here and I ain't gonna leave 'em."

"All right. We'll hide them with the others," offered Pete. "And then we'll call it a night."

Thunder rumbled in the distance.

"Well, let's hurry up before that storm gets any closer." Bobby reined his horse around to face Frenchy.

"Hell. I almost forgot." Pete tossed each man a small pouch. "Here's your share of last week's proceeds fellas. A man over Butte way paid a nice price for twenty head, and I made a couple other sales as well."

"*Merci*," muttered Frenchy, stuffing the pouch into his pants pocket. Every man trusted Pete. Honest as a judge.

Sammy and Bobby added their own verbal appreciation.

"Let's get them cattle and head home," reiterated Sammy. "Show us the way, Frenchy."

"*Oui*." Frenchy smiled wickedly, then whipped his horse around and headed across the range with the others following in his wake.

Frenchy had never believed in doing an honest day's work when late-at-night work paid so much better. Until someone caught on to this little operation, he'd stay put and line his pockets. At least until the snow threatened. He hated cold weather. Maybe he'd head down to Mexico again for the winter.

Chapter 13

Wednesday, June 19, 1889

Sunshine streamed through the kitchen window, and Maggie savored the warmth on her face, even knowing it meant a new crop of freckles would appear. For the first time in weeks she could take a deep breath and reflect.

She watched Sam and Patti through the window, wrestling with Rags in the backyard while Lucy buried her nose in a book on the swing. The younger children were adjusting to their parents' marriage with remarkable ease, but then there was Lucy. Her oldest stepdaughter continued to try her patience, but she and Luke hoped Lucy would realize soon that her temper tantrums and other antics were for naught.

The back door opened and Mike Armstrong popped his head inside.

"The buggy is hitched up, ma'am." Mike fidgeted with his crumpled hat. "I surely don't mind driving you to town."

"Did you hitch up a calm horse?" asked Maggie.

"Yes, ma'am, I did. His name's Bob, and if he were any calmer, he'd be dead."

Maggie smiled. "Then I won't have a moment's trouble. The children have been pestering me for a trip to town, and today's the day."

Mike plopped his hat on his head and tipped the brim. "Have a safe trip, ma'am." On his way out the door, he moved aside to avoid a stampede of small feet.

"Are we leaving for town now, Mama?" asked Sam, breathless from racing Patti inside.

Lucy followed behind them, scowling.

"Don't leave before I change my dress, Mama Maggie." Patti raced out of the kitchen.

"I won't go without you." Maggie turned Sam's jam-smeared face in her hands. "Fetch me a washcloth. You're not going to town looking like this."

Lucy brushed past her without a word.

"We'll be waiting in the buggy, Lucy. We won't wait if you aren't ready," warned Maggie.

* * *

By late afternoon, the sun had begun to descend toward the horizon, and Maggie adjusted her bonnet to shade her eyes. She waved goodbye to Elizabeth and flicked the reins. Bob shuffled forward, moving along at his own pace. Slow. No amount of cajoling, shouting, or rein-flicking could speed him up. But that's what she'd requested.

As the buggy rumbled down the main street, Maggie spotted Sadie Peterman, the banker's spoiled only-child, waving frantically from the sidewalk outside the bank. Sadie had recently completed her studies at the finishing school back East, or the high-strung young lady had been expelled. Knowing Sadie, either scenario was a distinct possibility. Maggie had heard someone mention Sadie was visiting someone in Miles City, but apparently she'd returned home.

Maggie halted the buggy, secured the brake, and climbed out. She stepped onto the sidewalk where Sadie stood glaring at her. "Why were you waving me down? Is something wrong?"

"There most certainly is!" The girl shook her lacy-gloved finger in Maggie's face.

"Whatever is the problem?" demanded Maggie, taken aback by the girl's rude behavior.

"You know perfectly well why I'm so angry." Sadie stood with hands on hips, her nose almost touching Maggie's. "You stole my future husband the minute my back was turned."

Maggie almost laughed in Sadie's face but caught herself. "I beg your pardon?"

"Since returning from that infernal finishing school, I decided Mr. Carlyle had mourned Catherine's death long enough." Sadie brushed an imaginary piece of lint from her custom-sewn traveling suit and readjusted the plume on her elaborate hat. "My social status in town and my finishing school diploma assure my suitability as the next Mrs. Luke Carlyle."

Maggie laughed; she couldn't help it. "I was not aware that candidates were vying for the position."

The bank's heavy wooden door flew open, and buxom Mrs. Peterman waddled toward her daughter. "Sadie Louise Peterman! What are you doing? I could hear you shouting at Mrs. Burns from inside your father's bank."

"Oh, but she's not Mrs. Burns, Mother. Haven't you heard? She's Mrs. Luke Carlyle!" Sadie fisted her hands. "This thieving witch stole him from me!"

"Sadie! I will not tolerate that language from you." Mrs. Peterman, breathless and red-faced, met Maggie's eyes. "Please accept my apologies. My daughter took it into her head to become Mr. Carlyle's new wife."

"And I would have married him, Mother, if you hadn't sent me off to Miles City." Sadie pouted. "The minute I leave town, she swoops in and steals him from me."

"Believe me, there was no swooping or stealing involved. It wasn't even my idea." Maggie blushed with the admission. "The marriage…just happened."

"You sought him out the minute I left town." Sadie stamped her dainty buttoned-booted foot on the wooden boardwalk. "Papa extended his blessing to Mr. Carlyle, approved of the widower courting me. And then Mother shipped me off to assist a friend with her new baby."

"I wasn't aware of any of this," mumbled Maggie, wishing she was anywhere but here, standing in the middle of town while a twenty-year-old spoiled brat publicly berated her. For a moment, she considered the possibility Sadie's claims held water. And then she recalled William's comments about every single fellow in town avoiding the little vixen at all costs. *No man in town would wish the girl on his worst enemy.*

"Sadie, come along home. What's done is done." Mrs. Peterman grasped her daughter's arm. "You've made enough of a spectacle of yourself for one day."

"I'm sorry, Mrs. Peterman," stammered Maggie. "Was Sadie betrothed?"

"No promises were made, no indication of a courtship even." Mrs. Peterman patted Maggie's arm. "Please forgive my daughter's unfounded accusations."

Mrs. Peterman dragged her daughter toward home. Although the street was deserted, curtains ruffled on the windows of surrounding establishments. No doubt, the confrontation hadn't gone unobserved. Lately, everywhere she tread trouble followed her as if she'd set out on a mission to destroy her standing in the community. Learning about the secret gambling loans, agreeing to a scandalous remarriage, and now stolen husbands-to-be. She stomped over to the buggy and climbed aboard.

Luke Carlyle, you have some explaining to do. In an effort to calm her nerves before collecting the children, she drove aimlessly up one street and down the other, paying no attention to where she was going and having no destination in mind.

"Maggie!"

She startled when she heard someone call her name. She swiveled on the hard wooden seat, searching for the source. Spirit Creek's newly-appointed sheriff, former deputy Franklin Smith, stood outside the jailhouse, waving to her. He stomped on his cigar butt with his boot while he watched her approach.

"Good afternoon," croaked Maggie, halting the buggy. Memories of riding past the jail on her wedding day flashed through her mind. She straightened her back and forced a smile. "How are you today?"

"I'm fine, but I sure miss William." Sheriff Smith helped her down from the buggy, tugged his Stetson off his head, and shook her hand. "I heard about your home. I was privy to William's gambling, but he swore me to secrecy. I should have spoken up. If you'd known…"

Maggie's eyes glistened with tears. "There was nothing either of us could have done. William made his own decisions."

"Do you need anything?" The sheriff stared at his boots.

Maggie heard the emotion in his voice, fighting a losing battle with his guilt most likely. Franklin understood her loss, but she couldn't acknowledge her appreciation without totally falling apart.

Her house was nothing more than wood and plaster, but she'd loved it so much. The new sheriff met her eyes, and she just shook her head.

"I'm renting your house. I've been building furniture: beds, table and chairs, cabinets and such." The sheriff twisted his hat in his hand.

"You're renting my house! You didn't buy it?"

"Already sold by the time I got around to making an offer. But the new owner willingly rented it to me, so I can't complain. I wanted a nice house for Ellie." The sheriff slapped his rumpled hat against his leg. "Dang it! I've gone and let the cat out of the bag."

"Your feelings toward Ellie Thomas aren't a secret, Franklin." Maggie smiled. "Was the person who purchased my home someone local?"

"Well, yes, ma'am," answered Franklin. "Luke Carlyle bought your house, and then rented it to me the very next day."

Maggie met his eyes, waited for him to admit 'I'm only joking'. Franklin just stared back at her.

"Luke bought my house?" she asked, incredulously. Her equilibrium wavered and she grasped the arm of the rickety rocking chair situated outside the jailhouse. She slowly lowered herself onto the seat.

It couldn't be true.

Of course, it was.

Franklin Smith had no reason to lie to her. But why would Luke marry her, if he bought her house? She revisited Luke's proposal in her mind. She had no home and no money, he'd said. Sam needed a father, he'd said. It was her only option, he'd said. But he'd bought her house. Surely, she could have remained living in her home and just worked for him. How could Luke deceive her this way? He'd needlessly forced her to marry him.

"Yes, ma'am. Luke told me the house was an investment, and he would rent it to me for as long as I wanted it. He was very particular about one thing, however. The house wasn't ever going up for sale."

Maggie straightened her spine. "It was a pleasure seeing you again, Franklin. But I must collect the children and head for home." She rose from the rocking chair and walked to the buggy on trembling limbs. The young sheriff offered her a hand up, and she settled her skirts before taking up the reins.

"Best of luck with your new position, Franklin. And I hope you'll be very happy in my house." Maggie almost choked on the words.

"Thank you, Maggie. You deserve all the happiness in the world. Luke's a good man, and you'll do well by him." The sheriff smiled and waved goodbye.

"Thank you," she replied. But considering what she'd just learned that seemed highly unlikely.

Maggie collected her children and headed out of town. Low-hanging, gray clouds travelled with the brisk wind across a somber sky which matched Maggie's mood perfectly. Sam and Patti, exhausted from playing with their friends, fell asleep on the back seat minutes after leaving town.

Lucy must have sensed something was terribly wrong shortly after she'd planted herself on the bench beside Maggie. She stared straight ahead while her fingers played with the lace trim on her dress.

Maggie caught Lucy peeking over at her. Her stepdaughter's eyes widened when she spied her stepmother's white-knuckled grip on the reins. "This has nothing to do with you," she offered, patting Lucy's knee and returning to the business of driving the buggy.

Lucy never uttered a word.

"I hope it doesn't rain before we reach home," muttered Maggie.

Home? She almost laughed at the irony. Seething with anger, she could spit nails. True, the banker had told her he'd sold her house. But discovering Luke's deception and betrayal hurt her deeply. She would never forgive him or trust him again. Her new husband was no better than William.

"I don't think it will rain," whispered Lucy, her voice trembling.

"Don't be frightened of my mood. I've just received some troubling news," confessed Maggie.

"Are you going to be leaving town?"

Maggie considered Lucy's question for a moment. "I just might be, after all."

Lucy's mood brightened, but neither of them exchanged another word for the remainder of the trip to the ranch.

Maggie pulled up to the hitching post alongside the main house. In a second, she set the brake and scrambled out of the buggy. "Lucy, help the children into the house. I've got something to discuss with your father."

"I wouldn't want to be in Papa's boots," whispered Lucy.

"No, my dear, you wouldn't." Maggie headed toward the horse barn, arms pumping and back straight. She noticed the slight smile that accompanied Lucy's comment. No doubt the girl believed she would soon get her stepmother out of her life. She just might at that.

Maggie stomped into the barn in search of her despicable husband who appeared to be nowhere in sight. But Mike stood ankle-deep in horse manure in an open stall.

"Where is Mr. Carlyle?" she demanded, hands fisted at her sides.

"He's cleaning saddles in the tack room, ma'am," blurted Mike, backing up a step.

"Thank you." She turned on her heel and headed toward the tack room. "Please tend to Bob and the buggy. You probably won't want to hear this."

"No, ma'am. Right now, ma'am." The young horseman stood the pitchfork against the wall and scurried outside.

Maggie threw open the tack room door. "Luke Carlyle, where are you? You miserable, thieving, lowdown…." She'd never before spoken to anyone in what her mother would have called *that tone using that language*. There was a first time for everything.

"Whoa, Maggie. I'm right here." Luke tossed a cloth aside and faced her.

"How could you be so cruel? I trusted you. I believed your intentions were honorable. Did you share a good laugh with that miserable banker?" Maggie had built up a full head of steam on the drive home.

"What are you talking about?" Luke removed his Stetson, scratched his head.

"I'm aware of your secret purchase." Maggie stood, hands on hips, shaking with anger. "I talked to Franklin Smith this afternoon. He wasn't apprised of your little secret, told me all about renting my house. The house Luke Carlyle bought out from under me. Oh, I'm so angry I could…"

"Let me explain…" began Luke.

She rushed forward, pounded his chest with her fists. He dropped his hat on the clean tack room floor and grabbed her wrists, which only angered her more.

"You made a fool of me, and a fool of William. Convincing me I must move out of my house and marry you. There were no more choices, no more options. All the while you'd set your sights on my home, probably bought it for a song. All of William's hard work, and I have nothing to show for it. Nothing." She crumpled to the floor, sobbing.

"Please hear me out." Luke squatted and laid a hand on her shoulder.

Maggie swatted his hand away and glared at him. "There's nothing I want to hear from your lying lips. You miserable scoundrel. You're no better than Banker Peterman."

"Ouch, now those words actually hurt. I'm nothing like Peterman; he's in a class by himself." Luke sat cross-legged on the floor. "Let me explain."

Maggie attempted to stand.

"You're going to listen to what I have to say." Luke gently pulled her down beside him. "I won't deny it; I bought your house. But I won't apologize for it either."

Maggie glared at the man who'd professed to care for her, care for her son. "How could I have been so blind? Was the house all you really wanted? Was this marriage only a means to a piece of real estate?"

"I bought the house with a partner," explained Luke. "I paid the two hundred dollars owing against the property and then I registered the deed in both of our names."

"You cooked up this little coup with that miserable banker." Maggie crossed her arms, daring him to deny her accusation.

"You're dead wrong, Mrs. Carlyle. I convinced Peterman he wasn't making a profit this time, considering the circumstances."

Maggie grimaced at the new title she detested at the moment. "If not Peterman, then who is your partner?"

"His name is Samuel."

"Samuel who?" asked Maggie, seething.

"I registered the deed in the new owners' names: Luke Matthew Carlyle and Samuel William Burns. I'm renting the house to

Franklin. He's fixing on getting married, and he wanted a suitable home for his new bride." Luke met her eyes.

For a minute, she couldn't grasp what he was telling her. He'd put her son's name on the deed? Sam was only a child! "But why would…" she began.

"Let me finish explaining. When our son turns eighteen, I'll remove my name from the title. Sam will own his pa's house, sole owner, free and clear. He can live in the house, sell it, or do whatever he wants with it. Meantime, the rent money's going into a special account at the bank to pay for Sam's college education."

Maggie gaped. Luke stood and pulled her to her feet.

"There was no way I'd allow a hard-working fellow like William Burns to lose his home over foolish gambling debts. A man should leave behind something for his son, and that house is Sam's legacy from his pa."

"Why wouldn't you just let me live there?" asked Maggie through clenched teeth.

Luke blew out his breath. "Because I knew you could only afford the taxes and upkeep if you were employed. You hadn't been able to acquire a job. And even if you managed to find something, once you bought food and clothes for yourself and Sam and the baby, there would be precious little left for those things. And being with child, it would be too tiring traveling out here and back to town every day to work for me, as you'd suggested. You even warned me there was a possibility you wouldn't be able to work for a spell due to morning sickness. How would you survive? The most sensible solution was for us to marry, and I rent the house to Franklin."

Maggie considered everything he'd said, hating to admit he was right. But what he'd done made perfect sense. Luke proved himself the gentleman he claimed to be. How could she have doubted his intentions? He'd rescued her and her children from living hand to mouth, and probably having to sell the house in the end anyway. Now, Sam would own his father's home someday; those precious four walls hadn't been totally lost after all. And marrying Luke in order for that to happen wasn't too big of a price to pay. Was it?

She felt herself redden to her hairline. "The names I called you! I'm so sorry."

"You're forgiven." Luke brushed her forehead with a gentle

kiss, and then wrapped an arm around her waist. Together they walked toward the main house.

"By the way, I experienced an unpleasant encounter with Sadie Peterman this afternoon. She is furious with me for stealing you away from her." Maggie kept a straight face. "You really should have warned me about all the hearts you were breaking by marrying me."

"For Pete's sake." Luke turned her toward him. "I should have warned you."

"I was so angry after I talked to Franklin, I was prepared to hand you over to her." Maggie sighed. Thank goodness, she'd demanded an explanation from Luke. What if she'd done something stupid like collect Sam and head back East without ever discovering the truth?

"Hand me over to her? Over my dead body. Sadie Peterman attempted every trick in the book to garner my affections, and her miserable father encouraged her. Probably hoping I'd take her off his hands." Luke shuddered.

"I don't know." Maggie grinned. "Finishing school graduate. Banker's daughter. Quite a catch. I'm surprised you let her slip through your fingers."

"A badger possesses a more agreeable personality." Luke tightened his grip on her waist. "I overheard Sadie berating the old fellow in the telegraph office. She almost had the man in tears because she hadn't heard back from some dressmaker. Sadie is definitely no catch."

"Well, she's turned her ire on me, now that I've stolen you from her. If looks could kill, I'd be six feet under." Without thinking, she leaned her head on his arm. His hand affectionately patted her cheek and she felt her face redden.

"I'd rather have remained a widower than saddle myself to the likes of Sadie Peterman. I'm no longer on the market, and Sadie will just have to turn her attentions elsewhere." Luke and Maggie approached the house. "If she annoys you again, I'll speak to her father."

"I pray I never encounter another Peterman," mumbled Maggie.

Tuesday, July 9, 1889

Maggie felt at her wit's end, and her hands shook with fatigue as she attempted to peel potatoes. How would she ever find the strength to prepare supper? Overcome yet again with nausea, she dropped the paring knife on the table and rushed out the back door.

Normally, she appreciated the outhouse being a discreet distance from the main house, hidden in a large cluster of pine trees and totally obscured from view. These days she found it impossible to reach the outhouse in time and vomited behind a flowering bush a few feet from the side of the house.

"This morning sickness will be the death of me," muttered Maggie, brushing a stray lock of hair from her eyes and wiping her mouth with her soiled handkerchief. She'd been violently ill and eating only dry toast and tea for almost two weeks. The very thought of food sent her running to what she now considered 'her bush'.

And there appeared to be no end in sight.

Composing herself after the nausea passed, Maggie stumbled back to the kitchen to face another go-around with those potatoes. She collided with Luke in the kitchen doorway.

"What's for supper, Maggie?" asked Luke, smiling. "Got a hankering for fried chicken."

"Oh, no," groaned Maggie and she raced out the back door.

* * *

"Where are you going?" called Luke, as his wife disappeared outside.

"Maggie's got stomach flu," explained Lucy, entering the kitchen. She set the book she'd been reading on the kitchen worktable. "She's been puking behind Mama's flowering bush. Make her stop! She's going to kill the poor thing."

"Could you please peel these potatoes?" Luke tossed his Stetson onto the kitchen table. He realized immediately what the problem was. "Maggie was attempting to prepare supper."

"See! She's useless, Papa! Send her away," demanded Lucy, as her father disappeared out the back door.

"Peel those potatoes!" he called over his shoulder.

Luke discovered Maggie crouched behind Catherine's

flowering bush, her entire body shaking like someone under-dressed in a snowstorm.

"How long has this been happening?" he demanded.

Maggie swiped her forehead with her sleeve. "A couple of days."

Luke crouched down beside her, grasped her chin in his hand, and examined her face: dark circles beneath haunted eyes, pasty complexion, and hollowed cheeks. "You're totally exhausted. This has been going on longer than a couple of days," accused Luke, standing.

Maggie struggled to her feet, unable to meet his eyes. "Perhaps it's been a week…or maybe two. But the last couple of days have been totally unbearable," she confessed.

"Why didn't you say something?" he whispered, incredulously.

"It's just the price a woman pays for a new baby."

"Any damn fool can see it's taking a toll on your health, Maggie." Luke silently cursed, knowing himself the fool. He'd dismissed her appearance as part of the grieving process, stress from the wedding, and moving to the ranch. Why hadn't he realized the seriousness of it all?

"The sickness will pass…eventually." Maggie attempted a smile, but failed miserably.

"How could I have been so blind?" muttered Luke. Maggie had mentioned morning sickness occasionally, but he had never suspected the extent of her misery or how serious the situation had become.

"Something will be done about this," vowed Luke, lifting Maggie into his arms and carrying her into the house. She wrapped her arms around his neck and rested her head on his shoulder. Her breath was sour, but he didn't care.

Luke bent down to grab a bucket off the floor in the back porch and then carried Maggie upstairs to their bedroom. "No more cooking in your condition. We can fend for ourselves tonight. I want you to rest for the remainder of the day, sleep if you're able."

"I can't let my duties slip. You hired me to…"

"I won't listen to another word. I've made up my mind." As Luke climbed the long staircase, Maggie felt as light as a feather and appeared white as a ghost. Her head rested on his shoulder, and he filled his lungs with her heady lilac scent. His heart beat in a jumbled rhythm, and he tightened his grip. In his current state, he just might drop her.

Reaching their bedroom, Luke set her on her feet and placed the bucket beside the bed. “Get some rest. I’ll ask Morning Star to bring you some tea. She used to give Catherine something when she was carrying the girls.”

Before Maggie realized what was happening, Luke embraced her and kissed her on the mouth. His hand caressed her cheek for a moment before he released her. Walking out of the room, he called, “I mean it, sweetheart. Get some sleep.” He quietly closed the door behind him.

* * *

For several seconds she stared at the closed door, barely able to breathe. Finally, she regained her wits, stomped across the floor, and sat on the edge of the bed. How dare Luke treat her like this? Ordering her out of her own kitchen, and forbidding her to perform the very duties he’d hired her for in the first place. And what about that kiss? For crying out loud, a man didn’t go around kissing his housekeeper.

“Of all the nerve. Why, he’s treating me like… like…like a wife!” she declared, aloud.

Every muscle ached, her head pounded, and she felt like she’d been run over by a herd of stampeding longhorns. She burst into tears and flopped back against the pillows. After a minute, she wiped her tear-stained cheeks with her handkerchief and then daintily blew her nose.

Having surrendered to a good cry, she should have felt better. But something didn’t feel right. A chill ran up her spine; she felt uneasy about her situation. Was there another reason why Luke had sabotaged her efforts to comply with their agreement? Had he changed his mind? She recalled his vow. *Something will be done about this.* Was Luke preparing to remove her from his home? Was he planning to ship her back East?

Well, Maggie Carlyle was not giving up without a fight. She’d worked too hard, returning this ranch to its original magnificence, attempting to make it her home, falling in love with his children, and watching the bond between Sam and Patti grow.

"I refuse to leave. Luke forced me into this situation, and now he's stuck with me. I will not be removed from my own kitchen," she whispered.

But Luke was right about one thing. She was exhausted. "I'll just rest for a few minutes. Then I'll prove I'm quite capable of fulfilling my end of this bargain." She kicked off her shoes and snuggled under the lacy throw.

Within seconds she was sound asleep.

* * *

Luke lingered in the hallway. A minute ago, he'd heard Maggie speaking aloud from behind the closed door. He couldn't distinguish her words clearly, but he could imagine the gist of her complaining.

Now, all appeared silent from within, and judging by his wife's exhausted state, he felt certain she'd fallen asleep. He raced down the stairs two at a time, charged into the kitchen and grabbed his Stetson off the kitchen table.

"Is she packing her bags? Are you sending her away?" demanded his daughter, pausing for a moment, holding a half-peeled potato in one hand and a paring knife in the other.

"Don't be ridiculous, Lucy. I'll be back in a few minutes with Ned to help you with supper," he explained as he headed out the back door.

Luke crossed the yard and entered the horse barn. "Mike, where are you, son?"

"Back here, Mr. Carlyle, tending Sugarfoot's sore knee." The young horseman poked his head up when Luke hung his arm over the stall door. "Did I do something wrong?"

"Nope. I need you to head into town right now. Go tell Florence Jones 'it's time'. She'll know what I'm talking about. I've got to find your pa." Luke charged out of the barn door.

"I'll leave right away," called Mike.

* * *

That evening Ned and Lucy prepared supper, the latter

grumbling the entire time. She even attempted to convince Ned to join her campaign to oust her new stepmother.

He wasn't having any of it.

Finally, Luke had had enough. "Stop complaining about Maggie. Or I'll send your new mare back to the Morgan ranch and tell Robert we don't need her anymore."

Lucy's mouth dropped open and she glared at her father. "How can you be so mean?"

"You're treating Maggie in an equally mean manner. Besides, you don't know the whole story, Lucy."

His daughter stamped her foot. "Uncle Ned?"

"Keep me out of this," he muttered, setting plates and cutlery on the table.

"What's it going to be? If Maggie stays, so does your mare." Luke stood arms crossed, hating himself for giving his daughter this ultimatum, knowing Maggie probably wouldn't approve. But he was at his wit's end.

His daughter's grousing ceased.

Sam and Patti washed up, slipped into their chairs at the kitchen table, and chattered non-stop. Lucy slumped into her chair beside Patti.

Maggie wandered into the kitchen and spotted Ned, obviously annoyed that he was wearing *her* apron and working at *her* stove. Luke hauled out the empty chair beside Sam, and Maggie seated herself.

"Now that you're all here, I have some news." Luke stood behind his wife and rested his hands on her shoulders. "Maggie is going to have a baby, Ned."

Maggie gasped aloud. Obviously, she hadn't expected his announcement.

"Children, you're going to have a new brother or sister," continued Luke, ignoring his wife's murderous expression.

Shocked faces stared back at him while everyone digested what they'd just heard.

"Mama's getting a baby?" asked Sam, incredulously.

"This is even better than a puppy," whispered Patti, beaming at her brother.

"Isn't that just wonderful!" Lucy rose from her chair and headed for the door.

"Lucy, get back here and sit down," ordered her father.

Lucy complied with his request but blurted, "You'll just spend all your time with Maggie and that stupid baby. You won't even notice me and Patti anymore."

Maggie gasped. "Lucy, don't for a minute think your father doesn't care deeply for you and Patti. He'll always make time for both of you. Whether or not Sam and I are here, that will never change."

"Maggie is right, Lucy. I love all of you very much. Nothing will ever change that. But your mother needs her rest." Luke heaved a sigh of relief. At least his two youngest children had taken the news well. "I've made some arrangements…"

A knock at the back door interrupted Luke. The screen door squeaked open, and Agnes Jones walked in carrying a small valise. "Hello, everyone. Have I arrived in time for supper?"

Agnes wore a faded calico dress, no bonnet, and a ragged, blue sweater. Florence Jones' fourth child stood almost six feet tall. With mousy brunette hair and dull brown eyes, no one would consider her pretty. But the plain-featured seventeen-year-old was sturdy and trust-worthy, and Luke recalled her mother saying Agnes and her twin sister were blessed with brilliant minds and hearts of gold. Qualities Luke valued much higher than appearance.

"Agnes, what are you doing here?" asked Lucy.

"I can explain that," answered Luke. "She is our new mother's helper. Your mama is clearly too ill for housework, so Agnes will carry out her duties."

"That's…not necessary," stammered Maggie, attempting to stand. Luke pushed her gently back onto her chair.

"Agnes will work for our family for a year until the baby arrives and your mama's back on her feet. Then she'll move out East and train as a nurse, like her sister Pearl before her." Luke smiled at Agnes. "Welcome to our home."

Luke habitually hired one of Florence's daughters each time his wife was carrying and then arranged for her education as payment. He'd done it each time Catherine was with child, and he'd do the same for Maggie. Some folks would say he was pampering his wife, but it was the only way to ensure Florence's brilliant daughters earned an education. The Jones family, poor but proud, wouldn't accept anything that hinted of charity.

"I'm much beholden to you, Mr. Carlyle, for this wonderful

opportunity." Agnes smiled at her new employer. "And I'll certainly hold up my end of our arrangement."

"Don't count on Mr. Carlyle holding up his end." Maggie glanced up at Luke. "You could be replaced at a moment's notice."

Agnes's horror-stricken expression moved Luke to quickly dispel her fears. "Don't be concerned that you'll be replaced. You'll be employed here until this child is born, and Maggie is fully recovered. Then I'll arrange for your nursing education, all expenses paid."

"Thank you, Mr. Carlyle," said Agnes, visibly relieved.

"Nothing will disrupt this agreement, Agnes." Luke shook her hand to seal the deal.

Maggie scoffed and muttered, "Good luck."

Chapter 14

Two days later, Maggie awoke with the distinct feeling she wasn't alone. She slowly opened her eyes and discovered a small multi-colored cat with four white socks sitting at the foot of the bed. Never partial to cats, Maggie screamed like a banshee. The cat sprang a foot in the air and flew off the bed, her feet slipping and sliding as she scrambled across the shiny plank floor and escaped out the door.

"What's wrong, Mrs. Carlyle?" asked Agnes, racing into the bedroom.

"There was…a cat…on the bed." Maggie's pulse raced, and she pressed her hand to her chest to keep her heart in place. She couldn't say exactly why cats frightened her so much. Perhaps a childhood incident that she couldn't recall was to blame.

"Goodness, ma'am," Agnes chuckled. "I found that little calico cat under Lucy's bed yesterday when I was mopping. Apparently, her name is Boots and she's a mouser."

"Is she now?" Maggie flopped back against her pillows and fanned her flushed face with the sheet. "Where'd she come from?"

"Lucy says she found her, wet and bedraggled, down by the creek a few weeks ago. Brought the poor thing home and claimed it for her own." Agnes assisted Maggie out of the bed.

"Miss Boots might be half way to Miles City by now, frightened out of one of her nine lives." Maggie donned a wrapper and sat at her vanity table.

Agnes grabbed a brush and began to battle with her employer's tangled locks. "She was headed toward the third floor when she raced by me. Don't worry about that silly cat. What's important is how you're feeling?"

Maggie twisted around to face Agnes. "I feel wonderful! I really do!" Until this very minute she hadn't considered her condition, due in part to her unexpected bedmate.

Morning Star had told her the story of having a vision about befriending flowers and plants during a high fever when she was only ten years old. Afterward, she'd learned medicinal healing from her aunt. The native woman's special tea that she'd insisted Maggie drink had done the trick. Her morning sickness was gone!

"I'll prepare some breakfast, if you're up to it." Agnes secured Maggie's hair into a bun and set the brush down.

"I'm starving."

"I'll make flapjacks." Agnes beamed.

"But I want another cup of Morning Star's magical tea. No sense in taking two steps forward, then one step back."

"Morning, Mama." Sam bounded into the room.

"Morning, Mama," echoed Patti, running behind her brother.

"Good morning, Mrs. Carlyle." Luke followed the children into the room. "How are you feeling? You were sound asleep when I slipped out of bed a half hour ago."

"I'm feeling wonderful today. And I'm joining you for breakfast downstairs." Maggie hugged Sam and Patti in turn. She suspected Lucy was pouting in her room since her stepmother wasn't being sent away. Luke had confessed his ultimatum with the new mare. Maggie considered the threat unfair, but what was done was done. And it had been effective.

"That's the best news I've heard all week," said Luke. "And if you keep improving, one of these days I'll give you your surprise."

"Do I get a hint?" asked Maggie.

"No. You will just have to wait."

Monday, July 22, 1889

Maggie dried the breakfast dishes, hung her dishtowel to dry, and neatly stacked everything on the breakfront shelves. With Agnes fitting into the household so well, Maggie found herself frequently at loose ends. She slumped into a chair at the kitchen table and rested her chin in her hands.

Agnes lugged an overflowing basket of wet laundry through the kitchen on the way outside to the clothes line.

"Do you need a hand with the door, Agnes?" asked Maggie.

"No thank you, ma'am. I'll just set the basket down for a second." Agnes stumbled through the door and disappeared outside.

When Agnes first arrived, Maggie believed Luke considered her lacking, incapable of performing the housekeeping duties comprising her part of their arrangement. But Luke insisted that an expectant woman exhausted from morning sickness would never toil in his household regardless of any agreement. There were plenty of strong young ladies eager for employment.

Now, Maggie was thankful for Agnes's help. With each passing day her nausea had decreased and she'd regained her strength. Although she grew increasingly restless, Luke insisted drying dishes, peeling potatoes, or mending and other needlework were the extent of her duties.

She was bored silly.

Suddenly, the back door opened and Patti poked her head around the corner. "Mama Maggie," she called.

"What is it, sweetheart?"

"I'm all dirty." Patti walked into the kitchen to prove it, leaving a trail of muddy shoeprints in her wake.

Maggie gasped. Her youngest daughter stood in a puddle of dirty water, mud sticking to her clothes, her hands encrusted with the black, oozing mess. "*What* did you do?"

"Sam and me made mud pies," she admitted in a whisper.

"Oh fiddle! Look at the mess you're making on Agnes's clean floor!" exclaimed Maggie.

Just then, an equally dirty Sam swept into the kitchen with a muddy-pawed Rags on his heels.

"No! Catch that puppy!" Maggie watched in horror as the two children gave chase to the canine who dashed straight through the kitchen into the rest of the house.

Maggie leapt to her feet and followed, in her haste slipping on the muddy mess they made. "Stop him before he makes it into the parlor," she called.

Sam and Patti giggled hysterically as they made several stabs at capturing the puppy who evaded their every attempt to catch him. They went left, the dog went right. The laughter continued with each new strategy. Finally, after a dozen futile attempts, Sam dove headfirst at the puppy, grabbed a hind leg, and held on as if his life depended on it. And it might. His mother could have throttled him at the moment.

The growing pup pulled Sam across the wet floor, coming to rest at Maggie's feet. Sam wrapped his arms around the wayward hound, getting a better hold. "Got him, Mama!" he declared, beaming.

There wasn't a square inch of hallway floor that wasn't covered in mud!

An hour later, with assistance from Morning Star and Agnes, Maggie's children were cleaned up, the floors were scrubbed again, and her children were seated at the kitchen table. Sam practiced printing his letters while Patti toiled over a sheet of sums. Neither child was happy. Morning Star had promised them an adventurous day searching for healing plants and medicinal roots followed by a picnic lunch by the creek. Maggie had canceled the outing as additional punishment.

"What are you to do if you get dirty playing outside again?" quizzed Maggie.

"Stand at the back door until someone comes to clean us up," replied Patti.

"Keep Rags outside with us," added Sam.

Maggie hugged each child in turn before settling into a chair across from them. "This punishment doesn't mean I don't love you. I love both of you to the moon and beyond. But you mustn't make additional work for Agnes and Morning Star."

"Yes, Mama," replied the children in unison.

The kitchen screen door squeaked open, and Luke strode across the floor. Maggie froze, her heart in her mouth. Her busy new husband never reappeared in the house before supper time, sometimes even later. What was he doing in the kitchen? Was someone ill? Had there been an accident?

"What happened?" Maggie leapt to her feet.

"Nothing's wrong." Luke glanced at the children. "Are these the jailbirds?"

Maggie smiled in spite of herself. "Yes. How did you hear about it?"

"Morning Star. But she promised to take the children with

her tomorrow, provided they behaved themselves the rest of today."

"We will, Papa," squealed Patti.

"We'll be very good," insisted Sam.

Agnes returned to the kitchen, having changed her clothes now that she'd finished cleaning up after the mud-making crew.

"Perfect timing, Agnes. You're in charge of these two. Come with me, Maggie." Luke reached for her hand and gently guided her through the house toward the entryway staircase. Both of them mindful of the still damp but decidedly cleaner floor. "Fetch your sunbonnet and shawl and meet me outside."

Maggie started up the stairs, and then stopped and turned. "What are you up to?"

"Remember the surprise I promised? Let me show you my ranch," said Luke, beaming.

"Your ranch is comprised of acres of barren landscape, thousands of smelly animals, and a collection of cowhands of questionable character." Maggie stood with one hand on her hip, her other hand resting on the railing. "You call this a surprise?" she teased.

Luke gaped. And then he noticed her mischievous smile.

"Are you going to stand there all day insulting my cattle and my men? Or would you prefer accompanying me on a tour of the Diamond C?" Luke slapped his Stetson on his head.

Maggie stood, head tilted in contemplation.

"Are you coming with me?" asked Luke. His expression told her he was afraid she might turn him down.

"Of course I am. I'm just considering which bonnet would be most appropriate for traipsing around the range." As she raced upstairs, she called over her shoulder, "I'll be down in five minutes."

Maggie hurried across the veranda, sailed down the front steps, and then froze in her tracks. Luke stood between two horses, holding their reins in one hand and smiling broadly.

"We're not taking the carriage?" she blurted.

"You can't go where we're going in a carriage. I checked with Doc when I was in town yesterday, and he assured me that even in your condition no harm would come from a horseback ride." He motioned her forward. "Let me introduce my friends. This little mare is Rosie, and she's as tame as a newborn lamb. As you know this magnificent fellow is Thunder."

By reason of his size alone, Thunder frightened the daylights out of Maggie. Smiling, she turned her attention to the complaisant mare. "Good morning, Rosie. I'm pleased to meet you, and I'm delighted to see you're wearing a side saddle. Otherwise, I'd have a time of it with my long skirts." Maggie patted the horse's neck and stared into her pretty brown eyes.

"Here. Let me help you up." Luke cupped his right hand and skillfully boosted her safely into the saddle.

Maggie rearranged her skirts, grasped the reins, and smiled down at her husband. "Thank you for your assistance. I'm looking forward to my tour."

Luke leapt aboard Thunder with the ease of a circus acrobat. "Are you ready?"

"Definitely. I haven't been riding since I attended Normal School." Maggie urged Rosie forward and they were off.

The horses climbed out of the valley, walking sedately. Maggie settled her bonnet lower on her head, shading her face from the glaring sun in hopes of preventing a new crop of freckles. But she had to admit the strong rays felt wonderful, penetrating her thin dress and shawl, warming her skin.

Soon, the ranch's corrals and buildings became dots below them. Buttes of varying heights—some gray and plain, others multi-colored layers of browns and reds—replaced the level, sage-covered valley. Luke and Maggie rode in silence for almost a half hour, slowing the horses for a brief rest and then returning to a canter, even galloping for a short time. Maggie considered the possibility Luke was testing her riding skills. Had she measured up?

As if he'd read her mind, he commented, "You're quite at home in that saddle. You've been holding out on me, neglecting to mention your skills as a horsewoman."

"I guess once you learn to ride, you never forget." Maggie smiled at three multi-colored butterflies playing tag amongst the clusters of colorful wildflowers. The mixture of floral scents, more intoxicating than the finest French perfume, teased her nose. "This landscape is one of God's natural works of art. At least there aren't miles of railway tracks stretching across your land. I noticed the tracks on my trip out West, a scar on the landscape and a permanent reminder of the price paid for industry and convenience," complained Maggie.

"Some folk consider the tracks an eyesore, but the Northern Pacific Railroad opened up the cattle industry for us. Shipping our cattle to market by rail is quicker with less hardship on the animals." Luke met her eyes and grinned. "This land is all free-range. Each year the Diamond C cattle mingle with other ranchers' stock. In the fall, with our neighbors' help, we round up all the cattle and sort them out by brands. We send the steers to market and winter over the cows. We brand the new calves in spring, and the whole business begins again."

"Have you branded all the spring calves?" Maggie leaned forward and patted Rosie.

"We branded calves about six weeks ago, once all the calves had dropped," answered Luke.

Maggie resettled her bonnet which had flipped about in the breeze. Thunder sidled up to Rosie and nudged her neck in an equine display of affection. Luke patted the stallion's neck.

"It's quite obvious…you love horses." Maggie smiled at her new husband, feeling quite comfortable with him.

"Blame that on Robert Morgan. Since we were children, we've been the best of friends. He's taught me so much about his Morgan horses, and I love them as much as he does."

"Such as?"

"Well, Morgan horses have been around for a hundred years, descendants of the famous Morgan stud named Figure. They have good stamina for working the range or pulling wagons and carriages. Thunder is a Morgan and he runs like the devil's licking at his heels. A good-natured disposition makes them ideal for pleasure riding, especially for children. Sam sure loves Spots," added Luke, chuckling.

"I assumed a horse was a horse, except for thoroughbred racehorses, of course. I have quite a lot to learn about ranching and horses and cattle." Maggie sighed.

"Don't worry. You'll learn it all in time."

A trio of small black birds darted in front of them, and Maggie gasped. Had she reached out her hand, she might have touched one. Neither of the well-trained horses even twitched an ear.

A fat jackrabbit darted across their path. Without a second's hesitation, Luke grabbed his pistol and fired. Maggie gaped as the animal flipped sideways in mid-air and then fell, still. She recalled childhood lessons on survival of the fittest and the food chain. Such was the harsh reality of prairie life.

Luke leapt from his mount to retrieve his prize and stuffed the rabbit into his saddlebag. Spotting the ragged edges of an arrowhead, he picked it up and twiddled it in his fingers. "It's a damned shame what we did to the Indian. Years ago, my father encountered a few Indians hunting his cattle. Through an elaborate display of grunts and his own brand of sign language, Father convinced the Indians they were welcome to a few cattle to feed their families."

"That was kind-hearted of him." Maggie listened intently to Luke's story.

"Father couldn't tolerate the idea of starving children. The red hunters killed three or four head, just what they required to feed the tribe. Unlike the white buffalo hunters who obliterated their food source, the Indians only killed what they required to survive. And they took the whole animal with them, using every bit of it for one purpose or another."

Luke mounted Thunder, and they moved on. A reddish-brown deer and her spotted fawn emerged from a thicket up ahead. The doe's ears twitched and she stood motionless for a moment. Catching a glimpse of the horses and their riders, the mother and baby bounded back to the protection of the trees.

Riding along in companionable silence, Luke and Maggie crested a grassy hill. Suddenly, Maggie detected a familiar aroma. Or was she imagining it? "Do I smell coffee?"

Luke turned in the saddle and pointed south. In the distance smoke spiraled slowly upward, like a snake charmed from a basket. "Cookhouse Charlie has the coffee on. Time for the noon meal. Let's ride down and say hello."

Luke nudged Thunder's sides urging him into a gallop, and Rosie accepted the challenge. While horses and riders raced across the range, the wind whipped Maggie's face and whistled by her ears. She smiled with the exhilarating feeling of freedom.

"Howdy, Charlie, got enough grub for a couple more?" Luke swung down from the saddle, and then helped his wife onto the ground.

Maggie recognized him immediately. Luke's Cookhouse Charlie and Codger Charlie, the disgruntled customer in The Joker's Wild, were one and the same. Would he recognize her?

"Charlie, I'd like to introduce you to my wife, Maggie. Sweetheart, this here fellow's the best trail cook in all of Montana Territory," proclaimed Luke, proudly. "Everyone calls him Cookhouse Charlie, even when he's fixing meals out on the range."

"Well, now, ain't she just as fine as wine on Sunday." The old fellow grinned broadly. "I'm mighty pleased to meet you, ma'am."

Maggie winced. He'd recognized her.

"Pleased to meet you, sir," she gushed, dipping into a quick curtsey, recalling he'd called her an uppity lady. Might as well give the old codger the full treatment.

Charlie guffawed. And then he slapped Luke on the back, sending him off balance. "I like her, Mr. Carlyle. She'll do just fine." The old codger returned to his cooking.

Luke uncapped a canteen and passed it to Maggie. While she drank deeply, a generous stream of water slipped past her lips.

"Whoa." Luke reached for the canteen. "That stuff's more precious than aged brandy on a hot day on the range."

Luke sent her, red-faced, to refill their canteens, while he chatted with the cook.

The crystal clear creek water reflected Maggie's image almost as well as the gilded mirror hanging above the entryway table at the Diamond C main house. She dipped her handkerchief into the cold water and wiped her face. Heavens above, it felt wonderful. Refreshed, she filled the canteens and strolled back to the cook wagon.

During their dinner—she couldn't have served up a better meal herself—Maggie observed the cowboys. Each man shoveled food into his mouth and swallowed, barely taking time to chew. Everyone talked with their mouth full. There was constant teasing, joking, and trick-playing, with Luke willingly participating in the tomfoolery. If she hadn't known he was the boss, she couldn't have distinguished him from the hired help.

After sharing the noon meal with his men, Luke shook hands with every one of them and spoke a few words of appreciation for their hard work. Before returning to their duties, each ranch hand tipped his hat to Maggie, respectful of the boss's new wife. She hoped none of these loyal and hard-working men were ever confronted by those cattle rustlers, perhaps even find themselves with an outlaw's pistol to their head. She shuddered at the thought.

Luke and Maggie shared a quiet cup of coffee with Charlie after the men returned to work. And then her husband helped her into her saddle, shook Charlie's hand, and mounted Thunder. With a wave to the cook, they continued on their way.

"Are you enjoying your day, Maggie?"

She smiled at her new husband's thoughtfulness. "I'm enjoying every minute, thank you. This is a wonderful surprise."

They rode for a short while, lost in their own thoughts, until they came upon a herd of Longhorns. The pungent scent of cattle dung floated in the air, and Maggie rubbed her nose, repelled by the offensive odor. She was a rancher's wife now. She'd better get accustomed to this.

"These cattle are descendants of the first herd Father drove from Texas. These feral, hardy survivors of the harsh winter two years ago will produce superior offspring in generations to come." Luke waved to the cowboys who'd been watching the herd while the others ate. A couple rode over to say hello on their way to the cook wagon for their noon meal.

When the ranch hands went on their way, Maggie inquired, "How many Longhorns do you own?"

"I'm not certain. We attempt to count them each fall during the round up. The cowboys are pretty wary and can report thefts right smartly. They know when even twenty or so are missing. It's uncanny sometimes. We've been missing quite a few lately. Cattle rustlers have moved into the area."

Maggie didn't relax until they rode on, wary of those dangerous curved horns that were the animal's necessary defense against predators.

As they crossed a verdant valley, Luke asked, "Are you tiring? We could stop and rest for a bit. Just say the word."

"I'm fine. No need to rest." Maggie smiled, appreciative of his concern.

A curious gray-brown prairie dog popped his head out of his hole. Luke's pistol instantly ended his life. Before Maggie could protest the sudden execution, Luke explained, "Those varmints are a nuisance. Don't be feeling sorry for him."

Annoyed that he'd read her thoughts so easily, she asked, "Why is he such a nuisance?"

"Prairie dogs dig their holes everywhere, and we've been

forced to put down a couple of horses that broke a leg stepping into one of their holes. My Morgan horses are a fair bit more valuable than a prairie dog."

They rode in companionable silence for a mile or two. Maggie heard a meadowlark's happy song in the distance, as pleasing to her ear as the finest classical tune played on a spinet.

Luke pulled up on Thunder's reins and dismounted beside a meandering creek. He helped Maggie out of her saddle, swung both sets of reins over a low-hanging branch. They strolled hand in hand beside the gurgling creek and her senses sharpened. She heard the pounding of her own heart and felt his calloused, warm hand reach for hers. So very warm. Butterflies performed acrobatics in her stomach, brought on by nerves and not a return of the morning sickness. Wouldn't that spoil the moment?

And then she blushed. What was she thinking? She'd already admitted being angry with William for leaving her penniless. Luke's respect for her probably hung by a thread as it was. She should pull her hand away, but she craved the warmth. Surely she deserved this one small comfort.

Was holding her hand having a similar effect on him? Don't be silly! He's simply ensuring she didn't stumble and fall. He dropped her hand without warning and wrapped his muscular arm around her shoulder, pulling her against him. The scent of horses and wood smoke from the cook fire clung to his clothing and drifted to her nose. She rested her head on his shoulder, and her eyes drifted shut. One moment of heaven wouldn't hurt.

"Remind me to teach Sam how to fish one of these days. There's some nice trout in here. Every father should teach his son how to fish."

Her eyes popped open, and she raised her head to meet Luke's eyes. "Sam would enjoy fishing. He loves anything involving the outdoors."

They circled back to the horses, and Luke pulled a blanket out from behind his saddle. Choosing a shady spot under a nearby cottonwood tree, Luke spread the blanket on the slightly damp ground.

"Let's sit awhile and rest." He removed his hat, motioned for her to join him on the blanket.

After a moment's hesitation, Maggie settled beside him and

yawned. "Thank you again, Luke, for my surprise. It's a blessing to just relax and enjoy the day."

"You're very welcome," said Luke.

* * *

Several minutes later, his new wife shifted onto her side with her knees slightly bent, resting her head on her arms. In a minute, her even breathing assured Luke she'd fallen into the deep restful sleep she needed.

Luke watched her chest rise and fall with each breath. Auburn tendrils framed her face, lying a few inches from his nose, and his fingers itched to touch them. He inhaled her ever-present lilac scent. For as long as he lived, he'd associate those spring blooms with Maggie. She stirred in her sleep and snuggled against him. Luke covered her with part of the blanket, thinking she might be cold.

She's so beautiful, he thought. Luke felt physically attracted to her—so tall, still slim despite the pregnancy, and so very pretty. What man wouldn't be? He dared to run his fingers down her arm. Her skin felt as soft and smooth as silk, and her pleasing, feminine scent teased his nose. Luke couldn't imagine Maggie's smiling face without the freckles she despised.

His new wife had attempted to hide her pain from him. But Luke had survived the loss of a spouse, too. When Catherine died, he'd plummeted into a dark chasm filled with heartache, depression, anger, and self-pity. Finally, he'd dragged himself out of that seemingly bottomless pit of despair and moved on with his life.

He admired Maggie's bravery: head held high, refusing to succumb to the pain. Perhaps the sudden dire circumstances following William's death had simply robbed her of the luxury of mourning him. But Luke hoped Maggie's tender heart, bruised by her husband's death and deceptions, would soon heal and she would feel ready to move on. To move on with him.

He thought about his new wife constantly while he worked, imagining what chores occupied her day. He'd wager a guess at what she'd instructed Agnes to prepare for supper. And then he couldn't wait to return home for the evening meal.

Ned saw right through him. *Yer the only feller I know spends his days pinin' after his own wife, like a dang schoolboy scared to ask a perdy gal to a dance*. Luke had attempted to deny it, but Ned wouldn't let the matter drop. *You've fallen for that little gal. It's written all over yer face. So, what ya plannin' on doin' 'bout it?*

Until that day, Luke hadn't realized the shocking truth: he'd fallen in love with his wife. How in hell had that happened? They'd been married only a few weeks. She wanted nothing to do with another man; she was still in mourning. And completely distrustful of men, including him. So what had he done? Gone and fallen head over heels in love with her!

He'd considered Ned's question, what was he planning to do about it? He'd spelled out the terms of their arrangement in order to free himself from housework: just a marriage of convenience that wouldn't be consummated until she felt ready. By his own doing the grieving widow became nothing more than his housekeeper. Now, he vowed to free himself from their agreement as soon as possible. He certainly needed a housekeeper, but he wanted a wife.

He wanted Maggie.

A small flock of geese winged low overhead; their honking shattered the solitude. Maggie awoke with a start, and blushed when she opened her eyes and realized she'd snuggled against the length of his body. She quickly moved away from him, wouldn't meet his eyes. Probably for the best. Otherwise, she'd notice how much his body desired her.

Luke led the way back to their horses, holding the blanket in front of him for obvious reasons, at least obvious to him. Maggie stomped along beside him, miffed about something. Had she felt his body's desire for her? He couldn't imagine how. She'd scrambled away from him like his flaming body burned through her thin dress.

Suddenly, she excused herself and scrambled behind a thicket of bushes. Luke discreetly kept walking in the opposite direction, wondering what she was thinking.

Chapter 15

A sudden wave of nausea surged through Maggie as she scrambled behind a clump of nearby bushes. She forced herself to relax by taking deep breaths, and the nausea passed. She felt purely mortified realizing she'd pressed her body against Luke's. The fact she slept soundly at the time didn't deserve merit. No doubt Luke believed her a fraud: expounding on her proper upbringing, playing the grieving widow, and then behaving like a hussy in her sleep. Had she ever snuggled close to him in their bed? Her cheeks flamed from the possibility.

Luke hadn't displayed one iota of concern about her shameful behavior, and that especially galled her. Had he failed to mention her inappropriate behavior because he held such a low opinion of her that he expected no better? Or did he consider what she'd done proper, them being married and all? Who knew how a man's mind worked?

She relieved herself behind the bushes, straightened her spine, and then strode toward the horses tethered some distance away. "Where are we off to now?" She kept her head down, feeling her cheeks ablaze, unable to meet his eyes.

"There's a special place I want to share with you on our way home." Luke spoke softly while he cupped his hand and boosted her into her saddle.

"Lead the way." Maggie settled her skirts and took up the reins. Was he attempting to reestablish their comfortable camaraderie? She considered the likelihood of that happening all but impossible. And it was all her fault.

Maggie's mind warred with her emotions, alternating between guilt and fury. Surely, she couldn't be held responsible for her actions while sound asleep. But why hadn't Luke discreetly moved away? Obviously, Luke Carlyle wasn't the gentleman she'd believed him to be. She almost told him what she thought of him but held her tongue.

Her temper simmered like a pot of stew atop a woodstove while they rode in silence for almost two hours. Finally, the horses crested a hill, and she spied a fenced-in area in the distance. She squinted while they rode closer, and her temper cooled when she realized what lay ahead.

An unpainted wooden fence enclosed the graveyard, one side leaning precariously. Luke dismounted and helped her down from Rosie, and they entered together through the open gate. The afternoon breeze rippled the waist high grasses covering the lettering on several of the wooden grave markers. No flowers or paths. A tangle of grass and sagebrush trampled in a few places evidenced the neglect.

The tallest marker stood guard over the others and simply read, MATTHEW CARLYLE. Luke moved his fingers across the row of dates recording his father's birth and death, like a blind person reading braille. The loving gesture, almost a caress, brought tears to Maggie's eyes and left her emotions raw. She should offer comfort, but no words could convey her feelings.

Maggie envied Luke. She'd never seen her parents' gravesites, never travelled back East since the day she'd left eight years ago to accept the teaching position. Her anger surged to the surface, recalling William's words: *we're living on a sheriff's wages, Maggie, no money for train fare*. She had to admit she wouldn't have traveled to Philadelphia anyway. She'd gone against her parents' wishes by coming out West. Returning home again would appear the ultimate act of hypocrisy.

"I often visit with my parents and Catherine." Luke brushed the dust from his hands. "Especially to discuss new ideas for the ranch, plans regarding the stock, decisions concerning the family." After a lengthy pause, he added, "I even asked Father's opinion before marrying you."

Maggie's gaze flew to Luke who turned and met her eyes, smiling.

"And what did Matthew have to say about that?" She held her breath, uncertain if she wanted to hear his answer.

"Insisted the matter was my decision alone." Luke reached for her hand, held it tightly.

She released her breath. Did he consider the decision he'd made to be the right one?

* * *

"Matthew approves of our marriage," said Luke, smiling. "Mother and Catherine, too. I just feel it."

Maggie withdrew her hand and wandered among the graves, pulling back overgrowth and reading markers. Luke noticed she paused in front of Ruth's grave, and again in front of Catherine's. She never uttered a word, just moved on.

In the far corner stood several crosses with faded names, recording the deaths of several men, some old and some young. "Who are these people?" she inquired, without looking his way.

"Ranch hands, passed on while in the Diamond C's employ. No kin, so we buried them together with their Diamond C family." He traced her steps, stood beside her, and they continued walking silently together.

Luke's breath caught when Maggie bent to read the small marker, and he braced himself for the words that were forthcoming.

"This baby passed when only a year old," she whispered.

"Little Ruthie, our second daughter, ten months old when she died from croup cradled in Catherine's arms." Tears slid down his cheeks, but it didn't matter with Maggie at his side.

"I'm so sorry." She tightened her grip on his hand.

"We were both devastated. Catherine cried for weeks, but eventually she pulled herself together. And then Patti came along and she helped to fill the void in our hearts." Luke sighed. "They reside together in heaven: Father, Mother, Catherine and Ruthie."

"To lose a child…I can't imagine the heartache." Maggie's head found his shoulder, and he buried his face in her hair.

"Catastrophe happens in threes: first my daughter's death, then thousands of our cattle perished, and then Catherine died. Surely, my life will take a turn for the better now." The breeze dried his tears, and he slipped his arm around her middle as he spoke.

Was Maggie a part of that turnaround? Would this remarkable woman's presence bring him luck for the future? Had fate brought them together? Was it all part of a bigger plan? When had his life become a collection of questions?

"I'm bringing the children out here to cut down the grass and plant flowers around the graves." Maggie gazed across the entire area. "And I should plant flowers around William's grave for Sam's sake."

"I'd be much obliged, Maggie. We've allowed the graveyard to deteriorate, like the rest of the ranch." Luke's voice caught, and he couldn't continue. She smiled at him and patted his arm.

Maggie knew that no matter how much time passed, the feeling of loss never totally disappeared. She'd lost her parents and her husband. If no one else understood how he felt, Maggie did. The thought brought him comfort.

Darkness descended upon them just as they arrived back at the ranch.

"Thank you for keeping supper for us, Agnes," said Luke, handing her the rabbit.

"And thank you for watching the children today," added Maggie.

"You're welcome. Thank you for bringing me this little fellow. Rabbit stew for supper tomorrow." The hired girl hurried away to dress the animal, delighted with her plans for the next day's evening meal.

Luke and Maggie devoured the simple meal of beef stew and biscuits.

"That was delicious," proclaimed Luke.

He noticed his wife's appetite had returned due in part to today's fresh air. And then he stretched and yawned, exhausted either from the fresh air or the emotional time shared at the graveyard.

Arms entwined, they climbed the long staircase.

Luke quickly pulled off his boots and socks. And then he stood, unbuttoned his shirt, slipped it off and climbed out of his denims. He noticed Maggie grimace as everything landed on the floor.

"I'll pick that up in the morning," he promised, avoiding a scolding.

Luke crawled into bed, settled the bedcovers around his chest, and then folded his hands behind his head. Maggie shrugged and turned her back to him. Was she too exhausted to insist he retreat to his study? If she asked him to leave, he would.

He hoped she wouldn't ask.

She didn't.

For the first time, Luke watched his wife undress for bed. She discreetly pulled her dress over her head and then tossed it onto a chair. Sitting on the chaise longue, she kicked off her shoes and removed her stockings. He'd never watched anything so seductive in his life, and his body reacted accordingly. She crossed the room, removed her nightdress from under her pillow, and slipped into it without removing her under things.

"Thank you for a wonderful surprise." She smiled at him. "I truly loved every aspect of the ranch: the cattle and the beautiful scenery, even sharing a meal with the ranch hands."

"I'm happy you enjoyed yourself." He smiled and yawned to cover his excitement, fearing his heart might beat its way right out of his chest.

Mesmerized, Luke continued to watch as she loosened the pins from her hair and tossed them onto the vanity table. She shook her head and an auburn waterfall cascaded down her back. She dragged a brush through her hair, crossed the room, and then crawled into bed.

"Good night, Luke." She yawned. "Thank you again for a wonderful day."

A minute later, she was sound asleep.

Luke wondered how he'd managed to make this beautiful woman his wife. "Good night, my love," he whispered.

There, he'd admitted it aloud.

He truly loved her.

* * *

The next afternoon, Morning Star raced into Patti's bedroom. "Maggie, what wrong with children? Ned storm into cook shack. Shout about sick children. Tell me come quick."

"We're not certain, Morning Star." Maggie's fingers worried the ends of her apron strings. "Sam and Patti started vomiting a couple hours ago. We settled them into their beds and sent Mike to town. Doc Benjamin's with Sam right now, and I'm praying he'll discover the problem."

Morning Star lowered herself onto Patti's bed and touched her little cheek. "What matter, sweet girl? You get fever again?" asked the native woman.

Patti grabbed the tin pail left within arm's reach on the bed and upchucked violently.

"The children don't have much fever, just terrible stomach cramps. And they're both vomiting something awful." Maggie teetered on her feet and reached for the wall to steady herself.

Patti groaned and held her stomach. "Mama, it hurts."

"I know, sweetheart." Maggie crossed the floor and tenderly kissed the child's forehead. "Doc Benjamin will give you some medicine soon."

"Open your mouth and stick out your tongue," said Morning Star.

Patti obliged and then groaned.

Maggie turned toward Morning Star and whispered, "I can't bear this again. The last time Patti suffered that fever was terrifying. This is ten times worse, and Sam's ill, too. Ned's gone to fetch Luke; I need him here." Tears welled in Maggie's eyes.

"We get children better. Don't worry." Morning Star patted her arm.

"Doc Benjamin's examining Sam, and he ordered me out of the room." Maggie brushed at the tear that slid down her cheek. "Agnes is assisting him. My son is in good hands, but I can't bear this waiting."

Doc Benjamin strode into the room and approached his patient, Agnes on his heels. "Is Patti still vomiting?" he asked.

"Yes, again a minute ago." Maggie met the doctor's eyes.

Just then, Lucy peeked into the room. "What's wrong, Patti? You look terrible."

Patti just moaned, and then bent her small head over the tin bucket again.

"Is my sister going to die?" blurted Lucy, her eyes filling with tears. She glared at Maggie. "What did you do to her?"

"No one is dying." Doc Benjamin mumbled, listening to Patti's chest through his stethoscope. "Your mother didn't do anything to her."

"She is *not* my mother!" Lucy stamped her foot. "This is all

Maggie's fault. She made my sister ill and I hate her."

"You're talking nonsense, young lady," blurted Morning Star.

"She poisoned my sister. I know it," insisted Lucy, shaking with anger.

"Oh, for crying out loud. We're going to the kitchen to brew tea," stated Agnes, dragging Lucy by the arm. "In times of crisis, Mama always makes tea. Please attend to Sam for me, Morning Star."

Morning Star slipped out of the room behind Agnes and Lucy.

Maggie sagged against the wall.

"She's just upset and worried," offered Doc, a sympathetic expression on his face.

"I wish that was all it was. She hasn't accepted our marriage. And I don't know if she ever will," whispered Maggie.

Just then, Luke charged into the room and rushed to her side. "Maggie, what's going on? Lucy was screaming and crying hysterically downstairs, something about you making Patti sick."

"Luke!" Maggie almost collapsed with relief, and he caught her in his arms. She buried her head in his shirt and burst into tears.

* * *

"Doc," Luke called over his shoulder while Maggie trembled in his arms and sobbed uncontrollably, her eyes wild with fright. "What in blazes is going on?"

"Good day, Luke." Doc Benjamin extended his hand. "Sam and Patti are ailing."

"What's the matter with my children?" he demanded, shaking the doctor's hand. He untangled himself from Maggie and settled her in a nearby chair.

"It doesn't appear to be influenza. There's no fever to speak of…" began Doc Benjamin.

"I don't care what it doesn't appear to be. What is it? What's wrong?" Luke's heart beat wildly while fear crept up his spine. Why was it that these children tried his nerves with one crisis or another every second day? If anything happened to any of them it would kill him.

"I have no idea, sir," admitted Doc Benjamin, scratching his head.

"Step away from my child." Luke pushed the doctor aside. "Morning Star!" bellowed Luke. When he'd charged upstairs, he caught a glimpse of the native healer in Sam's room.

"What is it, Mr. Carlyle?" called Morning Star from the doorway. "Something happen?"

"What's wrong with Patti and Sam?" Luke dragged his hands through his hair. If anyone could figure this out, he knew it would be Morning Star. She'd doctored the Carlyle family and ranch hands for years, and Luke held her medicinal potions in high regard. The native healer had been a godsend on more occasions than he cared to remember. Except once. No one had been able to save Catherine.

Morning Star glanced in Doc Benjamin's direction, and then met Luke's eyes. "I think children eat poison berries, Mr. Carlyle," whispered Morning Star. And then she dashed out of the room, calling over her shoulder, "I come back. Make better."

* * *

At ten thirty that night, Maggie slipped into her son's room illuminated by a low-burning lamp. With all that had happened this afternoon, she finally found the opportunity to talk to Morning Star.

The native healer stirred when Maggie entered. "I just close eyes for minute."

"How's Sam?" whispered Maggie, feeling totally exhausted.

"He sipped more tea. He good by tomorrow." Morning Star rubbed her eyes.

Maggie hugged herself with her thick woolen shawl. She couldn't seem to warm up. "How did you know the children ate those berries?"

"Patti tongue red. And she love berries."

"But how did you know which poisonous berries? There's dozens of berries growing in these parts."

"Children find snakeberry patch behind icehouse. Snakeberries pretty red color, and children like red berries. I tell Patti ask before eat berries, but today she forget."

"Her forgetfulness took a couple years off my life," admitted Maggie.

"I see children play near icehouse this morning. I know why sick. Snakeberries poison. Make sick. But no die. Mint tea stop sick."

"Thank you so much. Poor Doc Benjamin looked so embarrassed. He had no idea what caused their illness." Maggie smiled, remembering the red-faced medical doctor's stammered apologies.

"White doctor not know about snakeberries." Morning Star simply stated a fact. "I show white doctor what plant make sick. He know next time."

"You're so kind and humble, Morning Star. And you need sleep. Go home now. I'll sit with my son." Maggie gently pulled the native woman out of the chair and guided her toward the door. "Luke will sit with Patti."

"I don't mind stay."

Maggie shook her head. "Go home. And thank you again for all you did today."

Morning Star stood in the doorway. "Anything happen, come get me."

"We will, I promise. But I predict that those children will wake at dawn, leap out of bed, and demand their breakfast." Maggie hugged the Indian woman. "I owe you so much. Saying thank you seems rather inadequate."

Morning Star blushed. "No thank me. My job to heal."

"Good night, dear friend. Ned will be waiting for you." Maggie waved her out of the room and watched her descend the staircase before she returned to Sam's bedside, lowered herself into the chair Morning Star vacated, and wept.

"I heard you crying, sweetheart. Is everything all right in here?" asked Luke, massaging Maggie's shoulders.

"These are happy tears." Maggie looked up at Luke through a shimmering veil. "I cannot begin to thank Morning Star for her help today."

"Poor Doc Benjamin was pulling his hair out." Luke laughed. "It's amusing now, but at the time I could have throttled him. He didn't have the foggiest notion what was ailing our children."

"Did you hear him talking to Agnes, before he left for town?" Maggie tilted her head.

"No, I didn't. What did he say?" Luke's interest appeared piqued.

"He told Agnes that medical school never provided instruction on the proper protocol for assisting an Indian medicine woman." Maggie couldn't contain her laughter. "Benjamin assured Agnes his colleagues back East would receive an interesting letter in a week or two."

"Once Doc Fitzgerald hears about this, Doctor Benjamin Johnson will wish he'd never heard of Spirit Creek." Luke grinned. "The poor fellow will never hear the end of it."

"Doc Fitzgerald will rib him good-naturedly for a little while. Is Patti sleeping soundly?" asked Maggie, attempting to stifle a yawn.

"Yes, and Sam is sleeping just as soundly." Luke lifted her out of the chair and carried her from the room before setting her down on her feet. "Let's get some sleep as well. These children will be fine and Agnes is sleeping down the hall from them. It'll take more than a few poisonous berries to do in a Carlyle."

Maggie swatted his arm. "Don't ever mention poisonous berries in my presence again. These children are going to be the death of me."

"The joys of parenthood…" Luke opened their bedroom door and stepped aside allowing his wife to enter. "I recall on our wedding day telling you Sam and Patti were getting along famously, and they'd be getting into trouble together in no time. Remember the mud pies?"

Maggie rested her hand on her middle and turned around, meeting his eyes. "And we have another one on the way."

"Lord, give me strength." Luke smiled and shook his head.

The exhausted couple quickly prepared for bed, and then Luke extinguished the lamp.

"Good night, Maggie." Luke whispered in the darkness from the other side of the bed.

"Good night, Luke." She yearned to fall asleep engulfed in the safety and comfort of his strong warm arms. Instead, she snuggled under the covers on her own side of the bed and listened to her husband's slow even breathing. In a minute, he sounded asleep.

Maggie could never thank him enough for everything he'd done for her and Sam and the unborn baby. Luke's support today during their harrowing ordeal meant the world to her. She would never have survived it without him. In her opinion, there wasn't a man alive who provided better for his family, emotionally and financially.

But Luke didn't love her, she reminded herself. Their

marriage remained a business agreement whereby he provided a roof and a bed for her and Sam, and she provided a mother for his children. A tidy arrangement, absent of complicated emotions.

A tear slid down her cheek. Every day she found something new she admired about Luke, and her conflicted emotions rose in her mind like a serpent's ugly head. Raw emotions, new emotions, and not just rampant hormonal upheavals because of the baby, threatened her peace of mind.

Was she falling in love with Luke?

No, she admitted, she already loved him dearly!

How on earth had this happened? A sob escaped her lips, and she buried her face in the pillow to prevent waking Luke.

Clearly, Luke's sole priority centered upon providing a secure home for her and their family. Even sharing the same room, the same bed, he'd never shown any interest in her as a woman, as a wife. They'd shared a few chaste kisses for the children's benefit. In fact, she recalled catching Luke staring at Catherine's photograph in the parlor which only proved her suspicions. Luke was still in love with his first wife.

Maggie wasn't naïve; all men, including her husband, had needs. Did he frequent Darby's establishment or one of the other saloons to satisfy his urges? With several willing women employed in the town's saloons and brothels, Luke really didn't need her. And he would never love her.

But Luke's presence in their bed every night almost drove her to distraction. Lately, her body yearned for his touch, her mind filled with images of making love with Luke, and her heartbeat raced with anticipation. At this very moment, her body warmed with thoughts of her handsome husband. But she realized she longed for something that would never happen.

For her own sanity, she'd just have to fall out of love with Luke Carlyle.

Chapter 16

Wednesday, July 31, 1889

Agnes carried out her duties with limited instruction, instinctively determining what needed doing. Maggie enjoyed the personable young lady's company immensely, and they'd discovered a shared love of gardening. Today, they were weeding the vegetable garden.

"Let's take a break and enjoy a cup of tea." Maggie stretched her back. She'd regained her strength with the morning sickness under control, but she didn't want to overdo it.

Agnes straightened and set the hoe aside. "Isn't that the Waverly buggy coming up the drive?"

Maggie shaded her eyes. "Elizabeth's just in time for tea."

The ladies strolled toward the main house, waving as their visitor's buggy drew near. "Hello," called Maggie.

Mike scrambled across the yard from the horse barn and helped their visitor climb down from her seat. Elizabeth straightened her skirts.

"What brings you out our way?" asked Maggie, approaching. And then she gasped. Elizabeth's black dress and red, puffy eyes told the story.

"What's wrong, Elizabeth?" Maggie's heart stopped, and she reached for her friend's hand. "Don't tell me something has happened to Ronald?"

"No, Maggie, it isn't Ronald." Elizabeth sniffled into her handkerchief. "I don't know how to tell you this, dear. You two were exceptional friends."

"If not Ronald…who?"

"It's Doc Fitzgerald, Maggie. Doc Fitzgerald is dead."

Maggie's world tilted for a moment, and then slowly righted itself again. Surely she hadn't heard correctly. "I spoke with him in town a couple of days ago. He was teasing me and laughing and…" It couldn't be true. But Elizabeth would never joke about something so serious.

"I had to come and tell you myself. Doc loved you like a daughter." Elizabeth wrapped Maggie in her arms. "I'm so sorry, dear."

"I can't believe it." Maggie shook her head, her arms dangling at her sides.

"The whole town is in shock." Elizabeth lifted Maggie's chin, meeting her eyes. "Doc passed during the night. Doc Benjamin arrived at the store early this morning with the news."

"Surely, there's been a mistake. It can't be true," whispered Maggie, and then her eyelids fluttered. Mike caught her as she fainted and laid her gently on the strip of green lawn beside the curved drive.

"Oh, my. Oh, goodness. I should have foreseen this. Mike, please fetch Mr. Carlyle." Elizabeth fanned herself with her handkerchief.

"Mr. Carlyle's in the horse barn, ma'am." Mike headed toward the barn on the run.

"Agnes, help me revive Maggie." Elizabeth bent down and patted Maggie's cheek. "Can you hear me, dear?"

Maggie groaned but didn't open her eyes. She thought she heard voices in the distance and then everything went black again.

* * *

"What happened, Elizabeth?" called Luke, tearing across the yard with Mike at his side. "Is it the baby?"

"Doc Fitzgerald passed away last night, Luke, and the news of his death proved too much for Maggie's mind to handle." Elizabeth burst into tears.

Mike, head into town and fetch Doc Benjamin," requested Luke.

"Will do, sir!" Mike raced back to the horse barn.

Luke wrapped Maggie's arm around his neck and lifted her into his arms like she weighed no more than a feather. "Open the front door, Agnes," he called over his shoulder as he strode toward the house. "I'll take her upstairs to her bed."

"Do we have smelling salts somewhere in the house, sir?" asked the mother's helper, running ahead and flinging the door wide open.

"I have no idea." Luke carried his wife up the long staircase and through their bedroom doors. Her eyes fluttered when he gently laid her on their bed. "Open your eyes, Maggie," he commanded.

She rolled her head from side to side and muttered unintelligibly.

"Maggie, can you hear me?" Luke patted her cheeks.

Suddenly, her eyes popped open. "What…what happened?" She attempted to sit, but Luke gently pushed her back against the pillow.

"You fainted." He brushed her hair out of her face and searched her eyes. "How do you feel? Do you hurt anywhere?"

"I don't think so." Maggie shook her head and her hand moved to her middle.

Luke guessed by now she'd be in her fourth month and the bump there was now evident. If anything happened to her or the baby… No, he couldn't even think it. "Elizabeth brought bad news from town," offered Luke, encouraging her to remember why she'd fainted. He settled himself on the bed beside her.

Maggie met Luke's eyes, and she grasped his shirt with her hand. Her eyes filled with tears as she spoke, "Elizabeth told me Doc Fitzgerald was dead. That can't be right. He joked with me and promised to come for Sunday supper. Luke, please tell me someone made a mistake."

Luke grasped her hands. "Elizabeth wouldn't drive all the way out here if she wasn't certain."

"Doc's dead? He's truly gone?" whispered Maggie.

Luke watched as her world shattered. She buried her face in his worn work shirt and clung to him, sobbing uncontrollably. He wrapped her in his arms offering comfort. After several minutes, her tears subsided, and he untangled his arms from her while insisting she remain in bed.

* * *

Agnes arrived to sit with Maggie, a cup and saucer in her hands. Maggie accepted a sip of tea—it tasted like dishwater—and then she buried her head in the pillow. For another hour she wept under the watchful eye of the mother's helper. Exhausted, Maggie finally fell into a fitful sleep.

She dreamt of visiting Doc in his office. The old fellow sat in the familiar black leather-upholstered chair with his thin, wrinkled hands resting one atop the other upon his ample middle. His rich baritone voice reverberated around the room as he threw back his head and laughed at something she said. Doc reached for her hand…and she woke.

For a moment, she gazed around the moonlit bedroom, searching for her old friend. He'd been here with her a moment ago. And then she remembered.

Doc Benjamin entered the bedroom, his black doctoring bag in his hand. "How are you doing?" he asked, compassion evident in his voice.

"I can't believe he's gone," she whispered. A fresh batch of tears soaked her pillow while her heart silently broke.

Thursday, August 1, 1889

Doc's passing had sent Maggie tumbling into a deep, black abyss, and only Luke's unwavering care and concern brought her back. She still couldn't believe Doc was dead. William had been snatched from her life, senselessly killed in a second by a bullet. Again without warning, Doc slipped away. The dear old gentleman had become a member of the family. How would she bear saying goodbye?

She dragged herself back to reality, stared into the vanity mirror. With Agnes's help, she'd donned a black cotton dress, brushed her long curls, and swept her hair into a bun.

Tears welled in her eyes as Agnes slid her pearl-encrusted combs into place.

"I can't remember how many times Doc complimented me on how perfect these combs looked in my hair," she told Agnes.

"He was right, Mrs. Carlyle." Agnes wrapped a shawl around her shoulders.

Luke strode into the bedroom. "Are you certain you're up for this?"

"I'm coming with you," stated Maggie decisively, as Agnes left the room.

Maggie quickly brushed her tears away, hoping Luke wouldn't notice. What horrible sin had she committed to deserve losing so many of the people she loved? First, her parents, then William, and now Doc?

Her thoughts drifted to the many happy hours she had wasted away with Doc: discussing books and arguing philosophies and sharing dreams. The gentle old soul served as her honorary grandfather, although he would never divulge his age. She'd soaked up his wisdom like a thirsty desert plant sucking up the first hint of rainfall. Doc's intelligent conversations replaced the hours of discussions, and often arguments, she'd enjoyed with her father before moving out West.

"You're too pale for my liking."

Luke's words brought her back to the present. "The burial…just the thought of Doc in the ground…." Maggie met Luke's eyes.

"Stay home, go back to bed." Luke crossed the room and enveloped her in his arms.

She shook her head. "I dreaded William's burial, feeling certain I wouldn't survive it, but Doc never left my side. When he brought Sam into the world, I shook with fright, completely ignorant of what childbirth involved, but Doc reassured me, comforted me, and guided me through it. Such a kind soul. Nothing will prevent me from paying my respects."

"Doc would understand if you stayed home for the baby's sake." Luke held her at arm's length, searched her eyes.

"No, I'm going. I feel so guilty. I should have realized…" Maggie shook her head.

"Nobody knew he was ailing, and I suspect Doc wanted it that way." Luke took her hands in his. "You may come with me, but at the first sign of trouble I'm bringing you home. Agreed?"

She nodded.

Luke wrapped her shawl tighter around her shoulders.

"You're going to miss him dearly, but remember, no one seemed happier with his lot in life than Doc."

"I foolishly believed he would live forever," whispered Maggie, reaching for a fresh handkerchief and sticking it in her reticule. "Doc deserves more than my tears as a respectful goodbye. I need to be there at his graveside."

"Well, let's go then. Mike's waiting with the carriage." Luke led her from their bedroom.

* * *

A few minutes before ten o'clock, the Carlyle family arrived at the graveyard situated beside the Spirit Creek Church. Maggie and Sam spent a minute at William's gravesite.

"The flowers look nice, Mama," whispered Sam.

"Thank you, muffin." Maggie smiled at her son. "I imagine Papa likes them."

Sam looked up and met her eyes. "Does Papa know I'm living at the ranch now? Does he know I have a new papa?"

"I'm sure he does. And I know he's happy that you're safe and that you have a new family who loves you."

Sam nodded his head and whispered, "Bye, Papa."

Maggie fought back tears hearing the evidence that her son's heart was healing. He'd be fine surrounded by family and friends and the unconditional love they'd provide. She guided Sam toward Luke and the others standing beside Doc's simple pine coffin. Even in death, Doc hadn't wanted anything ostentatious.

Maggie fought back tears, awaiting the start of the ceremony while Luke watched her closely. "Stop worrying about me." She stood tall and patted her husband's arm to assure him she would hold up under the day's stress.

The mourners mingled in small groups, anticipating Reverend Gerald's arrival. A few folks approached Maggie and whispered their condolences which she acknowledged with a weak smile. If she spoke she feared she would burst into tears and wouldn't be able to stop. Her husband tightened his hold on her hand and thanked them for their kind words on her behalf. He instinctively knew she needed his support and he offered it without hesitation.

Reverend Gerald arrived promptly at ten o'clock. He

welcomed everyone and then began the ceremony with anecdotes about Doc's life. Everyone in attendance smiled at the wonderful memories of such a special man.

"Doc enjoyed a prank," the reverend spoke in summation. "But he doctored every patient with superior knowledge and unprecedented affection."

When the half dozen gentlemen lowered the coffin into the ground, most folks in attendance shed a tear. After the burial, Reverend Gerald requested everyone's attention.

"Friends, Sarah Grayson would like to say a few words."

Sarah stood beside the reverend, dwarfed by his six foot six inch height. She took a deep breath. "Most of you remember that Doc and my late husband were the best of friends and lifelong fishing buddies. The two of them shared many memorable times together. They regaled the entire town with tales of their angling prowess. And some of those stories were actually true."

Sarah paused until the ripple of laughter faded, and then she smiled as a tear slid down her cheek. "If there's a fishing hole in heaven, Graham will be waiting beside it for Doc."

"I'm certain there is, Sarah." Reverend Gerald rested his hand on her shoulder.

"Everyone is invited to my home for the noon meal in Doc's memory." Sarah fought to control her emotions. "Friends and neighbors, your presence is not only requested, it is expected," added Sarah, wiping away another tear.

"Thank you for opening your heart and your home today." The reverend patted her hand.

Minutes later, somber groups of mourners clustered around Sarah's back garden. Even the children respected the solemnity of the occasion and stood quietly beside their parents. Someone announced dinner and a serving line formed along both sides of a massive rectangular table laden with an assortment of sandwiches, pickles, cheeses, breads and preserves. Teenage girls poured cups of coffee, tea and milk for the mourners. The guests congregated in groups at a dozen large tables scattered around the garden, to devour the delicious meal.

"You look so sad, Maggie," observed Luke, popping a piece of cheese into his mouth.

"I was remembering when many of the folks here today were

gathered around these same tables a few weeks ago, happily celebrating our wedding." Maggie sighed. "And now, here we are…"

"Doc wouldn't want you to feel so glum," suggested Luke, reaching over and squeezing her hand.

"I know you're right. But it's just so difficult…"

Sarah's housekeeper and two hired girls served slices of cake and fruit pie for dessert. Afterward, the hired ladies collected the dishes for the washing up while the mourners conversed in small groups and sipped hot tea or coffee.

"Could I please have your attention for a moment?" Doctor Benjamin Johnson wended his way around the tables, and then stood beside his wife, Pearl. All conversation ceased while everyone eagerly awaited the young man's speech.

"Thank you." Doc Benjamin cleared his throat. "As most of you know, I'm the new doctor in town, and I've only known Doc Fitzgerald for a short time."

Sarah Grayson rose from her chair, a few feet away from him. "We're so pleased that you and your wife moved to Spirit Creek, Doctor Johnson. We're fortunate you're here."

"Thank you, Mrs. Grayson, but I'm not here by coincidence. In truth, when I received Doc Fitzgerald's letter extending the invitation to join his practice in Spirit Creek, I foolishly believed my wife and I would decide whether or not to accept his offer. I now realize Doc considered the whole idea a foregone conclusion."

Everyone chuckled.

"Doc possessed a persuasive nature," added a woman seated close by.

"In Doc's second letter, which he insisted I share with nobody, including my wife, the good doctor informed me his days on this earth were numbered. He'd contracted consumption."

Audible gasps erupted from several mourners.

"He wrote that for many years he'd doctored the people of this community, and contentedly so. He considered everyone his family. The possibility of dying without leaving someone to carry on the medical care of so many people he loved was unthinkable. My years of practicing medicine and my wife's experience as a trained nurse totally suited Doc's purposes." Doc Benjamin paused in this speech while his audience absorbed his words.

"Thus, we moved to Spirit Creek, and Pearl was delighted to

return home. Words fail me in describing the hug I received from her dear mother the day we stepped off the train in Miles City. My ribs still feel a little sore." Doc Benjamin smiled at his mother-in-law, Florence Jones, who blushed profusely but beamed with pride. "Everything worked out for the best," added Doc.

"Yes, it did," whispered Pearl, patting her husband's arm.

"Doc Fitzgerald insisted I tell no one about his illness." Doc Benjamin met Maggie's eyes. "Absolutely no one."

Maggie nodded and mouthed, "I understand."

"My wife and I shared Doc's home, and even Pearl didn't learn how seriously ill he was until a few days ago. I attended him until the very end, and he went quickly and at peace. His last words to me were, *I can accept my final rest knowing you will care for my patients.*" Doc Johnson fought to control his emotions.

Tears streamed down the cheeks of the ladies in attendance. Several older gentlemen, Doc's dearest friends, dabbed at a few tears of their own.

Doctor Johnson pulled an envelope out of his jacket pocket. "Doc Fitzgerald entrusted me with this letter, with strict instructions that I read it at his burial and not before." Doc Johnson tore open the sealed envelope and extracted the two sheets of paper within.

Maggie recognized Doc's personal stationery. Everything from a personal note at Christmas to an IOU after an evening of poker had been written on that special linen paper.

Doctor Johnson began reading…

Dear friends:

If you are listening to my young colleague read this letter, I have passed on to my reward, hopefully, heavenward and not the alternative.

I've enjoyed a long and rewarding life serving as your doctor, and I've loved every minute of it. Do not feel sad today; I have no regrets. Remember me fondly, but do not mourn my demise.

When I first hung out my shingle in your fine town, you welcomed me with open arms. I consider all of you family. My failing health troubled me; I couldn't leave you good folks without a doctor. Thus, I selfishly dragged Doc Johnson and his lovely wife to Spirit Creek. Benjamin is an excellent doctor and Pearl is a compassionate nurse, and I'm leaving you in very capable hands.

Doctor Johnson glanced up from the letter and discovered several heads nodding in agreement. "Thank you for your kind acceptance of Pearl and me. We appreciate your warm welcome to the community." Doctor Johnson returned to the letter, one finger scanning the page, searching for where he stopped reading.

"Good Lord, I can't believe this!" Doc Johnson's head whipped up and his eyes met innumerable startled expressions. "I apologize for the outburst, but you'll understand when I continue reading Doc's letter. Keep in mind, I'm reading its contents for the first time." Doc Johnson met his wife's eyes, smiled and then continued reading…

Now that I have enticed the Johnsons to our small community, I intend to ensure they remain here. As you know, I've never married and I'm without heirs. Therefore, all of you present today are witness to my decision. Benjamin Johnson, talented physician and gentleman of unquestionable honesty and integrity, I hereby bequeath to you my lovely home and all of its furnishings. As well, I bequeath to you my entire medical practice: the medical equipment, the medicinal stock, all of my books and texts, and my horse and carriage. In exchange for this act of generosity (some would call it bribery, me included) it is my sincerest wish that you and your lovely wife will remain in Spirit Creek.

It's a wholesome community, an ideal place to raise a family, and I truly hope, Benjamin, that you and Pearl will stay and raise a happy and healthy family here.

I've finalized all the legal arrangements with my barrister in Miles City. A copy of this letter is in his possession, and he'll forward the titles and other papers to you in the near future. Good luck, Benjamin, and thank you for putting my mind at ease.

Doctor Johnson brushed a tear away with his hand. His wife rested her head on his arm, while he finished…

Good citizens of Spirit Creek, I'll end this letter by saying I've shared your joys and your sorrows over the years. I've helped celebrate your successes and sympathized with your failures. I've assisted with your births and attended at the loss of your loved ones.

I'm confident Doctor Johnson is up for the challenge. He certainly made the passing of this old fellow quite bearable, and I thank him for that.

Think fondly of me from time to time, and I wish you all a long and healthy life.

Yours very sincerely,
Doctor James E. Fitzgerald

A period of silence followed while Doc Benjamin carefully folded the sheets of paper and slid them back inside the envelope. He hugged his wife and took a deep breath.

"Pearl and I have fallen in love with your community. Unaware of Doc Fitzgerald's generous gift, we'd already decided to make Spirit Creek our home. I would be honored to serve as your doctor for many years to come."

"Doc chose his successor wisely." Randy Barker strode across the yard and shook Doc's hand. "As mayor of Spirit Creek, allow me to formally welcome you and Pearl on behalf of the entire community." His words generated thunderous applause from everyone in attendance.

"I'll second that," said Luke, standing.

Sarah Grayson clasped the young doctor's hands. "Allow me to add my two cents, gentlemen. Doc Fitzgerald spoke highly of you, Benjamin, and I know you'll serve our community as proudly as your predecessor did."

"Thank you, everyone." Doc Benjamin smiled.

Those in attendance finished their tea and conversations in small informal groups. Maggie stood alone with Pearl and whispered in her ear. "Doc was like a grandfather to me. I just can't believe he's gone. I'd even hoped he'd bring this new baby into the world."

"Don't be concerned. My husband has attended at the birth of more babies than I can count," whispered Pearl, patting Maggie's hand.

Luke appeared at Maggie's side and wrapped a protective arm around her shoulders. "We should be heading home. This day has been very tiring for you."

"Perhaps we should be going." She experienced a moment of light-headedness as she spoke, but she refused to acknowledge it.

And she certainly wouldn't worry her over-protective husband about it.

* * *

Luke and Maggie walked arm in arm across the yard toward Doc Benjamin and Sarah while Pearl followed close behind them. Luke turned his attention from Maggie for a moment. "Thank you for opening your home to the community on this special day, Sarah. Graham and Doc were such good friends, your lovely garden seemed the perfect place to say goodbye."

"Luke, before you leave, there's something I forgot to mention," said Doc Benjamin. Pearl slipped her arms around his waist and he smiled at her. "Doc Fitzgerald entrusted me with a dozen or more journals he wrote, recording his adventures as a frontier town doctor. I've been reading the humorous and heartfelt stories within those pages. Do you suppose the old fellow would mind if I made inquiries, arranged to have the journals published as a book?"

"Doc would be honored, and Maggie and I would love to read the journals. We must be getting home, however. We'll discuss this further on Sunday after church." Luke guided his wife toward the carriage, but he realized something was wrong. Maggie wavered on her feet as if she'd sampled Darby's whiskey again. Her eyes fluttered and she groaned. When she fainted, he caught her in his arms.

Luke's heartbeat raced and perspiration formed on his brow. He mentally kicked himself for allowing Maggie to attend the funeral. The strain had proven too much for her, and her fainting spell was his fault.

Doc Benjamin and Pearl raced to Luke's side. The doctor raised one of Maggie's eyelids and Pearl grasped her wrist, checking her pulse while Luke held her in his arms.

"Carry Maggie up to one of the spare rooms. Doctor Benjamin, fetch your bag." Sarah shooed the young man into action.

Doc Benjamin raced to his carriage and grabbed his black doctor's bag.

"Here, let me help you, Luke." Pearl raced ahead to open the massive front door of the mansion Sarah had shared with Graham until he passed away some years ago, leaving her ensconced in their elegant home.

Luke climbed the long winding staircase, carrying an unconscious Maggie.

Sarah and Pearl settled Maggie onto the double bed in a spare room decorated in warm shades of pink. Sarah stood back and clasped Luke's hand in hers as Doc Benjamin's footfalls thundered up the stairs and he rushed to Maggie's side. A few seconds later, Pearl shooed Sarah and Luke out of the room, closing the door behind them.

"She'll be fine, Sarah. You'll see. She's strong." Luke paced the hallway floor outside the bedroom, awaiting news while Doc Benjamin and Pearl examined his wife.

"Of course, she'll be fine, Luke. She just fainted. Try not to worry." Sarah led a reluctant Luke down the winding staircase and out into the late afternoon sunlight.

Luke sent Ned home with Agnes and the children, assuring everyone he'd send word about Maggie's condition as soon as he learned something. At the same time, Sarah exchanged goodbyes with her remaining guests.

"I've got to get back inside, Sarah," croaked Luke, dragging his hand through his hair.

"Go on ahead. Almost everyone has left and the hired maids are busy cleaning up." Sarah waved Luke toward the house. "I'm right behind you."

Luke returned to his vigil outside Maggie's door. He paced for several minutes and then checked his pocket watch. Twenty minutes had passed since his wife fainted, but it seemed like hours. He glared at the door that separated him from his wife, silently willing it to open.

What was going on in there?

A minute later, Sarah struggled up the stairs. Her slow progress hinted that the day had been stressful and tiring for her as well. "Has Doc come out yet?"

Luke shook his head. "No, I'm concerned I'll wear a hole in your rug."

"I'll wear it out with you." Sarah patted his hand, and then lowered herself onto a nearby chair while Luke resumed his pacing.

"Sarah, Maggie is…she's…she's with child," confessed Luke. "William's child."

"I suspected as much." Sarah smiled. "You're a good man, Luke, for helping Maggie start a new life. No pun intended."

"We've formed a family, Maggie and me and the children. I'll raise her children as my own."

"I know you will. You're every bit the man your father was."

As the minutes ticked by on the hallway clock, Luke and Sarah became increasingly concerned. They silently exchanged looks, knowing each was thinking what neither of them dared to voice aloud. *Could she lose the baby?*

Finally, Doc slipped out of the bedroom.

"Let's go downstairs for a private conversation. Pearl will stay with Maggie while I'm away." One hand on the banister, Doc Johnson trotted down the winding staircase, with Luke and Sarah on his heels.

"Luke, show Benjamin into the library." Sarah pointed the way, excused herself, and headed toward the kitchen.

Luke followed Doc into the room, closed the door, and demanded, "How's Maggie doing? I want to know everything."

"Maggie came to, and she's feeling rather foolish for fainting in front of everyone." Doc Benjamin spoke calmly, without a hint of emotion, and Luke decided he'd overreacted. Perhaps the situation wasn't as dire as he'd imagined.

"Then she's going to be all right?" Luke thrust his hands into his pockets. "Just needs to return home and get a few days' rest?"

Sarah knocked, entered the library, and set a tea tray on the side table. She glanced in Luke's direction. "Just fill me in later," she suggested and slipped out of the room again.

Doc Benjamin crossed the room to the side table and helped himself to a cup of tea. "After a thorough examination, I've discovered Maggie is spotting, bleeding but not seriously."

Luke swallowed hard.

"There's no need to panic at this point. But Maggie's mind and body endured a great deal of stress today. Doc spoke so fondly of Maggie when I first moved here, I assumed she was his daughter. Pearl set me straight." Doc toasted Luke with his glass.

"Doc and Maggie became extremely close over the years. But what do you mean by 'no need to panic at this point'? At what point do I panic? I'm damned close to it right now." Luke started pacing, slowly losing the battle to remain calm.

"I'm concerned the bleeding might worsen. The fainting and the spotting could indicate Maggie's body simply reacted to today's stress. Or it could indicate more serious things are to come." Benjamin stared out the library window, not meeting Luke's eyes.

"What do you mean?" Luke's heart pounded, but he forced himself to voice the question his mind begged to avoid. "Will Maggie lose the baby?" he whispered.

"It wasn't my intention to imply that was a *probability*. But miscarriage is always a *possibility*. Let's hope it doesn't happen." Benjamin set his cup and saucer on the side table.

Luke met Doc's eyes. "Maggie believes this baby is a final gift from her late husband. If Maggie loses the baby…it will just kill her."

"There's no reason to believe a miscarriage will happen." Doc Benjamin removed a handkerchief from his breast pocket, wiped his brow, and thrust the small piece of cloth back into his pocket.

Pearl rushed into the room. "Benjamin, come quickly."

Before Luke could spit out a question, Benjamin and Pearl rushed out of the library and charged upstairs. Alone in the library, Luke paced the floor with a dozen thoughts racing through his mind.

And none of them good.

Chapter 17

Sarah knocked on the library door, bringing Luke back from his frightening thoughts. Maggie's best friend stood beside their hostess.

"Has there been any word?" asked Elizabeth, wringing her hands.

"Not recently. Thank you for coming." Luke sighed, and Elizabeth strode across the room and embraced him. He thought his ribs would crack, but her hug helped to eradicate his fears. Having Sarah and Elizabeth at his side convinced him all would be fine. A dozen frightening scenarios had raced roughshod through his mind, but he wouldn't allow himself to accept any of them as an actual possibility.

"I'm so worried about Maggie," admitted Elizabeth.

"She experienced a bit of difficulty, but according to Doc Benjamin there's nothing to panic about." Luke choked on the words.

"If Maggie's condition is nothing to panic about, Luke, I'd hate to see your face when you actually get to panicking," scolded Sarah, swatting his arm.

"Now tell us the truth. All of it." Elizabeth crossed her arms and glared at him.

"Maggie is…spotting." Luke felt himself blush clear to his hairline, but he'd gotten the word out in the ladies' presence. "Doc assured me her situation wasn't serious. At least, not yet."

Elizabeth's hands visibly shook and she slumped onto the chintz-covered sofa. "Doc Benjamin believes her condition could worsen?"

"Possibility." Luke blinked back the tears that threatened to embarrass him. "But not a certainty."

"I don't like the sound of this, not one bit," whispered Elizabeth.

Luke wondered if she meant to voice her concern aloud. Ever since he talked to Doc, the same thought plagued him. No, he decided, Maggie simply couldn't lose that baby.

"Luke Carlyle, sit down and try to relax." Sarah led him by the hand. "You're making me nervous with all this pacing."

Luke stumbled across the floor and flopped down on the sofa opposite Elizabeth. He checked his pocket watch and muttered, "Doc stampeded out of here more than an hour ago. I don't mind admitting I'm worried."

"Of course you are, dear." Sarah settled beside him.

"I don't know when Doc will let me see her." Luke rested his elbows on his knees, cradled his chin on his fisted hands, and stared at his boots.

"I don't care how long it takes, we'll wait together." Elizabeth's voice caught. Luke raised his head and met her eyes. She blinked back tears while her fingers played with an embroidered handkerchief.

"I'm going to brew some hot tea. And you need something in your belly, young man." Sarah patted Luke's knee and stood.

"I'll help you, Sarah," added Elizabeth. "Keeping busy will help."

The ladies bustled out the door, leaving Luke to worry in private.

Another hour passed while Luke and Sarah sat across from each other on the matching sofas and nibbled on sandwiches. Elizabeth slouched in an upholstered side chair, sipping tea. A small china plate held a half-eaten cookie, balanced on her lap. Her lips moved silently in prayer.

Doc appeared in the library doorway, startling everyone from their private thoughts. He rubbed his eyes with an index finger and thumb, looking extremely tired. "Evening, folks," he said, shoulders slumped.

"How is she, Doc?" Luke leapt to his feet.

Doc sighed and met Luke's eyes. "The bleeding's gotten

worse."

Elizabeth gasped.

"How bad is it?" demanded Sarah.

"I'm still hoping for the best. Pearl and I are trying everything we can think of to stop the bleeding." Doc rested his hand on Elizabeth's shoulder.

"When can I see her?" asked Elizabeth, standing.

"Maggie must remain calm." Doc grasped Elizabeth's hands. "I'd prefer she wasn't upset by visitors."

"You mean upset by the likes of me, and you're right." Elizabeth grimaced at the truth. "I'd be blubbering the whole time I was with her."

"Nothing is more important than that baby. We can wait until later to see her." Sarah stood and headed for the side table. She poured a cup of tea and placed a beef sandwich and oatmeal cookie on a china plate.

The doctor straightened his back and stretched, pulling back each shoulder in turn, and then slumped into a comfortable chair. Sarah passed the plate and cup of tea to Benjamin.

"Thank you, Mrs. Grayson."

"I'll go home for now, Sarah." Elizabeth moved toward the door. "Goodnight, gentlemen. Someone please send for me if there's any change."

"We will. I promise." Sarah patted Elizabeth's arm. "I'll see you out." Together, they shuffled out of the library. A few seconds later, Luke heard the front door close.

Doc balanced the small china plate on his lap, bit into the sandwich, chewed quickly, and swallowed. "I won't leave my patient for long. Mind you, your wife is in excellent hands when under Pearl's care."

"Doc, please tell me everything. Is there something you didn't share in front of the ladies?" Luke slid forward on the sofa, balancing on the edge. He nervously tapped his finger on the saucer, rattling the teacup.

"I've told you everything." Doc munched on his sandwich and washed it down with a sip of tea.

How could Doc remain so calm when anything might happen? Did the fellow truly understand the importance of a happy ending here? Luke barely stopped himself from shaking the man and forcing him to show some emotion. "You're certain there's nothing I can do?" Luke hadn't felt this helpless since the night Catherine passed away.

"I've doctored hundreds of women with bouts of bleeding. Most of my patients complete the rest of their term without any further problems. Of course, in a few cases I wasn't able to stop the bleeding, and then…an unfortunate ending." Doc strode across the room and reached for another sandwich. "But don't fret, Luke. At present, I don't foresee anything like that being the case here."

"But the bleeding worsened." Luke gritted his teeth. If this fellow wasn't telling him the truth, he'd beat it out of him. And then he grimaced, realizing fear was messing with his mind. He only used his fists on a man that deserved it. Doc Benjamin had no reason to lie.

"The bleeding doesn't mean a miscarriage is a certainty. I'm still hopeful the situation is not serious." Doc's hand brushed some cookie crumbs caught in his five o'clock shadow.

"Two years ago, my first wife fell ill with influenza. I told myself it wasn't serious." Luke glared at the doctor.

Doc Benjamin paled and cleared his throat. "I'm aware of your first wife's untimely passing, but this situation is entirely different. There's no illness, no fever involved. Maggie is young and strong. If she rests and remains calm, there's every reason to believe the bleeding will stop."

Sarah appeared in the doorway. "Gentlemen, my housekeeper prepared a room at the end of the hallway for you, Luke, and the room next to Maggie's for you and Pearl, Doc. I'll check that she remembered the towels." Sarah closed the library's double doors behind her.

For several minutes, Doc and Luke finished their tea in silence. Finally, the physician rose to his feet and placed his dishes on the side table. "I'll send Pearl down for a sandwich and a cup of tea while I check on our patient again." Benjamin snuck another cookie off the plate.

"Thank you, Doc. I'm confident you're doing everything possible for Maggie, and I appreciate it." Luke shook the doctor's hand.

"Get some sleep, Luke. I'll fetch you the second anything changes." Doc strode out of the library, passing Sarah in the doorway. "Good night, Mrs. Grayson," he called.

"Good night, Benjamin. There's fresh tea here for Pearl." Sarah set the rose-patterned china teapot on the side table, and then turned to Luke. Her freshly-brushed silver hair hung loose, and a flowered nightdress peeked out from under her lavender silk wrapper with matching slippers.

"Come with me, young man," she ordered, and Luke followed her upstairs.

"Thank you for your kindness toward Maggie and me." Luke attempted a smile.

"No need for thanks, Luke. I'll say a prayer for the baby." Sarah patted his arm.

"You're a very kind-hearted woman. Good night, my dear friend."

"Good night, Luke," whispered Sarah, heading down the hallway toward her own bedroom and closing the door behind her.

Luke entered the spacious guest room decorated in muted blues and grays. Sturdy curtains covered the open window and fluttered slightly in the cool night breeze. A lit lamp sat atop a small bedside table on the other side of the room.

He closed the door, crossed the floor, and perched on the edge of the bed to remove his boots. Standing, he unbuttoned his shirt and slipped out of his pants and tossed them onto the rocking chair in the corner of the room. Luke extinguished the lamp, crawled onto the bed, and tossed the quilt over himself. He punched the pillow beneath his head and then rolled onto his back.

For hours, he listened to his own breathing and counted the hallway clock's chimes.

* * *

"Luke. Luke." Someone gently nudged his shoulder, and his eyes flew open as he bolted upright in the bed. Sunshine streamed through the window blinding him for a moment.

"What is it, Doc? Is something wrong with Maggie?" Luke fought with the tangled quilt trapping his body. Freeing himself, he swung his legs over the side of the bed.

"Your wife asked to see you." Doc Benjamin turned and strode out of the room.

Luke pulled on his pants and struggled into his boots. He tugged his arms through his shirt sleeves as he stumbled out the bedroom door. Having counted chimes until he'd fallen asleep, one glance at the hallway clock told him he'd slept for four hours. He buttoned his shirt as he raced down the hallway to Maggie's room, and then he stopped outside the closed door.

He rested his head against the wooden frame, one hand grasping the doorknob. What awaited him inside? Why had Maggie finally asked for him? Was it bad news? Had Doc failed to save the baby?

Luke knocked softly on the door, paused another moment or two, and then slipped inside the room. Maggie rolled over in the bed, turning to face him. He noticed the crazy angle of the bed, higher on the bottom end, and then he closed the door and slowly crossed the floor.

He couldn't read her expression. Was she holding herself together for his benefit? His heart pounded so hard in his chest he was afraid it might pop out, and he felt certain Maggie could hear it beating.

"Come here." Maggie patted the side of the bed. "Doc and Pearl took turns sitting with me all night. They're having breakfast in the kitchen."

Luke lowered himself onto the bed, yearning to hug her until she begged him to stop. Her pale face and red-rimmed eyes told him she'd been crying. She'd just admitted she'd been up all night with one or the other of the Johnsons. Why hadn't she slept? He couldn't bring himself to speak aloud the question that he was itching to ask.

"There's still a lot of cramping and the bleeding hasn't stopped," whispered Maggie.

Luke blew out his breath. There was still hope. But his wife appeared ready to burst into tears. He reached for her hand. "That's not good. But we must think only positive thoughts. Nothing's going to happen to this baby."

"I tried to sleep, but I was so afraid." Maggie's eyes glistened.

"Doc told me not to worry." Luke searched her eyes. Had her condition worsened during the night? Why didn't Doc wake him, warn him? Was a miscarriage inevitable? His poor Maggie would never survive it. "Could you still lose the baby? Is that possible?"

"I don't know. Doc insisted that sleep would be the best

thing for me, but I couldn't bring myself to tell him the truth."

"What truth?"

"I didn't dare fall asleep, because I was worried that if I slept…I'd wake up and the baby would be gone," whispered Maggie, her eyes revealing just how terrified she felt.

"You mustn't think that way." Luke caressed her cold hand with his fingers.

"I'm being foolish, but I can't help it." Maggie wept softly.

"Why wouldn't Doc allow me to stay with you?" Luke wiped at her tears with his thumbs. Did Maggie instruct Doc to banish him from her room? Did she believe he didn't care what happened to the baby?

"I assumed you wouldn't want to stay with me. Not with the bleeding and all," admitted Maggie, blushing.

"I'm your husband. I'll stay by your side no matter what." Luke kissed her forehead hoping to comfort her.

Why did he feel so helpless? When he made decisions involving the ranch, he always felt in charge. He decided everything and managed the outcome. But trying to control this, he might as well attempt to stop the sun from rising.

"I'm happy you're here now. Please stay until Pearl or Doc returns." Maggie reached for his hand and clasped it to her bosom.

"I'm not going anywhere." Luke stroked her hand with his thumb and smiled. The hand of a rancher's wife, rough from gardening. He raised her hand to his lips for a kiss, felt her body tremble. "Are you cold, Maggie? Should I fetch another blanket?" Luke searched her eyes. For several minutes, their eyes locked on each other. What was she thinking?

* * *

"I'm not cold, Luke. I'm fine." An involuntary shudder had rippled through her body when Luke's soft warm lips touched her hand.

Her body's reaction stunned her, as equally shocking as Luke's concern for the baby. He appeared as worried as William would have been. But William represented her past; Luke was her future. And why wouldn't Luke be concerned about the baby? Wasn't concern for the baby's wellbeing one reason he suggested this silly marital arrangement in the first place?

"So, how is our patient?" Doc bustled into the room, sounding cheerful and refreshed after his hearty breakfast. Pearl followed close behind carrying a tray which she set on the bed in front of Maggie.

"I couldn't eat anything." Maggie blanched at Pearl's scathing look. "Oh fiddle, perhaps some tea."

"Butter her one of those biscuits, Pearl. The baby requires more than a cup of tea." Luke wagged a finger at his wife. "You need to keep up your strength."

"I agree." Doc grabbed his stethoscope. "Luke, you skedaddle to the kitchen for some breakfast while I take a peek at my patient. Sarah prepared enough food for an army."

Maggie noticed her husband's reluctance to leave. "I'll be fine, Luke. Enjoy your breakfast, and thank Sarah for her kindness."

"The second I'm finished eating I'll be back." Luke kissed Maggie's forehead again and walked out of the room.

Maggie sipped her tea and nibbled on a biscuit while Doc and Pearl examined her. The medical duo exchanged a series of mysterious looks during the poking and prodding process. Maggie became increasingly uneasy. What if she lost the baby? She wanted to know what they'd learned. And at the same time, she didn't want to know.

Eventually curiosity overcame dread, and she asked, "Is something wrong? Please tell me."

"The bleeding hasn't stopped. But the good news is there's no hemorrhaging." Doc patted her hand.

"Oh, thank goodness, but why the concerned expressions?"

"We'd hoped your condition would improve overnight, but there's still bleeding. You must stay in bed until it stops completely." The doctor rested his hand on Maggie's shoulder.

"What if you can't stop it?" she whispered as a tear slid down her cheek. "Will I lose the baby?"

"Don't expect the worst, Maggie." Doc Benjamin placed his stethoscope on her chest. "I'm convinced you fainted from the stress of the burial, but I can't say for certain that the day's events caused the bleeding."

"What else could it be?" Maggie discarded the half-eaten biscuit.

"Perhaps exhaustion from overdoing things at home contributed to your situation," he suggested. "Lifting something you shouldn't have."

"Agnes does all the heavy work. Luke insists I do very little: wash a few dishes, a bit of weeding in the garden, gather the eggs, some mending. Why won't the bleeding stop?" pleaded Maggie.

"Sometimes, there's just no explaining it. I won't lie to you, if the bleeding continues we could have a problem." Doc patted her shoulder. "But we're doing everything we can to stop it."

"You've propped up the end of the bed. You insisted elevating my bottom would help stem the flow, but it isn't working, is it?" Maggie peeked over her toes at Pearl, standing at the foot of the bed.

"We don't know if it's working yet or not. But it can't hurt, Maggie." Pearl tucked the sheet around her feet. "Now try to rest and don't worry."

"Luke can sit with you when he returns." The doctor wrote on his chart while he spoke. "Your husband's presence seemed to calm you. And you must get some sleep."

"I'll do whatever you say." Maggie's eyes filled. "How can I convey to you the importance of this baby?"

"I'm aware of what this baby means to you, Maggie. Every mother feels the same way. I'm going home for a while and check if there are any patients' waiting for me at the clinic." Doc kissed Pearl on the cheek and left the room.

"Lie here and rest. That's all I can do?" Maggie choked on her words.

"Some praying can't hurt." Pearl sat on the edge of the bed, took Maggie's hand in hers. "I've witnessed patients leaving for home two days after the doctors gave them hours to live. Conversely, I've seen patients suddenly pass away when there was absolutely no indication their condition was serious. Sometimes, we just can't predict an outcome."

"I'll rest." Maggie spoke heavenward. "I promise I will."

"We're all hoping for a happy ending, Maggie." Pearl patted her patient's hand. She stood, tucked the blankets around her patient. "Luke will be back soon. You get some sleep."

"Please, God," whispered Maggie, before she closed her eyes. Exhausted from the previous night's ordeal, she finally fell asleep.

Monday, August 5, 1889

Luke peeked into the bedroom where his wife had spent several excruciating days enduring a kind of hell no woman should face. Days of uncertainty, filled with fear that the worst thing imaginable could happen.

Maggie's eyes were closed, and he slipped into the room as quietly as possible while sorely tempted to race across the floor and envelope her in his arms. How could one man love a woman as much as he loved this one?

Leaning across the bed, he whispered near her ear. "Maggie, are you asleep?"

"Yes. Go away."

"Very funny."

She cracked open one eye.

"At least you haven't lost your sense of humor." Luke smiled. Her hair stuck out in a dozen different directions, but she'd never looked more beautiful. "How are you feeling?"

"The bleeding stopped a few hours ago." Maggie clasped her hands together. "Thank the Lord. And Doc is optimistic it won't recur. I feel wonderful!"

"Doc sent a man out to the ranch to bring me the good news, and I rushed to town the minute I heard. Ned's finishing my chores for the day so I can spend my time with you." Luke lowered himself onto the bed. "The minute I stepped inside the door, I spotted Doc smiling like a Cheshire cat. Only then did I believe the good news."

"When Doc told me, I burst into tears." Maggie reached for her husband's hand.

Luke felt himself beaming and he kissed his wife on the cheek. "The children say hello, and Sam insists you come home. He's taught Rags a new trick, and he can't wait to show you."

"I've missed them all terribly." Maggie stretched her slim arms above her head and touched the ornately-carved headboard. "I just woke up before you arrived. This lazing around like an old hound dog sleeping on a sun-filled veranda proved the best thing for me."

"Get accustomed to lazing around. Agnes is blissfully busy

with the gardening and preserving. Lucy's watching the children and helping with meals and cleaning house. You, my dear wife, will spend your days resting."

"But I can't just sit around all day doing nothing. I'd feel guilty, having Agnes and Lucy doing all the work." Maggie's shoulders slumped.

"I'll allow needlework, mending, reading to the children, but no strenuous work." Luke wagged his finger at Maggie, squelching any argument. "The baby's safety comes ahead of your sense of duty. I've aged several years these past few days. Thankfully, you will both be fine."

* * *

The next morning, Maggie stood outside Sarah's mansion, eagerly anticipating her return home to the family. She hugged Doc and kissed Pearl on the cheek. "Thank you both, so much. I couldn't have asked for better care."

"You're welcome. You're an excellent patient." Pearl hugged Maggie.

Sarah hugged Maggie next. "I'm happy everything worked out so well."

"Thank you for opening your home to us, and allowing Doc and Pearl to tend to me day and night. How can we ever thank you?" Maggie's eyes filled with tears.

"The only thank you I require is keeping that baby safe. Don't overdo now that you're heading home again," cautioned Sarah.

Luke handed Doc an envelope stuffed with bills. "You've earned every penny, Doc," he proclaimed and extended his hand.

"Thank you, Luke," replied Doc, shaking his hand.

Luke bundled Maggie into the carriage.

"Take care of yourself and no heavy lifting," warned Pearl while she tucked a quilt around Maggie's legs.

Doc Benjamin smiled. "We don't want another episode. I'll head out your way in a few days to check how you're doing."

"Don't worry. I can guarantee you Maggie's going to behave." Luke waved goodbye and took up the reins.

"Come for Sunday dinner," shouted Maggie, as the carriage moved forward. "Agnes will prepare something special."

"That sounds wonderful," called Pearl. "We'll see you on Sunday."

Luke drove her home to the ranch. When they neared the main house, Maggie craned her neck as they made their way down the winding driveway, watching for her children. Birds chattered in flowering bushes that swayed in the brisk wind and the flower garden's intoxicating perfume wafted on the breeze as they rounded the corner of the house.

"Home," she whispered.

Luke helped her out of the carriage, and she burst into tears. Sam and Patti raced outside, obviously excited to have their mama home again. Everyone received a hug and a dozen kisses.

"Why were you in town so long, Mama?" asked Sam, appearing confused.

"Young man, I told you why." Agnes ruffled his hair. "Your mama needed a little rest, and Lord knows she wasn't resting here."

"That's all going to change," Luke interjected. "We've established a clear division of household duties between Agnes and Lucy. Your mama will be doing very little, Sam, other than peeling potatoes and the like."

"I'll nap at the first hint of fatigue." Maggie slowly walked up the front steps.

"I'll watch over Mrs. Carlyle like a mama bear with a mischievous cub. Now, straight to bed, Mrs. Carlyle, no argument," ordered Agnes. Fussing like a mother hen, the hired girl ushered Maggie inside.

Chapter 18

Friday September 13, 1889

"Luke, you won't believe…" Through the vanity mirror's reflection, Maggie observed her husband sitting on their bed, deep in thought. She'd bet her best bonnet that his mood had something to do with those darn cattle rustlers. He'd seemed consumed with their capture for months now. The whole idea of her husband confronting a bunch of desperate thieves frightened her half to death.

"Did you say something?" he asked, glancing her way.

"What has your mind a million miles away?" asked Maggie, as if she didn't already know. Her auburn locks tumbled about her shoulders as she released her combs.

"It's this business with the cattle rustlers," admitted Luke, sighing. "It's become a messy affair. Something I never imagined possible."

She tousled her curls with both hands, and then dragged a brush through her hair. "It sounds serious."

"I seldom fire anyone, but I'm afraid I don't have a choice."

Maggie noticed the pained expression on his face. "Who are you going to fire?"

"Mike."

"Mike Armstrong?" Maggie almost dropped the brush, waited briefly for an explanation for his outrageous announcement. When none was forthcoming, she added, "You must be joking?"

Luke rested his head in his hands. "All indications point to Mike being guilty of cattle rustling. We've lost over a hundred head."

"How can you believe Mike is involved? That young man is…is…family!" exclaimed Maggie. "Why would Mike steal your cattle? The Mike I know would never do such a thing!"

"Every night when cattle have gone missing, Mike's been mysteriously leaving the ranch. I confronted him about it, but he insisted it was a private matter. He wouldn't tell me where he was going." Luke paced the length of the room. "He's guilty. There's no other explanation."

"Guilty, my foot! Mike is no more a cattle rustler than I am." Maggie tossed her brush onto the vanity table and grabbed her wrapper off the bed. Struggling into it, she headed for the bedroom door.

"Where are you going?" demanded Luke.

"To straighten out this nonsense," called Maggie from the hallway.

"Wait!" Luke launched himself out the door and called from the top of the staircase railing. "You can't go charging into the bunkhouse dressed like that. It's unseemly."

"I don't give a fig about propriety at a time like this." Maggie paused at the bottom of the stairs and glared up at her husband. "I'm getting to the bottom of things. Nobody will ever convince me Mike Armstrong is a cattle rustler!"

"Your loyalty to the young man is admirable." Luke raced downstairs, taking the stairs two at a time. He reached the front door, just as Maggie threw it open.

"What proof do you have? What if Mike leaves the ranch once in a while? If that was a crime, we'd all be guilty!" Maggie glared at him. "I left the ranch, went to town today. Are you going to accuse me of something?"

"Explain to me why cattle go missing every night that Mike leaves?" Luke reached out and snagged her arm. "That's too much of a coincidence for me."

"Coincidence wouldn't prove any man guilty in a court of law. And you know it." Maggie pulled her arm away. "Are you coming or not?"

"Stay here," ordered Luke. "I'll go fetch him."

Twenty minutes later, Mike, Ned, Luke and Maggie exchanged hostile looks across the kitchen table in the main house. Mike dragged his hands through his tousled hair, and Ned appeared in shock after hearing Luke's accusations.

"Mike, my boy, what ya got to say for yerself?" Ned placed a hand on his son's shoulder.

"It's a personal matter, Pa. But I can assure you I ain't been stealing no cattle. Any cattle." Mike glanced at Luke and then met his father's eyes. "I swear, Pa, I'd never steal anything."

"I believe ya, son." Ned turned to Luke. "There ya have it. Better be alookin' elsewhere fer yer cattle rustler. Cause he ain't sittin' at this table."

"Then how do you explain Mike's disappearance from the ranch? And how do you explain the reports that cattle are missing the very next day?" Luke leaned back in the chair and crossed his arms. "Seems mighty coincidental to me."

"I don't give a damn about yer coincidentals. My boy ain't no thief." Ned stood, preparing to walk out. "Mighty shameful way yer treatin' my boy."

"Mike, please just tell us where you go," pleaded Maggie, placing her hands on the young man's arm.

"I'm powerful sorry, but I can't tell you, ma'am." Mike smiled, weakly.

Maggie threw up her hands. "For Pete's sake, Mike, if you…visit…with one of Darby's ladies…"

"Mrs. Carlyle, it's nothing like that!" Mike turned beet red. "Dang it all. If you must know, I visit Miss Thomas, the schoolteacher."

"Mike! She's practically engaged to the sheriff!" gasped Maggie.

"I know that!" Mike reddened an even deeper shade. "She's teaching me to read."

"What?" asked Ned and Luke in unison.

"I'm kinda sweet on Agnes." Mike glanced at Luke and back at Maggie. "She's really smart, and she wouldn't marry up with a fellow who can't even read. But I figured, if I learned to read and cipher better…."

Luke grabbed Mike by the shoulders. "So, you're riding into town for reading lessons?"

"Yes, sir, I am." Mike met the older man's eyes. "And I'm not apologizing for it."

"That's wonderful, Mike." Luke slapped him on the back.

"Can I go back to bed now? Five o'clock is gonna come mighty early." Mike yawned, rose from his chair and headed toward the back door.

"Yes, son, go back to bed." Luke shook the young man's hand and held the door for him. "Sorry about the misunderstanding."

Mike stumbled out the door, and Luke and Ned returned to their seats.

"I told you so," muttered Maggie, smiling smugly.

"Who in tarnation told ya Mike was stealin' yer cattle?" demanded Ned.

"Frenchy reported cattle missing about twice a week now, for the past month. He mentioned Mike's been taking off for parts unknown the same evenings that someone's been stealing cattle off the Diamond C." Luke slumped in his chair. "I jumped to the wrong conclusion."

"And how in tarnation does Frenchy know cattle are missin'? Is he out on the range takin' a head count every night?" Ned glared at Luke.

Luke thought about Ned's questions for a moment. He straightened in his chair, and a broad grin crossed his face. "Are you thinking what I'm thinking?"

"Most likely I am." Ned nodded.

"That sneaky bastard." Luke turned to Maggie. "Sorry, I forgot a lady was present."

"You are forgiven, now that you've exonerated Mike from all wrongdoing." Maggie smiled sweetly.

"I'm sorry I doubted Mike." Luke reached for wife's hand. "Ned, Maggie refused to believe Mike had anything to do with this. She stood up for your boy like he was her own."

"Ma'am, I always figured ya was too good fer this feller." Ned snickered, looking pointedly at Luke.

"All right, I apologize. Mike would never do such a thing." Luke straightened his back. "Frenchy on the other hand. That varmint is another matter. Tomorrow's Sunday, so we won't bother the sheriff on the Lord's Day. But first thing Monday morning, I'm heading into town for a palaver with Sheriff Smith. One night real soon, Mike's going to town for a reading lesson, and we're going to catch us a cattle rustler."

Ned lumbered toward the back door. "If yer done

dishonorin' my family, I'll be off to bed now."

"Dang it, I apologized." Luke pleaded. "What else can I do?"

"Ya can do my chores fer a week." Ned chuckled, and the screen door slammed behind him.

* * *

A million twinkling stars occupied the sky while the moon appeared no larger than a sliver of light near the horizon. Frenchy's nag trotted across the rangeland, and the cattle rustler smiled, feeling secure in life.

Sammy rode up beside him and they shook hands under the clear sky. "How ya doing?" he inquired.

"*Très bien*," replied Frenchy, grinning.

"You're in a good mood," observed Bobby, riding up alongside the other two men.

Frenchy nodded. "With good reason."

"How so?" asked Peter, reining his horse closer to the other men.

"I bin hinting to that fool Carlyle that the foreman's son has been leaving the ranch in the evenings. Very mysterious this business. No explanation." Frenchy laughed uproariously. "I report cattle go missing when this boy is gone."

"You sneaky devil." Sammy had caught on right away.

"Talk about covering your tracks," said Bobby, grinning.

Frenchy threw up his hands. "What can I say? I'm helping the boss figure out the cattle rustler mystery. Letting him know this boy is up to no good. *Oui*?"

Sammy shook his head and chuckled. "Let's hope it works."

"No matter. By the time Carlyle and the others decide that Mike is innocent, it will be too late. *Non*?" Frenchy smiled wickedly. "We are too smart for these dumb ranchers. They will not catch us."

"I hope you're right." Sammy reined his horse in closer and tossed a pouch at each man. "Here's your share for this week, gentlemen. Most of the cattle have been sold. Only a few remain in the canyon and I'm certain they will be sold by next week."

"Then we should cull a few choice steers from each rancher's herd and then prepare to head south for the winter," suggested Bobby. "I ain't stayin' around here for six feet of snow and your piss freezes before it hits the ground."

"I hear ya," added Pete, grinning. "Sooner we leave for Mexico the better. Can't wait to spend time with some pretty senorita who's willing to scratch my itch."

"I can taste that tequila already!" Sammy rubbed his middle. "Gonna be a good winter, boys."

"Don't be counting your senoritas yet. We got steers to steal," said Frenchy, reminding his companions of their mission tonight.

"No harm in doing a little dreaming," muttered Pete.

"Yeah, well let's get at it." Frenchy headed off toward the far corner of the Diamond C where he'd seen some strays his fellow cowhands had missed. The others followed.

Monday, September 16, 1889

"We require more than me and a greenhorn deputy, Luke," argued Sheriff Franklin Smith, glancing toward his nineteen-year-old sidekick.

Florence Jones' fifth oldest had dreamt of joining the Pinkerton Detective Agency. When Randy Barker, in his capacity as mayor, promoted Franklin into the sheriff's role, he encouraged Ernest to prove himself and appointed him Franklin's deputy.

"No offence, Ernest," added Franklin.

"None taken, boss," replied Ernest.

"All the ranch hands at the Diamond C will help, and half a dozen of my neighbors have cattle missing. Their hired help will step up." Luke paced the floor of the small jailhouse.

Sheriff Smith stood and stretched his six-foot-four-inch frame. "We don't know if Frenchy is the ringleader, or if he's working for someone, or how dangerous these fellows are."

"I want every last one of them caught." Luke stopped pacing, faced the sheriff.

"That's my way of thinking, too, and I'm making this top priority. But we need to bring in more lawmen," insisted Franklin, demonstrating an uncharacteristic streak of stubbornness.

"There are enough ranchers and cowhands," argued Luke, not known for his patience when it came to cattle and horse thieves.

"Let's do this proper-like, Luke." The sheriff met the frustrated rancher's eyes. "We require duly-sworn lawmen to arrest these varmints, not a bunch of cowpunchers and their bosses."

"You're right," admitted Luke. "Our case against these bastards must be ironclad. I don't want some circuit judge setting them free because we didn't follow proper procedures when we captured their sorry hides."

"We'll catch them in the act," promised the lawman, heading for the door with Luke on his heels. "Let's get this rolling."

Five minutes later, Smith fired off a telegram to his colleagues in Miles City requesting their help with the rustlers' capture. The sickly old telegraph operator—sallow skin, bags under his eyes and clothes hanging on his skeleton-like frame—was sworn to secrecy, and he promised to take the information with him to his grave. Judging by appearances, it could happen sooner rather than later.

"Keep me posted, Franklin," requested Luke, shaking the sheriff's hand outside the telegraph office.

"You'll be the first to know when I receive a reply," agreed the sheriff, touching his hat brim and then heading back to the jailhouse.

Thursday morning, Luke's frustration level increased tenfold when Sheriff Smith informed him that he'd received a reply from a fellow named Jimmy George Barkley, a Miles City deputy who promised to travel to Spirit Creek with a few of his colleagues as soon as possible. Franklin Smith insisted that no action be taken until reinforcements arrived.

Luke promised to bide his time, hoping his patience would be rewarded in due course.

Monday September 23, 1889

Maggie's head whipped up from her sewing when she heard the main house front door crash against the hallway wall. Luke strode across the floor, glanced into the parlor, and froze in his tracks. Frowning in confusion, he glared at the assembly of women.

"Mrs. Carlyle, come to my study, please," he ordered.

Maggie excused herself and followed her husband down the hallway. She couldn't imagine why he was so annoyed. She certainly couldn't recall any mistakes she'd made in running the household.

Luke waited for her to enter the study and then closed the door. "What the hell are those women doing in my parlor?" he demanded, breathing heavily from his hasty entrance.

Maggie's heart pounded. She'd clearly done something wrong, but she had no idea what that something might be. Struck speechless, she wiped her sweaty palms on her skirts.

"I asked you a question." Luke glared at her, yanked his Stetson off his head and threw it on his desk.

Instantly, Maggie's own anger flared. Pounding heart be dammed, this was her home, too. "May I remind you that that is *my* parlor? Furthermore, those women are *my* guests! Have you forgotten our conversation? We're completing the quilt for Hattie Morgan's birthday gift. I won't tell you her age, but it's a special birthday year."

Luke began pacing, his body visibly shaking with fury. "I recall you mentioning it," he muttered, pointing in the direction of the dining room. "But you failed to tell me a dozen ladies would take up residence in my parlor."

"In *your* parlor?" Maggie fought to control her temper. She wouldn't tolerate having to defend her actions like some irresponsible teenager. Luke had better show her some respect or he'd be washing his own dishes again and she'd be long gone. "Do you recall bestowing upon me the title of lady of the house? Do you recall your decree that the Carlyle family should entertain again?"

Luke stood hands on hips, his eyes blazing. Maggie had never seen him so angry. Oh fiddle, what on earth had she done? She'd turned her easy-going husband into someone she barely recognized. Perhaps the title Mrs. Carlyle didn't entitle her to as much freedom in decision-making as she'd assumed. "I apologize, Luke. I shouldn't have shouted at you." She turned toward the doorway. "I'll send the ladies home at once."

Luke blocked her exit. "No, I'm sorry. I shouldn't have questioned their presence here." His voice softened.

"I should have reminded you again…I didn't think…" Maggie stammered, fought back tears. She felt like a school girl summoned to the headmaster's office.

"Maggie, you have every right to invite anyone of your choosing into your home." Luke reached for her hand, and she thought it prudent to not pull away. She searched his eyes for a clue to what had triggered his temper. Her easy-going husband never behaved in such a shameful manner.

"Is something…wrong?" she whispered, foraging for an explanation.

"Nothing for you to worry about. And certainly nothing concerning your quilting bee." Luke raised her hands to his shoulders and wrapped his arms around her. "Please forgive me for shouting. I shouldn't have taken this out on you."

Maggie pulled back from his embrace and searched his eyes. "You would tell me if something was wrong, wouldn't you?"

"I'm sorry, Maggie," repeated Luke, smiling weakly.

"If you're certain there's nothing you should share with me…" Maggie left the thought hanging in the air in hopes of an answer, but not expecting one. He'd sidestepped her question quite nicely by simply apologizing again, but something had happened to set him off.

Without another word, Luke strode across the room, grabbed several sheets of paper off his desk, grabbed his Stetson, and charged out of the study. A few seconds later, the front door closed behind him.

"Something is definitely wrong," she whispered aloud. If it wasn't anything she'd done, then the issue concerned the ranch. Problems with his prized horses? More trouble concerning the cattle rustlers? As she returned to the parlor to complete her obligation to her guests, she vowed she would learn the truth tonight.

By four-thirty the quilt was completed and the parlor was returned to rights. At five o'clock the ladies collected their children, exchanged goodbyes, and departed for home. Alone in the parlor, Maggie leaned back in her rocking chair and closed her eyes. Her head pounded from the ladies' constant chatter, and a dozen questions triggered by Luke's outburst still swirled in her head.

Sometime later, she awoke with a start, inhaling the wonderful aroma of beef stew and fresh-baked biscuits that drifted throughout the house. The side table clock indicated it was ten minutes past six, and she struggled out of her rocking chair. Being six months along and despite loose-fitting dresses, Maggie's condition was evident to everyone. The community ladies had extended their congratulations today.

Laughter greeted her as she stepped through the kitchen

doorway. Her family was enjoying their evening meal while teasing each other.

"You should have called me to the table." Maggie yawned and, due in large part to the little cat nap, she realized her headache was gone.

Agnes leapt to her feet and busied herself at the woodstove. "Sit down, and I'll dish up your supper."

"I dozed off." Maggie rolled her shoulders and took her place at the table. "I didn't realize quilting could tucker you out."

"We were busy stitching all day long, ma'am. Nearly tuckered myself out." Agnes set a plate of beef stew in front of her.

"Thank you. This looks delicious."

"You're welcome, ma'am." Agnes returned to her seat.

"Nobody asked if I wanted to help you," complained Lucy, passing her stepmother the biscuits.

Maggie's mouth dropped open. "It never occurred to me that you'd want to."

"Mama loved quilting, and she taught me some things," offered Lucy.

"You can work on quilts with me anytime," suggested Maggie, delighted that perhaps she'd finally found something in common with her difficult stepdaughter.

Lucy just nodded and continued eating.

"Early to bed tonight, Maggie, if you've been overdoing it," suggested Luke.

Maggie noticed he didn't even glance her way. Was he embarrassed by his behavior this afternoon? Well, he should be, she decided, as she savored the first flavor-filled mouthful. "Please pass me another biscuit, Lucy," she requested, smiling. With the absence of the morning sickness, she seemed constantly ravenous.

Ignoring the family's chatter, Maggie's mind returned to her speculations. What had triggered Luke's temper this morning? Was it a business problem he didn't want to divulge? Did Luke believe a woman couldn't understand business? Couldn't understand the finer points of free-range ranching?

"Mrs. Carlyle, if you're turning in early I'll bring you up some tea." At the mention of her name, Maggie was brought back to the supper conversation.

"Thank you, I'd appreciate that."

Maggie finished her supper and helped clear the table. With leaden feet, she trudged upstairs, changed into her nightdress, and brushed out her hair.

A short time later, Sam and Patti swept into the room, jumped onto the bed, and demanded their goodnight kisses. She hugged and kissed each child in turn. And smiled, listening to their footsteps as they raced each other upstairs to their own beds.

"Sam is so happy living on the ranch," she told Agnes, when the mother's helper arrived with her cup of tea. Maggie crawled into bed, bringing the quilting square she was currently working on with her.

"Very true. I'll go read the children a bedtime story." Agnes slipped out of the room, closing the door behind her.

Propped against her pillows, Maggie sipped her tea while stitching her square and waiting for Luke. "I'm happy here, too," she whispered aloud, stunned by the realization that the ranch had become her home. For the first time since she arrived on her wedding day, Maggie truly believed she belonged here.

William's death had cost her and Sam so much, but they had survived the turmoil. She would never allow another husband's secrets, lies or betrayals to almost destroy her life again. If she did, she'd be a bigger fool for trusting Luke, than for trusting William.

She must discover what Luke was keeping from her. But everything she'd imagined all day was probably far worse than the truth. She'd simply wait to hear a logical explanation from her husband's lips.

Someone knocked softly on the bedroom door, and Maggie called, "Who is it?"

Lucy poked her head inside. "Is it all right if I come in?" she whispered.

"Of course it is. Come and sit with me." Maggie noticed the girl carried a small basket with her. "What do you have there?"

"My sewing kit. Mama made it for me. I have needles and pins and quilting threads and a few buttons," explained Lucy, smiling for the first time since Maggie arrived at the ranch.

"My, you are prepared."

"I peeked at the quilt you made for Mrs. Morgan. It's very pretty. Mrs. Morgan was Mama's best friend. Thank you for being so kind to her," said Lucy, peeking out from under her lashes.

"Mrs. Morgan is my friend and many other ladies adore her, too. We loved making a special gift for her." Maggie reached over and touched Lucy's arm. "With all the materials in your sewing basket, you must be a quilter."

Lucy beamed. "Could you teach me something new? Maybe I could make my own quilt."

"I have a better idea." Maggie lowered her voice to a whisper. "Can you keep a secret?"

Lucy bobbed her head, a look of anticipation on her face.

"Then listen to this...." Maggie described her current project, and then suggested that Lucy join in.

Lucy giggled when Maggie finished her explanation. "This is going to be so much fun."

"Thank you for agreeing to help." Maggie opened her arms and her stepdaughter accepted her hug.

Suddenly, the bedroom door opened, and Luke startled when he spotted the two of them propped up in bed together. He appeared to quickly recover.

"Hello, Lucy. Maggie, I expected you'd be sound asleep by now." Luke closed the door, strode across the floor, sat on his side of the bed to pull off his boots.

"I was waiting for you." Maggie's heart pounded and her stomach fluttered with nerves. "And Lucy dropped by for some quilting talk."

"I'm going to sleep now," announced Lucy, scrambling off the bed.

Maggie set her quilting aside and winked at her stepdaughter. "We'll have to work on this some more tomorrow."

Lucy giggled. "All right. Sleep tight, Mama Maggie."

"Sleep tight, sweetheart," she called as Lucy closed the door behind her.

"It appears Lucy is coming around." Luke stood, removed his shirt, and tossed it over the back of a nearby chair. "But why would you wait up for me?"

"I deserve an explanation for your outburst this afternoon. If you weren't angry with me, then what set you off?"

"Must we discuss this tonight?" Luke tossed his trousers toward the chair, but his aim fell short. Muttering, he retrieved them and hooked them over the chair's post.

"Something's wrong, and I demand to know what it is." Holding her breath, she waited. Would he tell her the truth?

Luke paused beside the bed for a moment, and then one hand reached for the bedclothes and whipped them open. He crawled between the sheets and settled the covers around his chest.

"Don't lie to me," warned Maggie, sounding a lot braver than she felt at the moment. Submissiveness had its place, but this wasn't one of them. "Something's wrong. I will not tolerate secrets or being lied to by another husband..."

"Frenchy disappeared," blurted Luke.

"What do you mean…disappeared?" Maggie bolted upright in bed.

"When Ned noticed Frenchy's old nag was missing from the corral, he checked the bunkhouse. All of Frenchy's gear is gone. He's vanished." Luke's hand pounded his pillow.

"Have you told Franklin?" asked Maggie, stunned by her husband's revelation. No wonder he was in a foul mood.

"I sent Mike into town." Luke sighed. "Franklin sent a telegraph to the fellows in Miles City informing them something scared Frenchy off, or someone warned him we were on to the rustlers."

"I'm so sorry," whispered Maggie, reaching for his hand.

Luke raised her hand to his lips. "We were so close. Now we'll be looking over our shoulders…waiting for them to return after we've let our guard down."

"Do you think Frenchy will be back?"

"Oh, he'll be back. He'll wait for a few months and then get himself hired on at another ranch where no one knows him. And his cronies will be hired on at neighboring ranches. They'll be too greedy, too stupid to just let it be and move on."

Maggie noticed a change in Luke's expression. "Is there more? I can't tell what you're thinking?"

"All afternoon, I was thinking about you," confessed Luke, staring deep into her eyes as if he could see into her soul.

"About me?" Maggie almost burst into tears. She'd overstepped, asserting herself as lady of the house. Had it cost her everything: her new home, her happiness with Luke?

"I realized something after we spoke that rocked my entire being. And yet I should have seen it coming." Luke's expression hadn't changed.

"What was it?" whispered Maggie, fearing he'd reconsidered their arrangement. Fearing she'd proven herself unsuitable. Fearing she'd failed to measure up as Mrs. Luke Carlyle.

"You stood up to me, stood up for yourself..." he began.

"I'm sorry, Luke." Tears spilled down her cheeks, her fears confirmed. No one spoke to Luke Carlyle that way, not even his wife, apparently. "I should never have... I had no right to speak to you in that tone…"

Luke pressed his index finger to her lips. "You had every right. You're my wife, and I treated you shamefully. But in the midst of it all, I realized something."

Maggie brushed at her tears and searched his eyes for a clue. A stabbing pain pierced her heart, like a knife embedded in the depths of her being. Had he realized he could never love her? She loved him so much. If he sent her away now, it would surely kill her.

"The fact that you invited your women friends to your home without asking me first told me you've truly become my wife." Luke smiled and reached for her hands. "Not because a few months ago we spoke vows that meant nothing to us at the time. Not because the preacher wrote our names in the church register. But because in your heart you truly are Mrs. Luke Carlyle."

"You're not disappointed in me? You're not sending me away?" For some time now, she had loved him with all her heart. But she realized only recently that she loved him more than she'd ever loved William. Luke treated her the way a husband should treat a wife. She could rely on him. He was here for her, every day and every night. There were no secrets, no deceptions, and no lies. Luke was thoughtful and kind and loving in so many ways William never was. Luke and their children had become her whole world. She loved him, but more importantly, she trusted him.

"Maggie, you are Mrs. Luke Carlyle. Why would I send you away? *Till death do us part*, remember?" Luke slowly kissed one hand and then the other.

His lips were so very warm. She wished he'd kiss her properly. And she admitted to herself, she longed for more, for all of him. She never thought the day would come that she'd yearn to be loved by another man, touched in all the private places reserved for a husband.

"I love you, Luke, more than I've ever loved anyone." She whispered the secret she'd kept from him for weeks.

Luke hugged her close, whispered into her ear, "I've waited so long to hear those words. I've loved you almost since the day we wed." And then he kissed her the way a husband kisses his wife, stealing her breath.

His kiss burned her lips, and she greedily craved the warmth of his body. As if reading her mind, he pulled her against him; their bodies fit together perfectly. Her world tilted; she wasn't certain which way was up.

"Maggie?" whispered Luke, looking deep into her eyes. "Are you ready to take the final step? Are you ready to become my wife in every way?"

"No!" she exclaimed, pulling the sheet up to her chin.

"I'm sorry, Maggie." Luke's face paled. "I shouldn't have asked. I got carried away in the moment."

For several seconds, they just stared at each other like dueling combatants eyeing up the competition. Maggie saw the hurt in his eyes. Or was it disappointment? Why had she reacted so strongly? She longed to become Luke's wife, to belong only to him in every way. She'd dreamed of this moment a dozen times over

"I didn't mean that," she blurted, her face warming with the admission. "I mean…I want to…it's just that…"

"I caught you off guard." Luke smiled, opening his arms to her. "Let me ask you again."

"All right," agreed Maggie, slipping back into his embrace.

Luke slid further down under the sheets, urging her down with him. For a minute, they lay side-by-side, and he gazed into her eyes, unnerving her even more. One hand trailed up and down her arm sending a shiver of delight through her entire body. Another minute passed, and then he gently drew her closer and kissed her, deeply, completely. When she thought she'd burst into flames from the heat of the embrace, he suddenly ended the kiss and rested his chin atop her head.

Maggie closed her eyes, and let her fingers roam through his thick, slightly-damp curls. He must have bathed and washed his hair before coming to bed. She rested her cheek on his chest and the rapid tempo of Luke's heartbeat matched her own. He kissed her again, parting her lips with his tongue, demanding entry to her mouth. Their tongues performed a tango, and he crushed her against his body.

His need was undeniable, the evidence pressing against her. Tonight she would become Luke's wife in every way. She was ready; she was certain of it. But for some reason, her nerves jangled like those of a shy virgin bride.

Luke pulled his lips from Maggie's, pressed his cheek against hers. Slowly, he lifted his head and met her eyes. She wondered if he saw both her longing and her uncertainty.

"Sweetheart, are you ready to become man and wife?" Luke whispered. "I've waited so long. I don't think I can wait another minute."

Maggie's breath caught. The intense desire and urgent longing in Luke's eyes confirmed for her that his words of love were genuine.

Their time had come.

"You have no idea how much I love you," murmured Maggie.

"No more than I love you." Luke tightened his embrace. He kissed her quivering lips, and his hand found her breast.

"Make love to me," she whispered against his lips.

Their kiss deepened, and his tongue danced with hers. A moan escaped Maggie's lips, and she was swept away with emotion, with the need to truly become his wife. Luke responded to Maggie's need with urgency of his own. He fumbled with her nightdress, and she helped him slip it over her head. She lay back upon the sheets, naked and unabashed before him. The child growing inside her evident to his eyes.

"You are so beautiful." He whispered the words. And then he slipped out of the bed; his eyes never abandoning her.

Luke made no move to smother the lamp, and Maggie almost turned away. During her entire marriage to William, they had always made love in the dark; she'd never seen his naked body. As Luke shed his long underwear, she couldn't peel her eyes off of him. She admired his manhood and smiled with the knowledge that this magnificent being was her husband. And he belonged only to her.

Luke locked the bedroom door and then returned to her side. "I love the scent of lilacs," he murmured, nuzzling her neck. And then he met her eyes and cupped her chin in his hand. His lips found her lips, and his tongue slipped into her mouth, teasing and exploring. He mumbled, "You are so sweet."

Could he taste the sugar from her tea?

While he kissed her, Maggie's hands wrapped around his neck and her fingers entwined Luke's soft curly hair. Feeling brave, she lowered her hand. Her fingers trailed across his corded chest, and she inhaled the woodsy scent that lingered on his skin. And then his fingers began their own unhurried exploration.

Luke touched her, tasted her, covering every inch of her body in ways Maggie had never experienced before. Surely she would die from the pleasure of it. She touched him and tasted him, mimicking his movements. His breathing matched her rapid breaths. Could he hear her heart pounding? She shook her head to clear the deafening buzz in her ears.

The room was silent as a tomb, but invisible sparks snapped between them. And the unbearable torture continued, seemingly forever.

"Please, Luke," she begged with frustration.

And then he parted her legs, and she eagerly welcomed all of him. She suspected his brain was a muddle of emotion and need, but he was mindful of the child growing inside her. The child he'd promised to raise as his own, she thought, and smiled. He carefully moved his body with hers, bringing her pleasure and the release she craved while accommodating her swollen belly.

"Maggie." Luke whispered her name like a prayer, and together they travelled the time worn path to fulfillment.

Minutes later, Luke smiled at her, lying beside him. His finger traced the smile that creased her face. "That was wonderful, Mrs. Carlyle."

"Mmm, I agree," mumbled Maggie, sighing. She closed her eyes, feeling cherished and loved. More so than she'd ever felt before. William's lovemaking was usually rushed, and she seldom achieved her own release. But making love with Luke had been perfect because they had waited until they'd fallen in love. He'd touched her so gently, so thoroughly. She'd almost lost her mind with the sensations he'd created in her. His true affection for her shone through the words he'd muttered in the throes of passion, words of love. He'd been mindful of their child, of her feelings, of her satisfaction as well as his own. She couldn't love him more.

Luke's talent for lovemaking far exceeded William's, and her body tingled from head to toe. Her new husband was a demanding lover, but gentle. Her only regret was how long she'd foolishly waited to confess her love for him.

She opened her eyes and gazed deeply into Luke's. Everything she was feeling was reflected back at her in his eyes. "My wedding vows are no longer a lie. I promise to love and honor you until death do us part."

"I promise to love you for eternity." Luke rested his hand on her belly. And then the baby kicked, and his hand flew off her middle as if he'd burned himself on a hot stove. "Did you feel that?"

"I've felt it for some time now." Maggie placed his hand on her middle, and the baby kicked again.

Luke and Maggie made love once more, gently, slowly, lovingly. And again, they journeyed together toward an equally breathless conclusion. In time, Luke fell asleep, but Maggie lay wide awake. How quickly her life had changed. In a heartbeat a bullet made her a widow. In another heartbeat she'd lost her home. And then a miracle named Luke Carlyle had happened.

Maggie brushed a tear from her cheek. For now at least, she needn't worry about him being in danger, pursing the cattle rustlers.

Chapter 19

Wednesday, December 18, 1889

"Are you certain you're up for this?" asked Luke, his arms laden down with blankets and quilts.

"I'll stay in the sleigh, bundled up warm. I'll be fine." Maggie smiled. Nothing would prevent her from joining this family outing. The baby was due any day now, but even if her pains started, there would be plenty of time to return to the house.

"Let's go then," called Luke, heading out the back door. "The sleigh's all ready to go, and we're burning daylight."

Everyone clambered inside the sleigh, Ned flicked the reins, and the horses headed across the snow-covered valley.

The cold weather wasn't dampening anyone's enthusiasm. Pristine snow crunched under the horses' hooves, and the sleigh's metal runners glided across the barren land. Someone had attached bells to the horses' harness and they jangled with the animals' every step.

"It's warm in here, Mama." Sam beamed, wrapped in a quilt up to his chin.

"Very cozy indeed, muffin." Maggie tweaked his rosy-red nose.

"That's because we're prepared, Sam." Luke met his young son's eyes. "We heated six large stones in the wood stove, then wrapped the stones in canvas and set them in the bottom of the sleigh. Third and Mike piled in a thick layer of hay which we covered with blankets and buffalo hides. We'll stay warm for hours."

Lucy pulled her quilt around her shoulders. "Look at the frost clinging to the trees, Patti. Have you ever seen anything so beautiful?"

"It's very pretty," agreed Patti, smiling.

"Mother Nature provided an absolutely perfect day especially for us, Lucy," observed Luke.

Maggie squeezed closer to her husband, and he wrapped his arms around her. "Your horses are certainly enjoying their day out of the barn." With each lively step the harness bells shattered the silence of the vast countryside.

Agnes encouraged everyone to sing carols, and the miles flew by.

Suddenly, the sleigh jerked to a halt. "Is this a good spot?" asked Ned, turning around on the bench seat.

"Some nice pine trees over that way." Luke pointed to his left and then jumped out of the sleigh. "Sam, come choose a tree for the parlor with me."

"I'll help you pick one for your house, Uncle Ned," offered Patti. Ned stepped down from the seat and caught Patti as she jumped into his arms. He set the little girl on her feet and playfully swatted her bottom. "You better pick a good one."

"Could I pick a tree for our cabin?" inquired Belle, struggling out of the sleigh.

A few months back, Third married Darby's former soiled dove when the saloon owner abruptly terminated her employment when he discovered she was pregnant. Third was a regular customer at Darby's brothel, and he always had a special place in his heart for the girl. He hadn't hesitated to come to her rescue when he learned she was destitute and carrying a baby that could possibly be his own.

Maggie welcomed Belle to the ranch—the two women became instant friends—and no one ever mentioned the girl's past. Belle adjusted her hat, arranged her skirts, and glowed with pending motherhood.

"Yes, Belle, choose a tree for you and Third," agreed Luke, instantly. "We have lots of decorations. We can share with you."

"Thank you, sir. You and your family have been so kind. I've never had a home and a Christmas tree before," she whispered wistfully, swiping at a tear.

Lucy clambered out of the sleigh and tightened her scarf. "I'll select suitable trees for the two bunkhouses, and then I'm returning to this warm sleigh." Suddenly, a snowball exploded against her shoulder, and she yelped in surprise.

"I'm ever so sorry about that," gushed Agnes, with mock sincerity. "Truly, I was aiming for Mike."

"No you weren't." Lucy squished a handful of snow into a ball. The projectile hit Agnes square in the chest.

And thus the snowball fight began.

Soon Sam and Patti joined in the fun. Even Belle and Luke tossed a few snowballs. Maggie watched their antics with amusement and envy from the safety of the sleigh. Next year she'd join in when she wasn't expecting a baby any minute.

"Are you ruffians done wastin' a perfectly good day? These dang trees ain't about to hop into the sleigh by themselves." Ned stepped to the left, narrowly avoiding one of Luke's snowballs. "Now that's enough, Sonny Boy. Git over here and give me a hand with this."

"Children, you heard the old stick-in-the-mud," called Luke. "Let's pick out our trees and head for home. It'll get dark pretty quick."

Twenty minutes later, the trees were felled by Luke's best axe, and Luke headed toward the sleigh lugging a small tree under each arm. Mike and Ned followed close behind with a large tree each. And Belle and Lucy carried a tree, too. Soon, the bushy evergreens were loaded and securely tied down for the ride home. Everyone climbed into the sleigh and settled under the quilts.

"I'll have ya know, I ain't no stick-in-the-mud," muttered Ned, releasing the brake on the sleigh. Flicking the reins, he added, "In fact, I'd enjoy some more of that singin'."

Maggie closed her eyes and drifted asleep listening to her family's beautiful harmonies. She recalled childhood Christmases, alone with her parents. Each year Aunt Penny, Uncle Theodore and a few of her parents' adult friends shared dinner with them. But there were never other children around to share the holidays with Maggie.

When classes resumed, she listened to other children relating marvelous holiday stories: sledding parties the day after Christmas, drinking hot cocoa and popping popcorn over an outdoor fire, even ice skating on the river if the weather was cold enough. How she'd envied those children and fervently wished she was blessed with siblings. Maggie considered being an only child the cruelest twist of fate to befall a child.

Soon, the sleigh jerked to a halt in front of the main house.

* * *

Next morning, Sam tugged on his mother's skirts. "Why isn't Lucy and Patti going to school, Mama?"

Maggie set her tea cup down on the kitchen work table. Taking his small hand, she crossed the plank floor, lowered herself onto a kitchen chair, and pulled her son onto her lap.

"It's too dangerous and difficult for children to attend school in this cold weather. There are no classes until spring." Maggie squeezed her son as tightly as her protruding belly allowed. "Patti and Lucy can do lessons here, and there are lots of books for them to read. And you, my sweet, can practice your letters."

"I can print my name, Mama."

"Yes, you can. And I'm very proud of you." Maggie kissed the end of his nose. "Go play. I'll call you when Agnes is ready to make the Christmas cookies."

"Mama, can we string popcorn for the tree?" asked Patti, dashing into the kitchen.

"All right, but be careful. I don't want any accidents with a sharp needle." Maggie set Sam on his feet and struggled out of her chair.

"Lucy promised to help." Patti skipped out of the room with Sam on her heels.

"Have fun," called Maggie as the children disappeared through the door.

Maggie stared out the kitchen window, squinting in the bright sunlight that reflected off the foot of snow in the back yard. She closed her eyes for a minute, savoring the warm sunshine on her face. She rubbed her lower back as she waddled over to the woodstove.

Sighing, she poured herself another cup of coffee, set the pot back on the woodstove, and waddled back to her chair.

When was this baby coming? She couldn't wait for the child to arrive, but she couldn't help feeling a little nervous also. She'd been down this road before when she birthed Sam five years ago with Doc Fitzgerald at her side. Now, she'd arranged for the local midwife, Rebecca Simpson, to attend the birth. The Simpson ranch bordered the Diamond C and Rebecca could be here in a matter of minutes. And there was no guarantee Doc Benjamin wouldn't be away from town, attending someone else. She sighed, grimaced with the baby's busy movement. Was he or she dancing in there?

"Ma'am, did you hear me?"

Maggie jolted from her musings. "Did you say something, Agnes?"

"I'm looking forward to helping Morning Star prepare the trifle. Lord knows we've never had anything that fancy at Ma's house." Agnes sighed.

"We should make a trifle for your mother!" exclaimed Maggie.

"Now, Mrs. Carlyle, I wasn't begging for…" began Agnes.

"Not another word." Maggie waved away Agnes's argument. The Jones family was fiercely proud and would starve before accepting charity. "I've been stumped, thinking up a suitable present for your mother. We're making a trifle to thank her for sending me such a wonderful mother's helper. I couldn't be more pleased with your work."

"Now you've got me blushing," said Agnes, red-faced.

"Lucy and I have been organizing a basket of food: breads, jams, preserves and such. You've been working so hard preparing for the holidays, you should enjoy a reward for your labor."

"But…"

Maggie patted the girl's hand. "Consider the matter settled."

"Thank you, ma'am," whispered Agnes. "You're the kindest lady I've ever known."

"Just Christmas spirit, dear." Maggie laughed. "Now, we have everything to construct the trifles: pound cake, gelatin, custard, fruit preserves and whipped cream. We have plenty for two trifles. Morning Star mentioned a special crystal bowl brought from England by Ruth Carlyle. We'll find another bowl for your mother's trifle."

"Christmas dinner is organized. The goose is killed, cleaned and hanging in the root cellar. Let me think…potatoes, gravy, stuffing, carrots and turnips, pickles, bread and buns, plum pudding, and the trifle for dessert. Lucy can help prepare hot cider to serve in front of the fire after the dishes are done." Agnes stood hands on hips. "Is there anything I've forgotten?"

Maggie patted her middle. "You'll discover every one of us collapsed at the table, still groaning in agony, when you return to the ranch on the twenty-sixth."

"It's been a hard year for you. I hope you enjoy Christmas, ma'am." Agnes wrapped her arms around Maggie, and then she turned scarlet and quickly released her employer, realizing what she'd done.

"Hopefully, the new baby will be here. That will make Christmas special." Maggie patted Agnes's arm to convey forgiveness for her breach of conduct. If one of her mother's servants had ever hugged her mother, the poor girl would have been fired on the spot.

"And you'll have the whole family around you," added Agnes.

Everyone but her aunt, thought Maggie, wistfully. She should have sent a small gift and a newsy letter telling her aunt about her new family, but she'd forgotten. Too late now. She clasped the girl's hands and met her eyes. "I hope you and your family celebrate a wonderful Christmas, Agnes. Your ma will be delighted having you home for two days."

Maggie smiled, remembering the secret Luke shared with her last night: every year he and Buddy Maxwell, another well-to-do rancher, donated money to Reverend Gerald to purchase toys from the general store for distribution to less fortunate children in the community. No doubt, the younger Jones children would benefit from their anonymous gifts. As would many others. She had never loved Luke Carlyle more than when he'd told her, *no matter the parents' circumstances, every child within twenty miles of Spirit Creek will discover a toy or two under the tree on Christmas morning.*

"Did Mike carry down all the boxes of decorations from the storage room on the third floor?" asked Maggie.

"Mike and Third hauled down at least two dozen boxes this morning." Agnes laughed. "I've never seen so many decorations. They took the ones that were labeled BUNKHOUSES with them. The ranch hands must appreciate a bit of Christmas fuss."

"Most of the men don't have any place to call home, except the Diamond C. Apparently, Cookhouse Charlie prepares a special Christmas dinner for the men every year, and we'll send down a box of Christmas cakes, cookies and candy for them."

"That's very thoughtful, ma'am."

"Luke invited Ned, Morning Star and Mike up to the main

house for Christmas Eve and Christmas Day with us," said Maggie. "The Armstrongs are like family."

"That will be fun."

"No doubt Morning Star will insist on cooking Christmas dinner if I'm still recovering from delivering this child." Maggie laughed. "God forbid, the baby hasn't even arrived yet. I'm ready now."

"I'll pray for a timely arrival, ma'am." Agnes wiped her hands on her apron. "Well, let me round up my cookie-making helpers."

Soon, Sam and Patti were busy making cookies with Agnes while Maggie sat sipping a cup of tea.

"Sam, you're wearing more flour than went into the cookies," observed Maggie, chuckling.

Sam glanced at his dusty shirt and inadvertently tipped over the can of Roger's Baking Powder, spilling the entire contents onto the floor where Rags was sleeping.

"Oh, my!" exclaimed Agnes. "Thank goodness, there's a spare one in the pantry."

Maggie gasped as everyone watched Rags running through the mess.

"Rags, no!" yelled Sam, climbing off his chair.

Before anyone could stop him, the pup had made a path of white powdery paw prints throughout the kitchen.

Finally, Agnes snagged one leg, grabbed him round the middle and put him outside.

"I'm sorry Mama," whispered Sam, near tears.

"It's all right, muffin. Accidents happen." Including Patti in her gaze, Maggie added, "Seeing your smiling faces is more important than a bit of a mess on the floor."

Agnes grabbed a broom and started sweeping up. "Rags did look pretty funny, didn't he?" she asked, peeking over at Maggie and winking.

Realizing they weren't in trouble, Sam and Patti started to giggle. "Most of it fell on his head," said Patti.

"Will we have to give him a bath?" asked Sam.

"Hopefully, Rags will just roll in the snow and get most of it off. It's too cold to be giving a dog a bath." Maggie shifted on the chair, hoping to find a more comfortable position.

"If Rags doesn't get all of the powder off himself, we can

brush the rest of it out of his fur." Agnes swept the mess into the dust pan, tossed it out the back door, put the broom and dust pan away, and then washed up at the sink. "Now, we should get back to our cookie making," she suggested, drying her hands on a towel.

* * *

Luke heard all about the cookie-making antics. He'd spent a half hour brushing Rags' thick coat of fur out in the back porch before either of them were allowed into the house for supper.

Afterwards, the entire family gathered in the parlor to decorate the tree. Maggie shifted in her chair, searching for a more comfortable position. She'd admitted being troubled by almost constant back pain, but she wasn't one to complain.

"Did you leave some of the cookies for Christmas?" Maggie asked the children as she unwrapped delicate glass tree ornaments.

"Agnes gave us two cookies each and then she hid the rest of them." Lucy sat cross-legged on the braided rug beside Maggie's rocking chair while Sam and Patti continued making a colored-paper chain for the tree.

Luke described the history and significance behind each precious ornament—most had accompanied his mother from England—for Maggie's benefit. While unwrapping these family treasures this Christmas, he realized the pain of losing his parents and Catherine had lessened. He truly was healing. He hoped Maggie would soon find similar peace. Luke noticed she'd added a dozen of her own holiday treasures to their collection.

When the job of unwrapping the ornaments was completed, Luke rose from his rocker. "Let's hang these on the tree before it's your bedtime."

"Do you mean me or the children?" teased Maggie, handing him a beautiful crystal angel, one of his mother's favorites.

"Both of you," he countered, grinning.

As the last ornament was set in place, a loud knock on the front door startled everyone. "Are you expecting anyone tonight, Maggie?" asked Luke.

"I was about to ask you the same question." Maggie shrugged her shoulders and rubbed her back again. "Perhaps it's just Ned."

Luke stepped into the entryway and whipped open the front

door. A blast of cold air washed over him and Ronald Waverly stood there.

"What brings you out our way?" blurted Luke.

Ronald stamped the snow off his boots. "Invite me in and I'll explain."

"Of course, come in out of the cold. You know you're always welcome." Luke waved their visitor inside.

"I'm not alone," warned Ronald, stepping across the threshold.

Elizabeth rushed through the doorway, shaking snowflakes from her woolen hat. "It's an unexpected trip for us, but a special lady arrived in town yesterday."

Luke smiled at the elderly lady who'd followed Elizabeth inside. He'd never seen her before, but she looked vaguely familiar. White hair peeked out from under a fur-trimmed hat, hazel eyes twinkled with mischief, and her almost wrinkle-free complexion belied her age. She slipped out of an exquisite fur coat, handed it to him, and then passed him the matching hat. She nervously fluffed her tight snowy curls.

"Maggie!" called Elizabeth, shedding her own winter garb. "Come here! We have a surprise for you!"

Ronald hung his hat and coat on a peg in the entryway, and the three visitors removed their outer footwear while Maggie waddled in from the parlor.

"My goodness, what's all the fuss about?" Spotting the white-haired visitor, she gasped and grabbed Luke's arm for support.

"Hello, Maggie, dear. I do hope this isn't an inconvenience." The elderly lady stood, her hands cupped in front of her.

"I can't believe you're here!" Maggie recovered her composure and embraced the unexpected visitor in an awkward hug, her belly preventing much contact.

"I hope you don't mind, but I couldn't stay away."

"Oh fiddle! Where are my manners? Aunt Penny, this is my husband, Luke Carlyle." Maggie smiled at her aunt, and then met her husband's eyes. "Luke, this is my aunt, Mrs. Penelope Williamson, from Philadelphia."

"I'm so pleased to finally make your acquaintance, young man," stated Aunt Penny, beaming. Several seconds passed, and she whispered, "Maggie, are all the ranchers in Montana tongue-tied?"

"Oh, ma'am, forgive me. It's a pleasure to meet you." Luke felt his face redden as he stuck out his hand. Aunt Penny's firm handshake surprised him. He realized why she looked familiar. There was no denying she was his wife's aunt. In spite of the age difference, the resemblance was remarkable.

"Now that we've got the formalities out of the way, lead me to a warm fire." Elizabeth headed for the parlor.

Several minutes later, all the introductions were made, and Agnes dashed to the kitchen, promising everyone a cup of hot apple cider.

* * *

"Let me warm up these old bones, and then we'll sit and enjoy this lovely room." Aunt Penny stood close by the open fireplace with her niece at her side.

"Why didn't you write? Let me know you were coming?" asked Maggie, rubbing warmth into one of her aunt's ice-cold hands. "And more importantly, what in the world possessed you to travel way out here in the dead of winter?"

"I could have sent a telegraph, but I wanted to surprise you," explained Aunt Penny.

Agnes returned with a tray filled with cups of cider which Lucy helped her serve.

"Well, you succeeded. I couldn't have been more shocked if the King of England walked through the door." Maggie shook her head and grabbed her aunt's other hand. "Tell me how this came about?"

"It's all Sophie McCorkell's fault. You remember my housekeeper, don't you?" inquired Aunt Penny, sipping the warm beverage.

"That woman nearly frightened me to death as a child. How could I ever forget her?" Maggie shook her head.

"She hasn't mellowed over time," chuckled Aunt Penny. She turned toward Luke and added, "Sophie's never demonstrated a lick of patience with little ones, never having borne children of her own. Her husband died when she was only twenty, and she never remarried."

"My noisy brood would cause the poor woman heart failure."

Maggie glanced over at her children, teasing each other while they strung their paper chain on the lowest branches of the Christmas tree.

"A happy home requires children and a bit of noise." Aunt Penny patted Maggie's arm, motioning for her to follow her. Seated in adjacent rocking chairs, Aunt Penny continued her story. "Sophie received word that her mother was ailing. The woman is as old as dirt, nearly ninety, I believe. I gave Sophie the whole month of December off to be at her mother's side should something happen. Even paid for her ticket to New York and slipped a few extra dollars into her pay envelope. It was the first time I've ever seen Sophie speechless."

"You're generous to a fault." Maggie smiled at her aunt and peeked at her over the rim of her cup. "I suspect there were more than a few extra dollars in that envelope."

"Yes, well, Sophie's been extremely loyal; it was the least I could do. She hasn't taken a day off in years."

"I'm certain she appreciates your kindness." Maggie glanced at the clock on the fireplace mantle. "Children, it's your bedtime. You can finish the tree in the morning."

"No! Not already," moaned Patti.

"We're having fun," complained Sam.

"Children…." warned Maggie.

"Good night, Mama," sighed Patti. "Don't finish the tree until morning, please?"

"Good night, Mama," echoed Sam resignedly.

"We'll leave it for you to do," Maggie assured them as each child planted a wet kiss on her cheek and then on Luke's. They wished everyone a goodnight, and slowly climbed the stairs to bed.

"I'm helping Agnes clean up in the kitchen and then I'll turn in, too," announced Lucy. "I'll say my goodnights now though."

"Goodnight," said Luke and Maggie, smiling, as Lucy and Agnes headed for the kitchen with the tray of empty cups.

"Goodnight, everyone," called Agnes, over her shoulder. "I'll turn in, too, as soon as I wash up these dishes."

"Your children are so well-behaved, my dear." Aunt Penny beamed proudly at her niece. "Speaks volumes about their upbringing. You're obviously a wonderful mother."

"One of the reasons I married her, Aunt Penny," offered

Luke, settling himself in a chair alongside the newly-decorated tree.

"Now, what were we talking about?" asked Elizabeth, resting her hands in her lap.

"Aunt Penny was telling us what prompted her trip to Spirit Creek." Maggie adjusted the small pillow at her back.

"Yes, yes. Once I'd made Sophie's arrangements, I couldn't bear the thought of spending the holidays in that big old mansion all alone. On the spur of the moment, I decided to spend Christmas with my niece and her family in Montana." Aunt Penny shifted position in her chair. "I bought my train ticket the next morning, helped Sophie pack my trunks, and here I am."

"That's a rather extreme notion for a woman your age." Ronald whispered the words.

Maggie wondered if Ronald realized he'd spoken the thought aloud, but she shared his concern. Hadn't Aunt Penny celebrated her seventy-second birthday last month? But her aunt had arrived safe and sound, and Maggie couldn't be happier.

"When I learned that you'd remarried so soon after William's death, I realized the circumstances must be unusual." Aunt Penny's arthritic fingers worried a lacy white handkerchief.

"How did you learn about my wedding?" asked Maggie, overcome with guilt and silently berating herself for not writing. Her aunt must have been extremely concerned, not knowing what she might discover when she arrived in Spirit Creek.

"I have friends all over the world, Maggie. It wasn't difficult. By all reports, you were being well cared for, but I wanted to meet this young man and assure myself you were happy." Aunt Penny peeked over her spectacles at Luke. "He's certainly a handsome fellow, Maggie, but does he treat you well?"

"Exceptionally well, Auntie," said Maggie. She almost blurted that Luke was tenfold the man William had been, but caught herself.

"Then my concerns were unfounded, but these old eyes required proof." Aunt Penny's gaze moved to Maggie's bulging belly. "My sources failed to inform me that a baby was on the way. When is the child due?"

"Any day now." Maggie visualized the rapid arithmetic taking place in her aunt's head.

Aunt Penny glanced from Maggie to Luke and back. "That means…"

"It's a long story, Auntie. And I'll tell you everything tomorrow." Maggie yawned and struggled to her feet. "Ronald and Elizabeth, obviously, you're staying the night."

"I left the key to the store with Ellie Thomas." Ronald struggled out of his chair.

"With the school closed until spring, Ellie's been helping out two days a week. Gives me a chance to keep ahead of the housework and Ellie earns a bit of pin money," said Elizabeth. "That wonderful young lady doesn't spend much money on herself though. She bought several small presents and shipped them along with the mittens and socks she'd knitted to an orphanage in Boston. We gave her a substantial discount on her purchases and she burst into tears with gratitude."

"Good worker, that woman, for someone who grew up in an orphanage," added Ronald. "Or maybe she learned her excellent work ethic because she grew up there. Regardless, she'll operate the store tomorrow, since Elizabeth insisted we stay and visit."

"I think Franklin is going to propose any day now," whispered Elizabeth.

"I do, too." Maggie smiled and nodded her approval. The local sheriff and schoolteacher were perfect for each other. "The second-floor guest bedrooms are made up. I'll show Aunt Penny to her room, and then I'm turning in, too."

"Good night, dear," said Elizabeth, hugging her friend. "We won't be far behind you, and we can fend for ourselves."

"I'm certainly ready for a good night's sleep." Aunt Penny struggled to her feet. "Getting here has been a long journey, to say the least. But I'm delighted to arrive in one piece. I'm so pleased that I decided to come."

Maggie noticed the fatigue in her aunt's eyes. "I'm delighted you're here."

"Thank you for such a gracious welcome, my dear," said Aunt Penny, patting her niece's hand. "I feel right at home."

Maggie linked arms with her aunt, her only living relative in the world, aside from Luke and the children. Guiding the elderly woman toward the staircase, she called, "Luke, bring the bags up, please."

"I'll give you a hand, Luke." Ronald headed out of the room, muttering, "Those women brought enough trunks and bags to stay a year."

Agnes rushed into the entryway from the kitchen, drying her hands on a tea towel. "All of the bags and trunks are upstairs. I arranged for Mike and Scotty to bring them in from your buggy and take them up to your rooms."

"Agnes, that was so thoughtful of you." Luke smiled. "Thank you."

"Mr. Waverly, Mike informed me your mare is settled in the horse barn for the night, all fed and watered."

"And thank goodness for it, too. I wasn't looking forward to the task." Ronald winked at Agnes. "Thank that young man for me, next time you see him."

"I surely will, sir." Agnes blushed. "There's hot water in the pitchers and fresh towels and facecloths beside the basins. If there's anything else you need, let me know."

Elizabeth smiled, "You've thought of everything, dear. Thank you so much."

"Mrs. Carlyle, we put your aunt's things in the larger of the two second-floor spare rooms, assuming she'll be staying a spell."

"Thank you, Agnes. You are worth your weight in gold." Maggie lumbered up the staircase, holding the banister with one hand to steady herself. She thanked the heavens above that her time for confinement was nearing.

Aunt Penny paused on the second-floor landing and turned to Maggie. "Where did you find such a resourceful young girl?"

"Luke hired her as a mother's helper when I was experiencing some difficulty with morning sickness." Maggie smiled and squeezed her aunt's hand. "She's become an invaluable help and a dear friend, as well."

"I wish Sophie possessed a smidgen of her forethought. That woman must be thoroughly instructed in every little thing or nothing gets done." Aunt Penny shook her head.

"Must be the energy and eagerness of youth," suggested Maggie, kissing her aunt's cheek. "That's your room on the left. I see Agnes left a lamp burning for you. Sleep well."

"You too, dear," said Aunt Penny sweetly. In a split second her aunt's expression hardened. "First thing tomorrow morning, you're going to explain why you married that fellow without a word to me."

Before Maggie could utter a reply, Aunt Penny slipped into the spare room and shut the door in her face.

Chapter 20

Friday, December 20, 1889

Between the baby kicking, her sore back, and Aunt Penny's words echoing in her head, Maggie tossed and turned for hours. Did her aunt not approve of Luke? What could she possibly find lacking in the man? He exemplified a loving husband, a doting father, and a good provider. Her aunt must be concerned with something though, but Maggie was at a loss as to what it might be.

Eventually, she'd drifted into a fitful sleep.

A late-rising rooster woke her at eight o'clock, and she rushed through her ablutions. When she lumbered downstairs, she discovered Aunt Penny in the kitchen, serving her children flapjacks shaped like half moons, circles and triangles. Maggie remembered eating her aunt's special flapjacks as a child. She also recalled the devil of an argument Aunt Penny had with that nasty housekeeper to gain entry into her own kitchen.

"Good morning, Maggie. We're having some fun with our breakfast," greeted Aunt Penny.

"I can see that. Where's Agnes?" asked Maggie, pouring herself a cup of coffee from the pot on the woodstove. Aunt Penny's smile suggested she was having as much fun as the children.

"Agnes dashed out of here a half hour ago. Something about a trifle and someone named Morning Star." Aunt Penny finished cutting Sam's flapjacks into bite-sized pieces.

"There's something wrong with Agnes," said Patti, stuffing her mouth with a huge bite.

"What makes you say that?" inquired Maggie, sipping her coffee.

"Agnes was crying," whispered Sam.

"We asked why she was sad," added Lucy.

"She said she was happy." Sam shook his head. "I don't cry when I'm happy."

"Well, sometimes ladies cry when they're happy." Maggie kissed her son's cheek, wondering what on earth could have happened that brought Agnes to tears.

"The children finished their tree decorating while I prepared their breakfast, and Elizabeth is tidying up the parlor," reported Aunt Penny, pouring herself a cup of coffee. "Luke and Ronald mentioned something about a horse barn, and Agnes left me in charge of these rascals."

Sam leaned over and met Patti's eyes. "Are we rascals?" he asked, frowning.

Patti shrugged her shoulders.

"You two are," offered Lucy, adding indignantly, "Not me. I'm too old."

Maggie chuckled. "You are my three wonderful rascals."

"Finish up that breakfast," ordered Aunt Penny. "And then we'll find something fun to do."

"What a brave soul you are, taking on my children by yourself." Maggie smiled. When the children finished their breakfast, however, she intended to send them off to play and settle matters with her aunt. She was still troubled by her comment last night.

Maggie ate a hearty breakfast in spite of her nerves. As she popped the last bite into her mouth, there was a knock at the back door. Mike bustled inside and called, "Good morning."

"Good morning, Mike," replied Maggie. "What brings you to the main house?"

Mike whipped his hat off and poked his head into the kitchen. "I had a talk with a couple of ponies and a certain mare this morning, and they mentioned that they'd like some exercise."

"Yippee," shouted Sam and Patti in unison, hopping about in anticipation.

"We'll be ready in five minutes!" added Lucy, beaming.

In record time the three children were dressed warmly in coats, hats, scarves and mittens with Aunt Penny's help. Mike assisted them into their winter boots, and the youngsters eagerly accompanied him to the horse barn.

"Those children! If you could bottle that energy, you'd be wealthy," sighed Aunt Penny, slumping into her chair.

"We need to talk," began Maggie. She was an emotional mess, and she couldn't wait to clear up this matter. "What you said last night about wanting an explanation? Do you not approve of my marriage?"

"Heavens, that's not what I meant at all," said Aunt Penny, shifting forward in her chair and reaching for Maggie's hand. "If you're happy that's what matters."

"Then why demand an explanation? What have I done wrong?" Maggie prayed the tears wouldn't start; she'd be powerless to stop them.

"Maggie, why wasn't I invited to the wedding?" Aunt Penny straightened her back. "I was very hurt when I heard about your marriage. Of course, I would have declined your invitation, but it would have been a nice gesture."

"It all happened so quickly." Maggie shook her head. "Luke proposed on Wednesday, we married on Friday. My head was still spinning with William dying and the bank foreclosing on my house."

Aunt Penny nodded. "I heard that you'd been forced out."

"William owed the bank a considerable sum of money." Maggie brushed at her tears, having given up all pretense that her emotions were under control. "He was gambling…mostly, he was losing. And he borrowed money using our home as collateral. When he died, he left me penniless, homeless, with a child to raise alone and another on the way. If Luke hadn't proposed marriage…"

"My goodness, dear." Aunt Penny patted Maggie's hand. "You should have notified me immediately. I would have helped you."

"I would *never* accept your money." Maggie swiped at the tears she was powerless to stop and continued crying as she spoke. "Not after the heartless way I left all of you to come to Montana."

"Well, that's the thing, you see. I would have…"

Luke thundered into the kitchen and rushed to his wife's side. "Maggie, what's wrong?" He glared at her aunt. "What did you say to her?"

"Nothing untoward, we were just discussing…"

"I'm taking her up to our room." Luke helped Maggie out of the chair. "I won't have you upsetting my wife when she's so near to delivering our child."

"I'm sorry, dear. I meant no harm," whispered Aunt Penny, her eyes filling. Luke guided his sobbing wife out through the kitchen doorway.

* * *

Aunt Penny and Elizabeth poured themselves a cup of coffee and sat across from Agnes at the kitchen table where the hired girl was peeling potatoes for supper. "This coffee is delicious, dear."

"Thank you, Mrs. Williamson. How long do you plan on staying with us?" inquired Agnes.

Aunt Penny sighed. "That's the question of the hour. I was hoping I wouldn't wear out my welcome before early January, but there was an episode this morning with Luke. I wouldn't be surprised if he ordered me out of his house today."

"Nonsense, Penny," said Elizabeth, patting her hand. "You must be mistaken. That young man is far too well-mannered. Besides, Maggie is delighted you're here."

"I upset Maggie by discussing her sudden marriage. She was sobbing when Luke walked in on our discussion. He was terribly rude, wouldn't even allow me to explain." Aunt Penny dabbed at her own tears with an embroidered lace handkerchief.

Clearly, she was feeling sorry for herself, and hating it. She'd left Philadelphia with such high hopes: an adventurous trip across the wild frontier, a lovely surprise for her niece, spending Christmas with family. And now, she'd made a mess of the whole business on the first day. If Luke sent her packing, she could blame no one but herself.

She'd travelled so far and spent so little time with Maggie and wee Sam that she wouldn't leave unless Maggie told her to go. That new husband of hers didn't realize he was dealing with Penelope Margaret Williamson.

"Maggie's marriage was a very emotional time for all of us." Elizabeth sipped her coffee.

"Would you prefer to discuss this in private, ma'am?" asked Agnes, wiping her hands on her apron. "I can make myself scarce for awhile, Mrs. Waverly."

"You're not one to gossip, Agnes." Elizabeth waved her back to her work, and then she met Aunt Penny's eyes. "William's secrets and lies concerning his gambling debts almost crushed Maggie's spirit. And you know how strong our Maggie is."

"All of it must have been a terrible blow." Aunt Penny sighed, suddenly feeling every one of her seventy-two years.

Elizabeth patted the other woman's wrinkled hand. "Don't think badly of Maggie for marrying Luke. She had no more options at the time. But there was no impropriety. Luke insisted she wouldn't set foot on this ranch unless there was a wedding ceremony."

"Why wouldn't Maggie ask for my help?" Aunt Penny shook her head. "I could have sent her enough money to see her through and then some."

"Pride is a powerful thing. Sometimes pride pushes aside common sense." Elizabeth set her coffee cup down and met Aunt Penny's eyes. "Ronald and I suggested Maggie move back East, but she wouldn't hear of it. Spirit Creek was her home, and there was no telling her otherwise."

"Soon after her marriage to William, Maggie wrote me about her little house in glowing detail. Goodness, it didn't sound much bigger than a gamekeeper's cottage like the one I remember being on my grandfather's estate in England. But she was so proud of her home." Aunt Penny looked away for a few seconds, getting her emotions under control. "Maggie must have been heartbroken: losing her husband, losing her home. She must have felt so lost and alone."

"Shortly after they married, Maggie learned that Luke bought her house. She was as angry as a scalded cat," said Elizabeth.

"What a despicable thing…" began Aunt Penny.

"That's what Maggie thought. But young Sam's name is on the deed, and Luke rented the house to the new sheriff. Each month he deposits the rental funds into an account at the bank to pay for Sam's college education."

"Well, there's something good resulting from Sam's loss." Agnes dropped a potato into the pot. She reddened and whispered, "Sorry, I'm not supposed to be listening."

"You're family here, girl," chuckled Elizabeth.

"All the gambling debts were satisfied at the time of her husband's death?" asked Aunt Penny.

"No one ever came forward demanding money, except that miserable banker. I assume William honored his debts promptly." Elizabeth shook her head. "The gambling fever just grabbed him by the throat and as good as choked the life out of him. Every night was spent playing cards in The Joker's Wild Saloon."

"And Maggie never suspected a thing?" Aunt Penny sighed. "It makes one wonder what else he kept from her."

"I have it on good authority, William never drank a drop of liquor, and he never…" Elizabeth blushed profusely, and then whispered. "And he never visited with the women."

Aunt Penny turned scarlet. "Oh my! Well, that's something in his favor."

"William was a perfect gentleman, and he was an outstanding lawman. Not a soul alive ever had a harsh word for the man," continued Elizabeth. "If only we'd known about the gambling. Perhaps there was something we could have done."

"I doubt very much you could have swayed his interest in any way." Aunt Penny sighed and set down her empty cup.

"Well, Luke Carlyle has his head screwed on straight." Elizabeth refilled their cups, returning the coffee pot to the woodstove. "Of that I can assure you. I've never met a more responsible and compassionate fellow, pillar of the community. Luke dearly loves Maggie and Sam."

"Mr. Carlyle is a wonderful, kind-hearted, generous man." Agnes blushed. "Sorry, I just had to add that. He's been absolutely wonderful to Mike and me."

"Does Maggie love him?" asked Aunt Penny, holding her breath.

"In the beginning, the marriage was simply a means to provide their children with two parents." Elizabeth clasped her hands. "Right off, Sam and Patti got along famously. After a bit of a bumpy road, Lucy came around. And in time, Luke and Maggie fell in love. Maggie is absolutely over the moon in love with the man."

"Well, I've been needlessly worrying about Maggie and Sam." Aunt Penny smiled. "But I can't say this trip has been a waste. I'm delighted to meet you and your dear husband, Elizabeth. And you, too, Agnes. And this is the first time I've seen Sam, except in a couple of photographs."

"He's a handsome lad, is he not?" asked Elizabeth, beaming

like a proud grandmother.

"Sam is a beautiful little boy. Would it be in poor taste if I mentioned…" Aunt Penny hesitated. "Sam has the same brown eyes as Luke's, and the same curly brown hair. Have you noticed how much they resemble each other? Land sakes, if I didn't know better I'd mistake them for a true father and son."

Agnes laughed. "I've noticed the resemblance, too."

"Now that you mention it, the two of them do resemble each other." Elizabeth sighed. "I suppose it will serve them well someday."

"Hello, ladies." Maggie waddled into the kitchen, rubbing her back.

"Are you feeling rested?" asked Aunt Penny, smiling.

"Except for this backache, I feel wonderful." Maggie lowered herself onto a chair. "Is there any coffee, Agnes?"

"I'll get you some." Agnes filled a cup with coffee, added sugar and milk, and placed it in front of Maggie. "Ma'am, there's something I should tell you."

* * *

Aunt Penny and Elizabeth almost tripped over each other, making a speedy retreat from the kitchen.

"Those two must fear you'll confess something terrible and earn yourself an immediate reprimand," commented Maggie, smiling.

Agnes set the paring knife down and took a chair beside her employer. "Early this morning, Mike asked me to go for a little walk with him before I started breakfast."

"And…" encouraged Maggie, shifting in the chair.

"Mike walked me over to the big swing in the back yard and right there as the morning sun brightened the sky he proposed," whispered Agnes, her eyes welling with tears. "And I said yes."

Maggie smiled. "That's wonderful. Mike has been sweet on you for some time now."

Agnes blushed a dozen shades of red. "I've been quite fond of him since the day we met, and I'm so proud of Mike for working so hard and learning to read. He's a wonderful fellow and I love him dearly."

"I'm so happy for you."

Agnes shook her head. "My nursing plans were dashed the minute I accepted his proposal, however, and I dread telling my ma I won't be training as a nurse now. That will be the hardest thing I've ever done in my life."

"Won't she be happy about your marriage?"

"I imagine she will, once she gets accustomed to the idea." Agnes shifted closer to Maggie. "The best part is this. Mike and I searched for Mr. Carlyle and we found him in the horse barn. We told him about our engagement, and I asked him for a favor."

"And what was that?" Maggie hugged Agnes. "I'm certain he wants the both of you to stay here and work on the Diamond C."

"Oh, yes. That wasn't my concern, although I suppose it should have been." She frowned and then continued. "In lieu of my payment, now that I wouldn't be training as a nurse in the East, I asked Mr. Carlyle if he would consider sending my twin sister to normal school to become a teacher instead. That's all Angela has ever wanted for herself. Mr. Carlyle agreed to it, saying it was an excellent idea. And then I went and embarrassed myself by bursting into tears."

Maggie laughed. "Oh, don't worry about that. Men expect a few tears from their womenfolk once in a while."

"He made me so happy, I couldn't stop them." Agnes's eyes filled again.

"Have you decided when you'll marry?"

"I mentioned that I've always dreamed of a spring wedding. Your husband is such a kind-hearted man! He promised us one of the empty cabins to live in after the 'I do's' were spoken. And he insisted I work in the main house for as long as you need me." Agnes shook her head. "I can hardly believe it all."

"With four children and this big house and the garden and whatnot, you can believe this. Keeping up with it all will more than occupy every waking minute for both of us." Maggie reached over and patted Agnes's hand, while making a mental note to suggest to Elizabeth that the community ladies begin work on a bridal quilt for the hard-working bride-to-be. She deserved nothing less.

Agnes glanced at the clock on the kitchen wall and then met Maggie's eyes. "Goodness, look at the time! I've got to finish getting supper on the table. But I wanted you to hear my news from me, Mrs. Carlyle."

"Thank you, Agnes. I'm happy for you and Mike, and I'm delighted your sister will benefit from your generous offer. You're a wonderful young woman, Agnes Jones, and I'm pleased you'll be living here on the ranch permanently."

"Me, too," whispered Agnes, wiping a few tears from her cheek with her apron. "You folks are such wonderful people. I consider it an honor to live here with all of you."

By six o'clock, the family and their visitors were seated around the dining room table, enjoying the evening meal.

Luke cleared his throat, "Aunt Penny, Maggie explained your conversation with her this morning, and I apologize for my inexcusable behavior, wrongfully blaming you for my wife's tears."

"You're totally forgiven, young man." Aunt Penny waved off his apology. "Just proves how readily you'll come to her defense. Quite admirable of you. I hope her language wasn't too strong in setting you straight. She excelled in debating at school as I recall."

Luke chuckled. "Well, my ears aren't bleeding, so it couldn't have been all that bad."

Aunt Penny laughed heartily, and then regaled everyone with humorous stories of Christmas party mishaps involving her friends in Philadelphia. "Christmas with my friends was always such fun, but it certainly doesn't compare to celebrating with family." Aunt Penny beamed.

After supper, Luke and Ronald left the main house with a bottle of whiskey in search of Ned and Mike, to toast the groom-to-be. Elizabeth washed and Agnes dried the supper dishes.

"I'm so delighted you're here." Maggie hugged her aunt, seated with her at the kitchen table. "And you'll see the new baby when it arrives."

"It won't be too soon for me." Aunt Penny clasped her hands. "I haven't held a new baby in ages."

Suddenly, the back door flew open aided by a howling wind. Fluffy white flakes swirled about Morning Star's feet and followed her inside. "Someone close the door, please," she called, carrying Ruth Carlyle's crystal bowl filled with the trifle. She handed the bowl to Agnes who carried it down to the root cellar to keep until Christmas day.

"Wind angry tonight," offered Morning Star, slipping out of her deerskin coat and shaking snowflakes from her hair. "Sky promise lots of snow."

Maggie introduced Aunt Penny to Morning Star, explaining that the gifted native healer was married to Ned.

"Perhaps Ronald and I should head for town if you think there's a storm coming, Morning Star." Elizabeth glanced at the clock atop the breakfront. "It's already seven o'clock. Heavens, Ronald won't want to travel in the dark at this hour."

"Don't go to town. I think dangerous." Morning Star set the kettle on the woodstove and tossed a couple of logs into the fire. "But maybe storm gone by morning. Travel be good then."

"Ronald won't leave the store for long. The man never takes a day off, except for the Lord's Day, of course. He wouldn't know what to do with himself, if there wasn't work to be done."

"Tomorrow, I hope snow stop." Morning Star muttered, her expression not terribly convincing.

"Where's your trifle, Agnes?" inquired Maggie, when the girl returned from the root cellar.

"Morning Star and I prepared it yesterday so I could send it to town in the afternoon with one of the ranch hands, along with my gifts for the family, and your food basket," answered Agnes. "Fewer things to worry about when I leave Christmas Eve day."

"Agnes, you are so organized," said Maggie, shaking her head.

"How are you feeling, Maggie?" asked Morning Star.

"My back troubles me." She slowly rose to her feet. "Actually, I'm going to lie down for a little while."

"Do you need some help getting upstairs?" asked Elizabeth. "We don't want you falling."

"No, no, I'm fine." Maggie patted Elizabeth's arm. "I'll have a little rest, and then I'll challenge you to a game of checkers."

* * *

Luke and Ned returned to the house an hour later, whistling and in good humor. Ned was delighted with the prospect of having Agnes as a daughter-in-law.

Luke stepped into the darkened bedroom he shared with his wife. He could clearly distinguish the outline of her body atop their bed, fully clothed and covered by a quilt from the waist up.

"Maggie, sweetheart, are you asleep?"

"Mmm," mumbled his wife, sounding only half awake.

"Agnes sent me up with a cup of tea for you." Luke set the teacup on the bedside table and kissed his wife on the forehead. She looked so beautiful with her hair mussed and her hand resting on her belly, caressing their child.

"What time is it?" she mumbled.

"Eight-thirty. Elizabeth mentioned a game of checkers." Luke sat beside her on the bed. "Shall I extend your apologies, let you just sleep?"

"I think that would be best," replied Maggie, coming more fully awake and pushing the quilt aside. "I feel a bit strange."

"Is it your back? Are you in pain?" asked Luke.

"I'm not certain," answered Maggie, struggling to swing her feet over the side of the bed. "I should remove these clothes. Would you help me slip into a nightdress?" She stood up and immediately bent over, moaning in pain.

"Maggie, what's wrong?" Luke guided her back onto the bed, preventing a fall. "Sweetheart, have your pains started?"

"I…I think…maybe." Maggie forced the words out with some difficulty. "Let's wait awhile to be certain. I'll let you know when to fetch Rebecca."

"I'll send Morning Star up to sit with you. Rebecca attended Catherine's births, but Morning Star never left her side." Luke kissed her quickly and rushed from the room.

* * *

Maggie listened to Luke race down the stairs in search of Morning Star. She almost called him back. As quickly as the pain came, it disappeared. Perhaps it was nothing. She closed her eyes for a minute and dozed.

"Maggie, are you awake?"

"Yes." She forced her eyes open and attempted to sit up, but the native woman gently pushed her back against the pillows.

"Oh, ouch," groaned Maggie as another pain ripped through her body. She was definitely in labor; her time had come. The baby would arrive in the next few hours.

"You have pains," announced Morning Star. "I help. Make special tea."

"Did Luke send for Rebecca?" mumbled Maggie, sinking back against her pillows when the contraction subsided.

"I talk to Luke. Don't worry." Morning Star rushed out of the room.

Maggie prayed that Rebecca would arrive soon. The baby wasn't waiting much longer.

* * *

Morning Star slipped into the parlor and announced, "Luke, it's time."

"Then we'll fetch the doctor," said Ronald, leaping out of his chair.

"Maggie requested Rebecca. We'll send Mike. He's playing cards with Agnes in the kitchen," explained Luke. This is it, he thought. I'm going to become a father again, tonight. His pulse raced, and for a moment, he even felt a little light-headed.

Ronald and Luke charged into the kitchen. Mike leapt out of his chair scattering playing cards in every direction. "What did I do wrong, sir?"

If Luke wasn't so worried about his wife, he would have found the situation hysterical. The young man nearly jumped out of his skin when his boss charged into the kitchen like a bull with a bee sting.

"You didn't do anything wrong, son." Luke dragged a hand through his hair.

"Then why all the commotion?" asked Agnes, collecting the playing cards strewn about the kitchen table.

"Mrs. Carlyle is in labor." Luke forced himself to take a deep breath. "I need you to ride to the Simpson ranch and fetch Rebecca."

"I dare say with that storm in full gale, it's impossible to find my way anywhere, sir." Mike spoke, a pained expression on his face. "I nearly walked right past the house when I came up from Pa's cabin a few minutes ago."

Luke blanched. "There's a blizzard …"

Mike whistled. "A humdinger. I won't find my way back to the bunkhouse. I'd hoped to sleep on the cot in the corner over there."

"But Maggie's having the baby tonight. We need the midwife

now!" Luke grabbed his coat from the peg, stuck his Stetson on his head, flung the back door open, and stepped outside. Swirling white flakes landed on his hat, stung his eyes, and covered his boots and clothes.

All Luke could see was a blanket of white.

"My God…it's…it's a total whiteout," he stammered and stumbled back into the house. "You can't see your hand in front of your face."

Luke felt dazed. Ronald stepped up beside him, grabbed the door, and swung it closed. Someone took his coat out of his hand and guided him like a child toward a chair.

Aunt Penny and Elizabeth wandered into the kitchen. "What is all the fuss about?" asked Elizabeth.

"Maggie's in labor," whispered Luke. "She's having the baby tonight."

"Then send for the doctor," stated Elizabeth, hands on hips.

"Darling," said Ronald, crossing the floor and taking his wife's hand. "The storm has turned into a blizzard, a total whiteout. No one's going anywhere tonight."

Elizabeth's hand flew to her mouth.

"Merciful heavens," whispered Aunt Penny, slumping into a chair beside Luke. "What are we going to do?"

Ronald and Elizabeth each took an arm and guided Luke toward the parlor. Agnes, Mike and Aunt Penny followed closely behind.

* * *

"We should have sent for Rebecca sooner." Elizabeth's voice caught, and her eyes filled.

Agnes realized the poor woman blamed herself, and she reached for Elizabeth's hand. "We had no way of knowing," she whispered.

Elizabeth stood speechless and shook her head.

"We'll think of something," said Mike, shifting from one foot to the other.

"I make birthing tea for pains. Bring medicine up to main house several days ago to be ready," said Morning Star, poking her head into the parlor. "I not know about blizzard. Think Luke get

Rebecca. I say to Maggie 'not worry'."

"You did the right thing, Morning Star, telling Maggie not to worry. We don't want my niece getting herself all worked up," said Aunt Penny.

"Someone *must* help Maggie," mumbled Luke, slumping onto the sofa.

"I never birth baby." Morning Star whispered the admission. It was evident to Agnes that the imminent birth of Maggie's baby unnerved the normally calm native healer.

"I've never birthed a baby either, and I have no intention of starting tonight," stated Aunt Penny, frowning.

Every pair of eyes in the room turned toward Elizabeth. "Why, I'd faint dead away." She shivered, involuntarily.

"Need help me." Morning Star's voice rose an octave.

"I'll help you." Agnes's insides were tripping over each other, but she refused to admit her misgivings. "My mama's birthed a dozen babies. Being fourth oldest, I've witnessed birthing before. Why, I've even assisted Doc Fitzgerald the last time or two."

Elizabeth audibly gasped.

"Land sakes!" whispered Aunt Penny.

"Agnes, you help and I thank you every day I live on this earth." Morning Star grasped Agnes's hand and clutched it to her chest.

"I'll help you, Morning Star." Agnes repeated. "But we must remain calm and think this through." Her employer treated her like family. If anything bad happened to Mrs. Carlyle, she would never forgive herself.

"Thank you, Agnes." The native woman kissed her hands.

"We can do this." She spoke with more confidence than she felt. "Nothing's happening to this baby if I have anything to say about it."

"I live with my people seventeen summers. I see baby born many years ago. I don't remember what do."

"There's a rather…explicit…medical book, belonged to Mr. Carlyle's mother, on a shelf in his study." Agnes reddened, glanced around the room and whispered, "There's information on child birthing in it."

"Agnes!" Elizabeth blanched.

"I admit I read it…a couple of times. I'm interested in

medicine." Agnes held her head high. "It was my intention to train as a nurse, and I won't apologize for reading such material. There's nothing shameful in educating yourself. And Doc Fitzgerald encouraged me to read his medical textbooks, too."

Elizabeth patted her chest and took a deep breath. "Agnes, you're a godsend. Morning Star, are you certain this birthing tea will help Maggie?"

"As sure as sun will rise each day. And horsemint to assist afterbirth. And baneberry for Maggie's milk." Morning Star smiled. "My medicines work good."

"I believe you. We're having us a baby tonight, Morning Star. Get busy." Elizabeth shooed the native woman toward the kitchen.

At that moment, Sam and Patti skipped into the parlor. Luke bent on one knee and smiled at his children. "Sam, Patti, you could have a new brother or sister by morning."

Patti frowned and her bottom lip trembled. "Papa, I heard you say there's a blizzard. The stork won't find our house!"

"The stork brought twelve children to my mama's house, and some nights it was raining, and some nights it was snowing. That big old bird never got lost once! Don't worry, that smart old stork knows what he's doing." Agnes tugged on Patti's pigtails and was rewarded with a smile.

Luke met his oldest daughter's eyes. "Lucy, kindly read these two a story, listen to their prayers, and tuck them in for the night."

Sam's eyes widened. "And our new baby will be here in the morning?"

Luke kissed both children on the top of the head. "Off to bed with the two of you. There might be a new sister or brother here by morning."

"Yippee!" Sam shouted and raced Patti upstairs, with Lucy following close behind.

"I'll fetch that medical book." Agnes rushed out of the parlor, headed for Luke's study.

"We certainly don't need those two underfoot all night." Elizabeth stood, hands on her hips. "But do you think it wise to mention the baby, Luke? What if…"

"No negative thoughts." Luke shook his head. "The baby will arrive safe and sound. Agnes is an intelligent girl. If anyone can pull this off, she can."

"I found the book." Agnes returned to the parlor, sat on the unoccupied sofa, and placed the open book on her lap. "I'll browse the birthing passages again, and we'll split up the duties."

"Just tell us what to do." Elizabeth sat beside Agnes.

"We require two tubs of hot water to ensure things are clean and sterile and to wash the baby." Agnes peeked up, her eyes meeting Elizabeth's, and then she continued. "We'll need old towels and sheets. I'll fetch some from the linen closet."

"What else, Agnes?" asked Aunt Penny, motioning her to continue.

"Those old newspapers in the third-floor storage room, Mr. Carlyle. They'll be perfect for soaking up…." Agnes blushed. She almost said the blood and the afterbirth, but caught herself. "Please carry a box down to Maggie's room."

"Consider it done." Luke charged out of the parlor.

Morning Star popped her head through the parlor's open door. "Maggie's tea ready."

"Morning Star, the medical book recommends using ether for easing the pains." Agnes smiled at her friend. "But I'm putting my faith in your teas."

"Thank you, Agnes," whispered Morning Star, beaming at the praise. The native woman exited the parlor.

Lucy returned to the parlor and slumped onto the sofa beside Aunt Penny. "Sam and Patti were asleep before I finished the story. I carried Sam back to his room and tucked him in. I listened to their prayers beforehand, and they both asked for the baby's safe arrival. Sam requested a brother, and Patti wanted a sister." Lucy laughed. "One of them will be happy."

"Thank you, dear, for helping with the little ones," said Aunt Penny, patting Lucy's arm. "You should turn in for the night, too."

"I always read for a while first. And then I'll go up to bed." Lucy reached for her book sitting on a nearby table. She curled her legs under her and buried her nose in the book.

Agnes smiled, and then her expression turned serious again. "This is Maggie's second baby. The first one usually requires a great length of laboring time, but second and third babies come much sooner."

"Let's hope Maggie delivers this baby with little difficulty." Aunt Penny wiped her brow with her handkerchief. "We certainly don't want her in any greater discomfort than necessary."

"Agnes will sort out the linens while I get some water boiling," ordered Elizabeth.

* * *

In the upstairs storage room, Luke grabbed a large box overflowing with newspapers and lugged it down to the second-floor master bedroom. When he placed the flimsy box on the floor, one of the sides split open and newspapers slid across the floor and under the bed.

"Blasted thing," he muttered. He peeked over at his wife and the scattered newspapers were forgotten. White-knuckled, Maggie clasped the sheet to her chin.

Luke reached for her hand. "What's wrong, sweetheart?"

"Everything," whispered Maggie. "We can't send for Rebecca or Doc because of the blizzard. And there's no one to help me except Morning Star and Agnes."

"I know, sweetheart. But everything will be fine."

"I see the worry in Morning Star's eyes…the poor woman is trying to be brave…but she's frightened near to death. And Agnes is only seventeen. Luke, I've never been so scared in my life." A sob escaped her lips.

"You've had a baby before, Maggie. There's nothing to fret about. I'm certainly not concerned." Luke hoped she believed his lie.

"But what if something goes wrong? What if something happens to the baby?" Tears slowly trickled down Maggie's cheeks, and her shoulders shook.

Luke hardened his resolve. "Nothing will happen to the baby."

"I want to believe it, and I want to be brave," whispered Maggie.

"That's my girl. Agnes helped Doc Fitzgerald with birthing her siblings, and she knows what she's doing." Luke kissed his wife's forehead. "No more fussing, sweetheart."

"Agnes is not a doctor, not even a trained midwife. I'm entitled to some fussing, Luke," snapped Maggie.

"I'm going downstairs to smoke a cigar with Ronald. I'm not the least bit worried about you or the baby."

"Luke, please stay with me." Maggie's eyes pleaded with him, and then her tears flowed, which almost undid his resolve. But he couldn't show her how numb with fear he was. It would only frighten her more.

"You'll do fine." Luke kissed her cheek and exited the room.

Chapter 21

Luke hurried down to the main floor, strode directly to his study, and poured himself a generous shot of scotch, feeling as low as a snake's belly for the callous words he'd spoken to Maggie. He closed his eyes and prayed for the child's safe arrival. He swallowed the drink in one gulp and refilled his glass.

Ned and Ronald entered the room and slumped into the two chairs opposite Luke's desk.

"How are you doing?" asked Ronald.

Luke waved his hand, unable to put his emotions into words. Without needing to ask, he poured each gentleman a drink, distributed them, and then slumped into the oversized leather chair behind his desk.

"Sonny Boy, I can't imagine the thoughts athunderin' round in yer head right now. Morning Star and I weren't blessed with young'uns of our own, but we worried over Mike like he was our own flesh and blood. I know…it's not the same as worryin' over yer woman at a time like this." Ned struck a match, lit his pipe.

"Me neither, son." Ronald sighed. "Elizabeth and I never had children…it just never happened. We both wanted young ones around the house, but I guess it wasn't in God's plan."

"Oh, pooh!" scolded Aunt Penny, standing inside the doorway. "Birthing a baby is the most natural thing in the world. Maggie's young and healthy. She'll be fine."

"How many children have you brought into the world, Aunt Penny?" asked Luke, rising from his chair and heading toward the liquor table. He'd just assured Maggie she'd be fine a few minutes ago. Even hearing the same sentiment from Aunt Penny, he still didn't believe it.

"Children? Well, none actually. My husband and I were never blessed with wee ones. But I'm an excellent aunt, if I do say so myself." Aunt Penny's hands twisted the handkerchief she held, belying her previous convictions.

"Maggie would agree with you there." Luke picked up a clean glass. "Would you like some sherry?"

"Yes, dear, I believe I would." Aunt Penny moved across the floor and stood beside him. When Luke stemmed the flow, Aunt Penny tipped up the sherry bottle just a second or two longer. And then she patted Luke's arm, accepted the glass. "That's a good man."

"Would you kindly pour me one, please?" Elizabeth entered through the open doorway.

"Elizabeth, I didn't notice you standing there." Aunt Penny flushed from a healthy swig and turned to Luke. "Thank you, dear, that's excellent sherry."

"You're very welcome." Luke smiled. Apparently, Aunt Penny and expensive sherry were old friends.

"Thank you for the drink, Luke. Why don't we busy ourselves with a game of checkers while we wait?" Elizabeth smiled and clasped her glass in both hands.

"A splendid idea. Would you gentlemen care to join us?" inquired Aunt Penny on her way out the door.

"Ma'am, men folk cain't abide playin' checkers at a time like this," scolded Ned. "We'll take turns helpin' with the floor pacin' and the cigar smokin'."

"You two run along and enjoy your checkers." Ronald winked at Ned. "We'll just wait here with the soon-to-be new papa."

* * *

As soon as Morning Star ushered Luke out of the room, Maggie burst into tears. Her husband had just walked out with only a kiss to her cheek before essentially abandoning her. Everything was in God's hands anyway. She quietly cried and sipped her laboring tea.

Preparations for the birth were moving along nicely. Clean sheets were laid out for the bed and for wrapping the new baby. A pile of old towels were stacked at the foot of the bed, and Morning

Star straightened up the newspapers that Luke scattered across the floor. A small tub of steaming water stood ready on a table beside the bed.

"Why you cry, Maggie?" Morning Star piled pillows behind Maggie's back to provide a more comfortable position. "Birthing tea no work?"

Maggie shook her head. "It's not that. I'm not in much pain at all. Thank you."

"Have pillows on back good. You need more, you ask." Morning Star placed the back of her hand on Maggie's cheek.

"I'm not feverish, Morning Star."

"Then why you cry? Should be happy. Have new baby soon." Morning Star moved to the foot of the bed and began ripping old towels into long strips as per Agnes's instructions.

A sob escaped Maggie's lips. "You heard Luke. He doesn't love this baby, or he'd be worried sick about its safety."

"He worried," insisted Morning Star, nodding her head as she worked.

Maggie wanted to share the native woman's unwavering belief in Luke, but she wasn't convinced. "Luke told me he isn't concerned. But any number of things could go wrong. He just doesn't care."

"You believe that?" Morning Star tied a long strip of towel to the first bedpost.

"Yes, I'm certain. Otherwise, he never would have left my side."

"Silly talk," said Morning Star waving the idea away with her hand. "Do you believe something go wrong?"

"I don't want to, but Agnes is so young…" Maggie wiped her eyes. "I don't know what to think."

As if on cue, the teenager swept into the room. "Mrs. Carlyle, how are you feeling?" inquired Agnes, hugging the precious medical book to her chest.

"Please call me Maggie. If we're going through this birthing together, don't you think Mrs. Carlyle is a bit formal?" Maggie smiled, weakly. Agnes seemed so confident despite her age. She envied the girl, realizing she had never possessed such self-assurance in her entire thirty-one years.

"Maggie, it doesn't get more personal than one woman assisting with the delivering of another woman's baby." Agnes patted her arm.

"To answer your question…the tea's taking the edge off the pains."

"She be crying. Think Mr. Carlyle not care about the baby," blurted Morning Star.

"Well, judging by the expression on Mr. Carlyle's face when he charged down the stairs a few minutes ago nearly running me over, he's plenty worried about you and the baby." Agnes patted Maggie's hand. "Knowing Mr. Carlyle, he didn't want to frighten you by divulging how worried he really was."

"He looked worried?" Maggie bolted upright, but another pain struck at the same moment forcing her back against the pillows.

"Scared…to…death," corrected Agnes, patting Maggie's hand.

"Thank you for telling me that, Agnes. I feel a lot better," said Maggie, grimacing through the contraction. "You're right. He probably didn't want me worrying."

"I brew more tea. Be right back." Morning Star rushed from the bedroom.

* * *

With aching knees, Aunt Penny climbed the stairs to Maggie's bedroom and knocked on the door. Agnes pulled her inside, almost whisking her off her feet.

"Quickly, keep the heat in the room. We don't want Maggie catching a chill," stated Agnes, her expression serious. She turned, strode to the chaise longue in the corner, and buried her nose in her medical book.

"Maggie, dear, how are you doing?" Aunt Penny straightened her spine and patted her hair. The baby's arrival was a ways off and there was no call for nerves.

"I'm so happy to see you," said Maggie, setting her teacup on the night table.

"Elizabeth skunked me in checkers, three games in a row. So I came up to check on you, dear. If you prefer I leave just say so." Aunt Penny twisted her handkerchief in her hands.

"Nonsense. You may stay as long as you wish." Maggie patted the bed beside her.

"Well, all right. As long as I won't be in the way." Aunt Penny crept across the room and perched on the edge of the bed.

"Heavens, not at all. I appreciate your company," whispered Maggie, grimacing, and then a moan escaped her.

"Oh, dear." Aunt Penny sprang off the bed. "Is something wrong?"

"Just a pain. It'll pass." Maggie smiled, weakly.

Aunt Penny sat again and waited an eternity until her niece sighed.

"There now, it's stopped." Maggie lay back against the pillows.

"Dear, why are there strips of towels tied to the bedposts?" Aunt Penny frowned and looked at Agnes.

Agnes looked up from her book and glanced over. "The towels are for the final stage of laboring. Gripping the towels helps the mother bear down and force the baby out."

"My goodness, how clever." Aunt Penny attempted to relax. All this talk of bearing down and forcing babies out made her a little queasy.

"This birth will go smoothly, if I have anything to say about it." Agnes returned to the bedside and patted Maggie's brow with a small towel.

"You're a godsend, child." Aunt Penny rose and hugged Agnes.

"Chat with Maggie until her time nears." Agnes rested her hand on Aunt Penny's shoulder. "I'm going downstairs for a cup of tea and a Christmas cookie, but I'll be right back."

"Thank you, Agnes. I'll be fine until you return." Maggie waved the young girl on her way.

* * *

"Maggie, be honest with me now. How are you doing, truthfully?" Aunt Penny searched her eyes and Maggie felt like a child again. Her aunt sat with her hands folded on her lap, just the way Maggie remembered as a child.

"The pains are bearable, thanks to Morning Star's tea, and…"

"No, dear, Morning Star confided that something is bothering you." Aunt Penny grasped her hand. "Is it Luke?"

Maggie smiled as history repeated itself. Her mother had thrived on her charity events and social engagements; it never crossed her mind that her daughter might need her for anything. But Maggie could always rely on Aunt Penny's intuition when something in her life was amiss, and she would pour out her problems and her insecurities to the most important woman in her life.

"I thought Luke's indifference meant he didn't care about the baby. Agnes assured me his aloofness was all pretense. He didn't want to worry me, show me how frightened he really was." Maggie smiled through another contraction. "I'm feeling much better about it all now."

"So have things between you and Luke always gone smoothly?" Aunt Penny wiped Maggie's brow with the towel, mimicking Agnes's tender care.

"Our marriage began as an arrangement. I would care for the house and the children, and Luke would run the ranch. We were legally married, all proper of course, but there was no mention of…love." Maggie felt her face redden.

"Why on earth would you marry a man you didn't love?"

Maggie's eyes filled with tears. "Auntie, you deserve the truth. I had no more options. I needed a roof over our heads."

"I don't understand why you didn't contact me? Ask for the money you needed?" Aunt Penny shook her head.

"I was too ashamed. I'd moved to Spirit Creek against all of your wishes." It sounded like ancient history to Maggie's ears, but her mind recalled her family's disappointment in her defiant decision as if it were yesterday.

"But we kept in touch. Your letters assured me that you were insanely happy teaching the children. You were head-over-heels in love with that young lawman of yours." Aunt Penny smiled. "I understood your passion for the West. You made the right decision for yourself."

"My life seemed perfect." Maggie hiccupped with the remnant of her tears. "And then William was killed, and I discovered…"

"He'd kept secrets from you."

"William gambled, borrowed money against our home. After he died, the banker just demanded all monies owing. I was penniless, and I couldn't find a job. I lost my home." Maggie choked on the words.

"Dear, you should have sent a telegraph. I would have sent the funds immediately." Aunt Penny pulled her into a warm embrace.

Maggie dabbed at her tears with a corner of the sheet. Confessing everything to her aunt felt good. "I'd been such a fool for trusting William, and I couldn't take your money."

"I wouldn't have sent *my* money, dear. I would have sent *your* money," whispered Aunt Penny. "When your parents passed, God rest their souls, I handled all the arrangements for you, remember?" Aunt Penny searched Maggie's eyes.

"I was heartbroken, but I'm certain all of Philadelphia considered me a grand disappointment since I didn't even attend my parents' burial." Maggie sighed.

"Nonsense. I explained at the service that you were delivering their first grandchild any day, and you were unable to travel. Everyone understood the situation." Aunt Penny smiled.

Your money. Her aunt's earlier comment finally registered in Maggie's mind. "Mother and Father left me some money?" asked Maggie incredulously. "They were so angry when I moved out West, I assumed they'd disowned me and left everything to charity."

"Their wills left all their worldly possessions to their only child, Margaret Penelope Wentworth Burns. They loved you dearly, although they were never demonstrative people, were they?" Aunt Penny appeared deep in thought.

"They loved me in their own way, I suppose. Now that I have Sam, I can't imagine not loving him regardless of what he did."

"With the letter you sent giving me your power of attorney, I sold their elegant home and the furnishings and paintings, horses, carriages, everything. I deposited all the funds into a separate bank account in your name." Aunt Penny wrung her hands, unable to meet her niece's eyes.

"There's more, isn't there?"

"Yes, Maggie, there's more. You were living way out in no man's land with a perfect stranger." Aunt Penny took a deep breath. "I hired a fellow to travel to Spirit Creek and report back to me on your new husband's character."

"And what did this fellow report?" Maggie held her breath, although she wasn't certain why. William was a good lawman and a wonderful father.

"The fellow, a retired Pinkerton detective, assured me William Burns was a fine gentleman. Came from an army background. Honorable and a remarkable lawman. But the fellow reported that your new husband displayed a greater fondness for gambling than he did talent. I secreted your money away for a rainy day, knowing that if I forwarded the funds to you they would come under your husband's control. I never sent you a penny for fear he would gamble it all away."

"My goodness, in hindsight, I'm certainly thankful you made that decision." Maggie forgot her laboring discomfort with all that she was learning.

"With the sale of your parents' home and all. And with the cash your father held on deposit in the bank. And your mother's money from her parents. Well, it all tallied up to a considerable sum."

"I required two hundred dollars to pay the bank loan, an almost unimaginable amount on William's salary." Maggie grimaced with the painful memory of miserable Banker Peterman foreclosing on her home. "Would there have been sufficient funds to pay the banker?"

"Dear, there's over twenty-seven thousand dollars in your bank account," whispered Aunt Penny.

Maggie gasped. "That's a fortune!"

"My dear husband left me far more than your parents had, and that's also bequeathed to you when I pass. Maggie, you and your children will never want for anything as long as you live." Aunt Penny patted her hand.

"I didn't have to marry Luke, did I? If only my pride hadn't clouded my judgment, I could have paid the banker and stayed in my little house. And I would have had enough money to live on as well." Maggie dropped her head into her hands. "How could I have been so stupid? I let my foolish pride…"

"Do you love, Luke? Do you love those two sweet girls like there were your own?" Aunt Penny peeked over her spectacles. "Things happen for a reason, dear. There was a purpose behind your marriage."

"You're right, Aunt Penny. We're a family and I can't imagine my life without them." Maggie smiled. Luke was dearer to her than William had ever been. He never lied to her and he would never deceive her. She'd made the right decision.

"When I return to Philadelphia, I'll send your money to you. Luke is a man of means and of impeccable character. Your money will be quite safe in his hands." Aunt Penny kissed her niece on the cheek.

"Let me discuss this with Luke first. I refuse to deposit one penny of my money in the Spirit Creek Commerce and Trust Bank." As Maggie spoke, Mr. Peterman's face flashed before her eyes. Some wounds cut too deeply to heal, too deeply to forgive. "Luke has accounts with the Stockmen's Bank in Miles City, and I'd feel quite safe depositing my funds there, too."

"Excellent." Aunt Penny slapped her knees. "I was worried that you might decide to pack up and move back to Philadelphia. Forget about everything you've built here with Luke."

"I could never leave my home here on the Diamond C." Maggie knew it was the truth. Even with the knowledge that she was a woman of some wealth, her heart told her she belonged with Luke.

Suddenly, a contraction sliced through her middle, and she grimaced in pain. "I require another cup of Morning Star's tea."

With impeccable timing, Morning Star and Agnes bustled into the room. "How's Maggie doing?" asked Agnes.

"She's still having pains," piped up Aunt Penny, realizing Maggie couldn't speak at the moment. "Requires another cup of your marvelous tea, Morning Star."

"Let's have a peek and see how we're progressing." Agnes shooed Aunt Penny off the bed.

* * *

Elizabeth slowly climbed the staircase and headed toward Maggie's bedroom. Never in her wildest dreams had she imagined herself willingly doing this, even anticipating the experience. She'd never witnessed a baby's birth before, but she wanted to share this special time with Maggie whom she loved like a daughter. Penny hadn't returned, and if she could face the birthing, Elizabeth told herself so could she.

She gingerly knocked on the door and was quickly admitted by Agnes.

The first thing Elizabeth noticed was Maggie's distorted face. Knees wobbling, she almost bolted out the door. "Oh dear, is something wrong?" Her heart began racing, and she grasped Agnes's hand for support.

"Just a contraction. The pain will pass in a minute," answered Agnes, holding tightly to Elizabeth's trembling hand to reassure her.

"Everything ready. I be very happy when baby is out." Morning Star fussed with Maggie's pillows.

"We have every confidence in Agnes, don't we, Elizabeth?" Aunt Penny poked her new friend in the ribs. "This young lady is doing a fabulous job, Maggie. A midwife couldn't be more prepared."

"Yes, every confidence," mumbled Elizabeth, glaring at Penny. She wasn't entirely certain she wouldn't faint in the middle of it all, but she wouldn't worry anyone with her misgivings.

Agnes smiled at Morning Star and whispered, "Neither of them has a clue what we're doing, right?"

"Probably not," answered Morning Star, grinning. "But we doing a wonderful job."

"Well, I'm fairly certain I know what I'm doing," declared Agnes, standing a little taller. "I'm as ready as I'll ever be."

"That's the spirit," encouraged Elizabeth, feeling Agnes's confidence and bravery rubbing off on her. "Remember, this is the reason you wanted to become a nurse…"

"To help people and that includes birthing babies." Agnes finished her sentence for her.

* * *

"What time is it?" inquired Maggie, shifting positions yet again in an attempt to feel more comfortable. "Oh, fiddle! There's no end to this."

"It's one o'clock in morning. Babies no come at good hour," offered Morning Star.

"Let's take another peek and see how you're progressing." Agnes poked her nose under the sheet covering Maggie's private parts.

"How she doing?" Morning Star held Maggie's hand as she grimaced through another contraction.

"Oh my, the baby's coming. The head has crowned." Agnes took a deep breath. "This is it, ladies. Give me a minute, Maggie, and then you can push."

"Is it a boy or a girl?" blurted Elizabeth, clasping her hands together.

"I can't tell by the hair color, Mrs. Waverly." Agnes remained intent on her duties.

"Of course not, how silly of me," mumbled Elizabeth, plopping down on the vanity stool and wiping her brow with a lacy handkerchief.

"Now, Maggie, grab the towels and bear down with this contraction." Agnes peeked over the sheet and met Maggie's eyes. "Start pushing!"

Maggie pushed and pushed, certain her body would rip apart. She tightened her grasp on the towels and pushed some more. Finally, the contraction waned and she flopped back against the pillows. She drew in a deep breath and Morning Star wiped her brow.

Instantly, another contraction racked her body. She gripped the towels as if her life depended upon it and bent forward slightly before she bore down. Suddenly, she felt the baby slip out of her body, and the pains stopped immediately. She collapsed against the pillows and smiled in relief, still panting with a few tears sliding down her cheeks.

"It's a boy!" announced Agnes.

The room echoed with a cacophony of laughter and tears and Maggie was inundated with congratulations. She held her breath, waiting for the small cry, proof that her baby was alive and well.

Silence.

"What's wrong? What's happening?" she screamed, pulling herself onto her elbows. "Why isn't he crying?"

Agnes wrapped the baby in a clean towel and wiped his face. Maggie watched as the girl lifted him upside down and gave him a sound pat on his bottom.

Silence.

"Oh, no," whispered Maggie, her vision blurring with unshed tears. "Oh, no. Please, no."

Agnes slapped his bottom again eliciting a small whimper. And then a loud rousing cry announced the baby's displeasure at being thrust into such a cold, strange environment.

Maggie relaxed and closed her eyes. "Thank you, God," she whispered.

Aunt Penny kissed Maggie's cheek. "He's beautiful. His birth was a true miracle. I've never witnessed anything so wonderful."

"I'm just thankful that he's healthy. He is healthy, don't you think, Agnes?" Maggie had to raise her voice so Agnes could hear over the baby's crying. The new mother rose up on her elbows and peeked over her bent knees.

"If his lungs are any indication, then I would say he's healthy. Ten fingers and ten toes. He's the most gorgeous thing I've ever seen." Agnes laughed and met Maggie's eyes. "Mind you, I say that about all newborns."

Maggie burst into tears, and then Agnes was crying, too.

"Maggie, he's just so precious. I'm going downstairs to tell Luke he has a new son." Elizabeth headed for the bedroom door, paused and looked back meeting Maggie's eyes. "Thank you for allowing me to share this special moment with you."

"I'm so happy you were here, Elizabeth, and Aunt Penny, too," whispered Maggie, tears streaming down her cheeks.

"Tell Mr. Carlyle we'll send for him in a few minutes. He's not to come up here before then," warned Agnes.

"Agnes and Morning Star, I'm so very proud of both of you." Aunt Penny dabbed at her tears. "If you weren't here to help my niece, Lord knows what could have happened."

* * *

The two older ladies left the bedroom and hobbled down the long staircase in record time.

"Luke! Luke! Where are you young man?" called Elizabeth, discovering his study empty. "Where is everyone?"

"We're in the kitchen finishing off the cobbler you made for supper, Elizabeth," replied Ronald. He, Ned and Luke charged out of the kitchen and met the women in the hallway.

"What in tarnation is all the fuss about?" asked Ned.

"Luke, you have a brand new son!" Aunt Penny clasped her hands together. "He's the most beautiful baby in the whole world."

"Hot damn! Just what I was hoping for! I've got another son!" Luke danced around Ronald and Ned linking his arms with each man in turn.

"How'd you find out?" asked Luke. "I thought you were playing checkers in the parlor?"

"We witnessed the birth, the whole miracle. That was the most moving experience of my life." Elizabeth gushed and then burst into tears.

"I'll be talking about this for weeks." Aunt Penny smiled, swiping at her own tears. "Wait until I tell this story at bridge club when I return home."

"I've got to see him!" called Luke, heading for the staircase.

"You're supposed to wait…" Elizabeth gave up, realizing she couldn't have stopped the new papa if she'd tried.

* * *

Luke knocked soundly on the bedroom door and then barged into the room. He paled immediately. There was blood everywhere, or so it seemed. Maggie's face was as white as the sheet covering her top half, the bottom portion of her body was fully exposed. He quickly averted his eyes.

"I told Elizabeth we'd send for you when we were ready," scolded Agnes.

"It's not her fault. I couldn't wait." Luke met Maggie's eyes, and he felt his face redden as he hurried to her side. "Sorry to intrude, but I needed to see our new son with my own eyes."

"I haven't seen much of him myself," admitted Maggie, attempting a smile. "You might as well stay since you're here now."

"Here's baby boy. Agnes tie cord. I wash him." Morning Star beamed and turned the swaddled baby for his mother to view.

"I put a coin where the cord is tied so it stays flat like it showed in the book. Did you weigh him?" asked Agnes, still seated at the foot of the bed. "I know you snuck the scale up here from the pantry."

"He weigh seven and half pounds. Same as large chicken or puny goose," teased Morning Star.

"Stop making jokes and hand him over." Maggie felt exhausted and exhilarated in equal measure. She kept thinking they were forgetting something, but her mind would only focus on her new son.

Morning Star placed the swaddled baby in her arms.

"Hello there, precious child," Maggie whispered, smiling at the beautiful little eyes that peered up at her.

Luke's eyes misted and he whispered in awe, "He's so small, but he's perfect."

Maggie reached for Luke's hand. "I've never been so happy since the first time I held Sam."

"Luke, take the baby…downstairs…just for a while, please…." Agnes's voice trailed off, and Luke met her eyes. Agnes waited for him to take the baby from his mother.

"Go ahead, Luke. Show him to everyone. Then bring him back, and I'll try to feed him when we're all cleaned up." Maggie kissed the top of her son's downy-soft head and handed the baby to his father.

"I'll be careful with him."

"He won't break. Just make sure you bring him back. Once Elizabeth gets hold of him, you'll have to pry him out of her arms." Maggie smiled and flopped back against her pillows.

* * *

"Agnes, can I speak with you for a second?" whispered Luke, motioning with a nod for her to follow him out to the hallway. Luke carried the baby out of the room, holding him securely in his arms, like a priceless piece of crystal that could break at any moment. Agnes followed him out and closed the bedroom door.

"What's going on? There's something you're not telling me." Luke held his breath, uncertain whether or not he wanted to hear this. Whatever it was, he had to face it.

Chapter 22

"Dammit. Just tell me." Luke glared at Agnes, his frustration level building by the second. His beautiful new son was snuggled safe in his arms, but something was wrong. The image of all the blood he'd noticed when he first walked into the bedroom flashed through his mind. Was Maggie hemorrhaging? "I know something isn't right; I can see it in your eyes."

"It's just...we're waiting for..." whispered Agnes, unable to meet his eyes.

"What on earth are you saying? Are you saying there's another baby coming?" Luke teetered on his feet for a second and then found his balance.

"Heavens no. Nothing like that." Agnes took a deep breath. "It's the afterbirth."

"The afterbirth?" mumbled Luke.

"The placenta where the baby grew inside Maggie."

"I know what it is. I've helped birth hundreds of calves and foals. The afterbirth hasn't expelled?" asked Luke.

Agnes shook her head and blinked back tears. "I'm really worried, and I don't know what to do. If it doesn't pass soon...Maggie could..."

"This could threaten her life?" Removing a hand from around the swaddled baby, Luke touched the girl's arm, forcing her to meet his eyes.

Agnes nodded. "I'm sorry, sir. I did everything the book said. The birth went so smoothly. I can't imagine what's gone wrong now."

"I'm taking the baby downstairs to Elizabeth. I'll be back in a minute. We'll figure this out together." He shifted the warm bundle in his arms.

"Thank you, sir." Agnes sniffled. "I'm so sorry."

"It'll be all right, Agnes. Be brave." Luke flew down the stairs with the baby clutched to his chest, fervently praying. He couldn't lose Maggie now. Not after they'd come so far.

* * *

"Just burn all the old sheets and towels that were ruined during the baby's birth." Maggie smiled at Morning Star. Her mouth was dry; she would dearly love a cup of cold water. But she didn't feel it fair to ask, after all the help she'd received. "Thank you so much for the birthing tea, Morning Star, and for assisting Agnes."

"You welcome, Maggie." Morning Star blushed with the praise. "I don't mind wash sheets and towels. No need to burn."

"The linen cupboard is overflowing with new ones that have never been used. No need to toil over blood stains this time of year. That young fellow will keep you busy enough with his gowns, blankets, booties, and whatnot."

"All right," conceded Morning Star. "I just burn."

Agnes returned to the bedroom and marched straight to Maggie's bedside. "Mrs. Carlyle, there's a…a…a problem…"

"What is it? Is it the baby?" Maggie's eyes darted between Agnes and Morning Star. Why had she suddenly become Mrs. Carlyle? All through the birthing, she'd been Maggie. "What are you not telling me?"

"The afterbirth hasn't passed yet." Agnes grimaced and wrung her hands. "It's been a half hour, and it should have passed. I'm afraid something's wrong."

"The afterbirth!" exclaimed Maggie. "That's the thing that's been niggling at me. We've forgotten about the afterbirth."

"You read," ordered Morning Star, thrusting the medical book into Agnes's hands.

"I've read it a dozen times. It says the placenta should pass within thirty minutes." Agnes tossed the book onto the table. "Why hasn't it?"

Luke charged into the room and abruptly stopped as if

blocked by an invisible wall. "Has it passed?" he whispered.

Agnes checked. "Not yet," she answered, shaking her head. "I don't understand it."

"So, tell me what happens if it doesn't pass." Luke dragged his hands through his hair.

"There's surely going to be infection. And there could be bleeding, life-threatening bleeding," she whispered, hoping Maggie wouldn't hear. "If the placenta moves up it could press against vital organs and…"

"And what?" Luke met Agnes's frightened eyes.

"If it moves up and presses against her heart or lungs, she could stop breathing." Agnes took a deep breath. "Mr. Carlyle, we have to get it out. If we don't…it will surely kill Maggie."

"Oh, God." Luke wavered on his feet. He grasped Agnes's hand. "Just pull it out."

"We can't just pull it out. It must separate from inside the mother's body. I believe it has separated, but it's not moving down since Maggie doesn't feel the urge to push. Maggie must push, but if it moves up instead of out…"

"So, we have to guarantee that the afterbirth doesn't move up." Luke rubbed his chin, deep in thought. "I have an idea. I'll be right back."

"Where are you going?" Agnes rushed to the bedroom door, but her employer was halfway down the stairs.

"It will come, Maggie. It will." Morning Star touched her friend's arm.

"Agnes, I've heard of women bleeding to death…" Maggie paled. Everything had gone so well. Her new son arrived safe and sound, guided by Agnes's knowledge and skill. Why this? Why now? Was she being punished? Blessed with a beautiful baby, just to have her own life snatched away?

"I can't die, Agnes. I can't leave my children alone. Oh, my word. How will Patti survive if she loses another mother? And the thought of leaving Sam…" Maggie burst into tears.

"You're not going to die." Agnes grabbed her by the shoulders. "Do you hear me, Maggie Carlyle? You are not going to die! I won't allow it!"

Maggie collapsed against the pillows, crying softly. "What have I done to deserve this?"

Luke thundered up the stairs. The bedroom door swung back, crashing against the wall. "Let's try this and pray it works." He flung a clean strong rope onto the floor, unwound a length and grabbed the end.

"Is that rope?" Agnes leapt off her stool at the foot of the bed. "What on earth?"

"We tied Rags to the veranda railing when he was a pup so he wouldn't wander off to the barns and get trampled by a steer or a horse." Luke peeked up, grinning. "I washed it and wound it up last fall and then tossed it in the back porch. I've been meaning to take it back down to the barn, but I never got around to it. For once my procrastination has paid off."

Luke rushed to his wife's bedside. "Morning Star, help me lift Maggie enough so we can ease the rope around her middle. Then we'll tie it tightly. We'll help Maggie push and hopefully, things will move out and the rope will prevent it from moving up into her heart or lungs."

"Mr. Carlyle, that's brilliant." Agnes repositioned herself at Maggie's feet. "Morning Star, push on Maggie's middle when I give the go ahead. Mr. Carlyle, you push, too."

"The rope is tied snugly. When do we push, Agnes?" asked Luke, searching Maggie's eyes. Her eyelids fluttered from time to time, and he wasn't certain if that was a good sign or not. "Be brave, sweetheart," he whispered and kissed her forehead.

"Now. Push on Maggie's middle, and then slowly work your hands downward." Agnes moved the new mother's knees apart and watched.

"Help me," gasped Maggie. "Help me grab the towels. I'll push, too." Morning Star handed Maggie the towels tethered to the bedposts and then returned to her patient's midsection.

"Push however you can, Maggie." Agnes brushed her hair out of her eyes with her sleeve. "Do you feel the need to push at all?"

"I'm so tired, but I'll try." Maggie bore down with the towels, but she felt so weak. "I can't do it. I..."

"You can do it, Maggie. Think about that beautiful baby boy." Agnes shifted on her stool, watching for the afterbirth. "Keep pushing, Morning Star." A moment later she blurted, "I think it's working, Mr. Carlyle. Keep pushing everyone."

Luke closed his eyes for a brief second and prayed while he

pushed down on his wife's middle.

"The afterbirth's coming. Oh, thank goodness." Agnes squealed. "It's coming out, all in one piece. It's coming out."

Luke opened his eyes. "There's so much blood. Is that…normal?"

Maggie heard a dull thud as her husband hit the floor.

"Has the new father fainted?" inquired Agnes, dealing with the afterbirth at the foot of the bed. She wrapped it in newspapers, to be buried in the morning.

Morning Star peeked over the side and discovered Mr. Carlyle lying spread-eagled on the bedroom floor. "New father faint," she confirmed.

"This business is all a bit much for most men to handle. He'll come around in a minute. Let's get things cleaned up." Agnes met Maggie's eyes. "You're doing fine, Maggie. There's not even a hint of hemorrhaging."

"Thank you, Agnes." Maggie closed her eyes; she'd never felt so thankful.

"Mr. Carlyle's solution did the trick. I was at a total loss of what to do." Agnes smiled, weakly. "Doc Fitzgerald has passed, poor old fellow. Or I'd give him a piece of my mind for not discussing such possibilities with me. Mind you, I hadn't planned on doing any birthing on my own."

"You did very good job, Agnes." Morning Star patted her arm. "I forget horsemint tea. It help with afterbirth. All excited. I sorry I forget."

"I should have said something sooner, but I didn't want to panic Maggie." Agnes took a deep breath and sighed. "Frankly, I was panicking enough for both of us."

"I'll be forever indebted to you, ladies." Maggie smiled as happy tears trailed down her cheeks. "I couldn't have done this without you. And I've a perfect new baby boy. Thank you, thank you, thank you."

"Maggie, I enjoyed birthing this baby so much." Agnes stood back a pace and tilted her head. "Do you suppose I should train as a midwife?"

"Rebecca is getting up in years, but don't you dare tell her I said that." Maggie was exhausted but smiling. "I bet she'd love to train you."

"I'm happy about marrying Mike, but I admit I'm a little disappointed I won't be training as a nurse." Agnes smiled. "I've made up my mind; I'll become a midwife."

Luke finally came to. Blushing profusely, he dragged himself up into a sitting position. "Sweetheart, I apologize for leaving you high and dry in the middle of your ordeal."

"Luke, you're the one on the floor. Perhaps the ordeal was yours?" teased Maggie, laughing.

Red-faced, Luke stood. "I'll go fetch our son," he called, slipping out of the room.

* * *

"Finally, what took you so long?" Elizabeth glanced at Luke. The older lady, looking every bit the proud grandmother, cradled the baby in her arms. "Mind you, we've enjoyed our time with this little fellow."

"He's so precious, Luke." Aunt Penny beamed. "Just look at him. He's the spitting image of Maggie when she was born."

"I even held the little feller, Sonny Boy." Ned nodded. "He's a real whippersnapper."

"Thank you, everyone. Maggie's doing well, but she's looking for this little man." Luke stood hands on hips.

"Maggie came through the birth as expected? No mishaps?" Aunt Penny rested her thin, blue-veined hand on his arm.

"There was a bit of trouble with things at the end, but that problem has been handled. Let me hold my son." Luke reached for the baby, and Elizabeth reluctantly handed him over.

Luke snuggled the infant against his chest. "Hello there. Did you miss your old pa?"

"What's his name, Luke?" asked Ronald, beaming like a grandpa.

Luke's gaze flew to the older gentleman's. "I don't know. As far as I know, Maggie hasn't named him yet."

"We were a bit concerned with the goings-on up there. Heard a terrible crash at one point…something hitting the floor. I almost rushed up to investigate, but I didn't want to put the baby down." Elizabeth blushed with her admission.

"It was nothing to worry about." Luke felt his face redden to his hairline. His back hurt a smidgen and one elbow was throbbing something awful, but he wouldn't admit the why of it to anyone.

"What did ya need the rope fer, Sonny Boy?" asked Ned, laughing raucously. "Did Maggie threaten ta leave? Did ya tie her down?"

Luke was spared an explanation when Agnes stepped into the kitchen.

"Hello, everyone. Well, that was certainly enough excitement for one evening." Agnes flopped down onto a kitchen chair, brushing a strand of hair out of her face. "Takes one's breath away bringing a new life into the world."

"You did a marvelous job," whispered Aunt Penny, bending to hug the young heroine. "We couldn't be more proud of you."

"Thank you so much." Agnes smiled, meeting Aunt Penny's eyes. And then she burst into tears. Sobs racked her body, and she blubbered unintelligible mutterings into her handkerchief.

"Oh, my, did I say something wrong?" asked Aunt Penny, wide-eyed. "I apologize if I upset you, dear. I didn't mean any harm."

"I think the magnitude of it all has just finally set in." Elizabeth patted Agnes's hand. "Ronald, please be a dear and fetch the girl a glass of that sherry."

Ronald hurried out of the kitchen to do his wife's bidding. In a minute, he returned with a decanter of sherry and a clean glass. He crossed the room, and poured a few ounces for Agnes.

"Careful now," warned Elizabeth. "I don't imagine you're used to spirits."

"Mrs. Waverly, I've never drank anything stronger than coffee." Agnes grasped the small glass with shaking fingers and swallowed the contents in one gulp. Her eyes grew wide and then began to water ever so slightly. "That tastes rather wonderful, doesn't it?" Agnes shook her head once and then blew out her breath. "I believe I'd like some more, please."

Ronald glanced at his wife. Elizabeth nodded and Ronald poured the girl another shot. Agnes downed the second glass in two gulps. "That's much better. My nerves are steady now."

Agnes held out her glass, and Ronald refilled it again. "So, what's everyone been up to while Maggie birthed the baby?" asked Agnes, sipping on her third glass of spirits.

Aunt Penny met Elizabeth's eyes. Ronald glanced over at

Ned. Everyone in the kitchen, including Luke, turned toward Agnes and burst into laughter.

"My girl, you're something else," said Ronald, shaking his head.

"I'm taking this young man upstairs and see how his mother is doing. And I'll ask if he has a name." Luke kissed the baby's head and walked out of the kitchen.

"Patti and Sam are going to be so excited in the morning." Aunt Penny clasped her hands. "I'm off to bed now. I hope I can sleep after all this excitement."

"I'm turning in, too," said Agnes, polishing off her third glass of sherry. "Plenty enough excitement for one night."

"Bin a long night for everyone," declared Ned, following Agnes out of the room.

"Goodnight, Ned and Agnes," called Ronald, accompanying Elizabeth out of the kitchen and heading toward the entryway staircase.

"Night you two," added Elizabeth.

Before ascending the stairs, Ronald peeked out the entryway window. "I can't see a dang thing out there. Can barely see the veranda railing."

Elizabeth shook her head. "Listen to that wind howling. I'd hate to be out in that tonight."

"No sane man would venture out in that mess," agreed Ned. "Best go collect my missus and turn in. If'n I can git her to leave Maggie's side. She truly loves carin' for sick folk."

"Maggie's not sick. She's just given birth to a baby," argued Elizabeth, taking the stairs ahead of the men. "A few days abed, and she'll be as good as new."

"Good night, Ned." Ronald rested his hand on Ned's shoulder while the two men walked the stairs, side by side. "Let's hope the weather lets up by morning. Elizabeth and I should be getting back to town."

"Don't be frettin'. Ellie can run yer dang store fer ya. And we'll have that new young'un to take turns holding in the mornin'." Ned grinned from ear to ear.

"We'll teach him to say 'grandpappy'," chuckled Ronald, yawning loudly.

"Naw. We'll teach him a cuss word." Ned cackled as he

rounded the upstairs landing.

Agnes glared at the two men, blinking frequently in an effort to focus clearly. "Over my dead body. I brought that little fellow into the world and you two will behave yourselves around him." She teetered up the stairs toward the third floor.

* * *

Their bedroom was cleaned, and the blood-stained linens had been tossed into the trash for burning. Maggie, bathed and wearing a lovely pink nightdress, sipped a cup of baneberry tea that Morning Star had mentioned would help with the milk for the baby. The cradle was situated beside the bed. A persistent cry emitted from the bundle in Luke's arms as he moved farther into the room.

"I think someone misses his mama," suggested Luke, beaming.

"His mama certainly missed him." Maggie held out her arms.

"Little fellow sleep, you sleep, too," warned Morning Star. "I go now."

Maggie smiled, preparing to nurse her son for the first time. "I won't deny I'm bone tired."

"Don't worry." Luke tapped his wife on the arm. "I'll see that she gets some sleep. Go find Ned and get some rest; Elizabeth put you folks in one of the third-floor guest rooms. She probably left a lamp burning."

"Good night, then."

"Good night, Morning Star." Luke and Maggie called in unison.

The native woman walked out of their bedroom, closing the door behind her.

"At last, some time alone with my wife and new son." Luke crossed the room and set his pocket watch on top of his night table. He unbuttoned his shirt and glanced at Maggie who was successfully nursing their son. "I've been dying to ask you what you named him."

"Look in the top drawer of the writing desk." Maggie's eyes never left her son, now contentedly sleeping in her arms. Sitting up in bed, she covered herself and laid the baby on her lap. She opened his blanket and swaddled him tightly again. And then she met Luke's eyes.

Luke opened the desk drawer. A folded sheet of paper lay on top of the assortment of stationery. "What's this?" he asked, glancing over at Maggie.

"Open it and see." His wife smiled.

Luke unfolded the paper and read WILLIAM MATTHEW CARLYLE.

"You named the baby after my father?" Their eyes met, and he realized he loved her more than ever.

"No, actually, I have a second cousin named Matthew," teased Maggie, laughing at Luke's shocked expression.

"I thought Aunt Penny was the only…"

"Of course, I named him after your father, and after William. You'll be the only father he ever knows—the man who raises him, who calls him son, who teaches him everything he needs to learn—but he should carry his father's name."

William Matthew Carlyle. "It's perfect, Maggie." Luke kissed her lips.

"I thought about it a lot. And seeing his little face, the name suits him." Maggie lay back against the pillows.

"I have one question. How did you know it was a boy?" Luke strode across the room and gently lifted his son off her lap. He kissed one small pink cheek, and then settled the sleeping baby in the cradle. "What if you'd given me a daughter? She'd look pretty silly being called William."

"Not at all. I would have told you to look in my armoire." Maggie yawned and snuggled down under the covers. "I can't remember the last time I felt so exhausted."

Luke finished undressing, checked on the baby again, and then glanced at his wife. He listened to her slow even breathing—she was already asleep—and curiosity overcame him. Silently, he crossed the floor and opened Maggie's armoire doors. An identical sheet of paper lay in full view. Holding his breath, he unfolded it.

Bold black letters spelled ELIZABETH RUTH CARLYLE.

Luke's eyes filled with tears. She would have named their daughter after his mother and given her best friend a namesake. Elizabeth would have been beside herself with pride and cried a bucket of tears. This name would have been perfect, too.

Luke refolded the sheet of paper, slipped it back into the armoire, and closed the doors. "Maybe next time, sweetheart," he whispered aloud.

* * *

By the next morning the weather hadn't improved one iota. If anything, it had worsened. So much for Morning Star's prediction the snow would be gone. Fires blazed inside the main house fireplaces, keeping the family and their visitors warm and safe.

Luke relaxed in his favorite rocking chair situated close to the parlor fireplace, and the new baby slept peacefully in his arms. He couldn't pry his eyes off the little fellow, swaddled in a pale-blue blanket with only his tiny face exposed. Luke had been blessed with another son. His blood didn't run through the newborn's veins, but his new son already held a permanent place in his heart.

Fate brought Maggie into his life, and with her, two beautiful sons to call his own. He possessed everything a man needed: wealth and security, a loving wife, healthy children, and good friends. How fortunate could one man be?

"Ronald, I don't mind admitting I'm mighty content with life." Luke couldn't wipe the grin off his face. "Some days it's downright frightening how happy I am."

"Well, son, enjoy it while you can," advised Ronald, puffing on his pipe. He wandered across the room and stood beside the Christmas tree nestled inside the turret. "Before you know it, that young fellow will be asking your permission to ride Thunder."

"Nobody rides Thunder but me." Luke playfully wagged his finger at the sleeping infant.

Ronald peeked outside through the lacy parlor curtains. "The storm's still raging. Without Morning Star cooking for your ranch hands, the poor beggars must be getting a mite hungry by now." Ronald crossed the room and sat in Maggie's rocking chair.

Luke smiled at his honorary father-in-law. Just like Ronald to be concerned with everyone's well-being. "Every autumn Morning Star outfits the bunkhouses with tins of beans and dried meats and jars of preserves for just such an occasion. The men fend for themselves, cooking whatever they can slap together. Cookhouse Charlie is out there, so I doubt anyone's going hungry." Luke cooed and rocked the baby when he fussed. "But the fellow losing the most at poker will be cursing the weather."

"What about your horses and cattle?" Ronald relit his pipe.

Luke shifted the baby to his other arm. "There's a woodstove in the tack room, and some vittles and cots for them. Soon as a storm hits, the men draw straws to decide which fellows bunk down in the barns and feed the animals."

"I hope we don't see another winter like 86-87. Everyone lost a lot of stock that winter." Ronald set his pipe on the ashtray atop the mahogany table nestled between the rocking chairs. "Let me hold the little fellow for a spell."

Luke placed the sleeping baby in his honorary grandfather's arms. Restless from being cooped up in the main house, Luke began pacing. "The range animals are feral and hardy. When they sense a storm coming, they travel toward shelter and hunker down until it passes. Providing they don't come up against one of those barbed wire fences that we're being warned will be common practice here in Montana soon enough."

"Pure instinct, I suppose," suggested Ronald.

"I'm going to check the fire in Maggie's room," advised Luke, slipping out of the parlor. Keeping his wife and new son cozy and warm was upmost in his mind. With this weather there'd be no traveling to town for medicine if anyone came down with an ailment. As he took the stairs two at a time, memories of Catherine's sudden death flashed before his eyes and sent a shiver down his spine. Would he ever forget? Should he?

Luke quietly settled a few logs on the fire in the master bedroom. Maggie remained sound asleep, and he gently kissed her cheek. He slipped out of the room and wandered down to the kitchen which buzzed with activity. He poured himself a cup of coffee from the pot warming on the woodstove.

Everyone seemed in good humor, especially Patti and Sam. He smiled, recalling how they'd begged him to see their new baby brother after gulping down their breakfast. Even Lucy, who'd been so angry when she'd first learned another baby was on the way, raced upstairs to meet him. Wide-eyed and beaming, they each took a turn holding William. Patti was impressed that the stork found the house in the blizzard.

"What are you two doing?" asked Luke, tugging playfully on one of Patti's pigtails.

"I'm drawing a picture for my new brother," answered Sam,

holding up a colorful drawing of something resembling a horse. Luke reserved comment in case it was a dog, perhaps Rags.

Suddenly, a lump formed in his throat. Poor old Skipper had passed on in November, succumbing to the cold weather. Luke missed that old dog, and for the longest time things around the ranch didn't seem right without Skipper standing by his side, waiting for his master to scratch his ears. Thank goodness for Rags; the new pup helped ease the pain.

"Aunt Penny is helping me write William a letter," said Patti, bringing Luke back to the moment.

Apparently, the fact that the baby couldn't read hadn't crossed his daughter's mind. "I'm sure William will appreciate your picture and the letter," said Luke, downing the last drop of coffee and setting the cup in the dish tub for washing.

Aunt Penny met Luke's eyes. "Young William is quite the novelty. They even dragged Rags upstairs and introduced him to the baby."

"Rags likes William," added Sam. "But Mama wouldn't let him kiss my brother with his tongue, like he kisses me."

"Well, that's understandable," muttered Luke, heading back to the parlor to check on Ronald and the baby. "I'm quite surprised your ma entrusted us with your new brother."

* * *

"May I come in, Maggie?" croaked Agnes, the only person feeling less than jolly this morning. She tip-toed into the master bedroom and slowly lowered herself onto Maggie's bed.

"Are you not feeling well?" Maggie pressed her hand to Agnes's forehead. "You're looking a little peaked."

"I feel absolutely awful," admitted Agnes in a whisper, holding her head with one hand. "Too much sherry, I think."

"How much sherry did you drink?" asked Maggie, searching the young woman's slightly bloodshot eyes for an answer. Had Luke plied the young woman with spirits to celebrate the new baby?

"Three glasses that I can recall. I was so proud, successfully bringing your son into the world. I felt wonderful when I set off for bed, all relaxed and happy and a little woozy." Agnes blushed and attempted to smile. "But I woke up with Morning Star's ancestors beating war drums in my head."

"I'm so sorry," said Maggie, suppressing a smile.

"I'm getting their message. Don't drink sherry!" she attempted a smile. "Sam and Patti jumped onto my bed," continued Agnes, grimacing with the memory. "They went on and on about William. My foggy brain finally realized they were talking about the new baby. They were so excited, but I was rather short with them. I apologized immediately, of course, and when they realized I wasn't angry, they started shouting again. I thought my head would split in two."

"Poor Agnes." Maggie couldn't contain her mirth a second longer. She burst out laughing, and then quickly covered her mouth with the sheet.

"Go ahead. Have your fun. So soon people forget your good deeds." Head held immobile, Agnes attempted to slowly lift herself off the bed.

Maggie pulled her back down beside her. "I'm sorry. I can't thank you enough for helping bring William into the world. And I know how you feel, truly I do. The last time I partook of spirits, I fainted dead away in the middle of the floor in The Joker's Wild Saloon."

"What?" Agnes swung around facing Maggie and then grimaced. "Oh, ouch." Her hands flew to her head, no doubt attempting to keep it atop her shoulders.

"It's a long story, which I wish to forget." Maggie patted Agnes's knee. "But I have something to ask of you."

"Anything, as long as it doesn't involve sherry."

Chapter 23

"We've become very close friends, especially last night." Maggie reached out and stroked the girl's hair. Even with a head-splitting hangover, Agnes had brushed her flowing curls and tied them with a pretty ribbon. "After everything you've done, bringing my son safely into the world and all, it would please me greatly if you'd agree to be William's godmother. I can't think of a more deserving person."

Agnes's eyes welled, and she grasped Maggie's hand. "I'd be honored."

"Good, then that's settled."

"Thank you…for thinking of me…" Agnes stammered.

"You're welcome. I'm so pleased you've agreed. Now, go back to bed. Morning Star can attend to my needs and help with the baby."

"But Sam and Patti…"

"Surely, the collective efforts of Aunt Penny and Elizabeth can handle those two today. Lucy can help, too. Get some sleep; it's the best medicine. You certainly earned a day off last night."

"But, ma'am, I couldn't just…"

"Not another word. I insist." Maggie shooed the young girl off the bed and waved her in the direction of the door. "Off to bed with you. And if you're wise, you'll lock your door to keep you know who out."

"Thank you, ma'am, I'm eternally grateful for this small mercy." Agnes wobbled out the door, and Maggie thought she heard her muttering something about 'should I die before I wake'.

Tuesday, December 24, 1889

When the storm finally blew itself out, an almost magical calmness encompassed the ranch. Luke, Ned and Ronald ventured outside to check on things around the ranch. Ronald returned a half hour later to report snowdrifts, some as tall as a man, covered some of the barn doors, and the ranch hands were spending the morning shoveling. After two days holed up in the bunkhouses, no one was complaining.

Just as the group gathered around the kitchen table for the noon meal, a loud knock on the back door startled everyone. Luke strode across the floor and flung the door open. One of the Diamond C ranch hands stood there, his clothes caked in snow.

"Come in, come in." Luke ushered the fellow inside and quickly closed the door. They then moved into the kitchen.

"Sorry to bother you, sir, but I just rode in from town." The ranch hand removed his Stetson and the scarf tied round his face.

"Scotty! When did you ride into town?" asked Luke, sounding puzzled.

"Late last Thursday afternoon," he answered. "To pick up supplies for Ned. And Agnes sent a package and a letter for her ma with me, too."

"Tarnation, Luke!" exclaimed Ned, rising from his seat. "I plumb forgot I sent Scotty to town. Never inquired of the other men if he'd returned. It's a dang good thing the lad had sense enough to stay put durin' that storm."

"Actually, sir, I…I spent a couple nights in jail," confessed Scotty, blushing profusely and shifting from one foot to the other. "There was a bit of a 'discussion' at The Golden Garter Saloon, sir. And Sheriff Smith detained a few of us that were involved."

Luke's men occasionally spent Saturday night in a jail cell after a round of fisticuffs at one the town's saloons. But he'd never heard round-housing referred to as a 'discussion' before. Luke smiled at the young man's diplomacy, being that he was relating the story in front of the womenfolk. "Well, I'm glad to see you're back here in one piece."

"Thank you, sir. But there's…something else, sir," stammered

Scotty, averting his eyes and staring at the doorjamb.

Luke had never been addressed as 'sir' so often before during one conversation. Lord knows what else the boy had to confess.

"Good afternoon, Scotty." Maggie crossed the kitchen floor and stood beside her husband.

"Good afternoon, ma'am." Scotty nodded. "I'm real sorry to interrupt your dinner, ma'am."

"That's all right, Scotty. We were just sitting down, haven't started yet." Maggie smiled.

Scotty's eyes widened and he stared at her flatter middle. "You had the baby?" he blurted in a whisper.

"A little boy," replied Maggie, smiling.

Luke slipped his arm about his wife's shoulders, and then met Scotty's eyes. "You mentioned something else? Well, spit it out."

"Agnes's ma sent a box back with me." Scotty retrieved a wooden box from the back door and handed it to Luke. "Mrs. Jones insisted that under no circumstances was Agnes to venture into town for Christmas. Best she stays at the ranch, safe and warm."

"I'd hate for Agnes to miss out on Christmas with her family. I'll have one of the hands drive her into town." Luke passed the box to Agnes and then stood hands on hips.

"Well, now, sir," said Scotty, shaking his head. "There might be a problem with that, seeing as I barely made it out here on horseback. There's no chance of a wagon or buggy making the trip, not with them snowdrifts as high as my horse in places."

"The trail into town is impassable?" asked Luke, mouth dropping open.

"Well, in an emergency, you might get a fella on a horse through to town." Scotty sighed, tapping the toe of one boot on the floor. "But unless it was a true emergency, I wouldn't chance it for no amount of money."

"That bad," mumbled Luke. Most of his ranch hands, especially Scotty, would volunteer for almost anything if the price was right. The going must be treacherous, if Scotty wouldn't attempt another trip to town.

"We'll keep Agnes here with us then." Luke shook the young man's hand. "Thank you for bringing Agnes's parcel."

"There's another message, sir." Scotty peeked around Luke and met Ronald Waverly's eyes. "It's about the general store."

Maggie's eyes flew to Ronald. Everyone in town knew The Spirit Creek General Store and Elizabeth were Ronald's entire life. Had there been a fire? Or a robbery? Did something happen to Ellie while she was at the store? If it was bad news, Ronald would be devastated. Luke slipped his arm around Maggie's middle; he must have sensed her concern. No matter how bad the news was, I must stay strong for Ronald.

"Is there a problem?" asked Ronald, paling and leaping to his feet. "Don't lie to me, son, tell me the truth."

"No, sir," said Scotty, quickly. "Miss Thomas is running it right proper-like. She said you shouldn't worry about a thing. Said just enjoy Christmas." Scotty retrieved another box from the back door. "I brought the gifts Miss Thomas collected up from under your tree, knowing you'd never make it into town for Christmas Day."

"Thank you, Scotty." Ronald heaved a loud sigh of relief. "I'm mightily pleased things are running smoothly. And thank you for your kindness."

"She's doing a right proper job, sir." Scotty nodded. "She can cipher like nobody's business. Tallied up my order faster than you can kiss a duck."

"She is the schoolmarm," said Ronald, smiling. "I reckon she's good at ciphering."

"Well, I've said my piece and made the deliveries. Nobody else had any messages for you folks, so I'll be getting on down to the barn. My horse is a tad lathered up, plowing through those snow drifts. Better tend to him before he catches his death." Scotty slapped his hat on his head, touched the brim and hurried outside.

Luke closed the door and turned, meeting Agnes's eyes. "Are you disappointed, not seeing your family for Christmas?"

"I don't mind so much, Mr. Carlyle." Agnes smiled and then reddened. "Not that I won't miss my family. But I'll spend the holidays with Mike, and with all of you. You folks are family, too."

"I imagine your ma sent your Christmas present in that box. But it's too bad you won't be able to get to town." Luke patted her arm.

"Thank goodness I sent my family's presents with Scotty on Thursday, thinking I'd have less to worry about on Christmas Eve." Agnes smiled and met Maggie's eyes. "And I'm so pleased that I sent the basket of food and the trifle with Scotty, too, Mrs. Carlyle."

"I'm happy your family has the treats for Christmas." Maggie smiled.

"Thank you for thinking of them." Agnes blushed.

"Let's eat," announced Ronald, sliding his chair into the table. "I'm as hungry as a bear."

"You're always hungry." Elizabeth swatted at her husband's arm.

"Aunt Penny, would you say grace, please?" Luke grasped her wrinkled hand, meeting her eyes.

"It would be an honor, Luke. We have a lot to be thankful for," said Aunt Penny.

Wednesday, December 25, 1889

Everyone had enjoyed a lovely Christmas Eve: singing carols around the beautiful piano, drinking apple cider by the fire, the children hanging their stockings before heading off to dreamland. Mr. Waverly hung his stocking on the mantle beside the children's, and after he turned in, Elizabeth stuffed several pairs of home-made woolen socks and a handful of his favorite sweets inside.

Agnes had been up before the rooster to stuff the goose and prepare him for the oven. Mike rose early also to brave the cold and haul in armloads of firewood—all the bins were empty due to the inclement weather—in order to keep the fires going. As soon as the bird was in the oven, she and Mike shared a quiet few minutes to exchange their gifts.

"It's the most beautiful sweater I've ever seen," gushed Agnes, brushing the soft wool across her check.

"I paid Mrs. Waverly to knit it for you, but I picked the color. It matches your eyes perfectly," said Mike, blushing.

Agnes jumped up, almost toppling her chair, and peeked into the small mirror hung by the back door. She smiled and returned to her seat. "You're right…the perfect shade of blue. I love it, Mike."

Mike beamed and appeared overcome with emotion and unable to speak.

Agnes opened her mother's gift and discovered a box of homemade peanut brittle, her favorite treat.

"I hope you're going to share that," teased Mike.

"Of course." Agnes leaned across the table and kissed her fiancé on the lips. Her stomach did a little flip-flop. "Now, open mine."

Mike fumbled with the wrapping, finally unveiling a sturdy waistcoat and several pairs of woolen socks. "I'll look like a gentleman wearing such finery."

"Morning Star suggested the waistcoat; I bought it at the general store. But I knit the socks myself."

"You shouldn't have spent so much money on me," chided Mike.

"Mrs. Waverly gave me a discount being that I'm Maggie's friend, she said." Agnes laughed. "And that was before I delivered the baby."

"I'll keep the waistcoat for our wedding day," said Mike, his voice softening.

Tears sprang to Agnes's eyes. "Oh, Mike, I can't wait to become your wife."

"I can't wait until we're married either," added Mike, kissing her tears away. "Let's not wait too long. I don't want you to come to your senses and change your mind."

"Never," chuckled Agnes, kissing his cheek.

"Merry Christmas!" Aunt Penny charged into the kitchen with the energy of a much younger lady.

Mike and Agnes jumped a foot.

"Merry Christmas, Mrs. Williamson," said Agnes, blushing at having been caught kissing Mike in the kitchen.

"Merry Christmas." Mike leapt to his feet.

The elderly lady poured herself a cup of coffee. "Nervous as two long-tailed cats in a room full of rocking chairs," mumbled Aunt Penny, smiling wickedly. On her way out of the kitchen, she called, "Let me know if you need any help with breakfast. Mind you, all I can make is flapjacks."

Patti and Sam, wearing their pajamas and huge smiles, raced each other into the kitchen. "We have to eat breakfast before we open our presents," declared Patti, her expression turning into a small pout.

"Mama said," explained Sam, climbing onto his kitchen chair.

Agnes smiled. "Well, if *Mama said*, then there's no getting around it."

"I'll help, Agnes," offered Mike, winking at his betrothed. "Then everyone will be finished breakfast that much sooner."

"Yippee!" shouted Sam, clapping his hands.

"Do you think we'll get lots of presents?" asked Patti, sitting next to her brother.

"Have you been good children?" Agnes stirred a huge pot of oatmeal while Mike cracked eggs and added them to a sizzling frying pan.

Patti and Sam gaped, and met each other's eyes.

"We've been good," said Patti. "Except when we mess up mama's floors if we play mud pies. Or we forget and let Rags in the house with dirty feet."

"We ate those berries and got sick," whispered Sam.

"Mama said it was an accident." Patti nodded with her answer, her pigtails bobbing.

"I don't think it counts if it was an accident," offered Mike, cutting strips of bacon and tossing them into another pan.

"I'm sure there's some presents waiting for you." Agnes sliced bread for toast and whispered in Mike's ear. "Don't you want two just like them?"

Mike paled and swallowed hard.

Agnes burst into laughter.

"Well, someday," mumbled Mike, obviously shocked by his fiancée's comment.

"Someday," whispered Agnes, winking. "But there'll be no shenanigans, no little bundle on the way before we say our vows at the altar," she added.

Having experienced the wonder of bringing a new life into the world with Maggie, she couldn't wait to give Mike a son, too. She returned her attention to Sam and Patti. "Nobody opens any presents until breakfast is eaten and the dishes are done. I don't want to miss a thing."

Breakfast proved a noisy, laughter-filled affair. The ornate wooden parlor doors remained closed, and no one was allowed inside, creating much speculation as to whether or not there were presents under the tree. Sam and Patti fidgeted at the table, willing the adults to hurry with their meal.

Once the dishes were done, the entire household gathered in the parlor. The adults sipped coffee or apple cider while Lucy, Patti and Sam sat cross-legged atop an Axminster rug in the middle of the floor. Their new brother slept blissfully in Maggie's arms, totally oblivious to the goings-on, while everyone opened their presents.

"My word, you are fortunate children." Aunt Penny peeked over her spectacles, examining Patti's new doll. "You best take care of your new things."

"I will, Grandma," promised Patti. "Thank you for my book."

Agnes stood off to the side, observing the family celebration, and she knew Maggie's aunt was delighted with the new title.

Lucy closely examined the new sewing supplies she'd received. "This is the best gift ever," she declared and smiled at her stepmother.

"I thought you'd like it," replied Maggie and she winked at her oldest daughter.

"Sam, take care that Rags doesn't chew that book I gave you." Aunt Penny ruffled his hair. Sam jumped up and flung his arms around her neck, almost strangling her in a bear hug.

"Rags won't chew my toys, Grandma. He's not a bad puppy, and he's real smart," explained Sam, proudly.

"You've trained him well." Aunt Penny beamed, glancing toward Maggie. "You're a very good boy."

"Thank you for my book," said Sam, returning to his toys.

Agnes caught Luke glancing in Maggie's direction, a smile creasing his face. Maggie met his eyes, returning his smile. They know exactly what the other is thinking, she observed. She hoped she and Mike had a marriage like that someday soon.

She suspected Luke and Maggie were thinking how proud they were of that well-mannered, kind, loving little boy of theirs. Sam had become Luke's son, and her boss couldn't look more pleased. And Maggie treated Luke's daughters like they were her own flesh and blood. Agnes couldn't ask for kinder people to work for, and marrying Mike meant she'd remain on the ranch with these wonderful people.

Agnes and Aunt Penny each received a new quilt from Luke and Maggie.

Agnes's eyes filled with tears, and she quickly wiped them away. "It's lovely, Maggie. And just what a bride-to-be needs."

"Just what an old lady needs to keep warm on a cold winter

night," added Aunt Penny, hugging her new quilt to her bosom.

Ned and Ronald received new sweaters, each created with love by their wives. Elizabeth received a lovely embroidered tablecloth from Ronald, and Morning Star cherished the beautiful needlepoint picture of wildflowers that she received from Ned.

"We hired Sarah Grayson to make those presents for us," confessed Ned.

"That woman is a wonder with a needle," agreed Ronald.

"I've known Sarah Grayson for years. We write each other…" Aunt Penny paled, and her gaze flew to Maggie.

* * *

"So, Sarah is your eyes and ears in Spirit Creek," reasoned Maggie, shaking her head. The baby stirred in her arms, and she rocked him gently. "How on earth did you meet Sarah?"

"Sarah's sister, Mrs. Shelagh Bennett, lives in Philadelphia. Shelagh owns a very prestigious dress shop called Bustles and Bows, and she has custom-designed and sewn all my dresses for years. Shelagh introduced us when her sister was visiting several years ago. I've been friends and I've corresponded with Sarah ever since." Aunt Penny shifted in her seat.

Luke met Maggie's eyes, and he smiled. She smiled back at him. Luke knows how pleased I am, having Aunt Penny with us for Christmas, despite learning the name of her aunt's secret correspondent. It was uncanny how she sensed what her husband was thinking by looking into his eyes. She couldn't remember ever knowing what William was thinking, sharing that connection. Luke was definitely the right man for her.

Luke set a beautifully-wrapped present at Maggie's feet. "This one is from me." She handed the baby to Elizabeth and removed the wrapping, peeking inside the box. Clutching the lilac-patterned silk wrapper in both hands, she smiled, "Oh Luke, it's beautiful."

"Elizabeth found it in one of her catalogues. She showed me the picture, and I knew it was perfect for you." Luke met Aunt Penny's eyes. "Maggie's a bit partial to lilacs."

"Has been as long as I can remember," sighed Aunt Penny. Leaning over, she whispered in her niece's ear, "Your husband gives wonderful presents, too. I'd keep him if I was you."

"There's a present for you, Luke, behind the tree," said Maggie, pointing to the left. She peeked over at Lucy and winked. Lucy giggled and covered her mouth with her hands.

Luke fetched the present and returned to his rocking chair. The gift was enormous and covered his entire lap. "My goodness, what is this?" he mumbled.

"Hurry, Papa. Open it up!" exclaimed Lucy, appearing ready to jump out of her skin.

Maggie held her breath, watched Luke pull the wrapping off. Her husband stood, unfolded the quilt.

Everyone in the room gasped.

Luke studied the pattern for a moment. "It's beautiful, Maggie. I can't believe what you've done." Their eyes met, and he bent down and kissed her. Luke pulled away first and whispered, "Thank you so much."

Maggie reddened. Luke had kissed her in front of Aunt Penny, and God, and everyone. But somehow, it didn't matter. He couldn't take his eyes off the quilt she'd made, especially for him.

"I've been working on it for months, with some valuable help from Lucy. She's becoming quite adept with a needle. I'm very proud of her. But it was some job keeping it a secret from everyone." Maggie smiled at her daughter.

She and Lucy worked on their squares whenever possible, secreting them away every night before turning in. But all the hard work was worth it. Everyone had immediately recognized how special the gift was. The quilt depicted twenty different scenes on the Diamond C Ranch.

"Patti, look!" shouted Sam. "There's Rags, and there's our ponies."

"And there's the creek where we catch frogs," added Patti.

"There's Grandpa Matthew's swing, Papa," said Lucy, beaming. "That's one of my squares."

"This is the best present I ever received," whispered Luke.

"There's the Diamond C sign overlookin' the valley." Ned peeked over Lucy's shoulder for a closer look.

"Cattle, horses, the barns," said Elizabeth, shaking her head. "You haven't forgotten a thing."

"What's all this grassy stuff here?" asked Aunt Penny.

"That's Morning Star's medicine plants," whispered Maggie,

meeting the native woman's eyes. "The plants she brews into healing teas to make my children better when they're ill."

"Thank you, Maggie," whispered Morning Star, tearing up. "You not forget me."

"How could I forget someone as important to this family as you?" Maggie laughed. "Remember the day we first met?"

"Yes." Morning Star laughed. "I almost frighten you to death."

"We've come a long way," said Maggie, wistfully. "Friends for eternity."

"Where are these grave markers, Maggie?" asked Aunt Penny, examining the quilt.

"Let me tell you about them," suggested Luke, sitting beside the newest family member. Soon they were lost in conversation, Aunt Penny eagerly listening to Luke's stories about his parents and the beginnings of the Diamond C.

"I created the quilt for our bed, Luke, but let's hang it on the parlor wall for a few days," suggested Maggie. "To let everyone take it all in."

"That's an excellent idea, dear," agreed Elizabeth, shaking her head. "The hours you must have spent on this."

"I entertained myself for all those months when Luke wouldn't allow me to do anything because I was carrying the baby." Maggie winked at Luke, who looked her way at the mention of his name. "One night Lucy mentioned her mother had taught her some stitching, and she agreed to help me with my secret project."

Luke rose to his feet and wrapped his arms around his wife's neck, kissing her cheek. "I couldn't have asked for a better Christmas. You heeded my warnings, and as a result, I've been doubly blessed with a healthy new son and a wonderful Christmas present."

Maggie couldn't speak, choking on her emotions. She'd expected nothing more than a roof over her head from her arrangement with Luke Carlyle. But she'd been given so much more in seven short months.

She cringed, remembering all that she and Luke had survived together: Lucy's initial displeasure with their marriage, the poisonous berry scare, Doc Fitzgerald's death and the possibility of a miscarriage, and the distress surrounding and following the birth of their son.

Maggie paused in her thinking. She'd missed something. Oh, yes, her husband's devastating disappointment when the cattle rustlers eluded capture by disappearing. She'd only felt relief that he wouldn't be putting himself in harm's way. But he assured her they'd be back. She just needed to trust that Luke would be careful. *Trust him.* She could hardly remember a time when she didn't trust him. She would trust him with her life, her children's lives. Always and forever. He was such a good man.

And she'd been blessed with this wonderful new life: a loving husband who would never lie to her or betray her trust; four wonderful children including her healthy new son; dear Aunt Penny who'd forgiven her long ago; new lifelong friends like Morning Star, Hattie Morgan and Agnes whom she cherished with all her heart; and a home filled with happiness and love.

All because Luke had arrived at her door with his preposterous marriage proposal.

For a second she considered, what if she'd asked Aunt Penny for help? What if she'd moved back East? And then she recalled her father's advice, *never live your life wondering about what ifs.* Everything happened for a reason; she was meant to marry Luke. Her heart told her it was her destiny.

And thank goodness, she agreed to marry Luke. Her reward for that leap of faith was a happy ending: no more heartache, no more deceptions, and no more loneliness.

Every day for the rest of her life, she would be thankful for her many blessings.

The End

SPIRIT CREEK SERIES

historical western sweet romance,
NO MORE
NO TIME
NO CHANCE
NO TIES
NO WAY
NO HOPE

You can find Brenda at:

Website: http://www.brendasinclairauthor.com

Facebook: http://www.facebook.com/brendasinclairauthor

Twitter: https://twitter.com/bsinclairauthor

Email: mailto:brendasinclairauthor@gmail.com

Contemporary Romance Titles

Available on Amazon.com
by Brenda Sinclair
http://www.amazon.com/-/e/B007OXHMES

LOVE TO THE RESCUE
ebook and print book available
50% of the author's royalties will be donated to Humane Society shelters

A BANDIT CREEK MIRACLE
ebook and print book available

WHEN DREAMS COLLIDE
Sequel to A Bandit Creek Miracle

Escape to Alaska Trilogy
NOT WHAT IT SEEMS
ALMOST DOESN'T COUNT
NEVER A BRIDE

COOKING FOR COWBOY
(A Stampede Sizzler)
Warning: some adult content

SECRETS FOR COWBOY
(A Stampede Sizzler,
Sequel to Cooking For Cowboy)
Warning: some adult content

ABOUT THE AUTHOR

Brenda Sinclair writes historical American West and contemporary romance. She's a member of her local chapter of Romance Writers of America, a healthy lifestyle advocate and past leader of her TOPS weight-loss group, a gardening enthusiast and dog lover.

Brenda was raised on a farm in southern Manitoba and taught school on a semi-remote reservation in northern Manitoba where, during frequent visits to a nearby town, she met her husband, a Treaty Cree member of the local First Nations band. After working in the accounting field for over twenty-five years, she retired to write full time.

Brenda and her husband have been married for over forty years and raised two sons. She is extremely proud of her three wonderful grandchildren.

During writing breaks, Brenda enjoys walking the beautiful Fish Creek Park trails near her home in Calgary, Canada with her little dog, Kelly, checking out what Jack Abbott is up to on today's installment of The Young and The Restless, or snuggling with Kelly on the sofa and enjoying a good book.

Brenda believes life is good, and for days that life isn't so good, just get over it. There's always tomorrow.

31567722R00181

Made in the USA
Charleston, SC
21 July 2014